Praise for

"Ms. D'Alessandro ... keepers— the ... ures."
—*Affaire de Coeur*

"Ms. D'Alessandro brings new verve to the genre."
—*Romantic Times BOOKclub*

Cathy
Yardley

"Yardley has taken the opposites-attract theme and tailored it in such a way that it's not only fresh, it's also believable and truly romantic."
—*Romantic Times BOOKclub* on *Surf Girl School*

"Another winner from Yardley."
—*Booklist* on *Couch World*

Stephanie
Doyle

"Stephanie Doyle returns with *Baily's Irish Dream*, a truly amusing story of opposites attracting. The heroine's delightful and her hero is an absolute dream."
—*Romantic Times BOOKclub*

"Stephanie Doyle's deliciously satirical *Who Wants To Marry a Heartthrob* is a laugh-a-minute farce with some tender moments."
—*Romantic Times BOOKclub*

ABOUT THE AUTHORS

Growing up on Long Island, New York, *USA TODAY* bestselling author **Jacquie D'Alessandro** fell in love with romance at an early age. She dreamed of being swept away by a dashing rogue riding a spirited stallion. When her hero finally showed up, he was dressed in jeans and drove a Volkswagen, but she recognized him anyway. They married after both graduating from Hofstra University and are now living their happily-ever-afters in Atlanta, Georgia, along with their very bright and active son, who is a dashing rogue in the making. Jacquie loves to hear from readers! You can contact her through her Web site, www.JacquieD.com.

Cathy Yardley needs to get out more. When not writing, she is probably either cruising the Internet, sleeping or watching D-list movies and adding to her unnatural mental store of character-actor trivia. She can hum along with all the theme songs on Cartoon Network's *Adult Swim* and is learning Japanese from anime. She deems Daria a positive role model. Her family is considering performing an intervention for her addiction to pop culture. For those similarly addicted, drop her a line at cathy@cathyyardley.com.

Stephanie Doyle loves to create characters. A dedicated romance reader, she quickly fell in love with the idea of writing her own romantic stories——some funny, some adventurous, but all delivering the quintessential happy ending. At eighteen she submitted her first story to Harlequin Books and by twenty-six she was published. Now in her thirties, she struggles between the demands of her "day" job, her writing and trying to find a little romance of her own. She lives in south Jersey with her two cats, Alexandria Hamilton and Theodora Roosevelt. She wants to get a dog, but the cats have outvoted her. Stephanie loves any kind of feedback. You can contact her at her Web site, www.stephaniedoyle.net.

Jacquie D'Alessandro

Cathy Yardley

Stephanie Doyle

Come September

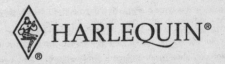

HARLEQUIN®

TORONTO • NEW YORK • LONDON
AMSTERDAM • PARIS • SYDNEY • HAMBURG
STOCKHOLM • ATHENS • TOKYO • MILAN • MADRID
PRAGUE • WARSAW • BUDAPEST • AUCKLAND

ISBN-13: 978-0-373-83723-6
ISBN-10:   0-373-83723-2

COME SEPTEMBER

Copyright © 2006 by Harlequin Books S.A.

The publisher acknowledges the copyright holders of the individual works as follows:

SUMMER BREEZE
Copyright © 2006 by Jacqueline D'Alessandro

SWEETER THAN WINE
Copyright © 2006 by Cathy Yardley

ICE CREAM KISSES
Copyright © 2006 by Stephanie Doyle

www.eHarlequin.com

Printed in U.S.A.

CONTENTS

This book is dedicated to my editor,
Alethea Spiridon, for giving me the opportunity
to write an older woman/younger man story.
And, as always, to my wonderful husband, Joe, who is
kind enough to forget that I'm several months older
than he is, and my terrific son, Christopher, who is
getting way too old to have such young parents.

Love you guys! xox

SUMMER BREEZE

Jacquie D'Alessandro

CHAPTER ONE

ELISE STANFORD SURVEYED the veritable mountain of cardboard moving boxes stacked in what would, after the unpacking, be the family room, and inhaled what felt like her first easy breath in months. Finally, after all the pain, she was ready to start over. A fresh beginning. Exactly what she and the kids needed.

Not that this change wasn't fraught with uncertainty. She now had an unfamiliar house that needed to be turned into a cozy home, new friends to make, a new environment to grow accustomed to, and a new job to settle into. But at least those uncertainties were of her own choosing and hadn't been thrust upon her by the sometimes unkind hands of fate.

Picking her way through the boxes, she walked into the kitchen then leaned her shoulder against the backdoor jamb. A gentle breeze, scented with a slight whiff of salt courtesy of the Long Island sound, ruffled her hair through the screen door. Bright, early-summer sunshine warmed her skin and she lifted her face, catching the golden rays.

Before deciding to buy this house, she hadn't been to Gateshead in fifteen years, yet Elise knew, in her heart, she was *home*. She'd always felt safe and happy, warm and loved in this sleepy town on the northeast end of Long Island where her family had vacationed for two weeks every summer when she was a kid. And home was now this outwardly unremarkable house whose kitchen and bathrooms and floors were thirty years out-of-date. It in no way resembled the executive house in the upscale gated community she'd sold in Westchester—a beautiful house, yet one too filled with ghosts of the past. Of happy times that would never be again. Even after almost five years, every corner of that house reminded her of Ian. Of what they'd had. And what they'd lost.

An image of Ian, the one she carried in her heart, of him smiling, laughing, handsome, robust, before illness had robbed him of his vitality, flashed through her mind. Ian's death had not only taken his life, but seemingly hers as well, leaving numbness where her heart used to beat. Cancer had stolen the man with whom she'd fallen in love twenty years earlier. The man who'd captivated her with his intelligence and infectious sense of humor. A man who had left behind a heartbroken son and a baby daughter he'd never see take her first steps. But if not for Jamie and Maggie, the fact that they needed her, that she was all they had left, she would have sunk into an abyss of grief from which she doubted she'd ever have emerged.

Over the past five years she *had* slowly emerged, at a rate some of her friends considered a snail's pace, but her grief support group had taught her that mourning was different for everyone, and required different amounts of time for everyone. That magic "one year" time period after Ian's death simply hadn't worked for her. But after five years of living nearly exclusively for her children, she was finally ready to start living for herself again. She'd made a few strides in that direction, had attempted several dates, and knew, in her heart, that this move, this change, was what she needed to move forward.

A shriek of childish laughter drew her attention and her gaze cut to Maggie, running across the backyard in pursuit of a soccer ball, her honey-colored curls flying behind her as Jamie chased her, purposely slowing his steps so as not to overtake his younger sister.

A smile curved her lips even as a lump lodged in her throat. Jamie seemed to have grown six inches since his eleventh birthday last month. Clearly he'd be tall, like Ian, yet he didn't just resemble his father in looks. He possessed Ian's intelligence and patience. His compassion. She watched him scoop up his sister and twirl her around twice before setting her back on her feet with a laugh. His glasses slid down his nose and he pushed them up with an unconscious gesture. He caught sight of her in the doorway and waved with one hand while executing a gentle pass kick to Maggie whose eyes shone with delight.

Maggie... How was it her baby was going to start kindergarten in the fall? In some ways the past five years seemed to have lasted a lifetime, but as far as the children growing up, they'd flown by on wings.

Elise waved back, then called out, "Snack in about thirty minutes, okay?"

Jamie shot her a thumbs up and Maggie yelled, "'Kay, Mommy."

Moving away from the door, she poured a cup of coffee then consulted the calendar she'd attached to the refrigerator. Her new bedroom furniture was scheduled to be delivered tomorrow, along with the kids' new beds, her new washer and dryer, and the comfy sectional they'd all chosen. Until then, they'd make due with folding chairs and blow-up mattresses. When she'd sold the house in Westchester, she'd sold most of the furniture as well. Maggie had been ready to move on to something less babyish while Jamie had wanted something with a desk and bookcases. And she had finally let go of the bed she'd shared with Ian, wanting a clean bedroom slate to go along with their new home and her new job.

Glancing at the calendar, she noted that the phone and cable companies were due later this afternoon. That gave her a few hours to get some more unpacking done. In fact, no time like the present. She'd just opened the nearest box, one labeled Kitchen, when the doorbell rang.

She maneuvered her way through the boxes then opened the front door. On the porch stood a smiling woman with snow-white hair, whom Elise judged to be in her seventies. In her hands she held a white bakery box and a sheet of paper.

"Good morning," the woman said, peering at her over the rims of her bifocals, her blue eyes dancing with interest. "I'm Frannie Cabot. I live next door. I know you must be swamped with unpacking, but I saw the moving van arrive yesterday and wanted to stop by to welcome you to Gateshead."

Elise opened the door wider, smiled, then introduced herself. "This is so nice of you. Would you like to come in? I just made some fresh coffee."

"I'd love to, but I'm afraid I'll need to take a rain check. I'm on my way to spend a day at the beach with my daughter and her family. But I'll be sure to pop over tomorrow or the next day. In the meanwhile, this is from Carson's, the best bakery in town." She handed Elise the square box. "Wish I could say it's fat-free, but believe me, you've never consumed calories that were more worth the cellulite than these."

Elise laughed. "Thank you." She lifted the box then breathed in. "Oh, yum. It smells like cheesecake. My favorite."

"And not just any cheesecake. It's called Chocolate Angel Silk Cheesecake and just so you know, it's addicting. We keep telling Gerald—he's the bakery owner —that he needs to start a twelve-step program. This is also for you." Frannie held out the sheet of paper. "It's a copy of what I call my 'Best of Everything' list. Best Chinese takeout, best pizza, best deli, best farm stand— all the food things. It also has all the best useful homey stuff, like best electrician, best painter, best general contractor. Of course, maybe you have a husband who's handy with that sort of thing—in which case, let me know and I'll add him to my list."

"No husband," Elise said. "I'm a widow."

Sympathy instantly filled Frannie's eyes and she laid her hand on Elise's arm. "Me, too, dear. Two years."

"Five years ago for me."

Frannie blew out a breath. "Everyone tells me it gets easier."

"The hole in your heart eventually mends, but I don't think the scar ever truly goes away."

"Well, we wouldn't want to forget the good things, the good people who have touched our lives, now would we?"

Elise shook her head. "No." Her focus lowered to the

list. "Thank you very much for this. There's so much I want to do with this house—updating the kitchen and bathrooms, building a deck."

"I saw your children playing in the backyard," Frannie said. "Remind me of my grandchildren. I have fourteen of them. Youngest is eight months and the oldest just graduated from high school. They visit me often and will be glad to know new kids have moved in. Your children will love it here. There're loads of youngsters in this neighborhood and the schools are great."

"The great schools are one of the reasons we moved here. I'll be teaching math at the high school starting this fall."

Frannie's smile widened. "Then you'll have a lot in common with Deidre Nelson who lives on the next block. She teaches science at the high school. I'll introduce you. In fact, I'll arrange a little get-together, something casual, maybe dessert and coffee, so you can get to know the neighbors. Let's see, I'm busy with the grandkids both nights this weekend and I play bingo on Mondays, so how about Tuesday evening?"

"That's perfect. Thank you. I bake a mean batch of chocolate-chip cookies."

"It's a date. In the meanwhile, about those renovations, call Seth McGuire. He's the best contractor around. Very reliable and does great work. Nothing slipshod with him. He's not cheap, but you get what you pay for."

Elise's brows rose at the name, which, while familiar, she hadn't heard in years. "Seth McGuire? I wonder if it's the same Seth McGuire I used to know when my family spent summers here. He was just a kid the last time I saw him, but that was fifteen years ago. I was friendlier with his two older sisters, Patti and Audrey."

"Yes, that's the same Seth McGuire," Frannie said. "One sister lives out west somewhere, and the other one's in Florida. His mother moved to Florida, too. The father died about ten years ago."

An image of Adam McGuire flashed in Elise's mind, his ready smile and even readier laugh. "I'm sorry to hear that. When my parents moved to South Carolina, we stopped spending summer vacations here and we lost touch with the McGuires."

"Didn't know the father myself as I only moved here six years ago, but if his son is any indication, he was a good man. Give Seth a call. He recently finished the Culpeppers' deck—they live just across the street—and it's beautiful." Frannie glanced down at her watch and made a *tsking* noise. "I need to get going, but I'll be in touch about Tuesday night. And I'll hold you to that cup of coffee."

"I'm looking forward to it," Elise said. "And thank you for the cake and the 'Best' list."

She watched Frannie cross the driveway and settle herself into a dark blue Honda Accord. After a quick wave goodbye, Elise headed back to the kitchen, where she slipped the bakery box into the fridge, then looked at the list Frannie had given her. She ran her finger down the typed words until she came to Seth McGuire, general contractor.

Elise instantly recalled the last time she'd seen him. It was the last summer she'd visited Gateshead with her family. She'd been twenty-five, her newly minted master's degree and teaching certificate in hand, and on the brink of becoming engaged to Ian. Seth had been about fourteen, a cute, lanky kid with unruly dark hair who loved the water and fishing and whose freckled nose was always sunburned. She'd watched him grow up over those summer vacations and vividly recalled how she'd barely recognized him that last summer as he'd grown so tall. She remembered teasing him about it and the bright shade of red he'd turned. She also recalled that he'd harbored a bit of a crush on her.

And now he was the best contractor in the area— exactly what she needed. With a smile, she reached for her cell phone. Time to see about getting the house remodeled and the rest of her life going.

CHAPTER TWO

"SETH, YOU GOING to Salty's tonight to watch the game?"

Seth McGuire flicked his gaze up from the nail he was about to shoot into the cedar deck plank to glance at his best friend Kevin, then shook his head. "Can't make it tonight." He shot the nail home, then looked around at the Longmore's deck, which was nearly finished. A very nice job, if he said so himself. Just a few more hours and the work would be complete. He reached for the next plank and set it in place.

"Hot date?" Kevin asked, from the other side of the deck where he was installing landscape lighting.

"Nope. An appointment to give an estimate on a deck and some home repairs." His heart lurched in a peculiar way, recalling his surprise at answering the phone earlier that morning and hearing a hauntingly familiar voice say *"Hi Seth, you probably don't remember me…"*

He blew out a quick breath. As if he could ever forget Elise Weller—or now Elise Stanford—the woman who had launched a thousand adolescent fantasies. Did any guy ever forget his first major crush?

"Dude, it's *Friday* night." Kevin's voice yanked him

from his thoughts and he looked at his friend who was shaking his head. "You're giving new meaning to 'all work, no play.' I've never known you to be such a dull boy. Especially since the tourist season has officially kicked off, and you know what that means—lots of scantily clad hot babes in town. Maybe those two we met last week—Amber and Tiffani—will be out slumming again."

Seth barely suppressed a grimace at the mention of the two young women. They'd been just like all the other women he'd met in recent months—attractive, but ultimately uninteresting, unable to discuss much beyond themselves, their former boyfriends, their wardrobe, and the drama in their lives. The thought of spending another evening with either woman, or another one like them, was more than a little depressing.

Setting down the nail gun, he reached for his bottle of water. After taking a long swallow, he wiped his mouth with the back of his hand and asked, "Don't you ever get tired of picking up women in bars?"

Kevin's brows rose and he simply stared. After a long silence, Seth asked, "Are you trying to decide?"

Kevin shook his head. "I'm trying to think up an answer that is *hell no-er* than *hell no*." His expression turned quizzical. "You okay? You've been acting kinda weird lately."

"I'm fine. It's just been a hectic week." True enough. And normally on a Friday night he'd be ready and willing to hit Salty's Bar and toss back a few brews and check out the newest flock of summer tourists, many of whom rented places on the more affordable North Fork rather than pay the insane prices the South Fork's Hamptons crowd laid down. In addition to the beach, quaint towns and great seafood, the North Fork had the added attraction of the local wineries, which drew impressive crowds. Many of whom were female. Which worked out great for a single guy like him.

But over the past six months—ever since he'd spent last Christmas in Florida with his mom, his sisters and their boisterous families—a nagging discontent had tugged at him. Something he couldn't name other than to call it *tired.* He was tired of hanging out at Salty's. Tired of meeting the same sort of women. Tired of transient relationships. Tired of going home alone. Waking up alone. In a nutshell, tired of being alone.

Spending that week in Florida with his entire family, seeing how happy both Patti and Audrey were in their respective marriages, how his mom was flourishing in her active retirement community, the great time he'd had playing with his nieces and nephews, had made his empty house seem even emptier. And lonelier.

Which was crazy. All he had to do was go to any of the local hangouts and he'd find someone he knew to talk to. Scaring up someone to go boating or fishing or beaching with required nothing more than a phone call. And on any given night he could go to any of the nearby bars or clubs and most likely score. And for the past few years, that had been enough—intermingled with several short-term and one long-term relationship.

Actually, when his year-long relationship with Andrea had ended last fall, he'd been relieved. He hadn't missed *her*—or the head games she'd played with him—but over the past six months he'd realized that he missed being in a relationship. Having someone to share things with. His glance flicked to Kevin who was looking at him as if he'd grown a third head. A *female* someone.

Maybe it was because his thirtieth birthday loomed on the horizon. A good time for a guy to take stock and reassess his life. And he'd realized that while he derived great satisfaction from his work, his personal life left a lot to be desired. But with a possible job offer in Florida, a change of scenery might be just what he needed.

Clearing his throat, he said, "Bob Wexford called me last night."

Kevin's brows shot up. "*The* Bob Wexford? Of Wexford Builders?"

Seth nodded. "The very one. He stayed at the Sperling estate in East Hampton last week. When he admired the deck and renovations to the pool house, Mark Sperling gave him my name and number."

Kevin looked suitably impressed. "What did Wexford want?"

"Said he'll be back in New York later this summer and wants to meet with me. To talk about possibly working for him."

"Here?"

"In Florida. Wexford Builders is based in Jacksonville."

Kevin set down the electrical wire he'd been working with and adjusted his Yankees baseball cap. "You thinking about moving to *Florida?*"

"You say that like it's Siberia. If he makes me a good offer, I'd certainly consider it. Especially since my sister and mom both live down there. It'd be nice to live closer to family again." Surely that would alleviate some of the loneliness gnawing at him.

Kevin's eyes bugged. "Dude, take it from me, having family nearby is highly overrated. Especially if you're single 'cause every relative feels this obsessive need to fix you up, and naturally never with someone who looks like Carmen Electra. I strongly suggest a distance of at *least* five hundred miles. Way I see it, you've got it made right here. With you in New York, Patti and your mom in Florida, and Audrey in Phoenix, it's the perfect Bermuda triangle of family distance."

Seth laughed. "You're only saying that because your folks and your sisters all live on Long Island."

"Exactly. So I know what of I speak. That cookout at my mom's two weeks ago? Holy crap, I barely made it out of there alive. All three sisters and my mom put on the full court press, firing questions about my love life, why don't I have a steady girlfriend, and 'I know someone who'd be perfect for you', blah, blah, blah." Kevin shot him a baleful look. "The least you could have done was come with me to run some interference."

"I would have—your family's great and I'm sure the food was outstanding—but I had to work."

"Yeah, sure they're great to *you*. You should hear my sisters talk about you." He adopted a high, falsetto voice. "Ooh, Seth is sooo dreamy. So handsome. So *hot*." He shook his head and looked skyward. "Give me a break. *I* don't think you're so hot."

Seth chuckled. "That's a relief. Too bad all three

sisters have husbands. If they didn't, I could marry one and we'd be in-laws. Then I could legally harass you at all the family functions."

"And I could legally toss you on your ass."

"You could *try*. As for your married sisters trying to fix you up, that's what they do. It's like it's their job or something. My sisters are the same way."

"Maybe. But luckily you've got that nice mileage bumper between you and them."

"I don't know about the lucky part." He shrugged and tried to put into words some of the frustrations he'd been experiencing lately. "Sometimes I think maybe I'm missing out on a great woman whose only crime is being friends with my sister. Well, that and living hundreds of miles away."

"Believe me, you don't want a woman who's friends with your sister. First of all, if you date her, then your sister is going to know all your business, and dude, you don't want to go there. Second, your sister doesn't fix you up with someone to have a one-night stand. Or even a weekend fling. Oh, no. She's fixing you up with visions of wedding bells in her head." Kevin visibly shuddered. "That's taking me to a scary visual place I don't care to go."

Seth took another pull from his water bottle, then again tried to voice something that had been roaming around in the back of his mind for a few months. "You might feel differently if you met the right woman."

He wished he had a camera to photograph the dumb-founded look on Kevin's face. After a full ten seconds of silence, Kevin said, "Okay, who the hell are you and what have you done with Seth?"

Feeling foolish for even attempting to broach the subject, he picked up his nail gun. "I'm just saying."

"Uh-huh. Well, *I'm* just saying that's a weird thing to hear from a guy whose definition of long-term, except for a few aberrations over the years, is five hours. Tops."

"Doesn't mean it'll *always* be that way. I mean, don't you want to someday find the right girl?"

Kevin waggled his brows. "Dude, I find her all the time. Usually at Salty's. On Friday nights. Just like you do. And it's clear to me that you badly need to go out tonight and get yourself some. Clear your head of whatever's messing you up and has you talking all crazy. Come down as soon as you're done giving your estimate. How long could it possibly take?"

"It might take a while," Seth said, setting the nail gun in place.

"Lot of work to be done?"

"Yeah. And it's for someone I used to know who's just moved to Gateshead. I'll probably spend some time catching up on old times and stuff."

"Yeah? Who is it?"

"Nobody I've ever mentioned. Her family used to rent the Kingston cottage for two weeks every summer when I was a kid."

"*Her?*" Kevin asked, his voice filled with unmistakable innuendo. "She hot?"

Seth couldn't help but laugh. "Do you *ever* think of anything else?"

"Nope. And don't act like you do."

Actually, he did, especially lately. But there was no point in delving further into that conversation with Kevin.

"So is she hot?" Kevin persisted.

"How would I know? I haven't seen her in fifteen years."

"Okay. *Was* she hot?"

She'd certainly made *him* hot, but not because of any overt actions on her part. "She was…classy. Uptown. But not snooty. And really smart." He vividly recalled the summer he was thirteen. He'd had to attend summer school because he'd flunked math. To his mortification, his sister Audrey had told Elise, but instead of looking at him like the crappy, screw-up student he was, Elise had offered to tutor him. Sitting close to her, listening to her soft voice, inhaling her flowery scent, he'd decided that failing math had absolutely been worth it. Blinking away the memory, he said, "She was older and hung with my sisters."

"How much older?"

"About ten years. But even if we'd been the same age, she was way out of my league."

"Yeah, but you know how it is—a lot of those classy 'out of my league' chicks dig the bad-boy thing." He grinned. "Which is why we do so well. No one would ever confuse either of us for investment bankers. You haven't kept in touch with this woman?"

"No. She stopped coming to Gateshead after she got married."

"Ah. Married. So it doesn't matter if she's hot."

"She's a widow. And has two kids."

Kevin grimaced. "Forty-year-old widow with two kids. Nope, that's definitely not hot. Something tells me you're going to need a beer after waxing nostalgic about the good old days. I say write up the estimate, get out of Dodge, then head to Salty's. I'll make sure whoever my hot babe *du jour* turns out to be, she has a friend for you so you don't have to play catch-up."

"Thanks, but I can find my own women."

And he could. But after years of playing the field, lately he just wished he could find *one* he really, really liked.

CHAPTER THREE

SETH SHIFTED his pickup truck into Park and stared at the small ranch house where Elise lived. Skeins of soft, early-evening sunshine glinted off the windows, mingling through the umbrella of shade cast by the huge weeping willow decorating the front yard. Knowing the houses in the area, he envisioned three bedrooms, two baths and a kitchen in need of updating. But it wasn't the prospect of taking on a kitchen job that had his heart skipping a crazy beat.

It was the thought, the anticipation of seeing Elise again. An image materialized in his mind, of the last time he'd seen her. With her bright smile and huge blue eyes and her thick, golden brown hair pulled back into a casual ponytail, her legs and arms bare courtesy of her shorts and sleeveless top, she'd been gorgeous, sophisticated and polished in a way that had simultaneously fiercely attracted and scared the crap out of him. He'd known her most of his life. Hell, Elise and his sisters had even babysat him a few times, but beginning with the summer he'd turned twelve, one look at her had rendered had him tongue-tied. He winced, recalling the major crush he'd nursed. His attraction to her had gotten even worse the following summer when she'd saved his sorry ass from flunking the summer-school math he'd been forced to take. And then the following summer, the last time he'd seen her, when he'd been fourteen, he'd thought of little except her, his mind endlessly imagining "what if" scenarios. What if he were ten years older? What if she were ten years younger?

She'd occasionally drifted through his thoughts over the years, always followed by the question *I wonder whatever happened to her?* Based on the news that she had two kids and had lost a husband, she'd clearly experienced joy and deep sorrow over the past fifteen years. *Haven't we all.*

When he'd answered his phone that morning, he'd expected to hear Kevin's deep rumbling voice. But instead, the soft, feminine voice he hadn't heard in fifteen years, the voice that had launched countless wet dreams had greeted him.

He'd asked about her family and hadn't been surprised to hear she had children, but the news that her husband had died five years ago had stunned him. No sooner had she told him than her call waiting had beeped and she'd said she needed to go—but would he be interested in stopping by around six o'clock to give her an estimate and maybe catch up on old times? He'd said yes—and now here he was. Feeling ridiculously out of breath, like a schoolboy facing his first crush. Which is exactly what she'd been. But he was no longer a schoolboy. So why did he feel so…discombobulated?

Hunger, no doubt. Because in order to finish the Longmore's deck today, he'd skipped lunch so he wouldn't be late for his appointment with Elise. Well, no big deal. He'd stop by Salty's on his way home and grab a bite.

After exiting his truck, he walked slowly up the cement path then climbed the three brick porch steps. The storm door was open, with only the screen door separating him from the small foyer. The scent of grilled meat wafted toward him and his stomach rumbled. He slid off his sunglasses, hooking them over the neck of his T-shirt then pressed the doorbell.

Instantly the sound of running feet reached his ears and seconds later a little girl with wildly curly honey-colored hair wearing shorts and a grass-stained T-shirt bearing an image of a unicorn skidded to a halt at the door.

"Hi," she said, studying him with clear interest through big blue eyes that he instantly recognized. By God, this little sprite looked like a miniature version of Elise. He judged her to be about the same age as his five-year-old niece Hannah.

"Hi," he said, smiling. "Is your mom home? She's expecting me. My name is Seth McGuire."

She studied him for several seconds through very serious eyes, then said, "Mommy said the last time she saw you, you were only fourteen. You don't look fourteen."

He laughed. "That's because the last time she saw me was a loooong time ago."

"Oh. Gotcha. 'Cause Jamie's eleven and you look much older than him."

"Jamie?"

"My brother. He's nice—*most* of the time. Unless I mess with his CDs or Xbox."

"And what's your name?"

"Maggie Stanford. I'm five and I'm going to kinder-garten in the fall."

"It's nice to meet you, Maggie Stanford. Do you think you could tell your mom I'm here?"

"Sure. She's in the backyard cooking dinner on the grill." She flashed him a gap-toothed smile that indicated a recent visit from the tooth fairy, then turned and streaked toward the back of the house. "Mommmmmmy! The man you said was coming is here." He heard the slap of a screen door. A few seconds later a figure walked toward him, shadowed by the sun's slanting rays, and he had to force himself not to press his face against the screen like a little kid. Then she emerged from the shadows, wiping her hands on a dish towel. She stopped in front of the door, then slowly opened it—and fifteen years slipped away, leaving him feeling like the same dorky schoolboy he'd been the last time he'd seen her.

She looked exactly the same…only better. Softer. Curvier. More…womanly. Just as when he last saw her, her shiny, tawny hair was pulled back into a ponytail, and she wore khaki shorts and a sleeveless top, this one a bright turquoise that accentuated the startling blue of her eyes. For several long seconds they simply stared at each other, and while he didn't have a clue as to what she was thinking, what he was thinking could be summed up in one word.

Wow.

In spite of going home to shower and change into clean jeans and a fresh T-shirt before coming here, he suddenly felt like a major-league slob. He curled his fingers inward to resist the urge to comb them through his windblown hair. Damn, Seth couldn't recall the last time he'd felt so self-conscious, as if he wanted to do a quick underarm sniff to make sure he didn't smell bad.

Surprise flickered in her eyes, and she blinked twice. Then her lips curved slowly upward, ending in the same bright smile that had always left him dazzled and speechless.

"Seth…hello." Holding the door open with her hip, she tucked the towel under one arm, then extended her hand. "How lovely to see you again."

He had to swallow twice to find his voice, a fact that surprised and slightly irritated him. Jeez. He was gawking as if he'd never seen a woman before. "Hi, Elise," he said, then reached out for her hand. Her palm met his and he swore tingles raced up his arm. "You haven't changed a bit."

She laughed. "And you obviously need glasses. You, I must say, have changed *a lot* since I saw you last."

"Considering that the last time you saw me I was a scrawny, moody, dorky teenager with braces and failing math grades, I'm going to hope that's a good thing."

"You've grown up very nicely," she pronounced with a smile, then pushed the door opened wider. "Please, come in."

He stepped over the threshold and, in spite of the stacked moving boxes, he could see she'd already made this house a home, placing little doodads that her children had clearly made here and there and framed photos on an oak coffee table.

"Come this way," she said, heading toward the rear of the house. "I'm grilling out back. Nothing fancy—just burgers and hot dogs. You're welcome to join us. Have you eaten yet?"

His stomach rumbled and he settled his hand on his abdomen to silence the sound, while all thoughts of grabbing a bite at Salty's vanished. "No. You sure it's no bother?"

"None at all. We can catch up with each other, then after dinner I'll give you the grand tour and tell you what I'd like done with the house. Sound okay?"

"Sounds great." He followed her through the kitchen then into the backyard.

The screen door closed behind him and he was immediately encased in the mouthwatering aroma wafting from the grill. The backyard was deep and large by Gateshead standards, surrounded by mature trees that cast the grass in pools of shade. He could see where flower beds had once lined the yard, but they were overgrown and the grass needed mowing. Maggie jumped up from where she sat on the cement patio beside a plastic bucket filled with sidewalk chalk. A dark-haired boy, sprawled in a lawn chair and wearing glasses, looked up from the book his nose was buried in.

Seth smiled at Maggie and she offered him her gap-toothed grin and a wave.

"Jamie, come meet Mr. McGuire," Elise said, flipping the burgers with the expertise of someone who knew their way around a grill.

The boy rose, settled his book on the chair, then crossed the patio. Seth judged the slim boy to be about eleven or twelve. He appeared somewhat shy and his glasses made him look studious. His feet and hands appeared too big for the rest of his body and Seth immediately commiserated, recalling the awkwardness of that age. While Jamie's eyes were the same blue shade as Elise's, Seth decided the boy must look more like his father.

"This is my son, Jamie," Elise said, pointing at the boy with her spatula.

Seth held out his hand and smiled. "Nice to meet you Jamie. I'm Seth McGuire."

Jamie held out his hand, unabashedly looking him over. "Hi, Mr. McGuire."

The boy's handshake was firm and brief. "Call me Seth."

"Okay." Jamie's eyes riveted on the anchor tattoo just visible below the white sleeve of Seth's T-shirt. "My Grandpa Tom has a tattoo like that. He got it in the Navy."

Since Elise's father's name was Bob, the boy clearly referred to his paternal grandfather. "That's where I got mine. My stint ended six years ago."

Maggie craned her neck to look at his upper arm, then shook her head. "Grandpa's anchor doesn't look like that. Grandpa's is all wrinkly."

Seth laughed. "By the time I'm a grandpa, mine will be all wrinkly, too."

"Grandpa says his hurt," Maggie said, reaching out a chalky finger to touch the tattoo. "Did yours?"

Not a bit, thanks to way too much tequila. "Enough so that I wouldn't care to do it again."

"I have a picture of my grandpa in his uniform," Jamie said, pushing up his glasses, "but it's still packed. After I find it, I'll show it to you. If you'd like."

Seth smiled. With those Harry Potter glasses and obvious love of reading, the boy reminded him so much of his nephew David, he had to squelch the urge to ruffle the kid's hair. "Sure. I'd like to see it."

"I didn't know you'd served in the Navy," Elise said from the grill.

"Just goes to show that a lot can happen in fifteen years," he said with a smile. "Can I help?"

"No, thanks. Have a seat and relax," she said, nodding toward the redwood picnic table. "I thought we'd eat outside since the weather's so great." She turned to the kids. "Jamie and Maggie—time to set the table."

The kids went inside and Maggie's firm voice floated out from the kitchen. "It's *my* turn to carry the drinks, Jamie, and *yours* to get the plates."

Elise smiled and shook her head. "We refer to her as 'General Maggie.' She's very shy and retiring, as you can tell."

He laughed. "She looks just like you. It's like someone tossed you in the dryer and shrunk you."

"We have the same temperament, too. We're both very bossy."

Seth straddled the picnic bench and watched her turn the hot dogs. He noted her shapely legs, then the womanly curve of her butt. It was nice to see a woman who didn't look like she starved herself. Whatever she'd been doing for the past fifteen years had obviously agreed with her. "I don't remember you as bossy."

She glanced at him and mischief danced in her eyes. "Uh, yeah, that's because I'm not. Nope, not at all. That's my story and I'm stickin' to it. How do you like your burger cooked?"

"Medium. You sure I can't help?"

"Well, you could grab the rolls from the grocery bag on the kitchen counter and the mustard, relish and ketchup from the fridge. The pickles, too. And bring out a tomato for me to slice."

"And you said you weren't bossy."

"I prefer to say I excel at giving detailed instructions. It's the mom and teacher in me."

"Good thing the Navy taught me how to follow orders." He stood, shot her a snappy salute and a grin, then headed into the kitchen.

Elise watched him walk toward the screen door then disappear into the kitchen. As soon as he was out of sight, she blinked and realized two things: she'd been holding her breath and staring at his butt.

She jerked her attention back to the burgers and cleared her throat. Well, who could blame her for ogling, er, looking? She wasn't sure what she'd expected Seth to look like; indeed, she hadn't really given the matter any thought. But she certainly hadn't anticipated that the skinny teenager she'd last seen fifteen years ago would have turned out to be so… so…attractive.

Not in a classically handsome way that would induce a woman to say, *Gee, he's really nice looking*. No, Seth McGuire, with his thick, mahogany, wavy hair that was a few inches too long, intense green eyes, dark stubble shading his square jaw, killer grin, and toned, muscular body that filled out his Levi's and white T-shirt to perfection would induce a woman to heave a gushy sigh and whisper, "Wow. He is steaming *hot*."

Not that it mattered, of course. He'd simply surprised her. Which was ridiculous. She'd known a grown man would show up. She just hadn't expected him to look like…*that*. To possess the sort of dark, bad-boy good looks that always garnered lots of female attention.

She flipped the burgers and idly wondered if he was married. There'd been no opportunity to ask during their very brief conversation that morning, and she hadn't noticed if he wore a ring. If he wasn't, women were no doubt lined up outside his house.

The murmur of his deep voice mingled with Maggie's and Jamie's drifted through the screen door and she inwardly smiled, imagining her daughter taking charge and directing Seth to where everything from the rolls to the relish were located. A minute later the trio emerged from the kitchen, all laughing at something, Seth leading the way, his arms filled with condiments. He held the door open with his shoulder, and Elise's attention dropped to his hands. They were tanned golden-brown and, like the rest of him, looked large and strong. He wore no ring. Her heart fluttered and she frowned. Obviously the heat emanating from the grill was getting to her.

Pulling her gaze from his hands, she looked up and stilled. Even though Maggie and Jamie had already passed, Seth remained in the doorway, looking at her with an expression that appeared decidedly...appreciative? Or maybe even...*heated?*

Her stomach performed an acrobatic maneuver and she blinked. Clearly she was mistaken, because when she looked again, he offered her a lopsided, friendly grin and moved toward the picnic table. The screen door slapped closed, the noise snapping her from whatever insane stupor she'd momentarily fallen into.

You idiot, her inner voice chided. *You're so unaccustomed to adult male testosterone—exuded from such a hunky adult male, no less—that a mere whiff of it renders you nutso.* Whatever look she'd thought he'd given her was obviously a figment of her imagination. And as for giving him the once-over *twice,* who could blame her? She'd be hard-pressed to name a woman, regardless of age, who wouldn't stare, given his starkly attractive, rugged good looks.

Inwardly chuckling at her momentary lapse, Elise scooped the cooked burgers and hot dogs onto a ceramic platter then headed for the picnic table. "Who's hungry?" she asked, setting the platter in the middle of the table.

"I am," answered three voices simultaneously.

While everyone helped themselves, she poured tall glasses of frosty lemonade. After all the plates were filled, she raised her glass. "A toast," she said. She looked at Maggie and Jamie. "To our first real meal in our new home, and…" she smiled at Seth, "to seeing old friends again. Cheers!"

Everyone clinked the edges of their acrylic glasses, then dug in. After swallowing her first bite of hamburger, Elise turned to Seth. "So what have you been up to for the past fifteen years?"

He squirted ketchup onto his burger. "The highlights? A year after graduating high school I enlisted in the Navy. As promised, they showed me the world—and let me tell you, seventy-five percent of the world is *water.* After putting in my time, I came back to Gateshead, bought a small house with my savings and started my own home-repair business."

"My next-door neighbor, Frannie Cabot—she's the person who recommended you—told me that your father passed away. I'm so sorry, Seth. He was such a nice man."

There was no missing the sadness that passed over

his features. "Yeah, he was. Thanks. It was very unexpected and incredibly hard on all of us, most especially my mom." His gaze met hers for several seconds, and she clearly read the sympathy and commiseration in his eyes. She'd told him this morning she was a widow, and although he didn't say the words, she could almost hear him thinking *You suffered loss as well...I'm sorry.*

She gripped her glass of lemonade to keep from giving in to the urge to reach across the table and lay her hand over his. Instead, she just looked into his eyes and said softly, "I understand."

"My daddy died, too," said Maggie, squeezing a blob of mustard onto her plate. "How did your daddy die?"

If Seth felt any discomfort at Maggie's blunt question, he hid it well. "He had a heart attack."

"My daddy got cancer. When I was a tiny baby. Were you a baby when your daddy died?"

"No," Seth said. "I was nineteen."

Maggie nodded. "You're lucky. I don't remember meeting my daddy, but I know I did because Mommy has pictures of us together. Jamie looks like him. Except for the glasses. My daddy didn't wear glasses."

Elise opened her mouth to change the subject, for while she encouraged the kids to talk about Ian, she feared Maggie's outspokenness might make Seth uncomfortable. But before she could utter a word, he said, "My dad wore glasses, but only for reading. We used to tease him because he constantly lost them, and you know where they almost always were?"

"Where?" Maggie asked, her eyes wide.

"On top of his head. Like this." He pulled his sunglasses from where he'd hooked them in the neck of his

T-shirt, slipped them on, then pushed them up, over his forehead until they settled on his head. "Then he'd do this." He frowned, pursed his lips and started patting his chest, moving down to his legs. "Now where did I put those glasses?" he asked in a deep, exaggerated voice.

Elise smiled, and both Maggie and Jamie laughed. "Mom does that with her sunglasses all the time," Jamie reported, reaching for the pickles. "So she went to the store and bought *six* pairs."

"And she *still* loses them," Maggie said with a giggle.

"And the car keys, too," Jamie added.

"And her cell phone," Maggie said in a singsong voice.

"Sometimes the only way Mom can find her cell phone is to call it from the house phone." Jamie snickered.

Elise shot her children a mock glare. "Okay, okay. It's not necessary to tell poor Seth *everything*, you know." She turned toward him and he looked highly amused.

"Glasses, keys *and* cell phone?" he asked, shaking his head. "You're a mess." He nodded toward his half-eaten burger. "But a really great cook."

"Mommy makes the best cupcakes in the whole world," Maggie enthused.

"And chocolate-chip cookies," Jamie added. "But she makes really *bad* fruitcake. Every Christmas." He screwed his face into a grimace and made gagging sounds. "It's gross."

"Everybody makes really bad fruitcake," Seth said. "I don't think there's such a thing as good fruitcake."

"My fruitcake isn't that bad," Elise protested.

"Mom. It's bad," Jamie said in a perfectly serious voice. "It's worse than Grandma's and hers is reaaaaaly disgusting." He turned toward Seth. "It's hard and has these icky sticky green things in it."

Seth nodded in complete understanding. "I'm feelin' your pain. My grandma uses the icky sticky *yellow* things and hers is always burned black on the bottom."

"Fine," Elise grumbled. "See if I bake any more fruit-cakes for you people."

"Great!" said Jamie. "I'd much rather have choco-late-chip cookies."

"Me, too," seconded Maggie, bouncing on her bottom.

Elise looked at Seth. "I take it you'd vote for choc-olate chip cookies, too?"

"Instead of hard, black-bottomed fruitcake? Heck, yes. Besides, chocolate-chip cookies are my favorites."

"Humph." She took a sip of lemonade, and noted how Maggie and Jamie were grinning at Seth. The awk-wardness she'd feared would permeate the meal at Maggie's mention of Ian's death had somehow magi-cally evaporated. Turning to Seth, she asked, "What are your mom and sisters up to?"

"Mom moved to Florida about eight years ago, after Patti gave birth to twins. She really needed a hand, es-pecially since she already had a two-year-old, and my mom was really lonely living here alone. I was in the Navy, and Audrey had moved to Phoenix. It took Mom a long time to get back into the swing of things, but she's doing great. Very involved in the golf community where she lives in Tampa."

"How many kids does Patti have?" Elise pictured Seth's vivacious oldest sister in her mind's eye.

"Three. She and her husband live about twenty minutes away from my mom. Patti's a full-time mother and totally involved with the kids' stuff. Coaches the boys' swim teams, is her daughter's Girl Scout leader. You name it, she does it. She and Rob—that's her husband— just celebrated their twelfth wedding anniversary."

"How about Audrey?"

"She's an R.N. and lives in Phoenix with her husband Alan, who's a cop. They have two kids."

"Do you have any kids?" Maggie asked Seth, dipping the end of her hot dog in the puddle of mustard on her plate, as was her habit.

"No kids," said Seth. "But I have pictures of my nieces and nephews in my wallet if you'd like to see them after dinner."

"Can I see now?" Maggie asked.

"After dinner," Elise said. "We don't want the pictures to get smeared with mustard."

Seth nodded toward the kids. "Well, I can see a couple of things that have kept you busy over the past fifteen years. Last time I saw you, you were getting ready to begin a teaching job. How'd that work out?"

"Great. I taught until Jamie came along, then stayed at home until he started kindergarten. I'd planned to do the same with Maggie, but…things didn't work out that way. I taught math at a high school near where we lived in Westchester, but it was time for a change. When the teaching position became available out here, the three of us agreed it would be a great adventure to live near the beach. Jamie was changing schools anyway since he'd finished elementary school, and with Maggie starting kindergarten, the timing was perfect all around."

"And your folks? How are they?"

"Terrific. They recently bought a house in Mystic, Connecticut, which means they're only an hour-and-twenty-minute ferry ride away."

"I can't wait to go on the ferry boat to visit them," Maggie said.

"Since your mom used to spend summer vacations here," Seth said to the kids, "she already knows how great Gateshead is, but believe me, you guys are going to love it. I grew up here, and even though it's a small town, there's lots to do. Aside from all the usual stuff like movies and bowling, there's swimming, boating, fishing, clamming, crabbing—everything the beach has to offer. And there's a great aquarium not too far away in Riverhead."

"My class trip two years ago was to the New York Aquarium," Jamie said. "It was way cool."

"Mommy said she'd take us for a boat ride—as soon as we get a boat."

"A little boat," Elise broke in. "Very little. Like a row boat."

"And teach us how to fish and sail—as soon as she learns how," Jamie added.

"We have a lot to learn," Elise said.

"I seem to recall you having an aversion to baiting a hook," Seth said with a teasing grin.

"Still do. But a mom's gotta do what a mom's gotta do."

"Well, if you need some help, I know how to fish and sail. And I have a boat."

"What kind of boat?" Jamie asked, leaning forward.

"A seventeen-foot Boston Whaler. It's great for fishing and waterskiing and just riding around."

Maggie's face lit up. "Will you take us for a boat ride?"

"Maggie, it's not polite to invite yourself," Elise admonished.

"Actually, I'd love to take you—if you'd like."

"Can we, Mom?" Maggie asked, employing her best puppy-dog eyes and wheedling tone.

"Yeah, Mom, can we?" Jamie joined in.

She turned to Seth. "It appears we'd like."

He smiled into her eyes and something that felt like warm honey eased through her. "Great. How does Sunday sound? The weather's supposed to be good."

"That sounds really nice," Elise said. "Thank you."

"It's a date," Seth said. Maggie clapped and Jamie's shy smile bloomed.

Elise's heart skipped at his words and she inwardly scowled. It was absolutely not a date. The thought of going on a *date* with Seth was—*tempting beyond all measure*—utterly ridiculous. While part of her "move on with her life" plan included a desire to more thoroughly dip her toe back into the dating pool, Seth certainly wasn't someone she'd ever date. He was too young. Too…bachelorlike. And far too sexy. And undoubtedly had a steady stream of gorgeous twentysomething girlfriends who sported navel rings and were cellulite and stretch-mark free. She needed to keep her sights on older men. Mature men who wouldn't be described by the words "eye candy."

She was already stressed enough about fitting into a new community, making new friends and starting a new job. She certainly didn't need to add to the pressure with an impossible and completely inappropriate attraction to a much younger man.

Seth was merely being kind, a much-appreciated gesture since they were new in town. And he clearly had a nice rapport with kids—no doubt he was a great uncle to his sisters' kids. She bit into her burger and listened while Jamie related the details of his class trip to the aquarium to Seth, who listened attentively and asked questions. It appeared that they'd all found a friend.

Now it would be nice if she could find an appropriate man to date.

And that man was absolutely *not* the hunk sitting at her picnic table.

CHAPTER FOUR

AFTER THE DINNER DISHES had been cleared away, and the kids were playing in the backyard, Seth stood in Elise's kitchen, his hips leaning against her Formica counter while he jotted down notes as she described the updates she wanted—joining the notes he'd already taken on the deck she envisioned. He made some suggestions, asked a number of questions, and was doing a damn good job, if he said so himself, of concentrating on the task at hand.

Until she reached up to illustrate the sort of upper cabinets she had in mind. Her shoulder brushed against his arm, and he was suddenly aware of how close she stood. He pulled in a sharp breath and her scent filled his head. She smelled really good. Soft and clean with a subtle hint of some kind of flower. As if she'd just stepped from the shower then wandered through a garden.

An image instantly materialized in his mind, of Elise standing beneath a steamy spray, water sluicing down her wet, naked body. Her eyes half-closed, lips parted, reaching up to slick back her wet hair. Then him stepping up behind her, fitting his wet, naked body to hers, sliding his arms around her waist, leaning forward to bury his lips in that delicious spot where her neck and shoulder met—

"Is something wrong, Seth?"

Her voice yanked him from his heated reverie. He blinked and realized he was staring. At that delicious spot where her neck and shoulder met. He jerked his head up but clearly she'd noticed his fascination, because she fluttered her fingers over her neck.

"Is there something on me?"

Yeah. My mouth. My hands. "Uh, no. I was just, um, thinking."

"About the cabinets?"

Cabinets? "Ah, yeah." He inwardly winced. He'd never been a good liar and he sounded like an idiot even to his own ears. "I mean, no. I mean, what about the countertop?"

"Definitely granite. I want to add a snack bar, and replace the floor with ceramic tile. Something with a terra-cotta look."

He nodded, scribbled a few more notes, then spent several minutes taking measurements. When he finished, he asked, "What's next?"

"The bathrooms. There are two full baths and they both need redoing." After taking notes and measurements on the bathroom Elise said would be mostly for the kids' use, she led him farther down the hallway.

"This is the master bedroom," she said, walking through the last doorway. "The master bath is attached."

He followed her into the room and noted the air mattresses on the floor. "Where's your furniture?"

"It's being delivered tomorrow. All brand-new—bed, mattress, dresser, the whole enchilada. Since I was moving into a new bedroom, I decided it was time for a new bed."

Do not, under any circumstances, think of her in bed, man. Unfortunately, the mental warning came too late, and before he could stop it, an image of Elise stretched out on the bed, wearing a seductive smile and not much else, popped into his mind. Damn. He needed a cold shower.

They stepped into the master bathroom and, like the kitchen and other bathroom, the fixtures were at least thirty years out-of-date. After describing the sort of vanity, sink and lighting she wanted, she pointed to the worn porcelain tub. "I want a jet tub in here."

Before he could stop it, another image popped into his mind. This one of Elise, her tawny hair piled loosely on her head, lounging in a swirl of bubbles in her whirlpool bath, her eyes filled with sensual invitation as she asked in a smoky voice, *Care to join me?*

"Yes," he said without hesitation.

"Yes, what?"

The image blinked away, and Seth whipped his head around. He found Elise regarding him with a questioning look.

"Yes, what?" she repeated.

He dragged his hand through his hair. "Uh, yes, I agree a jet tub is a great idea."

"I had one in the Westchester house and loved it. Very relaxing."

Without even trying, he could think of ten things he'd love to do with her in a bathtub—and none of them involved relaxing. Relaxing could be number eleven. Maybe.

Get a grip, his inner voice chided. *She's not one of*

the girls out in Salty's looking for some action. She's a mom, *for cryin' out loud.*

Right. A mom. He'd never had sexual thoughts about anyone's mother before. But hell, there was no denying the heat she inspired. Yet, it was more than heat. In spite of the discomfort caused by his inappropriate thoughts, he liked being here. A lot. Liked her house. Liked her kids. He'd enjoyed himself and felt more comfortable here with her and her children than he had in a long time.

"I plan to paint the bedrooms myself," she said, once again reclaiming his wandering thoughts.

"Enjoy getting all speckled with paint?" he asked with a grin.

"As a matter of fact, I do—something I hadn't realized until I repainted a few rooms in the Westchester house before putting it on the market. I promised the kids we'd head to Home Depot tomorrow morning so they can choose the colors they want for their bedrooms. As we've recently discovered, we all love Home Depot."

"You're singing to the choir with that statement. As far as I'm concerned, there's no store like it."

Her lips twitched. "Well, there's Bloomingdale's."

He adopted an exaggerated masculine "oh brother" look. "No comparison. Home Depot is like a department store for men. The scent of power tools, lumber, paint…" He drew a deep breath then released it with a satisfied *aah*. "It's like guy potpourri."

She laughed and her blue eyes twinkled. "Yes, I suppose it is, although as far as fragrances go, I'm afraid I prefer something a bit more flowery."

"You mean girly," he teased.

"Guilty." She led the way back to the kitchen, and, walking behind her, his wayward gaze traveled over her curves before zeroing in on her curvy butt. He had to admit that she had "girly" written all over her—in a soft, feminine, womanly way that had his pulse behaving as if he'd run forty miles instead of strolling forty feet.

Once in the kitchen, she leaned her hips against the counter. "Well, that's about it for the interior work I'm looking to have done."

"Anything besides the deck on the exterior?"

"Only the landscaping. I'm going to tackle clearing the flower beds and the planting myself. Or at least try to. I love gardening but unfortunately I don't possess a green thumb. I used to refer to my flower garden in Westchester as 'the cemetery.' It made a nice match to the mortuary for the tomatoes I tried to grow." She shook her head. "I'd hire a professional landscaper, but Maggie loves the garden and digging in the dirt, so I keep trying. It's become something of a quest."

"The soil here is good. Very rich and fertile. I predict loads of flowers in no time."

She smiled. "Oh? Are you psychic?"

His focus dipped to her curved lips. *Yeah. I also predict you're a great kisser.* Inwardly wincing at his runaway thoughts, Seth forced his gaze back up to her eyes. Which didn't really help because her eyes were as mesmerizing as her lips. *Say something, you idiot. Before she thinks you're certifiable.*

He cleared his throat. "Yup, that's me, the flower psychic. If you decide you need some help, let me know.

I'm pretty handy when it comes to yard work." The instant the offer passed his lips, he blinked. Maybe he *was* certifiable. What the heck was he thinking? He barely had enough time to keep his own yard looking decent.

"A kind and generous offer, but I've got it covered. Besides, I'm guessing you're not used to working in the garden with a five-year-old helper." She curled her fingers into air quotes as she said the word *helper*.

"Can't say I am."

"Let's just say that while Maggie definitely makes gardening more fun, she also makes it take a lot longer. And there's always a hose involved, so you can imagine what that means."

Seth grinned. "Oh, yeah. I know all about kids and hoses. My nieces and nephews are experts. As was I. In fact, I believe I still am."

A shriek of childish laughter drew both their attentions to the window. Maggie and Jamie were tossing a colorful beach ball back and forth in the yard. He turned back to her and said, "They're great kids, Elise."

She smiled. "Thanks. I think so, but I'm sort of biased. Of course, they were on their best behavior tonight. Believe me, things don't always go so smoothly. You already know that Maggie has a bossy streak—to go along with her drama-queen streak. And I'm starting to see hints of teenage behavior in Jamie—stuff that I'm sure will get worse after he starts middle school in the fall."

"Must be tough being a single parent."

She nodded slowly. "It is. Unfortunately, kids don't come with instruction manuals. It's hard, and often exhausting, to be the only one in charge. To not have someone else to share the responsibility." For several seconds her eyes took on a faraway expression. "And sad not to have someone else to share the joys."

"You're obviously doing a great job."

Her expression cleared and she smiled at him. "Thank you. Most of the time I feel as if I have no clue what I'm doing, but the three of us have muddled along pretty well so far."

"You don't have a boyfriend?" He tossed out the question in a casual tone and ignored the sudden tension gripping him.

She shook her head, and for reasons he refused to examine too closely, his shoulders relaxed.

"Truth be told, I've only gone on a handful of dates in the past few years."

"Not for lack of being asked, I'm sure."

She appeared startled by his compliment, then she laughed. "You're angling for some of my homemade chocolate-chip cookies, aren't you?"

"I wouldn't say no." *To anything you might offer.* He instantly shot his runaway libido a frown and forced himself to remain focused on the conversation before his thought process got totally derailed.

"I'll keep that in mind," Elise said. She then crossed her arms over her chest and shot him a speculative look. "You're single. Tell me, how can you stand dating?"

He couldn't help but chuckle at her bewildered tone. "I take it your dates didn't go so well?"

"With few exceptions, they were…not good. Completely awkward." She drew a deep breath. "But in all fairness to those men, *I* was the problem. They were all fix-ups by well-meaning friends that I accepted for the wrong reasons. Because I felt obligated to people who were trying to help. Because I listened to other people's opinions about how much time I needed to mourn. It took me a long while to work through everything, but over the past year, I've finally gotten to where I feel ready to wade back into the dating waters."

His heart seemed to jump over itself. "I wish you luck. Be careful for sharks. And for guys with too much chlorine in their gene pool."

"Ah. You met my last two dates," she said with a grimace, and he laughed.

"Of course, the biggest problem," she said, "is now that I finally feel ready, I can't seem to meet a man I'd actually like to go on a date with."

The words *how about me?* rushed into his throat, and he had to clamp his lips shut in order to keep from saying them. Jeez, he was losing his mind. Why on earth would a classy woman like Elise want to go on a date with him? She was the sort of woman who dated guys who wore designer clothes and drove fancy cars. Not guys who wore Levi's and T-shirts and drove pickup trucks. She was suited to men who smelled like stocks and bonds, not like sawdust and paint.

Their gazes held for several long seconds. Looking into those gorgeous blue eyes, Seth's mind went blank and he completely dropped the conversational ball. Instead he simply drank in the sight of her, softly gilded by the day's final rays of mellow sunlight. A lock of tawny hair had worked loose from her ponytail, and he had to clench his fingers to keep from reaching out to tuck the shiny strands behind her ear. And it occurred to him that he had only to reach out to do so…she stood no more than a few feet away.

Just as he was about to shake himself from his Elise-induced stupor and get the conversation going again, her attention shifted down to his mouth. That brief look jolted through his system like a bolt of lightning. Before he could recover his wits, the tip of her tongue peeked out to moisten her lips...a pink flick that completely fried the few remaining circuits the lightning bolt hadn't sizzled. Then she blinked and raised her eyes back to his.

"Well, *that* was more information about me than you ever wanted to know, I'm sure," she said with a short laugh that sounded decidedly self-conscious.

Probably it was just as well that he couldn't locate his voice, otherwise he most likely would have blurted out something that would make him sound like the schoolboy nursing a major crush that he'd once been. Something along the lines of *I want to know everything*. Problem was, he really *did* want to know everything. Which was crazy. And totally perplexing. He'd never experienced such a desire before.

The silence dragged on and Seth racked his brain for something to say. Something clever or witty, but since the only sentence he could think of was *I really, really want to kiss you* and that didn't seem appropriate, he kept his mouth shut. Which no doubt made her think he was a complete clod. Which he clearly was. 'Cause what sort of guy met a woman he hadn't seen in fifteen years and the only thing he could think about was learning every tiny detail of her life, kissing her sense-less, and getting her naked—and not necessarily in that order?

A rose blush stained her cheeks, a splash of color his

fingers itched to touch, and finally she broke the silence. "How long before you can give me an estimate?"

He had to swallow to locate his voice. "Estimate?"

She glanced significantly at the notebook he held. "For the work I want done on the house."

He barely suppressed a groan. Jeez, he really *was* a complete clod. Which was especially aggravating because normally he wasn't. Especially around women. But one look at Elise turned him into the same dorky, tongue-tied, horny dolt he'd been fifteen years ago.

"Right," he said, forcing himself to shift into business mode, a transition that felt decidedly less than smooth. "*That* estimate. I can drop it off tomorrow after work—if that's all right?"

"That's terrific. But tomorrow's Saturday. Don't you take weekends off?"

"Not if something needs to be done for me to stay on schedule. I lost time on a bathroom job earlier this week because of a delay in receiving a special-order sink and tub from the manufacturer. Saturday's my makeup day. I'll swing by tomorrow night when I'm done—not sure what time it'll be, probably around eight or nine. If you're not home, I'll just pop the estimate in the mailbox."

"We'll most likely be home. The furniture is being delivered tomorrow, which means lots of unpacking boxes and arranging things afterward."

"Great. Well. I guess I'll get going," Seth said, suddenly aware of how much he wanted to stay. But it was time to go. Definitely. He had friends to hang with at Salty's. Women to meet. "I'll see you tomorrow."

Still, he stood there, staring at her, not quite sure what

to do. A handshake somehow seemed a bit formal, but a hug—which sounded way too good—seemed too familiar.

He was spared from the decision when the back door opened with a bang and Jamie and Maggie dashed inside. Both kids sported sweat-darkened hair and their faces glistened with exertion. "Can we go out for ice cream, Mom?" Jamie asked, wiping his brow with the back of his hand.

Elise smiled and ruffled his damp hair. "I must say, you look like a man who could use an ice cream."

"I look like I could use one, too, Mommy," Maggie chimed in. "A really, really big one."

Elise laughed. "Yes, you do, sweetie." She turned toward Seth. "So where's the best place to get ice cream around here? It used to be Ferguson's Sweet Shoppe."

"Still is, only now it's called Ferguson's Sweet Shoppe and Café. A couple of years ago Dave Ferguson bought the storefront next door and expanded. Now, in addition to ice cream, you can get homemade soups, sandwiches, desserts, coffee, and my personal favorite, gelato."

"Gelato?" Elise repeated with the sort of reverence normally bestowed on royalty. "I *love* gelato."

"What's gelato?" Maggie and Jamie asked in unison.

"What's gelato?" Seth said in an exaggerated stunned tone. "Why, it's only the most delicious thing you've ever tasted in your life. It's like ice cream, only ten times better." With the kids looking suitably impressed, he threw a mock frown at Elise. "Clearly you've neglected the education of these poor children if they've never tasted gelato."

"I've never eaten it anywhere other than Italy," she said. "I've never even *seen* it anywhere other than Italy."

"Hey, Gateshead may look like a small, sleepy town, but let me tell you, we are on the cutting edge of frozen dessert treats," he informed her in a very serious voice.

Laughter danced in her eyes. "Obviously." She turned to the kids. "Go wash your hands and faces and I'll introduce you to the wonders of Italian ice cream."

Jamie grinned and dashed down the hall toward the bathroom, Maggie hot on his heels. With the sounds of their voices and water splashing echoing down the hallway, Elise asked, "Would you care to join us? We may be noisy, and we're sort of sloppy ice-cream eaters, but we're pretty harmless. Usually."

Seth quickly weighed his options. Cold beer and a fresh assortment of hot willing babes at Salty's—followed by steamy, no-strings-attached sex with one of those hot and willing babes. Or, ice cream with a mom with whom there was zero chance of getting laid, and her two—by her own admission noisy, sloppy eater—kids?

He was horny as hell.

His choice was clear.

He smiled into her blue eyes. "I'd love to have ice cream with you."

CHAPTER FIVE

AT NINE O'CLOCK the following morning, Elise and the kids had just finished unloading the cans of paint from their early jaunt to Home Depot—along with a dozen fresh bagels from Carson's bakery—when the doorbell rang. Hoping maybe the furniture delivery was early, Elise shooed the kids outside to the picnic table with their breakfast then hurried to the door. It wasn't the furniture deliverers but Frannie Cabot who stood on the porch.

"Good morning," her neighbor said with a smile. "Is it too early for that rain-check cup of coffee?"

"Of course not. C'mon in, Frannie. I have fresh bagels from Carson's, too."

After joining Jamie and Maggie in the backyard, Frannie told them all about her exciting day at the beach with her grandchildren during which they'd collected shells and built a huge sand castle. "And what did you all do yesterday?" Frannie asked.

Before Elise could answer, Maggie chimed in. "Mommy's friend from a long time ago, Seth, came over. He stayed for dinner and then looked at our house and then we all went out for…what was that kind of ice cream, Mommy?"

"Gelato," Elise said, inwardly frowning at the inexplicable warmth creeping up her cheeks.

"Oh, you must have gone to Ferguson's Sweet Shoppe," Franny said. "It's one of my favorite places."

"Seth's, too," Maggie said around a chewy bite of bagel. "He has a tattoo. Of an anchor. And his daddy died, just like mine did, 'cept his daddy didn't die of cancer like mine."

"He's taking us out on his boat tomorrow," Jamie added.

"He's going to show us how to catch fish," said Maggie.

"'Cause Mom doesn't like to bait hooks," Jamie said, with a touch of masculine disdain in his voice.

Elise, torn between amusement and mild dismay at their rapid-fire commentary, watched Frannie's gaze bounce back and forth between Maggie and Jamie.

But clearly, with fourteen grandchildren, Frannie was accustomed to such ping-ponging conversation. "Well, that sounds like a lot of fun. And like you've already made a new friend."

"Yup," Maggie concurred. "'Cept he's not really new 'cause Mommy used to know him. I'm glad she did. He's cool."

"I finished my bagel, Mom," Jamie said. "May I be excused?"

"Me, too, Mommy?" chimed in Maggie.

"Sure. Put your plates in the sink."

After the kids entered the house, Frannie said, "They're delightful."

"Thank you. I wish I had their energy. They can't wait for their new bedrooms to arrive today."

Frannie's blue eyes twinkled at her over the rim of

her mug. "It seems you took my advice and gave Seth McGuire a call."

Heat that had nothing to do with the bright sunshine suffused her at the unmistakable speculative gleam in Frannie's gaze. "I did."

"Quite the looker, isn't he? At least that's what we'd have said in my day. Young girls now would call him a hottie." She shot Elise a wink. "I know these things thanks to my teenage granddaughters."

A fiery blush warmed her face and she was saved from answering when Frannie continued, "Interesting that he joined you for ice cream. Especially on a Friday night. I hear he's a regular at Salty's, the local watering hole, and quite popular with the ladies. If he'd gone there, no doubt he'd have had half-a-dozen young chickies draped all over him."

"He probably went there after dropping us home," Elise said, trying not to imagine him with half-a-dozen young chickies draped all over him. Annoyance—at herself—rippled through her. What did she care how many women he had? She didn't. Not a bit.

"Has he given you your estimate yet?"

She shook her head. "He's dropping it off this evening."

Frannie's brows shot upward. "Really? Not tomorrow when he takes you all out on his boat?"

Elise wasn't sure if she was more embarrassed or amused by Frannie's very unsubtle hints. "He knows I'm anxious to get started on the renovations."

"My dear, if you think that handsome young man is making a special trip to your home on a Saturday evening to deliver something he could just as easily give you tomorrow when he'll be spending the *entire day* in your company, well, you need to wake up and smell the coffee." She saluted Elise with her mug. "Appears you made quite an impression on Seth."

"He was merely being polite due to our previous friendship."

"Uh-huh. And I'm the queen of England." She leaned forward and her expression turned serious. "I hope you won't think me too forward, but I find it best to speak my mind since at my age time is a precious commodity. I think Seth McGuire is a fine man, but a word to the wise, dear, especially as you're a teacher. Two years ago a huge brouhaha erupted when Julie Bartlett, one of the high-school teachers, took up with a construction worker from the crew hired to build a new track and tennis courts for the school. Unfortunately, Julie and her young man weren't discreet and were caught in a compromising position in the media center by Principal Mason himself."

Frannie scooted her chair closer and lowered her voice. "Julie was fired and moved away several months later. Based on what Deidre Nelson tells me—she's the teacher who lives on the next block I told you about—Principal Mason and the entire school board still remain up in arms about the entire incident. And scrutinize everything and everyone. *Humph.* Bunch of old busybodies if you ask me."

Elise sipped her coffee and recalled the morals clause in the employment contract she'd signed for her new job. "I appreciate your concern, Frannie, but Seth and I are only friends, and barely that."

"Of course, dear. But naturally we cannot predict

the future. One just must be discreet in these matters, is all. If Julie and her young man, who were both single, consenting adults, had chosen a more private setting than the school's media center to, um, show their affection, the entire unpleasant incident, along with the ensuing gossip and firing, could have been avoided. I've just always been of a mind that it's best not to give folks, especially in a small town like this, anything to talk about."

Frannie leaned back and smiled. "Now, about our dessert-and-coffee party Tuesday night—I'll provide the coffee, tea and soft drinks, and everyone brings a dessert to share. I have you down for chocolate-chip cookies. Eight o'clock, my house. How does that sound?"

Elise smiled. "That sounds perfect."

And while she appreciated Frannie's cautionary tale about the unfortunate Julie Bartlett, she certainly didn't have anything to worry about. Because she had no intention of risking her job in any way.

Or getting involved with Seth McGuire.

AT EIGHT O'CLOCK that evening, with the delivery men finally gone and the bulk of her belongings unpacked and put away, Elise stood in the doorway of her bedroom. The curtain panels she'd hung billowed in the breeze, and gilded ribbons of fading sunlight filtered through the sheer ivory material. All the new furniture—bed, night tables, dresser and chest of drawers—was whitewashed with a soft patina reminiscent of sugary Caribbean sand. The room perfectly exuded the casual, comfortable feel that she wanted for their new home.

It was the complete opposite of the more formal

cherry-wood bedroom set she and Ian had chosen
together the month before their wedding. She closed her
eyes and an image of them, laughing, flushed with happiness and love, wandering hand in hand through the
furniture store filled her mind. Kissing after they'd
chosen the bedroom set where they would sleep and
make love, laugh and cry for the next decade.

Opening her eyes, she looked at the swatch of the
paint color she'd chosen during her and the kids' early-
morning jaunt to Home Depot. She'd settled on a soft,
pastel turquoise that reminded her of a tranquil, tropical
sea. Again, completely different from the creamy-butter
yellow of the bedroom she'd shared with Ian, but different was precisely what she'd wanted. What she
needed. Ian would always live in her heart, in her
memories, and nothing would ever change that.

But she was ready to spread her wings again. To
continue with the strides she'd made, especially those
over the past year when she'd finally achieved a
stronger sense of emotional stability. Finally reached
the point where she wanted to meet new people and
make new friends—people who hadn't known her when
she was half of "Elise and Ian." And now that she and
the kids were settling into their new home, anticipation
nipped at her. It was time to start living again—as more
than simply a mom. As Elise.

Pushing off the doorjamb, she made her way toward
the kitchen, pausing outside Jamie's room. The thin
white cord slanting across his torso indicated he was listening to the MP3 player she'd given him for his
birthday. He appeared perfectly content, setting up his
collection of baseball cards and other sports memora-

bilia on his new dresser, softly singing to the tune pouring from his headphones.

A swell of love walloped her. He resembled Ian so much, right down to singing completely off-key. She was extremely proud of the young man he was becoming, but sometimes, like now, when she saw how tall and grown-up he looked, she missed the little boy he once was. The toddler who'd planted wet kisses on her face and fallen asleep in her arms.

Jamie caught sight of her and abruptly stopped singing. Blushing, he shot her a sheepish grin and waved.

Waving back, she asked, loudly so he'd hear her over his earphones, "Everything okay?"

He gave her a thumbs-up, and after smiling and returning the gesture, she continued down the hallway, pausing in the doorway of Maggie's room. Like her brother, Maggie was busy arranging her things, but in her case, it was the all-important placement of her collection of stuffed animals. Elise knew she'd have to remove all their knickknacks and shift the furniture when it came time to paint, but she didn't intend to begin that project until Maggie and Jamie left at the end of next week for their annual summer visit with her parents. In the meanwhile, she wanted all of them to feel settled in their new home and rooms.

"You can sit right here, Wally," Maggie said in her sweet, singsong voice, setting a gray furry walrus atop her dresser between a grinning alligator and a baby seal.

"How's it going in here, sweetie?" Elise asked.

Maggie looked up and frowned. "I'm not sure where to put Stripes."

After helping Maggie find a suitable place for her

well-loved tiger, Elise kissed her daughter's silky curls then continued down the hallway. Just as she approached the den, she heard the sound of a car door slamming, and the name that had drifted through her mind all day rose to her lips, quickening her heart in the most idiotic way.

Seth McGuire.

She huffed out an exasperated breath and looked toward the ceiling. Good grief, the frequency with which he'd entered her thoughts since he'd left last night was nothing short of ridiculous. But it was the *nature* of many of those thoughts that was truly appalling.

Oh sure, she'd wondered about the innocent details of his life—what he liked to do for fun, his stand on politics, his favorite movies, music and foods. She'd recalled how they'd all laughed at Ferguson's Sweet Shoppe. How great he'd been with the kids, sharing amusing stories about his childhood and asking them questions about their interests.

But to her consternation, she'd spent just as much time recalling the way he'd eaten his gelato. The long, slow sweeps of his tongue around the frozen delight and sugary cone had made her feel as if she sat in a steam room. That had led to imagining what he'd look like without his shirt. Without his pants. Wondering how he kissed. What his skin would feel like beneath her fingers. If his thick hair was as soft and silky as it looked.

What sort of lover he was.

She waved her hand in front of her face to cool the heat burning her skin. While she didn't recall the exact date of Seth's birthday, she did remember that it wasn't until late summer. Which meant he was only twenty-nine. And she was forty.

'Nuff said.

"You're turning into a veritable Mrs. Robinson," she muttered, shaking her head to erase the unwanted mental image of her palms coasting over his bare shoulders then down a ridged abdomen. "Put those lascivious thoughts of that…that *boy* out of your mind or you'll not only mortally embarrass yourself, you'll lose the best contractor in town." Not to mention running the risk of being the town's next Julie Bartlett and losing her job.

Laughing at herself for indulging in such crazy thoughts, Elise nonetheless found herself grabbing a quick peek at her reflection in the hall mirror. And reality returned with a thump. While she wasn't unattractive and tried her best to eat healthy and stay in shape—as much for herself as to set a good example for the kids—no one would ever mistake her for twenty-five. Which was fine under normal circumstances, but pretty daunting when faced with the prospect of re-entering a dating arena littered with young, nubile women who were wrinkle free and wouldn't know a stretch mark from a hole in the ground.

At the moment, she also looked like someone who'd been unpacking moving boxes all day. Knowing Seth was going to stop by, she'd contemplated changing into a nicer outfit, but had forced herself not to. No one unpacked boxes in cute clothes, and if she looked all spiffy, he might suspect she was trying to…something. Flirt. Or attract him. Which would only humiliate her and surely horrify him. Besides, he'd only be at the house long enough to drop off the estimate. Maybe thirty seconds. One minute, tops.

So she'd remained in her grungy clothes and cut herself some slack. After all, she certainly wasn't the only woman who'd ever fantasized about a sexy, younger man, and just so long as she didn't act on those fantasies, what was the harm?

One thing was for certain—these lustful thoughts Seth had inspired were just further proof she was indeed ready to get on with her life. To find a partner, a man to love and share her life with. Of course that man wasn't Seth, but he'd certainly relit the pilot light on her female hormones, which had resided in the dark for a long time. Now, when an appropriate dating candidate came her way, she was ready.

A knock sounded at the front door, and after drawing a calming breath she sincerely wished she didn't need, she moved toward the door. Seth stood on the other side of the screen. When he caught sight of her, he smiled and lifted his hand in greeting.

"Hi," she said, opening the door. Then she clamped her lips together to keep from gushing out a sigh of pure feminine appreciation.

Good Lord, he looked even better than he had last night—and he'd looked damn good then. His thick, shiny hair bore a trace of just-from-the-shower dampness. A black T-shirt stretched across his broad chest and was tucked into jeans which, based on the fascinating fade patterns across his groin, thighs and knees, were old favorites. Brown Top-Siders encased his feet…his very large feet. *You know what they say about men with large feet, Elise.*

She noted his gaze slowly sweeping over her, and she mentally kicked her own butt for not giving in to the temptation to change into something nicer than her denim shorts and lime-green sleeveless shirt. She gave her shirt a self-conscious tug and said, "This is what one looks like after unpacking moving boxes all day."

"Yeah? Then they should bottle it and sell it. You look great."

Even though he was clearly just being polite—or in desperate need of glasses—a warm blush suffused her. "Thanks. Back at ya. Installing bathrooms all day must agree with you."

He laughed. "You wouldn't say that if you'd seen me in all my grimy glory before I hit the shower half an hour ago."

Half an hour ago? How unfair was it that a man could go from grimy to gorgeous—*and* have arrived at his destination—in such a short period of time?

Reaching behind him, he slipped an envelope from his back pocket. "Your estimate."

"Thank you."

"If you have any questions about it, don't hesitate to call me." He peered over her shoulder into the family room. "Your new furniture came?"

"Yes." Holding the door wider she asked, "Would you like to come in?"

She fully expected him to say no, to make some polite excuse to escape and continue his evening, but instead he smiled, said, "Sure," then crossed the threshold.

His shoulder lightly grazed hers as he passed and tingles skittered down her arm. She sucked in a quick breath…a lungful of Seth-scented air that smelled so deliciously of freshly showered man that her knees turned woozy.

He walked to the center of the family room, then, settling his hands on his lean hips, he looked around. She absolutely didn't notice how big and strong his hands looked, or how his long fingers seemed to point directly to his groin. But just in case she *might* notice, she glued her attention to her new sectional sofa with the determined concentration a cat would bestow on a plate of tuna.

"It looks great," Seth said. "Very comfortable."

Before she could reply, he sniffed the air. "Do I smell cookies?"

She looked his way and laughed at his hopeful expression. "You sound just like the kids. Yes, you smell cookies. I baked a batch after dinner." She hesitated for a second, then asked, "Would you like some before you go?"

"Go?" He raised his brows and his lips twitched. "I've been here two minutes. Have I worn out my welcome already?"

"No, of course not," Elise said with an embarrassed laugh, then she winced. "I guess *I'm* not going to win hostess of the year. You're welcome to stay as long as you'd like."

"I'm not interrupting anything?"

"Not at all. I just figured you'd have better things to do on a Saturday night."

"Than eat home-baked cookies? Not a chance. There may be a guy alive who'd turn down an offer like that, but I'm not that guy. Any chance you'd offer a cup of coffee to go with them?"

"Absolutely," she said, her heart beating far more quickly than it should have or than she wanted it to at the prospect of him staying. "Actually, I was going to fire up the espresso machine and make myself a latte. Would you like one?"

"Sure." His eyes gleamed with mischief and he leaned closer, affording her another delicious whiff of his skin, then lowered his voice to a conspiratorial whisper. "Just don't let it get around at Home Depot that I'm drinking froufrou coffee drinks. The guys would razz me no end."

No doubt they'd razz him worse if they suspected he was hanging out on a Saturday night with a woman old enough to be his…older sister, but she wasn't about to kick him to the curb. "Your secret's safe with me."

A slow smile curved his lips, denting a pair of shallow dimples in his cheeks. "Great. Where are Jamie and Maggie?"

"Organizing their bedrooms. After several hours devoted to the task, their clothes are still piled on their beds, but the stuffed animals and baseball cards are nearly all put away."

"That's because stuffed animals and baseball cards are fun and clothes are booooring."

"So I've been told at least a dozen times already today. Would you like another grand tour now that there's actually something to show?"

"Lead on."

They stopped first in Maggie's room, where Elise watched her daughter's face light up at the sight of her new gelato-eating buddy, Seth. She took his big hand in her little one and led him around her room, proudly showing him her collections of animals and storybooks. When she finished, she said, "Mommy baked chocolate-chip cookies, the kind you said were your favorite. I helped."

Elise inwardly cringed. Maggie's statement made it sound as if she'd only baked the cookies because Seth said he liked them. Which wasn't true. Exactly. She would have baked them anyway. Probably.

Seth looked at her over Maggie's head, his green eyes filled with warmth and something else she couldn't decipher, other than to know it made her feel as if she were surrounded by hot coals.

"That was really nice of your mom," he said softly. "And you."

She forcibly dragged her gaze away from his. Good Lord, the man was potent. And without even trying. How irresistible would he be if he actually put any effort into it?

Best she not think about it.

"We'll all have cookies in a few minutes," Elise told Maggie. "I'll call you when we're ready."

"You're staying?" Maggie asked Seth.

"No way I'd miss out on chocolate-chip cookies."

They moved on to Jamie's room, and like Maggie, there was no mistaking her son's pleasure at seeing Seth again, especially after Seth proclaimed himself to be a die-hard Yankees fan.

"They're my favorite team, too," Jamie said.

"Yeah? I never would have guessed," Seth deadpanned, looking pointedly at Jamie's dresser where an entire lineup of bobble-head dolls dressed in Yankee pinstripes stood.

"Wanna see my baseball cards?" Jamie asked.

"Sure. I have a card collection, too. Haven't looked at them in a long time, though."

"Why don't you look while I get the coffees going?" Elise suggested, mostly for her own preservation. She needed a momentary break from the havoc Seth's presence was wreaking on her hormones.

"Sounds good," Seth said with a smile. He then turned his attention to the album Jamie handed him.

Elise escaped into the kitchen where she planted her palms on the counter and sucked in a deep breath. Okay, this was better. He'd just been too…close. He was just too…male. She just needed a little distance and a few breaths that weren't scented with sexy man and she'd be fine.

Damn it, she couldn't recall the last time she'd felt so flustered. It was totally out of character, as were the heated tingles warming her skin. Actually, they were more like hot flashes. Great. Probably all this sudden upheaval to her hormones had plunged her into menopause.

She'd just set the coffee grinder and espresso beans on the counter when she recalled the envelope Seth had given her. After pulling it from her pocket, she opened it, scanned the contents then raised her brows. The more she read, the further upward her brows hiked. When she reached the bottom line, she set down the estimate and headed toward Jamie's room.

Jamie and Seth sat on the floor, their backs propped against the dresser, a baseball-card album opened between them.

"Could I talk to you for a minute in the kitchen, Seth?" she asked.

"Sure." He rose and said to Jamie, "Great cards. You've inspired me to dig up mine and see what I've got."

"I'd like to see them," Jamie said.

"Then I'll be sure to bring them over."

"I'll call you when we're having cookies," Elise told her son, then led the way back to the kitchen.

Seth followed her down the hallway, sternly telling himself not to stare at her shapely denim-clad butt, but his errant eyeballs didn't listen worth a damn.

He'd thought of her more times today than he cared to admit. And not just today. He'd also spent a restless night, tossing, turning, staring at the ceiling, recalling in vivid detail her smile. Her laugh. The graceful way she moved. The teasing warmth in her gorgeous eyes. The way she managed to somehow make even a pair of shorts and a ponytail look elegant. The loving affection with which she brushed her hand over Maggie's hair or touched Jamie's shoulder. The way she blushed. *Blushed*, for cryin' out loud. He couldn't recall the last time he'd seen a woman blush.

And then there was the way she'd licked her gelato. Holy crap. The first swipe of her tongue over her icy treat had dazed him as if he'd been clocked with a two-by-four. He'd managed to suppress the fantasies watching her had inspired until he arrived home, but once alone in his bed, he'd let his imagination run wild. And gotten very little sleep as a result.

Anticipation had filled him all day today at the prospect of seeing her when he dropped off the estimate. He'd purposely suggested doing so in the evening in the hopes that she'd be home. He could just as easily have given it to her tomorrow before the boat ride he'd promised them, but he hadn't wanted to wait that long. Which was undeniably crazy. But definitely undeniable.

What he hoped to accomplish by seeing her, Seth had no idea. All he knew was that just being in the same room with her and her kids last night had made him happier than he'd been in a long time. He'd practically counted the minutes at work today. When he'd finally finished the job, he'd rushed home, showered and arrived here at warp speed, hoping all the while she'd be home. That she'd invite him in. Save him from another lonely evening, another meaningless night at Salty's.

He'd reminded himself at least three-dozen times in the past twelve hours that she was totally out of his league—and always had been. She was silk, he was denim. She was elegant—caviar and champagne, he was strictly pretzels and beer. She was a college grad and teacher; he'd barely squeaked through high school. Her husband had been a hotshot stockbroker who'd provided her with a fancy house in country-club territory. He worked with his hands, lived in a modest house and had never picked up a golf club. She had only to crook her finger and no doubt dozens of executive CEO types would line up for a shot at her. And unless he wanted to make a total ass out of himself, he'd better not forget it.

Yet here he was, unable to stay away.

When they reached the kitchen, Elise turned and looked at him. His heart performed the same crazy free-fall maneuver it seemed to execute whenever their gazes connected—this time with an added jolt of pleasure at the possibility that she'd baked cookies because he'd said he liked them.

Now why the hell would she do that? his inner voice jeered. *She baked 'em for her kids. You're just lucky enough to be in the right cookie place at the right cookie time.*

Right. Still, he wondered what she would do if he gave in to the gnawing craving to pull her into his arms and kiss her until neither of them could see straight.

He suppressed a humorless laugh. No doubt she'd hand him his gonads on a platter. Then tell him to never darken her doorstep again. Probably slap a restraining order on his ass.

And that would be that.

Definitely smarter to keep his hands and his lips to himself.

"What's this?" she asked, pointing to a piece of paper on the counter.

He glanced at it, then said, "The estimate I gave you."

"Uh-huh." Elise crossed her arms over her chest and gave him a look he bet had caused many a high school student to rethink the error of their ways. "Seth, I was told you were the best contractor in the area."

"At the risk of sounding conceited, I am."

"I was also told you don't come cheap."

"I don't."

"Then explain to me why your estimate is for *half* the amount of the other estimate I received."

Damn. He should have known she'd be smart and cautious enough to get more than one estimate. He shrugged. "I gave you the 'friends and family' discount. Did Greg Hutchins give you the other estimate?"

"How did you know?"

"Educated guess. Greg's the second-best contractor in the area."

"Are your prices and his normally comparable?"

"Pretty much."

"Then you've obviously made a mistake on your quote," she said, sliding the paper toward him and pointing at the bottom-line figure. "As much as I appreciate this 'friends and family' discount, surely it shouldn't be so much."

He glanced at the number. "There's no mistake."

"But comparing that to the quote from Greg Hutchins, you've barely covered the cost of materials. What about your labor?"

"My costs are covered just fine, Elise. I knocked a little extra off the price—"

"A *little* extra—?"

"—because I know you're anxious to get the work done and I'm guessing Greg can start within the next week or so?"

"Yes."

"That's because he has half-a-dozen partners. I prefer to do the bulk of the work myself and use only a few trusted guys on an as-needed basis. I already have jobs booked through the middle of August, and for now I'm not scheduling anything beyond that point because I might be taking an out-of-state job. That means in order to do your project, I'd be working here mostly in the evenings and on weekends, which would likely cause some disruption to your family. Which is something you need to consider."

"So you're compensating for any inconvenience by slashing your price."

"I wouldn't call it slashing, but, yeah."

"Well, I would." What looked like a combination of concern and confusion passed over her features. "Seth…clearly our previous friendship has made you feel obligated to make this overly generous offer. Good grief, between your other projects and this one, you'd be working nonstop. Please don't think I'm unappreciative, but why would you want to do that?"

Because I want to be the one who makes your home everything you want it to be. So that maybe when you look at it you'll think of me. Because I'd rather spend my evenings and weekends here, with you and your kids, doing something I love to do, than spend them alone. Or hanging out in Salty's, where, in spite of the crowds, I also feel alone. I'm just so damn tired of being alone. "Maybe I just want to do something nice for you. The way you once did something nice for me."

She frowned. "What did I do?"

"I would have flunked out of high school if you hadn't helped me pass math."

"Nonsense. Your parents would have hired a tutor—"

"Who I wouldn't have listened to. Any more than I listened to any of my teachers. I hated school and was a lousy student. For me, math was like being tossed in the middle of the ocean without a life jacket and told to swim to shore. *You* were what made the difference. You took the time to explain things to me—in a way I could understand." Unable to resist, he shot her a grin. "The fact that you were *much* better looking than my math teacher, old Mr. Brown, certainly didn't hurt."

A blush stained her cheeks, and Seth had to clench

his hands to keep from reaching out to brush his fingers over the wash of rosy color. "I'm guessing just about anyone would have been better looking than someone you referred to as 'old Mr. Brown.'"

"Maybe. But I definitely lucked out getting you as a tutor." He hesitated for a second, then figured what the hell—no harm in telling her after all this time. "Did you know I had a crush on you?"

"Yes."

He winced at her quick reply. "Was it that obvious?"

"Yes." Her lips twitched. "You were very sweet. Very cute."

He pinched the bridge of his nose and shook his head. "You mean dorky and awkward."

"That, too," she said, her voice gently teasing.

"That *splat* you just heard was my ego hitting the floor."

"Dorky and awkward—but in a very sweet and cute way. Don't worry. You outgrew it very nicely."

"Uh-huh." He crossed his arms over his chest and raised his brows. "So you're saying I'm not sweet and cute anymore?"

"No! I meant you're not dorky and awkward anymore."

He grinned. "So you still think I'm sweet and cute."

"No. I mean yes. I mean—" Her cheeks deepened from rose to bright red and she laughed. "We've gone way off on a tangent here. The point is, it was my pleasure to help you, Seth."

"And it would be my pleasure to help you, Elise. I've always wanted to return the favor. But I don't want you to feel obligated to accept. Greg could get the job done faster, and his men wouldn't be underfoot in the evenings or on weekends."

"But you're better."

"I am." He held up his hands, rotated them, then smiled. "Best in the business."

For several seconds she stared at his hands, which ignited fantasies she had no business thinking. Then she cleared her throat. "Actually, having you around in the evenings and on weekends won't disrupt anything as the kids won't be here. They're leaving Friday for Mystic, for a two-week visit with my parents."

"You're not going?"

She shook her head. "I think it's important that they have time alone with their grandparents. I'll spend a couple of nights there when I pick up the kids."

He went perfectly still, able only to stare at her while the words *she'll be here alone* reverberated through his mind. Damn, he didn't know if that was really great news, or really bad news. Certainly bad news as far as resisting temptation went. When he'd made his offer, he hadn't foreseen spending hours alone with her, without the buffer Maggie and Jamie would provide.

His better judgment told him in no uncertain terms that spending that much time alone with Elise would be torture. But his heart, his foolish heart that hadn't felt anything for such a long time, leaped with anticipation. He wondered how his heart would feel after a few dozen cold showers, because he sure as hell would need them.

"This out-of-state job you mentioned," she said, pulling him from his thoughts. "Where is it and how long would you be gone?"

"It's for Wexford Builders, a building company based in Florida. If I accept it, I'd move there."

Was that disappointment that flashed in her eyes? "That's a huge change."

"Yeah. But lately I've been feeling the need for a change."

"Something I understand completely. It's why we moved here."

"Everything's all up in the air right now—I won't even be meeting with the company's owner until August. But if he makes me an offer I can't refuse..." He shrugged. "In the meanwhile, I'd like to help you get your place fixed up." Forcing a lightness into his voice that he was far from feeling, he asked, "So whaddaya say? Think you can stand having me and my power tools around?"

"Think you can stand seeing me with my hair standing on end from stress as I work up lesson plans for new students at a new school where I don't know anyone?"

God help him, he'd take seeing her under any circumstances, hair standing on end or not. "Yeah, I think I can handle that."

For several long seconds Elise studied him through those big blue eyes, and he wished like hell he knew what she was thinking. Finally she smiled. "It appears you've made me an offer I can't refuse."

He released a breath he hadn't even realized he'd held. With a laugh Seth hoped didn't betray his relief, he extended his hand. "You've got yourself a contractor."

She shook his hand, and he absorbed the warmth of her palm against his. "A contractor—*and* a friend, I hope," she said softly.

"Absolutely."

And he'd make damn sure he didn't do anything stupid that would jeopardize that friendship.

But unfortunately, given how increasingly demanding the urges to touch her, to kiss her, were, he knew the effort was going to cost him.

CHAPTER SIX

WHEN ELISE AND THE KIDS arrived at Frannie's house with their platter of chocolate-chip cookies just after eight o'clock Tuesday evening, the dessert and coffee gathering was already in full swing. Frannie performed a quick round of introductions, told Jamie and Maggie all the kids were playing in the backyard, then returned to her coffee-pouring duties.

By nine o'clock, nearly two-dozen people filled Frannie's cozy house with conversation and laughter, and Elise felt as if she'd lived in Gateshead her entire life. She hit it off particularly well with the high school science teacher Deidre Nelson, who harbored the same love of chick flicks, romance novels and chocolate as Elise. With ten years' experience at the school, Deidre promised to show Elise the ropes and take her under her wing.

"School board's a bit stuffy," Deidre said, "especially after the whole Julie Bartlett fiasco—Frannie said she told you about it—but the school itself is great." She shot Elise a broad wink. "As long as you don't boink a construction worker in the media center you'll be fine."

"No problem," Elise answered with a laugh, meaning every word yet disturbed by the warmth that suffused her. It was obvious Deidre was only joking, but the words "construction worker" hit a bit too close to home, especially since Seth had been busy working on her deck when she'd left the house.

By the end of the evening, she'd accepted an invitation to a Tupperware party at Jillian Roth's house, who lived two doors down, had made plans to go shopping with Deidre, made a play date at the beach with Barb and Curtis Mackey and their two children, and had promised to host her own dessert gathering once the renovations on her house were completed.

When she and the kids left Frannie's house, Elise noted that Seth's truck was no longer parked in her driveway, and a wave of relief hit her, as the man was occupying her thoughts far too much. The relief was instantly followed by disappointment that she wouldn't see him, which meant it was best that he was gone. This desire to spend more time with him was becoming increasingly difficult to fight.

On the short walk back to their house, the kids chatted nonstop about all the new friends they'd made at the party. After closing the front door behind them, she hugged the kids and smiled. Their new lives in Gateshead had officially begun. And they were indeed home.

AT NINE O'CLOCK the following Friday evening, Elise surveyed her newly painted bedroom with an air of satisfaction. Perfect. The pale blue-green walls made her feel as if she waded in the warm, soothing waters of the Caribbean.

The phone rang and she carefully stepped over the

paint tray and can to snatch up the cordless handset from her drop-cloth-covered dresser. She smiled when she looked at the caller ID display.

"Hi, Mom," she said, tucking the phone between her chin and shoulder. "How're things going?"

"Wonderful," came Anne Stanton's soft-spoken voice. "The kids loved the ride on the Cross Sound Ferry," she said, referring to the boat service between Mystic, Connecticut, and Orient Point, the easternmost tip of Long Island's north fork. "They both thought it was 'way cool' that we were able to bring the car on the ferry. We've already been shell collecting and to the video rental store. I'm taking a breather while they're outside with your dad catching fireflies."

Elise smiled. "I'm glad you're having fun. But I miss them. The house is so quiet."

"And we love having them here. The house is so delightfully noisy. How's the painting project coming along?"

"I just finished my bedroom. I'll start Maggie's room tomorrow."

"And what about the rest of the renovations?"

"The cabinets and countertop will be delivered on Monday and Seth will begin work on the kitchen then. Hopefully it'll be done before the kids come home. In the meanwhile, he's working on the deck."

"I was so glad when you told me Seth not only still lived in Gateshead, but that he was doing your renovations. It's always nice to know someone when you're new in town, and the McGuires were such a lovely family. You mentioned he'd be working evenings. Is he there now?" This last was asked in a casual tone—a bit too casual, perhaps?

"Yes. He's outside, working on the deck." As she spoke, Elise was drawn to the window, as she'd been more times than she cared to admit during the past few evenings. And was treated to the same sight that had given her palpitations each time she looked—Seth, dressed in faded jeans and a T-shirt, working on her deck. Looking at him now, muscles straining, his shirt clinging to his damp skin, she actually felt her nipples tighten.

Good Lord, even dirty and dusty and sweaty, he was the stuff of fantasies, something she'd been indulging in with disturbing frequency. To her annoyance and consternation, in spite of her best efforts to exorcise him from her mind, the man stubbornly remained embedded in her thoughts, as if branded there. Which utterly confused her. Guys like Seth—hunks who were a little rough around the edges and exuded gobs of sex appeal—had never been her type. She'd always gone for preppy, executive, clean-cut men.

"Maggie and Jamie have been filling us in on their new friends and also all the things you've been doing with Seth." Her mother's voice drifted through the phone as Seth lifted a length of decking then set it in place. "They seem to like him very much."

They're not the only ones. "He, um, has a nice way with the kids," Elise murmured, her focus glued to Seth's broad back. "Thanks, no doubt, to all his nieces and nephews."

"They told us about the boat ride he took you on last Sunday."

Her heart skipped just thinking about it. Seth had been the epitome of the perfect host—attentive, amusing, and patient with the kids. He'd explained boat safety, and answered the barrage of rapid-fire questions Maggie and Jamie had shot at him. After a fun ride they'd beached the boat in a small harbor, gone swimming, built sand castles and eaten the picnic lunch she'd packed.

The sight of Seth in swim trunks had made her mouth go dry, and she'd thanked the Patron Saint of Stupefied Women that dark sunglasses shielded her eyeballs, which regardless of how hard she tried to focus them elsewhere, followed him everywhere.

With his broad, muscular chest and well-defined abs, he looked as if he belonged in an ad for exercise equipment. When he'd risen from the water after a shallow dive, his strong arms raised to push back his wet hair, the sun glinting on the water sluicing down his body, she'd done what any living, breathing female would have done—she'd nearly swallowed her tongue.

And based on the admiring glances he'd received from the female occupants of the other boats nearby, she clearly wasn't the only one who'd noticed. He seemed oblivious to the attention, however, and more than once she found herself studying him and wondering why such a criminally sexy man was unattached. Probably one of those commitment-phobic types. Not that it was any of her business. And she certainly wasn't about to ask. If she did, he'd likely think she was attracted to him. *Which you are, dimwit,* her inner voice sneered.

Fine. She was. But hey, show her a woman who *wouldn't* find him attractive and she'd show you a woman without a pulse. As for her unwise attraction to him, *he* didn't have to know about it. Elise cringed, imagining his reaction—horror mixed with pity that the

older woman to whom he'd offered kindness and friendship wanted to rip off his clothes and have her wicked
way with him.

But as they'd spent time together this past week, she
was impressed with more than his good looks. He possessed an easy-going, personable manner that the kids
naturally responded to and she greatly enjoyed—and
would have appreciated more if he didn't have her
hormones in such an uproar. Still, in spite of how flustered he made her, she enjoyed his company very much.
Too much. So much that she was beginning to doubt her
ability to remain calm and cool in his presence and not
make a complete and utter fool of herself.

Thank goodness she had her budding friendships
with Deidre and Frannie and the other neighbors to
keep her more or less on track. Still, it irritated her that
she simply couldn't stop thinking about Seth. She
should have been concentrating on her lesson plans. Or
gathering her materials for the upcoming teachers'
meeting at the high school for which she now only had
four days to get herself organized.

But what was she doing? Going on boat rides with
and fantasizing about a man who was so completely not
her type as to be laughable. If the school board had any
idea the sort of lascivious thoughts she was entertain-
ing about Seth, they'd invoke the moral clause of her
contract and fire her before the school year even began.

"Elise…did you enjoy the boat ride as much as the
children?" her mother asked in a tone that suggested a
long silence had passed.

Her eyes slid closed and another image of Seth rising
from the water filled her mind. "Sure did."

"Maggie said you baked Seth's favorite chocolate-chip cookies and that he's eaten dinner at the house *every night* this week."

Elise's eyes flew open at her mother's far-too-innocent tone and heat rushed into her cheeks. "Chocolate chip is also your grandchildren's favorite cookie," she said lightly. "As for the dinners, feeding him before he puts in more hours of work after an already full day is the least I can do given the amount of money he's saving me."

"Of course it is. The discount he gave you was *very* generous. Between his kindnesses to both you and the children, he sounds like a very fine young man."

"He is—with *young* being the operative word, Mom," she stated, feeling the need to remind herself, as well as squash the matchmaking thoughts her mother's tone hinted at. "*Too* young."

"Too young for what, dear?"

"Too young for whatever that is I hear in your voice." Her mother had been gently encouraging her to expand her social horizons for quite some time, but lately her hints had become broader. And more frequent.

"There's nothing in my voice. I'm simply asking what it is you think a man of thirty is too young for."

"*Twenty-nine.* He's only twenty-nine. And the thing that a man of twenty-nine is too young for is a woman who's forty."

"Forty is the new thirty, Elise. All the talk shows are saying so. Is he…unattractive?"

"He's…" *Sexy as hell. And has gorgeous green eyes I could stare into for hours. And one of the most beautiful smiles I've ever seen.* "Nice looking."

"If he were forty, would you date him?"

In a heartbeat. Although she wasn't sure if the naked, sweaty things she wanted to do with him would actually be called a *date.* "He's *not* forty, so it's a moot point. Good grief, he's not even thirty!"

"So the age difference—that's the only reason you wouldn't date him?"

"Well, there's also the fact that he hasn't given me any reason to believe he's interested in me. In fact, every time we're alone for a minute, he seems... nervous." Great. In spite of her best efforts not to, she probably was throwing off "I'm hot for your body" vibes that made him want to head for the hills.

Her mother chuckled softly. "Oh, honey, you're so wrong if you think he's not interested. No man, whether he's thirteen, thirty, or one hundred and thirty, does all the things Seth has done—for both you and the children—unless he's interested. Why, Jamie told me how Seth taught him to drive his boat and how he found his old baseball-card collection to show him. And Maggie told me that he played some sort of Barbie video game with her. Now *that's* a patient man."

Yes, it was. And her heart had turned to goo watching her children's delight.

"Elise," her mother said softly, "there's a reason he's devoting so much time and attention and energy to you and your family. Don't you want to know what it is?"

"I know what it is. He told me he wants to repay me for tutoring him all those years ago and helping him graduate from high school."

"A debt that's way past paid by now."

"He's just being a good friend."

"What if he wants something more than just friendship from you?"

Her heart seemed to skip over itself, leaving her with a dizzying combination of trepidation and anticipation. Then common sense returned. "Why would he, Mom? He must have hordes of gorgeous, nubile twentysomethings fighting over him. The mere thought of being with someone that much younger makes me feel lumpy, bumpy, clumpy, dumpy, grumpy, frumpy and schlumpy."

Her mother laughed. "Sounds like the new seven dwarfs."

"Yes—in a really depressing middle-aged fairy tale."

"Honey, forget middle-aged. How does anyone know when they're middle-aged? You could live to be one hundred and ten, in which case middle age is years away. You're a beautiful woman, Elise—something you've obviously forgotten. Something you need to remember."

After a brief pause, her mother continued quietly, "You've been alone for such a long time and more than anything I want to see you happy."

"I am happy. I'm making new friends and fitting in here very nicely."

"You're not dating anyone."

"But I will, as soon as I meet someone I like. My new friend Deidre mentioned fixing me up with a cousin who'll be visiting her later this summer. There's also a teachers' meeting next week. Who knows—maybe I'll meet someone there."

"That's good, although you should be wary of getting involved with a coworker. You know what they say about fishing off the company pier—it's not a good policy.

There's nothing but gossip to contend with while you're dating and nothing but awkwardness after you stop."

"And you don't think there'd be a boatload of mortifying gossip if the new high school teacher was dating a hot contractor ten years younger than her?" The mere thought made her cringe even before she visualized the disapproving frowns of the school board.

"Oh? So you think Seth is hot?"

Elise pinched the bridge of her nose and cursed her runaway tongue. "Mom, please. I'm already stressed enough about the renovations and the new job. I'm not about to add the stress of dating someone completely inappropriate."

"Honey, what's inappropriate about dating a decent, hardworking man who's good to you and your children?"

She blinked, nonplussed. She opened her mouth to reply, but shut it when no words came out. What, exactly, *was* inappropriate about that?

Nothing, her heart whispered.

Everything, her mind countered, *when the man is a decade younger than you, which would lead to gossip that would mortify not only you but the school board, too.*

"I strongly sense that you're attracted to Seth," her mom continued, "and from what you've told me, it's obvious he's attracted to you as well."

Her pulse skipped. "You think so?"

"Yes, I do. And I say go for it. You have the next two weeks completely to yourself. It's the perfect opportunity to find out if there's any spark between you."

Elise tried to dismiss her mother's words but couldn't. *Could* Seth be attracted to her? She didn't know, but suddenly she desperately wanted, needed to know. *Go for it.* Did she dare? Her gaze shifted to the window and settled on Seth once more, and she nearly groaned. *Go for it.* Lord, she wanted to. So very badly.

She couldn't recall the last time she'd done something just for her. Of course, there was every chance she'd make an idiot out of herself and he'd recoil in horror at the thought of a date with her. But if there was any chance this attraction wasn't one-sided...

Two weeks—to date a man who made her feel as if steam pumped from her every pore. Then, if things even lasted that long between them, she'd go back to being Elise the mom, Elise the teacher, Elise the woman ready to start dating men her own age.

"I suppose," she said slowly, "I could ask him, very casually, to join me for a glass of wine."

"Exactly! You don't have to worry about the children—don't think of anyone except you. Of what will make you happy."

"That sounds lovely, Mom, but I'm not a single entity anymore. I couldn't be happy in a relationship if Maggie and Jamie weren't happy."

"No, but you need to remember that your children love you just as much as you love them, and if you're happy, then they'll be happy. And it's clear they already like Seth. Besides, no one is saying you have to marry this man. I'm merely pointing out that you're both single, he's apparently a hunk, and since you're on your own for the next two weeks, it would be a perfect time for you to have some adults-only fun. Get your groove back."

A laugh sputtered in Elise's throat and she wondered if her mom knew what getting one's groove back entailed.

"And yes, I know what getting your groove back means," her mother said, in that scary I-can-read-your-mind way she had. "And I think it's high time you did so."

"I…I don't know what to say."

"Say, *I've met a nice man who I want to get to know better.*"

Elise drew a bracing breath, then pushing aside all the reasons she shouldn't, she said in a rush, "I've met a nice man who I want to get to know better."

Dear God, she'd actually said it. Out loud. To her mother, who would never let her renege.

Now the questions were: how did she intend to proceed and what would Seth's reaction be?

AFTER SETH HAD PUT AWAY the last of his tools, he drew a deep breath, then walked slowly toward Elise's back door, mentally repeating the speech he'd already practiced countless times. Damn it, his heart was racing, and he felt downright nervous. Which was crazy. He was never nervous around women. In fact, the only one who'd ever made him feel this way was—

Elise.

First fifteen years ago, and then ever since he'd knocked on her door one week ago. Yet in spite of his jitters, he'd felt happier and more alive in the past week than he had in years. Yeah, she gave him jitters, but they were *good* jitters. Jitters he wanted to explore further. And with her kids away, the timing was perfect. He only had two weeks and he refused to waste even one night. He was going to ask her for a date, and if he made an ass out of himself, well, at least he'd tried. He'd certainly made an ass out of himself for lesser things than a shot at being with Elise. At least this time the risk would be worth the reward. And as a famous hockey player had once said, "You miss one hundred percent of the shots you never take."

He might miss. God knows there were loads of suave, college-educated, executive suit types who'd fall over themselves to be with a woman like Elise. But if he missed, it sure as hell wasn't going to be because he didn't take a shot.

Seth entered the kitchen and had just finished washing his hands when Elise entered.

She appeared startled to see him and a rosy blush rushed into her cheeks. Then she smiled and said, "Hi."

That's all it took—one word, one smile, and every thought in his head scattered. He took in her paint-speckled clothes—a dingy gray T-shirt that proclaimed in faded yellow letters *You can fool some of the people all of the time and all of the people some of the time, but you can never fool MOM,* baggy sweat pants complete with a hole in the knee, old sneakers, and a tattered baseball cap that looked as if it had seen the world. She looked…perfect. Adorable. Gorgeous. And sexy as hell. Heat coursed through him and his heart thudded in slow, hard beats, as if she'd appeared wearing a black lace teddy.

Whoa. Do not, under any circumstances, think of her wearing black lace—at least not until you say what you need to say.

Right. Because one thought of her in black lace and he'd forget how to speak English.

He swallowed then shot her paint-spattered clothes

a pointed look. "Did you manage to get any paint on the walls?"

She raised her chin, which bore a streak of pale turquoise. "You'll eat those words when you see how fabulous my room looks. Want to take a peek?"

"Sure. But not now. I'll track sawdust all over the house."

She looked toward the ceiling. "Are you kidding? I have two kids, remember? Trying to keep a house clean with children is like shoveling snow before the blizzard stops." She grabbed his hand and led him down the hallway. "C'mon."

His fingers closed around hers and warmth spread up his arm. Seth looked down at her small, paint-smeared pale hand clasped in his and decided he really liked the way it looked there. And felt there.

When they arrived in her room, she slipped her hand from his, and he immediately missed the sensation of her palm pressing against his.

"What do you think?" Elise asked.

I think you're the most amazing woman I've ever met and I hope like hell I don't mess this up. He looked around the room then nodded his approval. "Great job. And I like the color. Makes me feel like I'm on a beach in the Caribbean."

Her full smile dazzled him. "That's exactly what I was going for."

Silence fell between them and he drew in a deep breath. *Now or never, man. Take your shot.*

"I was wondering—" they said in unison.

They both laughed. "Go ahead," he said.

She moistened her lips then said, "I was wondering

if you might like to stay for a drink. A glass of wine, or a froufrou latte if you'd prefer."

Surprised pleasure rippled through Seth, along with hope that since she'd issued such an invitation, she'd accept one.

"It's funny you should ask," he said, "because tonight is my buddy Kevin's birthday and I promised him I'd stop by Salty's—Gateshead's most popular bar—for a drink. I was going to ask if you'd like to join me. The place is always packed on Friday nights," he rushed on with his much practiced sales pitch, "so I could introduce you around. You'd meet some of the locals, that sort of thing."

There was no missing the flicker of surprise in her eyes, but then she smiled. "That sounds like fun. I'd love to go."

He barely refrained from pumping his fist in the air. "Great. I'll head home and grab a shower then swing back to pick you up. How much time do you need?"

She looked down at herself and grimaced. "Yikes. At least a week. But I'll do the best I can in an hour. That will give me enough time to clean myself up and call the kids to say good-night."

"Great. I'll see you in an hour."

She walked him to the door and, with a wave, he headed out to his truck. Just in case she was watching, he waited until he'd driven away and her house was out of sight before he pumped his fist in the air.

CHAPTER SEVEN

SALTY'S PULSED with noise and energy, and while it felt undeniably liberating to be out, Elise couldn't help but also feel a bit intimidated. She hadn't been to a bar in a long time and she was woefully out of practice. Yet her fear of being the only person over thirty quickly dissipated as one look around showed that Salty's clearly drew a mixture of all ages.

A sea of humanity seemed to stretch before her in the huge, dimly lit room. Rock music throbbed from a band playing on a stage in the corner. A half-dozen pool tables occupied another part of the room, and another held tables and booths crowded with people eating.

"I see Kevin," Seth said close to her ear, his warm breath shooting tingles down her spine. "Follow me."

How he could spot anyone in the crush of bodies she had no idea. He grabbed her hand, his fingers wrapping warm and strong around hers, and led her through the crowd. When they arrived at the bar, a handsome young man with shaggy light brown hair whom she judged to be in his mid-twenties clapped Seth on the back.

"Thought you'd never get here, dude. We started the party without you. Everybody's over at the usual pool table." The man's gaze slid to Elise and there was no missing the curiosity in his eyes.

After Seth made the introductions, Kevin shook her hand and said in a loud voice to be heard over the noise, "Nice to meet you."

"Same here," she hollered back. "Happy birthday."

"Thanks. Seth tells me he's doing some renovations for you. He's the best contractor around here."

"So he very modestly keeps reminding me," she said with a laugh.

Kevin flagged down the bartender. "Jimmy, I need two beers and…" He looked at Elise. "What's your pleasure?"

Normally she preferred wine, but when in Rome… "Beer's fine, thanks."

A feminine squeal sounded directly behind them. "Ooh! Seth! Long time, no see, Gorgeous."

Elise turned and watched a beautiful young blonde who barely looked old enough to buy her own beer loop her arms around Seth's neck, press herself against him, and lean in for a kiss, clearly heading for his lips. He quickly turned his head and she left a bright red lipstick stain on his cheek instead.

He immediately reached up and disentangled the blonde's arms, then stepped back. "Tiffani. I'd like you to meet Elise."

Tiffani turned and looked at her with an expression that so clearly said *who the hell are you?* Elise had to bite back a laugh. And she thanked God for that urge to laugh, because it was the only thing masking her discomfort. Not to mention the ridiculous twinge of jealousy, an unwanted feeling that had little to do with the fact that this young woman was stunning and possessed a drop-dead figure displayed by low-rise jeans and a barely there tank top. No, it was because of the familiar, intimate way she greeted Seth. Obviously they were...acquainted.

And while she couldn't blame him for Tiffani's overly friendly greeting, nor could she deny that he'd clearly not encouraged her, neither could she ignore that the young woman's presence was a much-needed slap, forcing her to recall the differences between her and Seth. A reminder of the sort of woman he should be with—young, bouncy, nubile—and the sort of man she should be looking for—namely someone her own age. And that this wasn't a date. That Seth was a friend and nothing more. And that even though she suddenly felt like going home, she wasn't a quitter. But she did need a minute to regroup.

She gave the young woman her brightest smile. "Hello, Tiffani."

"Hi." Clearly summing up Elise as "not competition", she dismissed her with a flick of her long hair and returned her attention to Seth.

Before she was forced to witness any further familiarities, Elise asked Seth, "Where are the bathrooms?"

Stepping away from Tiffani, he nodded toward the far corner, past the dance floor. "I'll walk with you—"

"Nonsense. Stay with your friends."

Before he could persist, she melted into the crowd. And prepared to regroup.

SETH WATCHED Elise disappear into the crowd, and frustration rippled through him. Damn it, he hoped she didn't think—

"How about we hit the dance floor and get this party started?" Tiffani said, pressing herself against him again and giving a little shimmy.

His frustration doubled and was joined by a big dose of annoyance. Stepping back, he lightly grasped her shoulders to keep her at arm's length. "Tiffani, Elise is my date."

She studied him for several seconds with a look that bordered on disbelief, then shrugged and laughed. "Maybe next time."

"She'll be my date next time, too." At least if he had anything to say about it.

Tiffani's brows shot upward, clearly unaccustomed to being on the receiving end of a brush-off. But then she shrugged again. "Okay. Fine. Whatever." After flicking her hair over her shoulder, she turned and disappeared into the crowd. Seth didn't doubt she'd forget about him in five minutes.

He turned and found Kevin staring at him with an expression that suggested he'd sprouted a third eyeball in the center of his forehead.

"Holy crap," Kevin said. "Did I really just see you give that insanely hot woman the heave-ho?"

Seth shrugged. "Not my type."

"Since when?"

"Maybe I'm looking for more than just casual sex."

Kevin's eyes goggled. "Are you running a fever?"

He laughed and reached for his beer. "How's your birthday going so far?"

"Fine. Would be better if an insanely hot woman like Tiffani draped herself all over me."

"Night's young." He scanned the area near the restrooms, but he saw no sign of Elise. As soon as she returned, he'd make certain she understood that there was nothing going on between him and Tiffani.

"So what do you think?" Kevin's question yanked his attention back.

"About what?"

Kevin shook his head. "Dude, I've been talking to you for the past five minutes about hanging in the Hamptons tomorrow."

"Can't. I'm working tomorrow."

"How about Sunday?"

"Working."

"At Elise's house?"

"Yeah."

Kevin studied him over the rim of his beer mug for several long seconds, then said, "She's pretty."

"I agree."

"So is she really your date or did you just say that to get rid of Tiffani—who, in case you didn't notice, *is insanely hot.*"

"Maybe I think Elise is the one who's insanely hot."

"Dude, I'd be willing to go so far as to say she's beautiful, in that cool, elegant way some women have. But insanely hot she is not."

"I disagree. But I'm actually relieved you don't think so, because it would be awkward if you did."

"But you don't care if I think Tiffani is hot enough to light a firecracker underwater."

"Nope. She's all yours."

"If only," Kevin muttered. "Dude, you've got it bad."

Just then Seth spied Elise making her way through the crowd and his heart jumped. Yeah, he had it bad all right.

He watched her weave her way through the tight-knit throng, mouthing an apology when she bumped into someone. He noticed a number of men checking her out, one of whom spoke to her. He was older—maybe late forties, and wore dark dress pants, a white dress shirt and a loosened tie. Probably just arrived from Manhattan for the weekend after a tough day on Wall Street. Probably graduated from some Ivy League school. Probably exactly Elise's type.

Gripping his beer bottle, he watched them chat for a moment, after which she smiled and shook her head, then nodded toward the bar. The guy handed her what looked like a business card and she continued on her way.

Damn it, he wasn't sure what annoyed him the most—the fact that the guy gave her his card, that she tucked it into her purse, or the way the bastard ogled her as she walked away. A sensation he didn't like at all crawled beneath his skin, and he couldn't call it anything other than what it was.

Jealousy.

Damn, he really *did* have it bad. But who could blame him? He'd thought her gorgeous when she was flecked with paint and wearing grungy clothes. What the hell chance did he have when she wore a pale green top with thin, crisscross straps that left her arms and shoulders bare? When she outlined her eyes with some sort of smoky pencil that made them seem larger and more luminous than usual? When her black pants showed off her curves, and combined with her high-heeled, strappy sandals, made her legs appear endless?

"She's almost here," Kevin said, nudging him in the ribs. "You might want to wipe that look off your face."

"What look?"

"The one that's making it clear you'd like to toss that guy who just talked to her on his ass."

Yeah. Right after I told him to get lost. In an anatomically specific way. Irked at the transparency of his feelings, he took a long pull of his beer, watching Elise all the while. "When the hell did you become so observant?"

"About the same time you became so interesting to watch. And, um, you also might want to wipe *that* look off your face."

"What's wrong now?"

"You're staring at her like she's a sheep and you're the big bad wolf who really, really wants to gobble her up."

Damn. Even though that pretty much described the situation, Seth attempted to wipe all expression from his face but wasn't sure he succeeded.

When she rejoined them, he searched her eyes for any sign she was upset about their encounter with Tiffani, and relief filled him when he saw none. He knew damn well if Tiffani had been his date, she would have made a federal case out of the situation.

Still, he wanted to make certain there wasn't any misunderstanding. With his eyes steady on Elise's, he said, "Just so you know, she means nothing to me. I'm completely unattached."

She studied him for several long seconds, then said, "Good to know."

Good to know. Three little words that revved up his heart rate and pumped heat to his every nerve ending.

She nodded toward the bar. "Is that my beer?"

"Yeah." After handing her the frosty mug, he asked, "Do you play pool?"

"I haven't in years."

"Good," he said with an exaggerated evil grin. "That'll make it much easier to win money from you."

Interest kindled in her eyes. "How much do you play for?"

"Five bucks a game. Wanna watch me whoop Birthday Boy's butt?"

"Hey, you can't beat me on my birthday," Kevin objected. "That's in the official Birthday Boy Handbook."

"I'll play you," Elise offered Kevin with a smile. "I have five bucks I'm willing to lose."

Kevin smiled. "Sounds good to me."

Thirty minutes later, Elise pocketed Kevin's five bucks, and Seth was torn between pure admiration for her skill, pure lust at the picture she made bending over the table to hit the ball, and flat-out laughter at Kevin's disgruntled expression at his unexpected loss.

"Got your butt whooped, Birthday Boy," he said to Kevin.

"Where'd an uptown girl like you learn to play pool like that?" Kevin asked Elise, grudging respect glinting in his eyes.

"College. Pool is really nothing more than applied geometry."

"Seth told me you're a math teacher. I guess that helps."

"I guess it does." She cocked an eyebrow at Seth. "You ready to get your butt whooped next?"

"Sure," he said, grabbing a cue stick. "But first, let's play some pool."

Two hours later, Elise sank her final ball to best her latest challenger, Ricky Winstead, and Seth applauded, along with the crowd who had gathered around the table.

With a smile and her face flushed, Elise bowed then accepted the five-dollar bill Ricky presented her with a flourish. "Makes me wish I'd paid more attention in geometry," Ricky said with a laugh. "I probably would have if you'd been my teacher."

Claiming fatigue, Elise surrendered her cue stick then walked to the nearby corner where Seth had taken up residence. As she approached, he held out the tall glass of water from which she'd been sipping.

"That was amazing," he said. "You sure were a hit—and I'm damn proud to know you."

"I bet you say that to all the women who lighten your wallet at the pool table."

"Since you're the only one who has, I couldn't say. By my calculations, you won yourself sixty bucks."

"That's right." Her eyes gleamed with mischief. "And you think you're not good at math."

"I had an excellent tutor," he said, fighting the urge to yank her into his arms. "So what are your plans for your ill-gotten gains?"

"Don't know yet. I'm thinking that since it's found money, I might just splurge on something I wouldn't ordinarily buy."

He instantly wondered if she ordinarily bought black lace lingerie. And with that thought the desire to touch her, hold her, morphed from *want to* into *need to—now*. "Would you like to dance?" he asked.

She surveyed the crowded dance floor and for a brief second a faraway expression flitted across her face. "I haven't danced in a really long time."

"That's what you said about pool—and look how good that turned out." Pushing off the wall, Seth grabbed her hand and led her toward the dance floor. Some guardian angel must have been looking out for him because as soon as they arrived, the band switched to a slow song.

Sliding one arm around her waist, he splayed his hand low on Elise's back then drew her slowly in, until their bodies lightly bumped. Heat sizzled through him at the contact and when she rested one hand on his shoulder, he raised her other hand and settled it against his chest, right over the spot where his heart thudded as if he'd sprinted the length of Long Island.

He wanted to say something witty, something intelligent, maybe even something flirtatious or romantic, but she looked up at him with those big blue eyes and all he could do was look back. And absorb how perfect she felt in his arms. Their thighs brushed, shooting desire through him, desire that doubled when he saw her pupils dilate.

Unable to stop himself, he pulled her closer, until they touched from chest to knee. The feel of her soft curves, her full breasts, pressed against him, even through the layers of their clothes, dragged a low groan from his throat.

He was helpless to stop his body's swift reaction, but instead of pulling away as he feared, she snuggled closer and rested her cheek against his shoulder. Tenderness and desire and want and need all swirled inside him, creating a tornado of feelings the likes of which he'd never experienced.

Lowering his head, he closed his eyes and brushed his lips over her soft hair, breathing in the subtle, clean scent of her shampoo and the delicate floral fragrance clinging to her skin. She smelled so good, felt so good.

Lifting his head, he slipped his hand from atop hers where it lay against his chest and gently nudged her chin up until their gazes met. The heated look in her eyes told him everything he needed to know, and with his heart rapping against his ribs, he lowered his head.

He brushed his mouth over hers, once, twice, savoring the warm softness. Her lips parted, and he sank slowly deeper into the kiss, a soft, leisurely glide into heaven. His tongue touched hers and everything faded away…the music, the crowd, the din of voices. Everything except Elise, who wrapped her arms around his neck and rose up on her toes, pressing herself tighter against him.

God help him, no woman had *ever* felt like this. Felt this good. This right. He slid one hand into her silky hair while the other hand skimmed lower on her back to cup the curve of her bottom while his tongue explored the delicious, velvety smoothness of her mouth. She rubbed her tongue against his and he moaned, low and deep, pressing her tighter against his erection.

She squirmed against him and he swore he was going to lose his mind. As slowly as their kiss had begun, he ended it, lifting his head and opening his eyes.

She looked at him with a glazed, utterly aroused expression that perfectly reflected how he felt. And if he'd been capable of stringing together a coherent sentence, he would have told her so. Instead he framed her flushed face in his not-quite-steady hands, brushed his thumbs over her soft cheeks, and said the only two words he could manage—and prayed she'd agree.

"Let's go."

CHAPTER EIGHT

ELISE STARED into Seth's eyes. He regarded her with a breath-stealing, knee-weakening, heart-fluttering intensity as his words reverberated through her mind. *Let's go.*

She knew very well what agreeing to those two little words meant. The practical side of her hesitated—the person who for so long had been only a widow, a teacher, and a mother. A person who worried about pleasing everyone, about what other people thought. But then the woman inside her, who'd been buried and denied, ran from the dungeon where she'd been kept prisoner, desperate for freedom, delirious at the thought of escaping to run in the sunshine once more. A woman who, for the first time in a very long while, greedily wanted, just this once, to please herself.

"Let's go," she whispered.

There was no mistaking the flare of fire—and relief—in his eyes. Without hesitation he clasped her hand and walked off the crowded dance floor. They paused only long enough to retrieve her purse and say a quick goodbye to his friends. Then he led her to the parking lot.

Once they were seated in the cab of his pickup, Seth looked at her and she nearly melted from the fire simmering in his eyes. "My place?" he asked, his voice a soft rasp in the quiet car.

Heart racing, she nodded.

The five-minute drive to his house felt like an eternity…an eternity during which she had too much time to think. To question her decision, his desire, her ability to sexually please either of them, the enormity of actually making love again. With a man who wasn't Ian.

In theory it sounded reasonable, but now that the moment was upon her, all the fears and insecurities she'd abandoned on the dance floor grabbed her in a vise grip. By the time he'd closed his front door behind them, her ardor had cooled, leaving uncertainty in its place.

Clearly he sensed her withdrawal, because instead of pouncing on her, Seth led her into the family room then lit several lamps. Soft light illuminated a taupe sectional sofa, matching recliner chair, and a low-slung entertainment center, complete with a flat screen TV. A set of weights were stacked in the far corner. A T-shirt had been tossed haphazardly over the back of the sofa and a large pair of beat-up sneakers lay where they'd been kicked off next to the weights. A dark blue ceramic mug, bearing a trace of coffee in the bottom, rested on the end table, next to a stack of rumpled newspapers. Something about the room, perhaps that lone coffee cup, squeezed her heart. It somehow felt…empty. Lonely. Two feelings with which she was painfully familiar.

He joined her in the center of the room and loosely linked their hands. "Elise," he said softly, brushing his thumbs over the sensitive skin of her inner wrists. "Tell me what's wrong."

She looked into his beautiful eyes, glittering with a combination of banked desire and tenderness. He'd tasted so good, felt so good. And he made her want so much. Too much. "I...I'm afraid."

"Of what?"

Admit the truth, Elise. To yourself and to him. Drawing a deep breath, she said in a shaky voice, "Of so many things. I...I've forgotten how to do this. How to be with someone...like this. I'm afraid of disappointing you. I haven't been with anyone since Ian died."

He nodded slowly. "I figured as much." He raised her hands and pressed them against his chest. His heart beat hard and fast against her palms. "Feel that?" he asked. After she nodded, he said, "My heart pounds like that every time I'm near you. Just thinking about you does this...." He dragged one of her hands down and pressed it against the hard ridge of his erection. Desire gushed through her, quickening her breath.

He once again settled her hand on his chest. "If you don't want to make love with me because you're not ready to take that step, or because it's too soon, or because you've decided you don't want me, I understand," he said, his voice low and husky, his serious gaze steady on hers. "But please don't let the reason be because you think you'll disappoint me. I promise you there is a *zero* percent chance of that happening."

"This is a big step for me."

"I know. And I want to take it with you."

"Maybe you shouldn't. I should warn you, I have stretch marks. Cellulite."

"I'm hardly Mr. Universe."

She huffed out a laugh. "Shows what you know."

His lips twitched. "I can't imagine any part of you not being beautiful."

Good Lord, with the women he was accustomed to, he'd most likely never even *seen* a stretch mark. "I'll probably cry."

"Then I'll just hold you until all your tears are gone. Until you feel like smiling again."

"That might take a while."

"I'm not in a rush."

No, she could see that. Tell that he wouldn't push her to do anything she didn't want. Something inside her clicked, and Elise knew this was the right time. And the right man with whom to share this. That he, they, would be discreet. And that if the lights stayed off, darkness was a great age equalizer.

She erased the distance between them with a single step. And inwardly smiled at the fire that flared in his eyes when their bodies touched. "I, um, should also warn you that there's a risk that after not having sex for so long I might be rather…insatiable."

One corner of his mouth lifted. "A chance I'm willing to take. I'll do my best to keep up. So to speak." He lowered his head until his lips hovered just above hers. "You certainly haven't forgotten how to kiss."

She slid her hands up, over his broad shoulders, to encircle his neck. "Really? I think we should try it again…just to be sure."

"Oh, I'm definitely all for being sure."

And then he kissed her, with that same bone-melting, brain-liquefying perfection he'd demonstrated at Salty's. Her blood raced thick and hot through her veins, reawakening her passions, igniting nerve endings that had long lain dormant, arousing each of her senses, re-discovering how incredible it felt to be touched by a man, and to touch in return.

Her fingers sifted into his thick hair, and she pressed herself closer, drowning in the feel of his hard body against hers. Warm…he was so warm. The clean, masculine scent of his skin intoxicated her and the erotic sensation of his tongue mating with hers pumped want through her until she could feel the thrum of her heartbeat everywhere. In her temples. At the base of her throat. Between her thighs.

His hands skimmed down her back, then, without breaking their kiss, he bent his knees and lifted her. She clung to him, her feet dangling as he walked down the hallway, presumably to his bedroom, and reveled in his strength. After he set her back down, his lips left hers to blaze a hot trail down her neck.

"Seth…" His name whispered past her lips, ending on a thick moan of pleasure when his hands skimmed under her shirt and cupped her breasts.

Her head fell back and she luxuriated in the magic his fingers and lips wrought. He slowly removed her clothes, kissing, caressing each new bit of skin he uncovered, murmuring soft words of praise that blew warm against her overheated skin, until she stood before him naked.

"You're beautiful, Elise" he said softly, his thumbs tracing drugging circles around her nipples, still hard and damp from his clever mouth. "So damn beautiful. And soft. I've never felt anything as soft as your skin."

The raw heat burning in his gaze incinerated any lingering modesty and ignited her need for him to a fever pitch. Settling his hands at his sides, she murmured, "My turn," then proceeded to remove his clothes with the same lack of haste he'd treated her to. She basked in his every groan. The way his muscles jerked when she traced her fingers along the dusky ribbon of hair that bisected his torso. The obvious effort he expended to keep from touching her, to allow her to explore. To touch and kiss. To lick and taste. His soft, husky words of encouragement further released her inhibitions. When she encircled his erection with her fingers and gently squeezed, he sucked in a sharp breath and warned, "I won't last much longer if you keep doing that."

With a wicked grin, she gently squeezed again, and with a growl, he scooped her into his arms and carried her to the bed, following her down onto the mattress. He paused only to roll on a condom, then covered her body with his.

With his weight propped on his forearms and his eyes locked on hers, he slowly entered her. A long moan of pleasure escaped her and her eyes slid closed.

"Look at me," he said, gliding out with an erotic pull that dragged another moan from her.

Elise opened her eyes and he slid deep once again. Then again, and again, stronger, faster, each thrust pushing her closer to the edge of her control, until she cried out, her climax overtaking her, throbbing through her system. She felt him thrust a final time, then shudders racked him as he buried his face against her neck.

Delicious aftershocks still rippled through her when she felt him raise his head. She dragged her eyes open and his beautiful face loomed above her. Reaching up, she combed her fingers through his wildly mussed hair then laid her palm against his cheek. Seth turned his head and kissed her palm. And hot tears pushed behind her eyes.

Before she could stop them, they spilled over. He moved, as if to roll off her, but she tightened her legs and arms around him and shook her head.

"Don't go," she said. "I like you right where you are."

"Right where I want to be." He gently brushed away a tear. "Are you all right?"

"Yes." And she truly was. Yet the neeed to explain, to try to verbalize everything she was feeling overwhelmed her. "For so long I believed I'd never make love again—would never want to—and that if I did, it would be filled with sadness for what I lost with Ian. That by sharing myself in this way with another man I'd forget the man I'd loved so deeply."

She pulled in a deep breath, then continued, "But making love with you wasn't sad. It was…joyous. Miraculous. Beautiful and passionate, tender and exciting. And healing." She lifted her head and brushed her lips over his. "Thank you."

"The pleasure was all mine."

"Not all yours, believe me. I…I'll never forget this."

"Neither will I." He touched his forehead to hers. "I haven't stopped thinking about you since the minute you called me last week."

A fresh wave of tears filled her eyes. She nodded and their noses bumped. "Me, too."

He lifted his head and kissed her damp cheeks. "More tears?"

"These are happy tears."

"I'm glad."

"I'm, um, thinking I'd like to shed a few more." She bumped her pelvis upward against his. "You free for the next couple hours?"

"Sweetheart, I'm available for as long as you want me. How do you feel about a nice warm shower for two…for starters?"

She smiled into his eyes. "Now that's an offer I can't refuse."

CHAPTER NINE

THE NEXT TWO WEEKS flew by so quickly, Elise could barely catch her breath. Her days were filled with painting the kids' rooms, chatting with them on the phone about their latest adventures, clearing the garden of weeds, digging new flower beds, working on lesson plans and rediscovering Gateshead. She and Deidre went shopping several times and she discovered a fabulous bookstore Jamie would love and a craft shop that sold handmade Barbie clothes that Maggie would want to visit daily.

Frannie came by for coffee twice and they'd chatted for hours about every topic from movies to losing a spouse. Her neighbor clearly suspected the nature of her relationship with Seth, even though they took pains to be discreet, keeping his truck in the garage when he spent the night. Frannie didn't question her, only saying, "I'm happy for you, dear. Just don't give that uptight school board any reason to complain."

Elise also attended the meeting at the high school, where she met the other teachers, who all welcomed her into the fold, as well as the board of education, the latter a stern reminder that she needed to keep her private life private. Of course, once Maggie and Jamie came home the point would be moot as Seth would no longer be spending the night.

Yet as fun and fulfilling as her days were, they couldn't compare to the nights. With Seth.

Seth…his name shivered a thrill of anticipation down her spine. He arrived late each afternoon, always greeting her with a toe-curling kiss. Sometimes he stopped at his house to grab a shower before coming to her. On those occasions, they never made it to the bedroom, and she'd breathlessly learned he was as talented making love in the foyer as he was in the bedroom. Not to mention the kitchen. Or the family room.

Other times he came to her straight from whatever other job he was working on. On those occasions he'd shower at her house—and bring her along for company. Then, after reminding her what an incredible lover he was, he'd spend several hours working on her renovations.

She'd cook them dinner, and they'd talk and laugh, sharing stories of their lives, their hopes and dreams. She discovered his love of classic rock, action movies, animals, Italian meals, and stargazing. Learned when he tried to teach her to play his guitar—at which she had *no* talent whatsoever—that he was patient to a fault, and a good singer. Realized he was awful at trivia games, but unbeatable at poker. Especially strip poker, which, she decided after her resounding loss, still made her a winner. Although probably her favorite discovery was that underneath all that masculine brawn, he was ticklish.

Some nights they walked along the beach; other times they ventured out for ice cream or a movie; others they just curled up on the sofa. But every night was a beautiful, exciting sensual adventure. Making love, exploring new ways to please each other. Seth was a playful, generous lover and it didn't take her long to rediscover the sensual, adventurous woman she'd once been. Afterward, she'd fall asleep, wrapped in his strong arms, reminded each time of how much she loved being this close to someone. And how much she was going to miss it again when Jamie and Maggie came home.

How was it possible that he'd become so important to her so quickly? That wasn't in her plan. He was merely supposed to be the young, sexy guy who helped her get her groove back. Reintroduce her to the dating game. Prepare her for men her own age. But each minute she spent with him planted seeds of feelings that threatened to grow and blossom into deeper emotions she wasn't certain she was ready for. Especially with a man ten years younger, with whom an affair could threaten her teaching position. And one who might be accepting an out-of-state job. It was one thing to feel ready to get on with her life but quite another to experience the whirlwind of unexpected emotions that Seth inspired.

He hadn't initiated any conversations about the future, and since she didn't want to think beyond this short, magical time, she'd avoided the subject as well. But now, on their last night together before she left to pick up the kids the next morning, as they lay on her sofa, her head nestled against his shoulder, she knew the subject couldn't be avoided any longer.

"I'm going to miss being with you like this," she said.

Seth's heart clenched in that odd way it had every

time he thought of her visit to her parents to pick up Maggie and Jamie. "Me, too. But you'll only be gone three days." Yeah, three long days that stretched out before him like an empty desert. He'd known he'd been lonely, but it wasn't until Elise had entered his life that he realized just how lonely and unfulfilled he'd been. At least he had plenty of work to keep him busy until she returned.

She twisted in his arms so she could look at him. "I've really enjoyed our time together," she said softly.

"So have I." Something in her voice, in her eyes, made him add, "But you make it sound like this is goodbye."

"In a way it is—to the unlimited freedom we've had these last two weeks." She turned and sat up. "Seth, we can't continue to see each other like this after I return home."

"What does 'like this' mean?"

"Like we have been. You spending the night here."

He nodded. "I can understand that."

"Us sleeping together."

He frowned. "Do you mean 'sleeping together'—or having sex?"

"Both."

Seth sat up and turned to face her fully, unease spreading through him. "You want us to stop seeing each other?"

"Well, obviously with the renovation work we'll be *seeing* each other, but…" Elise twisted her fingers together. "Seth, this time with you has been wonderful, something I realize I needed—time for myself, away from the kids. But once Maggie and Jamie come home, they have to be my first priority. I need to set an example for them. And the example I want to set isn't one of carrying on an affair."

"I completely understand them being your first priority," he said. "But they shouldn't be your only priority. Your happiness is important, too. We obviously won't be able to be together as freely as we have been, but that doesn't mean we can't be discreet." He tucked a stray curl behind her ear. "We can find the time, make the time to be together."

"I suppose we could, but to what end, Seth? Where could this possibly go?"

"I don't know. But I want to find out. Don't you?"

"Not at the risk of exposing my impressionable children to their mother having an affair. Nor do I want to give the school board any reason to disapprove of me."

"Why would they disapprove of you having a social life?"

"There's a difference between having a social life and carrying on an affair."

"You make it sound as if we're doing something wrong."

"It hasn't been wrong for the last two weeks because there was only you and me to consider. But when the children come home, that will no longer be the case. We both know, deep down, that this can't go anywhere. I'm *ten years* older than you."

"So what? You've been ten years older these past two weeks, too. Didn't seem to matter then."

"It did."

"Not to me." Seth raked his fingers through his hair and his insides tensed with an unpleasant sensation, as if everything he wanted was slipping through his fisted hands and he couldn't stop the flow. "Look, if I was ten and you were twenty, there'd obviously be a problem. Even if I was twenty and you were thirty, I'd agree because at twenty, I was…lost. A complete jackass. But me at thirty and you at forty is not a problem. Hell, if *I* was forty and *you* were thirty, we'd never even have this conversation."

"I suppose not. But the age issue is only part of the problem. The bottom line is that as much as I've enjoyed being with you these past two weeks, I wasn't planning that our affair would go beyond that time frame."

Her words hit him like a sucker punch. "Why not?"

Instead of answering, Elise asked, "Were you?"

"I sure hadn't put an end date on it. Why didn't you think we'd go beyond these two weeks?"

"Well, for one thing, I figured you'd be tired of being with an old broad like me by now. Would be ready to go back to the Tiffanis of the world."

"Well, you'd be wrong." He dragged his hands down his face. "These insecurities about your age—I don't know how to reassure you other than to say that you're the most incredible woman I've ever been with. Would it help to know I've got my own insecurities where you're concerned? I'm well aware I'm not one of those college-grad, suit-wearing, briefcase-toting Wall Street types you're probably looking for."

The blush that colored her cheeks told him he'd hit a nerve. And damn it, that hurt. And pissed him off.

"A college degree is not the measure of a person, Seth. You're a wonderful man—"

"Here comes the *but*." Anger laced his voice.

"But I'm just not ready to have a sexual relationship with my children around."

"With someone ten years younger than you."

"With *anyone*. Especially with the beginning of the new school year only a matter of weeks away." She blew out a sigh. "But yes, most especially not with someone ten years younger than me. Our age difference is just so…intimidating to me. And it can't be changed. This has all happened too quickly for me. All I can offer you from now on is friendship. Do you think you can be my friend?"

Seth felt as if she'd kicked him in the stomach. Anger and frustration and hurt collided inside him and he wanted to snap out *no,* he couldn't go back to being just her friend because he damn well didn't want to. The fact that she did made his heart feel…numb.

But her blue eyes held a plea he couldn't ignore. Damn it, he didn't know if he could only be a friend. All he knew was that he didn't want to lose what they'd found together. Didn't want to push her permanently and completely away by trying to talk her into something she obviously wasn't ready for. That maybe he wasn't ready for, either. His mind said maybe she was right. Things had moved quickly. Maybe too quickly. Maybe friendship was the way to go.

But his heart didn't agree. His heart knew exactly what, and who, it wanted.

Unfortunately, Elise's did not. And even though he made his living fixing things, he wasn't sure he'd be able to fix that.

CHAPTER TEN

JULY ZOOMED BY, a kaleidoscope of hot, sunny days and warm, star-filled nights. Elise spent her time with the kids, cavorting on the beach, visiting the library, furthering her friendships with the neighbors and their children. By the time July melted into August, a stream of neighborhood kids were constantly parading through the house, playing Xbox or Barbie—depending on whether they were Jamie's playmates or Maggie's. Frannie was a frequent visitor as was Deidre and Alison Culpepper from across the street, whose two daughters were four and eight. But of all the friends they each made, Seth was, by far, their favorite.

Jamie thought he was "way cool" and showed all his friends the cool deck his cool friend Seth had built for them. And he'd won Maggie's heart when he'd played the Barbie video game with her and two of her little neighborhood friends.

As for Elise, she also thought Seth was "way cool," and he'd slowly but surely won her heart as well by keeping his "just friends" promise. He still came to the house each day, sometimes in the late afternoon, sometimes early evening. He'd brought Kevin with him a few times, as well as his friend Ricky, and with their help, the renovations moved along at a fast clip.

She always invited him for dinner, and sometimes he accepted, but not always, and on those nights, she jealously wondered if he was having dinner with some sexy twentysomething whose metabolism hadn't yet slowed to a snail's pace and who hadn't experienced what gravity could do to a woman's butt. Maggie, with all the tact of a five-year-old, hadn't hesitated to ask him, "Who do you have dinner with when you're not with us?"

He'd smiled and said, "Usually my friend Kevin."

The relief that had swept through her at his response was nothing short of ridiculous, although she couldn't help but notice he'd said *usually*. Not that she blamed him. He was perfectly free to have dinner—or whatever—with whomever he chose. As was she. The problem was that she didn't want to have dinner—or whatever—with anyone except him. Which was not good. In fact, if she were brutally honest, she had to admit that as much as she was glad they were friends, it was basically torture to be in the same room with him and not touch him. To no longer share the intimacies they once had.

She fought a daily battle not to stare at him, a fight made more difficult because she so often caught him looking at her, with a heated expression that whooshed fire through her. And made her want to drag him to some deserted corner and rip off his clothes. With her teeth. Yup, the school board would love that.

"Kevin's nice," Maggie had proclaimed in response to Seth's answer to her dinner question, "even though he calls me *dude*. You should bring him here for dinner. Then we wouldn't have to miss you. Because we miss you when you're not here."

Seth's eyes had met hers over Maggie's head and he'd said, "I miss you, too."

And, oh Lord, she missed him, too. Missed the feel of his hands on her. Of hers on him. Of snuggling on the sofa with him. Falling asleep in his arms. She'd find herself scheming, thinking up ways to meet with him, to steal a few minutes alone for a quick grope—like a drug addict sneaking a fix—and she'd force herself to stop. To remember that there was nowhere for an impractical relationship with a hot young hunk to go, except to heartache. And that was a place she had no desire to go.

Yet seeing him every day was a bittersweet torment. Spending time with him only made her want him more. It was a maze of complicated feelings from which she just couldn't seem to find her way out.

By the end of the first week of August, the renovations were finally finished. On the evening Seth completed the last bit of touch-ups, Elise served a platter of chocolate-chip cookies.

"Here's to Seth," she said, raising her cookie. "Thank you for doing such a wonderful job and for turning our house into our beautiful home."

Everyone tapped their cookie edges, then, around a mouthful of chocolate-chip cookie, Jamie asked him in a worried voice, "You're still going to come over, right?"

Seth hesitated for several seconds then said, "You're still going to have cookies, right? Yeah, I'll be around."

After only a few cookie crumbs remained on the

plate, Seth said he needed to leave, then asked Elise, "Walk me out to the truck?"

"Sure," she said, her heart pounding in the most ridiculous way at the thought of a few minutes alone with him.

After saying goodbye to the kids, he exited the house and she followed him to the driveway. Darkness had fallen, and the sound of cicadas rang in the warm, humid air redolent with the pungent scent of freshly cut grass.

He leaned against the hood of his truck and regarded her through serious eyes. "I wanted to tell you that I won't be around for the next couple of days. I'm going to Florida."

Concern washed through her at his solemn tone. "Is something wrong? Your mom—?"

He shook his head. "No. I met with Bob Wexford today."

Her stomach tightened at the familiar name. "The builder from Florida."

"Yeah. He's flying me down to his corporate offices so I can see his operation."

"Do you think he's going to offer you a job?"

"I'm pretty sure he is."

She felt as if the bottom of her heart gave way. "I…see."

He stared at her for several long seconds, then asked quietly, "Do you miss me?"

Suddenly the air felt too thick to breathe. Before she could even process his question, Seth reached out and clasped her hands. Heated tingles raced up her arms, and she had to press her lips together not to sigh with pleasure at his touch.

"Because I miss you, Elise. I'm trying my damned-est to do as you asked, to only be your friend, but just in case you were wondering, I wanted you to know that I miss you. To the point of pain. It hurts like hell to be near you yet unable to touch you. Hurts like hell to be away from you. I just hurt. All the time."

The anguish in his hoarse voice, in his eyes, lodged a lump in her throat. As he spoke, he'd moved closer to her, erasing the distance between them until only a breath separated their lips. Her pulse pounded in anti-cipation and her body involuntarily arched into his.

His arms came around her and with a groan his mouth slanted over hers in a hot, hard, possessive kiss that tasted of hurt. And need and want and frustration. But as quickly as he'd started it, he ended it, pulling away and stepping back, leaving her shaken and trembling.

His eyes glittered in the moonlight. "That didn't even begin to describe how much I miss you. You think about that while I'm gone. I'll call you when I get back from Florida."

She remained rooted to the spot and watched him drive away. And wondered how she'd be able to think of anything else. Except perhaps to wonder how the simple physical act of getting her groove back had turned into something so emotionally complicated.

THREE DAYS LATER, Seth knocked on Elise's front door, and recalled the first time he'd done so two months ago. And just as she had two months ago, Maggie ran to the door. The sight of her, honey curls flying, made his chest go hollow. It wasn't just Elise who'd stolen his heart—her kids had wormed their way right in, too.

Unlike two months ago, however, this time after she opened the door, Maggie launched herself at him, giving him a huge hug and a smacking kiss on the cheek. His heart melted and his arms went around her. Lifting her off her feet, he spun her around until she squealed with laughter.

"Whatcha been doin', Miss Maggie?" he asked, setting her down.

"I have a new loose tooth," she reported. "Look!"

He examined the tooth she indicated then nodded solemnly. "Won't be long now," he predicted. "Where're Jamie and your mom?"

"Backyard." She grabbed his hand and tugged. "We're playing horseshoes."

They walked out the back door, and his gaze immediately found Elise. Dressed in white shorts and a crisp, sleeveless orange top, she somehow managed to look cool even though the temperature hovered around ninety. She was laughing and ruffling Jamie's hair.

And in that instant, seeing her with her son, her affectionate touch, he could no longer deny putting a name to the maelstrom of feelings she inspired. He loved her. Probably had since the minute he'd seen her two months ago. Certainly it had been building since that moment. He loved her and wanted to be with her.

But what if she didn't want the same thing?

He needed to know. Had to know. Today. Now.

Just then she caught sight of him. She appeared to go still for several seconds, then she waved. When Jamie saw him, the boy grinned and trotted over to shake his hand. "Got some new baseball cards yesterday," Jamie said, pushing up his glasses. "Wanna see?"

"Sure. But I need to talk to your mom first, okay?"

"'Kay."

The kids went back to their game, and he and Elise walked into the house.

"Would you like something to drink?" she asked.

"No, thanks. I wanted to tell you…" *That I love you. And need you. And more than anything want to be with you.* "About my trip to Florida."

"How did it go?"

"Bob Wexford offered me a job."

Was that a flash of disappointment in her eyes? He sure as hell hoped so. "It's an incredible opportunity. The salary is three times what I'm making here on my own. Plus perks, medical insurance, retirement plan, paid vacation, even a company car. It's basically an offer I can't refuse."

"I…see."

He stepped forward and clasped her hands. And tossed his heart into the ring. "Give me a reason to refuse it."

Her eyes widened. "What?"

"Give me a reason not to move to Florida. Tell me you want me to stay here. And be more than just your friend."

The loudest silence he'd ever heard stretched between them. Finally she said, "Seth, this decision, it has to be yours and yours alone. I wouldn't, couldn't ask you to forgo such an opportunity because of me."

"And I can't think of a better reason to forgo it." He squeezed her hands and tossed his soul in to join his heart. "I love you, Elise. I don't want to just have an affair with you. I want to be a permanent part of your life. Maggie's and Jamie's lives. I want us—all of us—to be together. To make a future together. To be a family. The kids already like me and I'm crazy about them."

She looked stunned. Dazed. "I don't know what to say."

"Say I have a reason to stay here."

Several long seconds of silence passed, and Seth realized he was holding his breath. Then she shook her head. "I can't."

He felt as if she'd gutted him. "You said you were ready to move on with your life."

"I am. Just not this…quickly."

A humorless sound escaped him. "Quickly? It feels like I've wanted you forever."

"It took me a long time to get to this point, Seth. The thought of moving from having barely dated to asking a man ten years my junior to turn down this incredible job offer is a step I'm simply not prepared to take."

"There're those damn ten years again. Years that mean nothing to me except that they're something I can't change. And something that I apparently can't erase your insecurities over, except to tell you again that they don't matter to me. But I think I finally see what the problem is. It isn't that you don't want to move on with your life. It's that you just don't want to move on with *me*."

Tears glistened in her eyes. "I…don't know."

He released her hands. "The fact that you don't know by now…I guess that's my answer right there. Because I knew the minute I laid eyes on you. I didn't see someone ten years older than me. I saw the most beautiful woman I'd ever seen. It was like I'd been struck by lightning. I only wish we'd both been struck." His throat tightened and he knew he had to get out of there before he made even more of an ass out of himself. "I've gotta go. Tell the kids I said goodbye."

Elise watched him walk away. Listened to the front door close. The hum of his truck's engine. And then silence. And then she sank to her knees on her new kitchen floor, buried her face in her hands and cried.

She wasn't sure how long she'd knelt there before the back door banged open. Jarred from her misery, she lifted her head and met Jamie's wide-eyed gaze.

"Mom, what's wrong?"

"Nothing," she said, wiping her eyes.

Jamie grabbed a handful of paper napkins and handed them to her. "Why are you crying? Did you and Seth have a fight?"

She wiped at her wet cheeks. "No. Why would you think that?"

"Where is he?"

"He had to leave." *And he's not coming back.* A fresh supply of tears pressed behind her eyes. "He told me to tell you he said goodbye."

Jamie sat down next to her. "When's he coming back?"

"I don't know. He's going to be busy. Looks like he's moving to Florida." Another batch of tears dribbled from her eyes.

There was no missing Jamie's distress. "Florida? But…but I don't want him to go."

"Neither do I." And the instant she said the words, she realized how true they were. How the thought of not seeing his smile every day left a hole in her heart.

"Then why don't you ask him to stay here? I bet he would. He likes you."

"I like him, too."

"Yeah, but I think he like *likes* you, Mom."

"*Like* likes?"

"You know, like a boyfriend."

She stared at him, noting his earnest expression. "What makes you say that?"

He shrugged. "I dunno. I guess the way he smiles when you're around."

"He smiles at everyone."

"But he smiles different at you. Do you *like* like him?"

She drew a shaky breath. "If I did, how would you feel about that?"

Jamie pondered for several seconds. "It'd be cool. Do you think he might be my…dad?"

Before she could think of an answer to his startling question, his shoulders slumped. "Dumb question. He can't be my dad if he moves to Florida."

Elise's heart seemed to lurch sideways in her chest. No, he couldn't. He'd be gone. Taking with him all the fun and warmth and happiness he'd brought into their lives. And she'd have lost him. A wonderful, loving, caring, generous, sexy man who's greatest flaw was his age. A wonderful, loving, caring, generous, sexy man who wanted a future with her and her children and who loved her and who—

She loved.

She squeezed her eyes shut as the undeniable truth smacked her. After letting the realization settle for a moment, she said carefully, "If we asked Seth to stay here, we'd have to be sure we really wanted him. All of us. Maggie, too."

"Maggie loves Seth," Jamie said. "She told me."

As if mentioning her name conjured her up, Maggie dashed into the kitchen. She skidded to a halt when she saw Elise and Jamie sitting on the floor, then planted her hands on her hips.

"Hey, no fair, you guys are having fun in here without me."

Elise laughed and held out her arms. Maggie scooted into her lap then asked, "What game are we playing?"

"No game," Jamie said. "We were talking about Seth."

"Maggie, I was wondering…" Elise's voice trailed off as she struggled to find the right words.

"Seth might move to Florida," Jamie interjected matter-of-factly, "and Mom might ask him to stay, but only if we all want him to stay and maybe be our new dad. I said I want him to stay. What do you want?"

Maggie's bottom lip quivered. "I want him to stay." She looked at Elise with huge, pleading eyes. "Seth doesn't have a family here, Mommy. He needs us. He'd be a great daddy. Better than Alicia's." She made a face. "He won't even play Barbie video games with us."

Elise laughed and shook her head. Out of the mouths of babes.

"Me and Maggie want him to stay," Jamie said, giving the official tabulation of the votes. "What do you want, Mom?"

She wrapped an arm around each of her children and hugged them close. And said the words that she knew would change their lives.

"I want him to stay."

AT THREE O'CLOCK the following afternoon, Seth was loading his tools into his truck when he heard his cell phone ring. Tired, hot and sweaty, not to mention cranky after a sleepless night, he was in no mood to talk to anyone and ignored the sound. When he finished loading his tools, he checked his phone and saw that the missed call was from Elise.

He retrieved the message, disgusted at himself for the way his heart pounded just listening to her recorded voice. *Hi, Seth, it's Elise. Sorry to bother you, but the kitchen sink is leaking pretty badly, and I was hoping you could stop by and take a look at it. Please call me back.*

Since she'd only called a minute ago and he was less than five minutes from her house, he just drove over. He knocked on the door, and when Elise answered, he tried not to stare. Dressed in a bright yellow sundress, with her hair loose around her shoulders, she looked amazing.

"Looks like you're going to a party," he said, crossing the threshold, trying hard not to think of her at a party wearing that dress for some other guy.

"I am," she said with a smile. "You are, too."

That's when he noticed all the balloons in the room. "What's all this?"

"A party. For you."

"Me? What for? My birthday isn't for another three weeks."

"Not your birthday. It concerns your new job."

Realization dawned. "A going-away party." He should have been pleased by the gesture, but damn it, as far as he was concerned, his going away was no reason to celebrate. He craned his neck in the direction of the kitchen. "And the leak?"

"A little fabrication," she said, holding her thumb and index finger close together.

Seth ran his hand over the back of his sweaty, gritty neck. "Listen, Elise, this is very nice but—"

"It was Jamie and Maggie's idea. They each made you a card."

Jeez, how many more times could his heart break? "Where are they?"

"Next door at Frannie Cabot's house. I'll call her to bring them over in a few minutes. But first I wanted to give you my present." She took his hand and led him toward the sofa. Once he was seated, she picked up a rolled scroll of paper from the coffee table and stood before him.

"My gift is a treatise I wrote. May I read it to you?"

Mystified, he said, "Sure."

After unrolling the paper, she cleared her throat. "My treatise is entitled, The Advantages of an Older Woman or I'm Not Older, I've Simply Marinated in Life Longer Than You. 'Advantage number one—an Older Woman has the intelligence and ability to talk about anything— most likely because she's lived through it. Advantage number two—an Older Woman is emotionally stable— although she may occasionally require reassurance that she is not saggy, baggy, or draggy.'"

Elise looked up from her reading. "Actually, she may require that reassurance more often than 'occasionally.'" Looking down again, she continued. "'And lastly, an Older Woman knows what she wants—although in some cases, it may take her a while to figure it out.'" Raising her gaze to his, she said softly, "But she does eventually figure it out. And what she wants is a wonderful, patient, kind, beautiful man who loves her and is good to her children. What she wants is *you*."

She waved her hand to encompass all the balloons. "This isn't a going-away party. It's a please-stay party. If you—"

Seth didn't give her a chance to say anything else. He shot to his feet, snatched her into his arms and kissed her with all the pent-up love and frustration and passion crashing through him. When he finally raised his head, she cupped his face between her hands, and he looked into blue eyes brimming with love.

"Will you?" Elise asked. "Will you stay?"

"Sweetheart, you had only to ask."

"You know," she said, "what the problem boiled down to was I'd hoped to someday find a man to share my life with. But just a *regular* man. You—you're spectacular. You threw me totally off-kilter. It took me a while to get back in alignment."

"And I was looking for someone spectacular—and I found her."

Tears shimmered in her eyes. "I love you. I'm sorry it took me so long to figure it out."

Happiness filled all the spaces where despair had so recently dwelled. "You know, when you're ninety and I'm eighty, I'm going to look just as baggy, saggy and draggy as you." Seth brushed his thumbs over her cheeks. "I love you, Elise. Maggie and Jamie, too. Will you—all of you—marry me?"

Her eyes filled with tears, but he knew from her brilliant smile that they were happy tears. "Now that's an offer I can't refuse."

SWEETER THAN WINE
Cathy Yardley

CHAPTER ONE

CHAD MCFEE'S PHONE VIBRATED in the pocket of his black Hugo Boss suit. The call display showed the name of his sister, Violet. He glanced around. There were several other people in the lawyer's office, all chatting amongst themselves—mostly older people, and a few of his cousins. Walking out into the hallway, Chad answered the phone. "Hello?"

"So, what'd you get?"

He rolled his eyes. "Vi, this isn't a good time. Besides, they haven't even read the will yet. And that question is tacky."

Violet made a rude noise. "Great-Uncle Charles was ancient, and you know it. It's not like any of us were that close."

At three years younger than he was, his "kid" sister was twenty-seven. Neither of them were children. Still, she could be pretty childish when she felt like it. "He obviously felt close enough to me to leave me something," Chad said, feeling a little badly that he hadn't been closer to the older man after whom he was named. That didn't stop him from being curious as to what Great-Uncle Charles had left for him. A small, guilty part of him hoped that it was money. Great-Uncle

Charles had been wealthy, and considering the McFees were one of the wealthiest families on the West Coast, that was saying something.

"I'll bet he left you something dumb and sentimental. Like a pocket watch," Violet said, bursting his bubble and bringing him back to reality.

"Probably," Chad admitted.

"Mom and Dad hope it's money," Violet added. "Especially after your little indie movie fiasco."

Chad growled. "That was six months ago. Aren't they going to let that go?"

"You nearly wiped out your trust fund with that, you know. Did you really think they were just going to laugh it off?"

"I've still got some money," he said. "Not that it's any of your business. Or theirs, really."

"It is if you keep getting money from them," Violet pointed out.

"You're the one who keeps getting them to pay for your stuff," Chad said defensively, hating that she was dragging him into this conversation. She loved stirring up drama. He suspected it was just out of sheer boredom, like when she couldn't find a friend to go shopping with her or she'd broken up with her latest boyfriend du jour. "Didn't they pay for your birthday party in Hong Kong? And your car?"

"Yeah, but they don't care about stuff like that," she laughed. "The McFees are supposed to spend money and enjoy themselves. Besides, people like hearing about the latest things I've bought." Violet paused a beat. "At least I don't embarrass them by throwing money at little projects that keep failing. How many 'business ventures' have you been in, anyway?"

He shut his eyes and counted to ten. "Don't you have a club to go to or something? Some fashion show to attend? Or someone *else* to annoy?"

She laughed again. "No comeback for that one, huh?"

"I'm hanging up now."

"Mom and Dad are going to want to talk to you when you're done. That's all I was calling to say."

"Wonderful." Chad rubbed at his temples. He was starting to get a huge headache. "Fine. Message delivered. Beat it."

"Bye." She hung up, and he shut off his phone. He'd call when the whole thing was over, but he wasn't looking forward to it.

At least I don't embarrass them by throwing money at little projects that keep failing.

He walked back into the lawyer's office and sat down, arms crossed. He loved his family, and they did have a point about his last few investments. But he was getting sick of being considered the black sheep of the McFee Empire simply because he'd taken a few chances. They hadn't always been a multi million-dollar family, he consoled himself. If his great-great-grandfather McFee hadn't hit it rich in gold and turned it into a string of very successful restaurants and then frozen foods, his parents would be broke, too. It took risks to make it big. He just hadn't picked the right risks, that was all.

Chad looked around the room. His cousins were in one corner, looking like they were arguing amongst themselves. They were all in their thirties and forties, wearing chic black clothing and matching stern expressions. There were also a few people who looked like businessmen—Great-Uncle Charles was known for being on the board of directors for several corporations.

Finally, the lawyer stood up and began the reading of the will. The bulk of the fortune went to Great-Uncle Charles's children, who looked moderately happy at their share of the pie, although they still glared at one another. Chad imagined they would probably get their own lawyers to squabble out the details. It was a sizable fortune, so he guessed he couldn't blame them, and they *were* brothers and sisters. Hell, he'd considered hitting Violet with a lawsuit or two, just because she annoyed him so much. He thought back to his phone conversation with her. They'd never really gotten into rough-and-tumble fights when they were younger, but they'd fought fairly intently. That hadn't changed a lot as they got older, though they still spoke often.

"And to my great-nephew and namesake, Charles 'Chad' McFee…"

Chad shook his head to clear his thoughts, and then focused on what the reedy lawyer standing at the podium had to say. Everyone else seemed curious to see what he was doing there.

Violet was probably right, he thought, trying to squash hope. He was probably getting a pocket watch, or some antique paperweight.

The lawyer adjusted his glasses and read directly from the will. "'I know that we haven't been that close, all things considered, over the past few years.'"

Chad felt a pang. He'd been busy, but he really should've spent a little more time visiting the guy. A little late now, he thought with remorse, and for a second his eagerness to find out what he'd inherited was eclipsed by guilt.

"'The McFee fortune is large, but some things are more important than money. I learned that the hard way. And, if what your parents have been telling me is accurate, so are you.'"

The cousins chuckled maliciously at that little commentary, and Chad scrunched down in his seat a little. *Good grief,* he thought. *Am I supposed to be getting lectures on my spending habits from beyond the grave, now?*

He was probably getting a calculator, at this rate. Or maybe an *Investing for Dummies* book. *Yuk yuk, isn't that hysterical?* The family would be talking about it for years.

"'So to you, great-nephew, I am giving one of my favorite possessions,'" the lawyer continued, clearing his throat. "'You are now owner of the Honey Ridge Vineyard, in Napa.'"

Chad blinked, not sure that he'd heard that one right. A vineyard? He hadn't even known Great-Uncle Charles liked wine, much less owned something as friv-olous as a vineyard!

"'It has been a joy for me, in my old age,'" the lawyer said, and his voice warmed, as if Great-Uncle Charles himself was channeling through the thin old man. "'I give it to you with only one stipulation—that you allow the current vineyard team to finish out one last vintage, should you decide to sell it. They're good people who work hard, and they deserve that much.'"

There was a murmur that went through the small crowd at that point. Everything up to that point had been given away with no strings attached, so this seemed odd.

The lawyer was obviously skimming ahead, because he cleared his throat with even more gusto, as if hesitant to continue. Finally, he said, "'I give this to you because I know, of all the family, you will understand and honor my dying request…instead of bringing lawyers into it and trying to have it all your way.'"

Ooh. Chad glanced over at the cousins, who were now looking guilty and scowling instead of looking smug. *Score one, Great-Uncle Charles!*

The rest of the will reading was short and to the point—various items and knickknacks. When it was done, one of his cousins, Eldridge, came over.

"I can't believe he gave you the vineyard," Eldridge said without preamble.

"Me neither," Chad said, honestly enough. "I didn't even know he had a vineyard."

"He bought it about ten years ago, after Mom died," Eldridge said. "He was a bit silly about it, to be honest. It was sort of a retirement hobby, I think."

Chad was curious. His great-uncle hadn't seemed the type to have hobbies, considering he'd kept making money right up to the day he died. He didn't think the man had ever retired.

"Anyway, too bad you can't sell it right away," Eldridge said. "Unless you're planning on keeping it?"

"I just found out about this," Chad pointed out. "I have no idea what I'm planning on doing with it."

"It's a money-loser." Eldridge waved his hand dismissively. "You'll want to ditch it, first chance."

Chad nodded, eager to get home at this point. "Uh, okay," he said, then put out his hand. "I'm so sorry for your loss."

Eldridge looked nonplussed for a moment, then shook his hand. "Thanks," he mumbled, sounding a little choked up, then quickly walked away.

Chad sighed. There might be more to life than money, he thought as he grabbed his coat. But money was a lot easier for his family to deal with.

LEILA FAIRMONT HAD DONE a lot for Honey Ridge Vineyard. She'd stayed up countless nights, working heaters to make sure the grapes didn't freeze during frosts. She'd contacted the best agriculturalists in the business during the blight that struck some of their prize Merlot grapes, year before last. She'd supervised the business, farming and winemaking aspects of the entire enterprise since she was twenty-five years old, now nearly four years. She couldn't feel closer to the vineyard if it were her own child.

Still, she'd never gone up to a total stranger's house and introduced herself before.

She had gotten news from Charles McFee's lawyer that the vineyard had been given to his nephew, Chad McFee. She'd never met Chad. For that matter, she'd barely met Charles. He was responsible for the continued survival of Honey Ridge, though, and for that, she was very fond of the man, who had seemed very old and very, very serious on the occasions he'd visited the vineyard. Charles McFee had been an old-school, tweed-and-pinstripe business type, who apparently had developed a passion for being a vineyard owner late in life. He'd given them tons of money and never balked at costs or disasters. He had been a true patron, and he'd let Leila, and her parents before her, run the place as their own.

She drove through the unfamiliar streets of San Francisco, feeling frustration at herself for getting lost—and even more frustration at being nervous. If Charles were anything like his uncle, he was a quiet, stuffy, pleasant sort of investor. He probably had the same wire-rim glasses, though not as thick, and his idea of a good time was checking out stock prices while sitting in the bathtub. The image made her giggle.

Leila found the condo, finally, in a nice neighborhood in Nob Hill. He likely had a gorgeous view. He was also obviously very rich. The trick here was going to be convincing him that Honey Ridge was, indeed, a good investment.

She parked her beat-up van on the hill and got out, straightening her very best business suit and praying for strength. Honey Ridge had been in financial straits for the past two years, and only love had kept Charles McFee giving money to the cause. She couldn't thank the man enough for his patience. Her parents had been head vintners of Honey Ridge since she was a child, and when they left to start a new vineyard in Australia, Leila had begged them to intercede on her behalf. Even though twenty-five was an unbelievably young age for a head winemaker, she had grown up on wine and had studied winemaking in college. She'd done everything necessary to one day run the vineyard she'd fallen in love with. Charles McFee had taken a chance on her, based on her parents' recommendation.

Now, the vineyard was recovering slowly, first from blight, then from last year's drought, which had hit all the independent vineyards hard. She just needed another year or two to bring it around.

If only Charles hadn't died!

Still, she thought, as she walked up the concrete stairs that led to the front door of the condo, the man had been ninety if he were a day. It was selfish of her to expect him to hang on just to bail her out.

She rang the bell and, after a moment, a puzzled voice came over the intercom. "Yes?"

"Mr. McFee?"

Another pause. "Yes. Who is this?"

"My name is Leila Fairmont. I'm from Honey Ridge Vineyards—"

"I'm not interested in buying anything today," he said quickly.

"Well, you're already the owner," she said, with a little chuckle. He thought she was some kind of door-to-door solicitor! "I'm so sorry to be barging in unannounced like this, but I left you several messages, and I was hoping for just a few minutes of your time."

A slightly longer pause. Then, "Yes, of course. Leila Fairmont. Give me a second, I'll get you."

She smiled. He was probably in the middle of some business plan or something, she thought with a grin, and didn't want to be disturbed. She took a deep breath, standing up straight, and held her slim briefcase in front of her. She knew she looked the picture of professionalism. Now, to just…

He opened the door, and Leila couldn't help it—her mouth fell open.

He looked like a frat guy. He was wearing a pair of sweats and a tank top that left little of his body to the imagination. His arms were chiseled and nicely muscular, without being obnoxious or overly bulky. His waist was slim, and she'd bet anything his stomach was ironing-board flat, probably rippled with muscle. His hair was a rich reddish-brown, and it was tousled and mussed in a way that had nothing to do with artistic sculpting gel. It just looked…

Sexy. Natural, just-got-out-of-bed sexy.

Her mouth went dry. "Mr. McFee?" she croaked in disbelief. "*Chad* McFee?"

"You must be Leila Fairmont," he said, as if it were the most natural thing in the world for him to greet her this way. He opened the door, gesturing her in. "I've been meaning to call you. I'm sorry I didn't sooner—things have been a little crazy. I just got back from a birthday party, actually."

"Oh?" She couldn't help it. She sneaked a quick look at his butt as he walked into his living room. Was *nothing* on this man less than perfect? When he turned, she made a show of glancing at her watch, to make sure that he didn't catch her scoping him out. It was four o'clock in the afternoon.

Had he been out all night, then?

"Have a seat," he said, gesturing to two huge gray leather couches. "I'll just be a second. I need to get a cup of coffee. And an aspirin." He laughed. "Can I get you anything?"

She shook her head, sitting on the couch, feeling dismayed. She was expecting a tweedy business nerd, not some party-hearty poster boy!

And certainly not a sexy one.

Chad came back out with his coffee. "Sorry. Jet lag always hits me this way," he said, by way of explanation.

"Jet lag?" She couldn't track what he was saying.

That wasn't a good sign. "I thought you'd just been to a party."

"Yup. It was in Ibiza. Spain," he clarified, taking a long sip of the coffee. "Ah, that's the stuff. So you're from the vineyard I inherited. How's it going?"

She blinked, thrown by…well, everything. "It's going okay," she said guardedly.

"Well, that's good."

Leila sat there a minute, staring at him as he smiled at her sleepily. Maybe this was a bad idea. Maybe he'd just be like Charles—keep writing the checks and stay out of her way. Anybody who just jetted off to Spain for a birthday party had to be doing okay financially.

"How's the harvest coming?" he asked.

"Uh…well, it's only July," she said. "We're planning on harvesting in September this year. That's a little early, but I want to have the time to age the Merlots, which we're famous for, and experiment with some blends."

She stopped as she saw his eyes glaze over. Now, he was the one who wasn't tracking.

Apparently, he didn't know anything about wine at all.

"Anyway," she said, feeling stupid for deciding she had to meet the new owner, "I just wanted to see who our new investor was, and answer any questions you might have about, er, the vineyard. But I see this is probably an inconvenient time for you. Anytime you'd like to come by Honey Ridge, though, I'd be more than happy to give you a tour."

She was staring full into his face when she said it, which she realized was probably a mistake. He was looking sleepy, so his amber-brown eyes were low lidded, like he'd just come out of bed...or he was still in it, and wouldn't mind company. His slow smile was sinfully handsome.

"That could be nice," he said, and his voice was low, rubbing over her skin like raw silk.

"Um. Yes," she said, fidgeting with her briefcase. "Right. So, no questions?"

He frowned for a moment, thoughtful. "Actually, yes, as long as you're here. How's the vineyard doing financially?"

Leila blinked. Then she opened her briefcase and got out the little presentation she'd meant to go through, back when she'd assumed Chad was Mr. Tweedy Nerd. "Here is a snapshot of our financial picture, as well as our plans for future expansion and growth."

He reached over, his fingertips inadvertently brushing against hers as he collected the slim report. She shivered, and felt like an even bigger idiot. Leila watched as he breezed through the pages.

"Hmm," he said. "Well. This will take me a little time to go over, but I appreciate you having it pulled together so neatly."

She wondered if he'd really read it, or if he'd chuck it into a desk somewhere. A house this big, a guy this rich, had to have some huge mahogany desk, even if he just used it to play video games or seduce women with by saying, *Let me show you my study.*

Her mind flashed a picture of how he might seduce her—and how big that mahogany desk might be, with two people on it—for just a moment before she stopped herself. *Knock that off. He's the new owner, you idiot!*

"Well, I guess I'll be going," she said, standing up quickly and putting out her hand. "I appreciate you taking the time to meet with me, Mr. McFee."

"Call me Chad," he said easily, with that quicksilver smile. "And Ms. Fairmont?"

"Call me Leila," she said, to be fair.

"Leila," he said. She'd never heard anyone say her name the way he did. Man, did she have to get out of there! "I think it's only fair to warn you that I am very serious about my investments. I'm going to take you up on that offer of yours."

"Which offer would that be?" she squeaked, then cleared her throat with a frown.

That smile turned lethally sexy. "I'll be out for a tour, at the very least," he said. "But I think I'd like to really investigate what makes your vineyard tick. I mean, I'm the owner, right? I shouldn't be in the dark about it. I have a ton to learn, I'm sure."

"Uh…" This wasn't going the way she'd planned. At all.

"And I'm sure you'll show me," he said confidently. "Can I count on you?"

"Er…all right," she said uncertainly. "I mean, of course. Of course, you're welcome to come anytime you like."

He smiled and shook her hand, his palm warm and solid over hers. "I'm looking forward to it," he all but purred.

She took her hand back, still feeling his warmth on it, and then fled with a nod and a hasty goodbye.

Going back to her van, Leila was surprised to find herself trembling a little. Instead of a kindly old man, she had a young man to deal with now. A rich, jet-setting, socialite guy, sexy as all get out, who might or might not have intentions of being hands-on when it came to her vineyard. Which gave her two sources of concern.

One: how was she going to convince a guy who knew nothing about wine not to just barge in because he was bored…and how was she going to convince him not to drop them when he got bored of this new toy?

And two: more disturbingly, as she thought of his smile and his handshake…just how hands-on was her new boss planning on being?

"CHAD, WHAT ARE YOU thinking about?"

"Hmm?" Chad looked over the family dinner table toward his mother, who had asked the question. "Sorry, what?"

"You're so distracted lately," his mother noticed. "Anything going on? Some girl maybe?"

"As long as it's not another investment," his father muttered, from the far end of the table, causing his sister Violet to smirk. Chad was surprised to see Violet there, actually. She'd been at some resort for the past week, or so her tan seemed to suggest.

"So which is it, Chad? A girl, or an investment?" his mother continued, in her gently relentless way.

A bit of both.

Leila Fairmont had dropped by his house a few days before. He couldn't get her off of his mind, and he wasn't sure why. She was cute, of course—honey blonde, five-six, with a trim body that had curves in the right places without suggesting any kind of surgical enhancement. But while she was cute, she wasn't what he'd consider beautiful. He'd seen enough porcelain-perfect near-model socialites to know the difference. But there was something about her—fidgeting with that leather briefcase of hers, or tugging on her business skirt—that seemed adorable. That, and the fact that she was obviously concerned about her livelihood, the vineyard.

"I think I'm going to be gone for the summer," he ventured carefully.

"Really?" His father looked up from his beef stroganoff at that point. "You know we're going to the lodge in Scotland. Are you going to be in Europe? You should swing by if you are."

"You'd better not be in Mazatlan," Violet said sourly. "I don't want to keep running into you at parties."

He sighed. If he'd realized his family was going to be out of the country, he might've kept his mouth shut and saved himself the trouble. But he'd already put his foot in it, and now they were all expecting him to break the news.

"Actually, I'll still be in the country. I just won't be around my condo, that's all," he clarified.

"Oh. Well," his father said, and turned his attention back to eating his dinner.

"That sounds good," his mother said, frowning at her husband. "Where will you be then, darling? On your friend's yacht? That was lovely, as I remember."

"Ah, no," Chad said. "Actually, I think I'll be out in Napa for a while."

"Napa? That's nice," she enthused. "I haven't been in wine country for…well, years now. At least, not in the United States." She turned back to Chad's father. "Do you remember when we spent those months in France, at that château right by that charming little vineyard—"

"Vineyard," his father said, and Chad could see the wheels turn and the connection finally click. "Your great-uncle Charles's vineyard. Don't tell me you're actually going to stop by and see the damned thing."

"It's my vineyard now, actually, Dad," he said, keeping his voice mild and eating his own dinner.

"You *are* selling the thing, though, right?" His father made it sound like a leper colony. "You're getting rid of it as soon as possible."

"Part of the provision of the will," Chad said quickly, trying to head off his father's tirade, "was that the current vineyard team gets to finish out this harvest, and bottle it. I can't sell it until then."

"You probably could," his father grumped. "If you'd just let me call our lawyer…"

"Dad," Chad warned.

His father sighed. "Your uncle knew he had a sucker in you," he finally said. "So, what exactly are you going to check out at this little vineyard of yours?"

"I don't know," Chad admitted. He hadn't planned on looking at it, in all honesty. He had just planned on waiting until he got the okay that the last bottle was finished, and then he was planning on dumping the whole thing on a Realtor or something. But then, he hadn't met Leila. "I've always liked wine."

"Yeah," Violet snorted. "*Drinking* it."

Chad ignored that little jab. "So I thought I'd see what sort of wine cellar they have, what the grounds are like, stuff like that. Get a sense of the place," he said. "If I'm going to know what it's worth to sell, I ought to check it over."

He figured that was what it would take to placate his

father, and he was right…for the moment, anyway. His father simply harrumphed and went back to eating, giving his son a baleful stare every few minutes.

Chad got the feeling he wasn't going to be getting off that lightly, but he was glad for the reprieve. He spent the rest of the evening listening to Violet spin stories about her rich friends and their various feuds and gossip. His father tuned that out, too, although his mother was able to keep up, even adding little bons mots of her own from her older social circle. "Just try not to give them anything nasty to write about in those social columns, Violet," his mother concluded. "The way I keep reading about those Hilton girls…it breaks your heart, it really does. It's just embarrassing. And then to turn around and hear they think they're making their own money!"

Chad frowned. "Don't they have a clothing line or something?"

He shouldn't have. His father took the opportunity to pounce. "They might be embarrassments, but when they put their money into something, at least they're successful at it."

"Dear," his mother warned. "Please. Not at the dinner table."

"I just want our son to realize that I keep having to hear about his little hobbies every time I go to the gym or the yacht club," his father replied. "Violet might be burning through her trust fund and going to every soiree in the Western hemisphere, but kids your age, in your social circle…who isn't expecting that?"

Chad rolled his eyes. "You're still mad about the movie not making money, huh?"

"All of it, Chad," his father growled.

Violet stopped looking smug when she realized her father wasn't just doing his usual posturing—he was well and truly steamed, and he was about to unleash it. She sat up in her chair, her eyes darting toward the door. "Um…excuse me," she said, and fled.

"First there was your little Internet business, that you shelled out half your bank account for," his father said.

"That was just before the bust," Chad argued. "I wasn't the only one who got burned."

His father held up a hand for silence. "Then there was your real estate brainstorm."

Chad squirmed. He'd gotten taken for a lot of money, from a friend of a friend who had conned a bunch of them. "That was a mistake," Chad admitted. "But it did teach me to be much more careful about research and who to invest in."

"Then, there were those cars…that cruise ship…and finally a movie. What the hell do you know from movies?" His father shook his head. "You just meet these people, and they're so happy, and you think it'll be so much fun that you dive in without thinking. Dammit, Chad!"

He crossed his arms. "I know I've been overenthusiastic," Chad said. "But dammit, Dad, what am I supposed to do? Get a job over at the family company?"

"Lord, no," his father said, with an undertone of *Lord knows what damage you'd wreak if I let you go there!* Chad felt his chest burn with humiliation. "If you just keep your spending reasonable, you don't have to work. Ever. Do you know how many people would love to be in the position you're in?"

Chad clenched his jaw. He knew it was unreasonable. He knew that he could just sit in the lap of luxury and cruise for the rest of his life, if he wanted to, just as his father had said. The thing was, he was bored—bored with parties, bored with traveling, bored with the same old thing. He knew it was pathetic, the old "bird in a gilded cage" dodge. But when he invested…he supposed the closest thing to what he experienced would be gambling, but it wasn't just the risk. It was feeling like a *part* of something.

Unfortunately, the things he kept choosing to be a part of were usually stuff his friends pulled together, and while they meant well, they usually had the attention span of a gnat. He'd learned, the hard way, that the next time he invested in something, he was going to not only know everything about it, he was going to develop it himself.

"Just remember what I said, son," his father said, finally concluding his lecture. "Stop trying to be something you're not. Just…I don't know. Buy a car or something. And knock off trying to be Mr. Tycoon, okay?"

Chad swallowed his humiliation and pushed away his plate. "Thanks for dinner," he said in a monotone.

His mother looked thankful that the discussion was over. "Would you like some dessert?"

Chad shook his head. He'd had enough for one family dinner.

"Well then, have a fun time in Napa," she sang out brightly. "We'll call you as soon as we come back in September, okay?"

CHAPTER TWO

THAT FRIDAY, at noon, Leila gathered her motley crew of vineyard workers and assorted staff to meet their new owner. She paced awkwardly in the courtyard, feeling nerves course through her. Most of them were due to the fact that Mr. "Call Me Chad" McFee had probably read her report on the state of the vineyard by now, or at least, there was the possibility he could have…and by this point, he might've decided to simply sell the place, which was probably the most logical conclusion. For all she knew, he'd called to tell her he'd be showing up to "inspect" the place as a final courtesy, before pulling her aside and dropping the ax personally. It didn't seem likely, but weirder things had happened.

Of course, on a purely personal level, she admitted that at least part of her nervousness had nothing to do with the vineyard…and everything to do with seeing Chad again, for whatever reason.

If that wasn't stupid, she didn't know what was.

Leila glanced at her watch. She could deal with droughts and blight—hadn't she had to face them both, in the past two lousy seasons? She'd even face a swarm of locusts, if it came to that. But this was her last chance at bringing back the vineyard she'd grown up with. Her last chance at making her parents proud.

She might not have had a lot of boyfriends, but she did know that they could be distracting. And a man as distracting as Chad McFee was one disaster she really had to be wary of.

She was still thinking this when he walked up to her. She jumped, startled, when he tapped her shoulder.

"Sorry," he said with a roguish smile. "Didn't mean to scare you."

"Surprised me, that's all," she quickly corrected, even though her heart was still trip-hammering a mile a minute. "Let me get the gang all assembled. I told most of them this morning that you'd be stopping by to check us out. I mean, to check out the vineyard."

Shut up, you're babbling. In an effort to get back her bearings and what was left of her dignity, she rang the community bell, a deep, resounding bell that she'd gotten in college, from an Asian monastery. The gong rattled her rib cage, but it also got all the farmhands in, which was the point. Pretty soon a throng of people were gathered in the "courtyard," the grassy area beneath an almond tree by the main house.

"Well, here he is," she said, by way of introduction. "Chad McFee, our new owner, and Charles McFee's... great-nephew, was it?"

He nodded.

They stared at Chad. Chad looked back at them, and she could sense him squirming under their attention.

"Um, perhaps you'd like to say a few words?" she prompted, wishing this could be easier. Charles hadn't ever addressed the vineyard, but then, he was content to deal with Leila, and before her, Leila's parents. He'd never wanted to "check things out" the way Chad did.

"Sure," Chad said, shrugging, and he smiled at the crowd. People smiled back, friendly, but Leila knew them enough to read their expressions. In his white T-shirt and jeans, and his sneakers, he looked like just plain folks. But his T-shirt was obviously expensive, not something you bought in a three-pack at a discount store. Same with his jeans, some name brand that probably cost hundreds. And the sneakers—white leather with black-and-red trim, and an expensive logo. They were a dead giveaway.

"Er, hi," he started, waving. It was just this side of shy, sort of goofy. Utterly disarming. "Glad to meet you all."

There was an echo of responding greeting, murmurs and waves.

"I have to admit something," he said, shifting his weight nervously from one foot to the other.

Leila felt her heart clench. *Oh, please don't tell them you're thinking of selling the place.* She'd considered the possibility, but thinking the worst and actually witnessing it were two completely different horrors.

"I am not a winemaker. At all. Or is that vintner? Isn't that what you guys are called?" Chad looked at Leila for clarification.

Leila nodded, feeling a little relief seep into her system.

"All I know about wine is how much I usually pay per bottle," he continued, with a nervous chuckle. They didn't laugh in response, causing him to clear his throat awkwardly. "So I want to see exactly what goes on at a vineyard, and what it's like to work here. I'm in your hands completely, blank slate, totally at your disposal. Whatever you tell me to do, I'll do, until I learn what goes on here. Does that sound fair?"

It was charming, Leila thought.

It was also, unfortunately, probably the worst thing he could have said.

Julio, the head of farming, had a wicked smile in his eyes that did not register in the rest of his impassive expression. "Well, the best way to learn about winemaking," he said, in a voice that sounded much older than his thirty-four years, "is to start from the ground up."

"That's what I had in mind," Chad said enthusiastically. "So, what's the ground, metaphorically speaking?"

The man had no idea what he was asking for. "Uh, Julio," Leila interrupted, "Chad isn't really…I mean, he shouldn't be doing hard labor."

Julio shrugged innocently. "The man said he wanted to learn, Leila. I'm just trying to help him out."

She knew where that would lead. Chad would be doing the roughest, crappiest manual labor that needed doing. Call it hazing.

If Chad had any lingering thoughts of getting rid of Honey Ridge, a day full of the torture that Julio and his crew would dish out might be the deciding factor in tipping the scale toward ditching the vineyard completely.

"I think what Chad means is more of an overview," she countered, frowning intently, trying to will Julio to read her mind. *Please, don't screw with him.* "He ought to learn, yes, but—"

"If I may?" Chad interrupted.

She turned, surprised at the tinge of anger in his voice. "Yes, of course."

"Chad here knows exactly what he means," he said, in a way that clearly illustrated what he thought of being referred to as if he wasn't there. Leila felt her cheeks heat with a blush of embarrassment. "You don't need to coddle me. Sure, I haven't worked on a farm, but I'm in good shape, and I'm not completely useless." His words had a particular bite on that last word.

"I never meant…"

"If it'll help me learn what it's like to work here, and what goes into our product, then what the hell. Bring it on," Chad said fearlessly. "I'm sure I can handle it."

Oy. She felt a tinge of worry. *I'm sure I can handle it* were famous last words. *Infamous* last words. Right up there with *How bad could it get?*

"Well, then. We're getting ready for harvest and for bottling," she said, shifting her voice back to business. "This year, we're getting the Cabernet and the Pinot Noir in by end of September, gang."

There was a loud chorus of grumbling at that announcement, quickly diverting attention from their new owner/whipping boy.

"What's the rush?" Vince, one of the farmhands, complained.

"We got nailed with that frost last year, and it took out half our crop," Leila reminded him, the pain of the loss still fresh. "That's not going to happen again this year. This year, more than ever, we're going to get the vintage perfect, got it?"

"Yes, ma'am," Vince drawled.

"That was just a fluke, sweetie," Marisol, Julio's

mother and a part-time cook at Honey Ridge, said with concern. "Things happen that you can't control, especially with wine. You know that."

Leila sighed. Marisol was the closest thing she had to a mother here in Napa, since her own had moved to Australia. "I know, Marisol. But…" She glanced at Chad, not sure how much to divulge. "Well, I want to make sure the things we can control go perfectly."

Marisol nodded, although she still didn't look convinced.

"Okay, enough gabbing. You guys know what to do," she said, knowing that was true.

"Come with me, Chad," Julio said, his voice equal parts amusement and a wickedness that Leila didn't trust. "We'll get you started on something easy."

She saw Chad disappear toward the vats, and went to Marisol, who wordlessly hugged her.

"I miss my parents all of a sudden," Leila said against Marisol's shoulder.

"I'm sure they miss you, too," Marisol answered. "You know, you could've just gone with them. I hear that vineyard they're running is really coming along."

"You know what this place means to me," Leila said. "And they fought to convince Charles I was good enough to run it, even though I was young. I couldn't leave."

Marisol just shook her head. "I'm going to make some lunch," she said. "Tell that new owner of ours that he's welcome to a bite. I imagine he'll be starving after a few hours with Julio."

Leila smiled weakly as Marisol disappeared into the house. Then she turned toward the vats, but saw that

Chad was already out and headed toward the fields. This time, he had a pitchfork and a wheelbarrow.

He also had his shirt off, she noticed. Her mouth went dry.

He wasn't kidding when he'd said he was in shape. He had a lean physique that was cut out of marble. *Gorgeously golden, tanned marble,* she thought, knowing she shouldn't stare, but she was somehow unable to stop herself. She knew he was good-looking. She'd done some belated research on him, and seen photos of him online. She'd even seen him in sweats. But she realized none of that did him justice, now that she was seeing him, literally, in the *flesh.*

As if sensing her gaze, he glanced over at her, shooting her a quick "what, me worry?" grin before disappearing into the rows of grapevines.

Leila blushed and quickly turned back to the house. She needed to get this under control. She couldn't afford to lose focus. A gorgeous new owner with a killer smile was not on her list of things to do.

At least she wouldn't have to worry about the attraction tonight, she thought grimly. The guys were going to work him for hours. If his muscles could stand it, that would be one thing. But without his shirt, she was fairly certain that by dinnertime, he'd be burned scarlet as a lobster. In fact, if today went as badly as she feared, she might not be seeing him at dinner. Or after. Or possibly ever.

BY THAT EVENING, Chad was tired. No—he was exhausted. Actually, he couldn't even come up with a word to describe adequately how physically wrung out he felt.

In the course of his "orientation" they'd been true to their word, giving him no deferential treatment. He'd polished the stainless-steel vats that held the wine, he'd "punched" down the frothy mixture of fruit pulp and grape skins that rose to the top of the vats, he'd swept the cellars. He'd even picked a few grapes by hand, although he was bad enough that they stopped him almost immediately. They hadn't been vindictive, which was good. He even suspected they were being tolerant, since he was no doubt slower at the menial tasks than any of the experienced staff. And they weren't being mean. He was grateful that Julio had sent him to the main house to get some sunscreen and forced him to take water breaks, or else he would probably be suffering from heat stroke. Julio hadn't even commented on Chad's obvious stupidity, but instead had merely suggested that keeping a shirt on might be a better plan. The rest of the crew only grinned a little. For the most part, though, they'd offered helpful advice, and accepted him with a good-spirited-ness that he'd never experienced before.

When he'd "checked out" his other investments, and asked to learn about them, he now realized he'd been humored, pampered and, for the most part, snowed. They didn't want an owner getting involved and mucking things up, so at the movie, they'd let him hang out in the actor's trailer (right then, he should've known that with their budget, getting the guy a trailer was a costly mistake) and look through the camera lens. And the real estate stuff was so dodgy, he'd never even seen the site. These guys apparently had no qualms about letting him really learn what it was they did. And they loved it. Chad could tell that immediately. They wanted him to love it, too.

Of course, if his father wanted him to sell... He shook his head. They would all be out of a job if he sold the place, he realized. And with the little disasters Leila had mentioned, this place was not doing well financially. He'd do better, personally, if he just sold the place—the land itself was more valuable than the grapes.

It was more than he wanted to think about. In fact, all he wanted to do right now was drive back to his hotel, order room service and soak in a hot shower for an hour or so. Of course, that would require standing. Chad wondered absently if the hotel had a suite with a Jacuzzi tub.

As he was walking past the main farm house, headed for his car, he saw that a picnic of sorts had been set out on a few tables, on a grassy patch by the cabernet vines. The vintners and farm hands were putting out food from the kitchen, and Julio was pouring red wine out of their bottles and into funny-shaped glass pitchers.

"Hey, Chad," Julio said, grinning and still continuing the slow wine transfer. "I meant to ask you...would you like to stay for supper?"

"Uh..." Chad thought of his aching muscles. "I don't want to impose," he said instead.

"You're the new owner," Julio answered. "You can impose all you want. Besides, we do this every other week or so, especially during harvest. Nobody wants to go home and cook after a long day." Julio had finished pouring, and he held up the empty wine bottle displaying a competitor's wine label. "Also, it's still business. Sort of. We try different wines to see what the other guys are doing."

Chad noticed that, while the other workers looked busy arranging food, they were obviously listening for his reply.

It would probably be rude not to stay, Chad thought. And he'd probably look like a wimp if he bowed out. Or he might look like he wasn't interested in the vineyard—which he was, more than he'd even expected to be. He really did want to learn.

But if you get close to these people, and you wind up selling the place anyway...

He sighed to himself. His life had been a lot less complicated, just a few weeks ago.

Just then, Leila emerged from the house with a platter of vegetable crudités and three kinds of dip. "Oh, Chad," she said, her violet eyes opening wide. "I didn't know you were still here. I thought you'd be long gone by now." Then her cheeks went rosy, as if she realized that what she said could be considered rude. "I mean, you put in a long day. I figured...I thought you'd want to go sleep or something."

"Julio asked if I wanted to stay for your picnic," Chad said, smiling. He wasn't sure what flustered her so much around him, but he had a few guesses, and it was cute as well as sexy.

"Oh," she said. "Um...of course you should stay. We should get to know our new owner, right?"

He grinned, a slow, inviting grin that he knew she couldn't mistake for anything else.

She nearly dropped the platter. Recovering, she put it safely on a table and muttered, "I'll go get more food," then dashed back to the house.

He turned back. "I'm staying," he told Julio. *Oh hell yeah, I'm staying.*

Vineyard or not, he knew he'd never have gotten this personally involved in one of his investments if it hadn't been for Leila Fairmont.

Chad noticed that Julio was no longer smiling at him, but instead was giving him a thorough, almost disapproving, once-over. Chad suddenly wondered if maybe Leila and Julio were an item. Or if Leila and *anybody* were an item. He hadn't seen a ring, and hadn't gotten the impression that she was involved with anyone, but he'd been wrong before. He should probably be more careful until he knew, one way or the other.

Leila came back out and walked over to him, still giving off that vibe of tension—and awareness. "I'll be honest," he said. "I'm pretty whacked, so I can't stay too long."

She smiled, and Julio lightened up a little. Chad relaxed a little, too. He watched as Leila poured herself a glass of red and took a few slow sips, closing her eyes.

Damn, she's pretty.

Deciding to make the best of things, Chad changed the subject. He pointed to the decanter she'd poured her wine from. "What's that all about?"

"You see how wide the base is? That's to help the red wine breathe. It increases the surface area, so more air can touch more wine. Pouring it from bottle to decanter helps mix air into it, too."

"Seems like a lot of trouble," he said.

Her warm, gentle smile hit him like a fist in the stomach. "Hey Julio, what is this? The Jordan Cabernet?" At Julio's nod, she continued, "Do we have any still in the bottle?"

Julio grabbed a still-corked bottle out of a box and handed it to her. Chad watched as she deftly removed the cork and poured him a small amount in an empty glass.

"Taste this," she said, "and tell me what you think."

He drank it, aware more than ever of the scrutiny of the people around him. "It's nice," he ventured. "Better than most of the wine I drink, I guess."

Actually, it didn't taste much different than the wine he drank at almost every party his friends gave.

Leila didn't laugh, although Chad could've sworn Julio snickered. Instead, she took his empty glass, and poured from the open, "breathing" decanter. "Now, try this," she said, staring at him with interest.

He was momentarily sidetracked by her intensity, but forced himself to focus. He took a tentative sip, wondering what the joke was. Then he blinked in surprise. It was as if the taste of the wine took up all the room in his mouth. His brain scrambled to process it.

"This is the same stuff?"

Now several people did laugh, but it was a happy sound, Chad noticed. Like when introducing a friend to your favorite restaurant, and being happy he liked it. Leila's smile was like liquid sunshine. "Pretty cool, huh?" she asked, with a wink.

Another farmhand, Ted, walked up, a little hesitant. "You should try that with the food. It complements the flavors unbelievably."

"Thanks," Chad said, feeling a little foolish. Now that he thought about it, he *was* hungry. Probably from doing the first hard labor of his life, he thought with a grin. He went for a chunk of Gouda cheese.

"You don't want that," Ted said immediately.

"Why not?"

Julio stepped in again, with a glass of white wine. "Cheese takes the edge off of terrible wine. Something about the cheese-making process, I don't know. But if you've got a really lousy vintage, eat a chunk of cheese with it, and it tastes less sour." He grinned. "That's why you see all those pictures in France, with a peasant drinking out of a jug, holding a big old hunk of cheese."

Leila grinned. "And that's why they usually serve it at wine tastings. So your taste buds get psyched out and you won't realize the wine's not that great." She crossed her arms, looking smug. "We never serve cheese at our tastings."

"Of course we don't," Chad said feeling a little foolish, but also intrigued. "So why do you have cheese here?"

"Some of our competitors put out some real 'cheeseworthies,' so we put it out to save our taste buds," she explained, eliciting an appreciative laugh.

Chad nodded. There was a lot to learn…and after a full day of hard work, his brain felt as slow and achy as his body. He liked the atmosphere, liked the education—but hated feeling like the slow kid, the obvious idiot.

"So you didn't know anything about wine before you got the vineyard?" Ted asked innocently.

"Well, not the process, but I've had plenty of wine," he said, with a laugh.

"What's been your favorite?" Julio asked.

Chad saw his chance. "Well, I don't have a favorite," he said, trying to sound worldly, "but I've had the 'sixty-eight Chateau Vincente Bordeaux."

He tossed that out with quiet pride, knowing that the stuff cost nearly nine hundred dollars a bottle. He knew this because his friend Lester had pointed it out when he'd poured it at his dinner party. And since they were all connoisseurs here, from the looks of it, he figured that *they'd* know. He'd been around good wine, all right!

"When'd you have it?" Julio asked.

When? "Uh…a year ago, I think," Chad said. This wasn't the impressed and awed reaction he was going for.

"Too bad," Leila said, taking another sip of wine, shaking her head slightly. "I hope you didn't pay too much for it. That wine peaked four years ago." At his blank look, she added, "It would be slowly turning to vinegar, and the taste would be way off."

"I…a friend bought it, actually," Chad said.

"Do you know some people actually paid six hundred dollars a bottle for it, back in the day?" Julio said, with a chuckle. "Amateurs. Just because a wine's expensive doesn't mean it's good."

Chad thought about Lester's nine-hundred-dollar boast, and decided to keep silent. He'd made a big enough fool of himself for one day.

Leila smiled at him gently. He couldn't win, he thought. He just couldn't win.

"I guess I'll be driving back to the hotel now," he said, wishing she would smile at him with admiration instead of tolerant amusement.

"So soon? You haven't eaten anything."

"That's fine," he said tightly. "I think I've had enough for one day."

"I'll walk you," she said, and followed him to his car. "How are you feeling?"

"Tired." He realized she looked concerned, so he added, "But it's a good tired."

"Don't let it bother you."

He didn't make the jump in logic. "Don't let what bother me?"

"Not knowing about wine," she said. "Nobody's born knowing. You'll pick it up."

"Oh." Chad squirmed. "I just don't like feeling slow, that's all. Especially since I own the place now."

She put a hand on his arm as he reached for his car door. Her palm felt warm, warmer than even the heat of the day. "You're a fast learner, I can tell," she said. "If you want, I can go over some stuff with you privately, so you don't have to feel embarrassed in front of the whole gang."

He was about to say no, since that would actually make him feel even more foolish—and she was the last person he wanted to look foolish in front of. But then it occurred to him. Private lessons. Maybe, just maybe, that was the best way to find out more about not only wine, but his favorite vintner.

"Okay," he said. "How about over dinner?"

"Dinner?" she asked, her voice sounding stunned.

"Yeah. Maybe tomorrow night?" He thought about his aching muscles. If they hurt like this now, by tomorrow, he'd barely be able to walk, much less…

Much less what? What were you planning on doing with her?

"Not tomorrow night," he amended. "How about next Tuesday?" He grimaced as a spasm of pain rippled his back. "I should be feeling human again."

She made a smile of sympathy. "Sure thing," she said, and he felt a little guilty. "Next Tuesday. I'll make dinner here, and go over wine stuff."

"Sounds good."

He had a date—of sorts, he thought, as he got into his car and drove away.

He shook his head. Apparently, he was just complicating his life now for the hell of it. But from what he'd seen of Leila…

He smiled. She might be worth the headache. But he'd still better see just how salvageable this new vineyard of his was, or he'd be hurting the very people he was getting to like.

CHAPTER THREE

"YOU KNOW, he's not that bad," Julio said. "Except for the whole, you know, not-knowing-anything-about-wine thing."

Leila grimaced, leaning against an oak barrel they'd just finished sealing. "If it weren't for a bunch of bankers and insurance salesman and other novices that didn't know squat about winemaking, California wouldn't even have the kind of wineries and vineyards it has today."

"I know that," Julio said with a gentle grin. "Your parents taught me that, same as they did you, remember?"

"Yeah, well," she said, realizing that he was just teasing. "He's just self-conscious, that's all. You should've heard his voice when he said he couldn't come in today. I'll bet he couldn't even walk."

Julio nodded, leaning against another barrel. "I'll bet. He might not know much about wine, but the guy's kind of a nut when it comes to enthusiasm. I've never seen anything like yesterday, with him trying to do all the chores we piled on him."

"Yeah, why *did* you guys haze him so hard?" she asked, crossing her arms.

"Didn't mean to," Julio said. "He just wouldn't say

no, so it became kind of a test, I guess. And most of us could do the stuff. He was just too stubborn."

"Well, you might've been more careful, is all I'm saying." Leila could still hear the pain and, worse, the embarrassment in Chad's call this morning. "He needs time."

Julio shot her a sly look. "Really? You're not this careful with most of our new hires. Got a thing for him?"

She could feel her cheeks heating and quickly turned to another barrel so Julio wouldn't notice. "I'm just saying, this is the guy who's going to be cutting our checks," she pointed out. "We might not want to cripple him."

"You've got a point there," Julio admitted. "Think he's going to sell the place?"

Now Julio's voice took on a note of concern. He'd been there as long as Leila had been. They'd grown up together. She'd lived in the farmhouse since she was six, and he'd been born just a few miles away—Marisol still owned the house. More importantly, Julio had a wife and two kids to think of.

For Leila, this place was a dream come true…a way to prove herself as a master vintner, a way to justify her parents' faith. For the others, it was a living…and that was way more important. *Just one more reason I can't let this vineyard fail,* she thought, worry gnawing at her stomach.

"I don't know," Leila said honestly. "He genuinely likes the place, which I think is a good start. We just have to convince him that it's worth saving."

"Now, now, don't get stressed about it," Julio said. "I know you. I can hear the gears grinding in your head from here."

Leila smiled weakly. "I keep trying to think of what

else we can do. The Merlot was great last year—even if we lost half the crop. And we're still bottling some of the best wine in the valley," she said, with defensive pride.

"Nobody's saying we're not," Julio soothed. "Nobody blamed you for the blight or the drought or the frost. Things just happen. That's nature, you know?"

"I know," she said, "but…"

"No buts," Julio said sternly. "You're like my kid sister, you know that. Everybody who's worked here knows how hard you work. But they also know that…" He paused, clearing his throat.

"Know what?" she asked, curious.

Julio took a deep breath and motioned her to sit down. She sat on a barrel, waiting for his reply. "We all love wine here," he said slowly.

"Well, duh." She rolled her eyes.

"But you're getting a little mental about it," he said, and put up his hands defensively when she made an irate squawk of disbelief. "Hey! Don't tell me you're not obsessed, *chica*. When was the last time you had a date?"

"What does that have to do with the price of tea in China?" Leila said impatiently. "I work hard. And where would I meet somebody anyway?"

"We have friends. People try to set you up all the time. My wife's tried to set you up three different times in the past year alone," Julio pointed out.

"I hate blind dates," Leila moaned. "And your wife just sort of sprang them on me. At family gatherings, no less!"

"Okay, Angelina's not very subtle," Julio agreed. "But if you don't like the people we're coming up with, why not Internet date or something?"

"What's with the sudden interest in my love life?" Leila crossed her arms, feeling even more vulnerable.

"You're unbalanced, Leila," he said. "Girl cannot live on wine alone."

Leila sighed. "Listen, when I get the guarantee that we've got financial backing, when I *know* that Honey Ridge is going to be okay…then I'll date. I'll see whoever you want, I'll set up a profile online. I'll take out a billboard. But until then…" She struggled to find the right words. "If Honey Ridge goes under, and I feel I didn't do absolutely everything I could to try to save it, I think it would wreck me, Julio. It would be beyond awful. I just can't face the thought."

Julio sighed. "You take things too seriously," he said. "You always did."

"I know," she said.

"It's amazing your wine is as good as it is, actually," Julio added.

Leila frowned. "Thanks a lot," she said, hurt.

"No, you're phenomenal. Don't even try to pretend you have self-doubt," Julio scoffed. "But to be a good winemaker, you've got to have a sense of fun. Risk. Adventure," he said, waving his hand flamboyantly. "Otherwise, you go all corporate, and it tastes…awful."

She nodded. She knew exactly what he meant.

"So maybe," he said persuasively, "if you spiced up your love life, your wine would be even better, huh?"

She stared at him. "You sneak. You're trying to get me to agree to dating just to save the vineyard."

"I'm saying if you're serious," Julio said piously, "you'll consider all options."

"What, I should 'take one for the team' to improve my vintages?" Leila asked, laughing with bewilderment.

"Of course not," Julio said. "But hey, if something comes up that stirs your interest, why not see where it goes? It could only help the wine, after all."

"Oh, yeah," Leila laughed. "And where exactly am I supposed to find some handsome, sexy guy who…"

She suddenly stopped laughing as Chad's face popped into her mind, like a blinding flash of clarity. She gasped.

"You keep thinking about it," Julio said drily, "and tell me if you come up with anything."

"I *couldn't*," Leila whispered, scandalized. She glanced around to see if anybody else could hear them. "He's the owner, for pity's sake! He could decide to sell the place tomorrow, for all we know! And even if he didn't…I have to work with the guy! What are you—crazy?"

"I can't help but notice that none of your reasons include that you're not attracted to him," Julio said.

Leila's blush could've toasted marshmallows, she felt quite sure. "That's such a dumb idea, I can't even…I won't even acknowledge it," she muttered.

"I'm not saying marry the guy," Julio said. "I'm not even saying sleep with the guy, honestly. You're probably right about that. But he's obviously interested in you, and you've had your hormones in deep freeze for so long they probably don't even remember what to do."

He had a point there, Leila thought, biting her lip.

"Wine's romantic. Flirt a little, play a little, loosen

up. You don't have to be so tense all the time. It wouldn't kill you to think about something other than work."

"Don't you have to check soil or something?" Leila asked.

Julio laughed. "Just think about what I said." With that parting shot, he went back to the vineyards.

She sighed heavily. The thing was, she didn't know how to just play. There was too much to think of, too many things that could go wrong. Too many ways that everything could go to hell in a handcart, with her at the wheel.

And playing with somebody like Chad McFee?

Well, that was playing with fire.

IT WAS AROUND TWO-THIRTY when Chad picked up his cell phone, dialing the number he knew by heart.

Renaldo picked up the phone. "Hey there, Chad," he said, his voice as casual as if he were talking to a friend. "How's it going? And please tell me you don't need a huge amount of money for some new project of yours. I'm a financial adviser, not a miracle worker."

"Ah, but you've worked so many miracles," Chad said, chuckling even though he meant it. Renaldo had been his financial adviser since he was fifteen years old, strangely enough—when his father had given him ten thousand dollars and told him to learn about the stock market.

"Well, what is it this time?" Renaldo said, with a long-suffering sigh. "Ostrich farm in Bakersfield? Ski resort in Idaho? And please tell me it's something you'll actually let me research this time," he added with a note of disapproval. In some ways, Renaldo was harder on him than his own father was. "I told you, if you keep making these wild agreements, you're going to blow through your trust fund like a class-five tornado."

"This isn't really my fault," Chad protested, only to get cut off by Renaldo's snort of disbelief. "I...*ow*." He winced as he stretched too far to get his glass of water, causing his arm muscles to scream.

"What was that? You hurt yourself?"

"Actually, yes. I've been working." Chad groaned as he sat down on the corner of his hotel bed.

"Working?" Renaldo said the word as if he couldn't recognize it. "Doing what?"

He sighed. "Remember that vineyard I inherited?"

"Well, yes..." There was a long pause. "You're actually...wait a minute. What exactly are you doing there? I thought you'd go take a peek, grab some bottles of wine, play lord of the manor."

"Not this time. Not even close," Chad grumbled. "I told them I wanted to understand the vineyard from the ground up."

"So, what, did they make you tour the entire place or something?"

"This week, I'm a cellar rat," Chad informed him.

"You mean, you're doing actual *physical* labor?"

He closed his eyes, rubbing his temple with his free hand. "If I didn't know better, man," he said, "I'd swear you were laughing at me."

"Just with delight," Renaldo said. "A cellar rat. My God. That's brilliant. So what menial chores have you been learning?"

"I've punched vats, I've cleaned, I've hung grapes. I've harvested grapes, for that matter," he said. "They're really careful here. Nothing automatic—nothing that gets trampled. Costs more, but it's worth it—you can taste the difference, since there's no fungus or mustiness that creeps in when you have flat-dried grapes or grapes that have been crushed too early by a harvester." He rattled off everything he'd gleaned from his talk with Julio and Ted.

Another pause. "You even sound like a vintner," Renaldo said, and his tone was more admiring. "And you've spent how much this week?"

"Not a dime…unless you count the cost of maintaining the vineyard, I guess," Chad said. "I haven't been drawing a salary or anything."

He thought briefly about Leila. He wondered how much the vineyard paid her. It couldn't possibly be that much—with the expenses, he knew, they didn't make much profit.

Still, it's better than selling the vineyard and firing her, since then she's not going to make anything at all.

"Well, I am happy for you," Renaldo said. "So, other than making my day—since I'm going to be laughing my butt off at you for at least the next hour—what did you need from me?"

"Actually," Chad said, unsure how to broach the subject. "I wanted you to do me a favor this week. I need you to run some numbers."

"That's what you're paying my retainer for—that, and being your on-call shrink," Renaldo joked. "Numbers for what?"

Chad took a deep breath. "I want you to run some profit-and-loss numbers on Honey Ridge."

Renaldo let out a low whistle. "It's not great, from what I recall," he said slowly. "But don't worry—when it gets bought out, the company buying it isn't going to care about profitability. They'll be buying it for the land, to expand. And I'll make sure you get a good price, don't even sweat it. You should be ahead, even after the indie movie disaster. That's got to be a comfort."

"That, er, wasn't what I meant," Chad said. "I meant….how bad would it be if I, you know, kept it?"

The pause this time was so long, Chad wondered if his cell phone had cut out. "Hello? Renaldo, you still there?"

"I'm sorry, I want to make sure I heard that right." Renaldo's voice was tight. "Did you just ask me to run numbers in case you wanted to *keep* the vineyard?"

"That's right," Chad said stoutly. "I know. I know it seems crazy."

"More than seems," Renaldo said. "You don't know anything about wine. Damn it, I didn't even know you *drank* wine. So, what, after a week of hard manual labor you've decided to become a man of the land? You're going to chuck your hard partying ways, and become a farmer?"

"Vintner," Chad said, noticing the sullen edge in his own voice.

"Come on, Chad. I'm sure you're having fun, but let's be reasonable."

"Are you kidding?" Chad spit out. "I'm not having fun! I've been working my butt off! The people here are great. I don't know if you'd understand, but they're all incredible. They love what they do. They work hard, and they all work together. And everybody knows why they're here, and what they need to do, and they all pitch in…"

And he'd been part of it. Through his weird deal

with Leila, he'd been allowed to become a small part of the Honey Ridge family. He knew people by name. The work itself was grueling, yeah, but at the end of the day he still felt better than he did any day at his family's companies. Hell, most of the time, he knew that people at his family's companies didn't even want him there. They were just humoring him because he was an heir, not because he could contribute anything valuable.

"I see," Renaldo said. "Is this guilt, then? Because you're going to be putting these people out of business?"

Chad let out a breath. "Yeah, that's part of it. A big part of it."

"Well. I have to say, it's nice to see this side of you." Renaldo managed to not sound patronizing about it. At least, not much. "But you've got to be reasonable. It's amazing that Honey Ridge has stayed alive this long. Your uncle Charles threw a lot of money at it, which helped. And it was starting to turn a corner, but some bad stuff happened. I'll need to look at it. Bottom line— it's a brutal time to be an independent vineyard, Chad, and they have to know that. If it weren't you putting them out of business, it'd be somebody else. They're grown-ups, they know the score."

Somehow, that didn't make Chad feel better. Especially when he remembered Leila's face when she talked about Honey Ridge, what it meant to her. When he remembered all the faces out there in the courtyard, looking at him expectantly.

"Just do me the favor, and run the numbers, okay?" Chad said, and it came out a little more belligerent than he meant it to.

"It's futile, but if looking at the actual numbers will

help, then okay, I'll run the numbers," Renaldo said. "It sounds like this place is really affecting you."

Chad closed his eyes, and pictured the vineyard in the setting sun, just before he'd driven off. Leila had been walking slowly toward the house, back in from the grapes. She'd paused to smell a rose from one of the thorny bushes that grew at the end of a row of grapes. She hadn't even looked back at his car, he remembered. She'd looked beautiful, and completely at home.

"Yes," Chad said. "This place is definitely affecting me."

THE FOLLOWING TUESDAY, Leila waited on the porch of the yellow farmhouse, watching as various farm hands and winemakers got into their cars and drove home. She had finished checking the Cabernet blend that afternoon, and then she'd knocked off early, an uncharacteristic gesture. She was still remembering what Julio had told her.

Relax. Play a little.

Flirt.

She was supposed to see Chad tonight, and teach him about wine and winemaking. She was even making dinner, a simple stew in the Crock-Pot and fresh-baked bread, thanks to Marisol. When she'd come in from the fields, she'd taken one look at herself and winced. Of course, Chad had already seen her like this and she wasn't trying to dress up, or anything. But there was no sense in both of them sitting there grungy, was there? Besides, she felt dirty, and her palms had purplish-red stains from the grapes. She would just get a little cleaned up, since she had the time before he showed up.

If he even remembered—for the rest of last week, and even yesterday, he'd gone home as soon as work was over.

Two hours later, she was scrubbed clean and smelled like lavender and mimosa, thanks to the lotion she had smoothed on her skin. She usually didn't have the time or the patience, but she was running early, Leila justified to herself. Besides, it was relaxing, and Julio had told her to relax.

It'll make the wine better, she told herself. She'd do a lot to improve the wine. Ask anybody.

She saw Chad, walking in from the vines with Julio. He was wearing jeans, the same expensive type he'd been wearing that first day, but now they were marked with dirt and wine stains. His black T-shirt had a dusting on it, as well, and his hair was ruffled by the wind. He should've looked grubby, but Leila got the feeling there was no way this man could look anything less than…

Delicious, her mind supplied. She suppressed it.

Chad was listening intently to Julio. "So when there's a mutation in the grape vines," Leila heard Julio explaining, as they got closer to the house, "it changes the flavor ever so slightly. Same with the environment. We call the mutated grape vines 'clones,' and—"

Julio broke off lecturing when he saw Leila. He grinned, taking in her appearance. Not that she'd done anything special. She was just wearing clean jeans and a soft periwinkle tank top that was more feminine than what she usually wore. And her hair was up. No big deal, she assured herself, crossing her arms.

"Looks like you guys worked hard today," Leila said, struggling to keep her voice light and easy.

She knew exactly when Chad focused in on her. He seemed to drink her in with intensity, studying her from the crown of her head to the toes of her slip-on shoes. She looked down at the plank boards beneath her feet, feeling warm.

"You look nice," Chad said, and she smiled in response.

"I should get going," Julio said. "My wife's waiting for me, and the kids start school soon…you know how that goes."

Leila nodded, feeling a little wistfulness at the picture of Julio's domestic bliss—marriage, family. *Something other than work.* She cleared her throat. "Tell Angelina I said hi, and the kids, too." Then she looked over at Chad. "You mentioned that you wanted to learn more about wine. I made some dinner, if you want." Then, when she saw Julio's eyes gleam, she quickly added, "But if you're tired, it can wait. And it sounds like you've done a ton today."

"No, no," Chad quickly assured her. He didn't notice Julio's little smirk as he walked away. At least, Leila hoped he hadn't. "Thanks for remembering."

She shrugged, nerves making her want to fidget. "Come on in. Welcome to my house."

She could feel his presence as he followed her in, large and warm. Her heart beat a little more rapidly. "Julio and the gang tell me you've been working really hard," Leila said. "They're impressed."

"Didn't think I had it in me, huh?"

She could hear the edge of bitterness in his voice, surprising her, and she quickly shook her head. "Even experienced farmhands have trouble keeping up with a fully operational vineyard and winery, if they've worked in other types of crops," she said. "You've picked things up very quickly. Especially for someone outside the business."

He nodded, the bitterness evaporating as he accepted the compliment. "It's fun." His voice suggested that even he was surprised at that statement. "I enjoy it. A lot."

She started to lead him into the kitchen, but stopped when she realized he was lingering in her living room. "What's wrong?"

"I guess I never put it together that you actually live here," he said, as he took in the overstuffed couch in front of her fireplace, the wrought-iron wine rack, and the stained-glass lamps. "It's nice."

"Thanks. It's the head winemaker's house—just another one of the perks of the job. My family became head winemakers when I was little, so I've lived in this house a long, long time."

Chad accompanied her to the kitchen, where the scent of the herbed beef stew wafted in the air, interwoven with the fresh, yeasty smell of newly baked sourdough bread. They both laughed when his stomach growled.

"There's plenty," she said, putting everything out on her rustic maple kitchen table. "Please. Dig in."

Leila poured them both a glass of the Honey Ridge Merlot and, as requested, he dug in.

"So…you've been here about a week and a half," she said slowly. "What do you think?"

She had to wait for an answer, since he had taken a huge bite of stew and was slathering butter on the still-warm bread. "This is heaven," he answered instead, then sighed. "Sorry. What was that?"

"I asked what you think of the vineyard," she repeated.

"It's fantastic."

Leila waited for him to expand on the thought. Instead, Chad continued to shovel in stew as if he hadn't had food in a month.

She smiled at his obvious relish. "What do you think of the wine?"

He took a gulp, then sighed. "I'm probably not enjoying it as much as I should. I can't remember ever being this hungry," he said, by way of apology.

"It's the work," she said, chuckling a little, "and the fresh air."

She let him finish the bowl of stew and bread in relative silence, keeping the talk light. Then, she asked him if he wanted to sit in the living room and finish the wine he'd barely touched.

He settled on the couch with the wine. She started a fire in the living room, then sat on the couch, careful to sit on the other end.

"I really appreciate the opportunity to learn, and to work hands on here, Leila," Chad said, and he really did sound grateful. "I had no idea it would be like this."

"Like what?" Leila asked, thinking that his tone sounded promising.

"Absorbing." He took a slow, considered sip from his glass. "Wow. This is really great."

She smiled. "Our Merlot. The movie *Sideways* makes it sound like Merlot is for rubes, but there are some nice vintages out there."

"And this is one of them," he said enthusiastically, taking another sip. "Am I doing this right?"

She nodded. "I like to smell the wine first." She put her nose in the glass and took a deep breath. "Then, you swirl the wine around—check the color, see if it clings to the glass."

"Okay." He followed her instruction.

"Then, take a sip, keep it on your tongue, and take a deep breath," she said. "Let the air flow over your tongue. The taste of a wine is just as much about the aroma as the actual flavor."

He did as she directed, his eyes closed as he almost frowned in concentration. It made him look like a harsh dreamer. After a long moment, he finally opened his eyes, smiling at her.

"It tastes good, but I don't know what I'm looking for."

"All that matters is that you enjoy it," she said. "You'll develop a palate in time. It takes a while, but if you really love it, you'll begin to taste all kinds of things you didn't realize before. Honey, violet, fruit, smoke… it's going to open up a whole new world for you."

"Wow." Chad shifted his weight a little, getting more comfortable. "You know, I've never seen anyone with as much passion for anything as you have for wine."

She shifted a little too, and then realized that the gap between them had closed—not a lot, but enough. She swallowed, hard.

"In fact," he added, leaning ever so slightly closer to her, "I've never met anyone quite like you, period, Leila."

She took a deep breath. He looked so serious and sounded so good.

Her mind emitted one quick alert but was drowned out by the overwhelming sensations she was experiencing. She leaned forward. She could smell the musky scent of him, like freshly turned earth and an expensive, spicy cologne. She could smell the Merlot on his breath. His breathing quickened, matching her own.

She kissed him…first, just a slow brush against his lips, like an accident, a test. Then she held her breath and went for it, kissing him with intensity.

Leila wasn't sure if she moved to close the gap, or if he pulled her closer, but she was practically in his lap, his strong arms banded around her like steel. Not that she was trying to escape. If anything, it was as if she was trying to melt into him, meld with him, become one person. She hadn't been kissed like this in a long time. Hadn't kissed anyone like this in…well, ever.

She pulled away after what felt like a long time—or the blink of an eye. She'd lost all sense of time. No. She'd lost all *sense*.

"I'm sorry," she said quickly, edging back fast enough to hit the arm of her couch sharply. "I shouldn't have…that was my fault."

"Shh," he said, pursuing her, moving toward her end of the couch and reaching for her. "I'm not sorry at all. I've wanted you since I first saw you. I still want you." Chad stroked her shoulders. "I want you, now."

She blinked. She'd just kissed him, and enjoyed it. But he seemed to be talking about a lot more than kissing.

Relax. Play a little. Flirt.

She could do those things. But what he was asking for, she couldn't do casually. Especially not in light of who he was. What he was.

You don't sleep with the owner.

"I, uh…wait a second," she said, dodging his lips when he moved in for another kiss. Even as part of her body desperately wanted it, she forced herself to stand up and walk to the far side of the room. "This is too fast. I'm sorry," she repeated.

He frowned. "I'll go slow, don't worry. It's okay, Leila," he said softly, as if he were talking to a frightened animal. "Don't overthink it. It's no big deal."

"Which part is no big deal?" she asked quietly. "The part where I kiss the new owner of my vineyard, and my employer—or the part where we would've slept together?" She shook her head. "Either way, it seems like a pretty big deal to me. To anybody who was looking at this from a business standpoint, it would seem like a major mistake. In fact, it'd look downright dumb."

"I wasn't being dumb," Chad growled in frustration. "Listen, it's not like I go around sleeping with people whose companies I invest in, you know."

"So you agree this was a bad idea," she said quickly.

"I wasn't just learning about the vineyard to sleep with you," he said. "This isn't just some *hobby*."

"I'm really, really sorry." She bit her lip. "You'd better go. I really am…"

"Don't apologize again," he snapped. "Thanks for a lovely dinner. I'll see myself out."

She watched as he closed the door with some force and drove away. Her body ached, but her head ached more.

She should've known better, Leila told herself bitterly. Now, instead of loosening up, she'd only made things worse.

"CHAD! BACK FROM the wilds of Napa!"

Chad took in Lester's shouted toast with a wan smile. He had driven into the city because he knew Lester would be having one of his parties, Tuesday or not. Lester always had a party going. If you wanted to have a good time, Lester was your hookup for good, old-fashioned, drunken debauchery. There was nothing serious about Lester, except his pursuit of a good time.

He'd understand what "no big deal" meant, Chad thought with asperity.

He was still stinging from his little dinner with Leila. He'd kissed her. No, she'd kissed *him.* And now she was acting as if she'd committed treason, and the fact that he wanted to sleep with her was also tantamount to some horrible crime. What the hell was her problem, anyway? He didn't make a habit of it. He told the truth: he'd never slept with anybody he'd invested money with.

Granted, they were all men. But he wouldn't have, anyway. He took his investments seriously. Of course, getting involved with her did create some issues, and she probably had a point.

But she'd pushed away from him like he was a leper, and treated him as though he should've known better and he hadn't thought things through. As if he didn't understand what it meant to be in business. That rankled him more than anything.

Lester introduced him around to the gang of party-goers. Most of the women were "Lester specials"... cookie-cutter gorgeous, with perfect bodies and porcelain faces with identical chiseled cheekbones. The best that plastic surgery could deliver, he realized, wondering how long he'd been this cynical. The one thing that all that sculpted perfection couldn't erase was the calculating looks in their eyes: the ones that seemed to absorb his clothes, his stature, and somehow extrapolate his bank balance and his possibility for marriage.

Maybe *that* was why Leila's reaction seemed so out of line for him, he thought bitterly. He was used to a more transactional type of relationship—you wanted something; she wanted something, an exchange was made. Leila wanted something from him, namely Honey Ridge. And it had to be obvious that he wanted something.

Namely, her.

But did you really want things to go that way? His conscience pricked him mercilessly. *From what you know of her, did you honestly think that's how she wanted things to go?*

If you did—man, she's right. You are *dumb.*

"I've got the full bar going tonight, buddy," Lester said, obviously noticing Chad's unusual reticence and trying to cheer him up. "And, of course, I've got wines too…now that you're Mr. Vineyard."

"Don't call me that," Chad said absently, knowing that it only emphasized the fraud he felt like. Then curiosity got the better of him. "What kind of wine do you have?"

"Let's see," Lester said, snapping his fingers at the busy bartender and causing Chad's embarrassment level to inch up a tad. "Barkeep! What sort of wine have you got open?"

The bartender smiled politely, although his eyes seemed full of disdain. "Red or white?"

"Red," Chad said quickly, and Lester nodded imperiously in agreement.

The bartender addressed Chad from then on, ignoring Lester completely. "We've got a Beaujolais, a Cabernet, and a Syrah," the man said in a dry monotone.

"Any of them local?" Chad asked.

The bartender's eyebrows went up. "The Syrah is from Napa. From the Far Niente vineyard."

"Do you recommend it?" Chad asked, but Lester interrupted.

"Is that the expensive one I ordered?"

"No, sir," the bartender said, and Chad could almost hear the man's teeth clenching. "That would be the Beaujolais. It's French."

"Go for it, Chad," Lester said, giving him a gentle nudge. "Nothing but the best, to buck up my buddy."

"Actually," Chad said, "I'd rather go with the Syrah."

Lester looked at him. "What, you've got something against French wine?" He paused. "Or just expensive? I told you, I'm covering all this."

Chad shook his head. "Just because it's expensive doesn't mean it's any damned good, Les," he said, with a little laugh. "If I learned anything this week, it's that."

"Well—" and Lester sounded irritated "—obviously *somebody* thinks it's good, if it drove the price up."

Chad shrugged, feeling like an idiot as the bartender handed him the glass. "I'm still learning," he conceded.

Lester was still talking when Chad took the glass, taking a deep breath, just as Leila had shown him. He then swirled it around. It had a good color, he thought— that deep garnet tone, clinging slightly to the crystal. Then he took a sip. It was okay. "Has this had any time to breathe?" he asked.

The bartender shook his head. "You might want to let it sit a minute," he said, with obvious approval.

Lester had finally shut up, as Chad swirled the wine around in his glass, trying to get the air to mix in. "You're not kidding with all of this," Lester said.

"Kidding with what?"

"You're keeping the damned thing," Lester crowed. "You *are* Mr. Vineyard!"

"Why are you riding me about this?" Chad asked irritably. "So I like wine. I've always liked wine."

"Yeah, but you weren't a poster child for pretension." Lester crossed his arms. "You used to order a few bottles—of the *expensive* stuff—and get plastered. Just like the rest of us," Lester said, gesturing to the rest of the party. "You used to have *fun*. What happened?"

Chad surveyed the party. The place was chock-full of the usual suspects—other socialites, hangers-on, trust-fund kids and the nouveau riche alike. They were all staring, circling like sharks. There was none of the camaraderie Chad had felt in the short time he'd spent at Honey Ridge. Granted, then, he'd felt like an outsider—and a wine idiot. But at least he could sense that the people there genuinely *liked* each other.

These people didn't necessarily hate each other, but again, it was transactional. Mutual back-scratching. People of the same station, with the same mind-set, getting drunk, escaping from whatever in their lives wasn't worth facing.

Am I like these people?

Was that what he was doing? Spending money, trying to be a "part" of something?

He didn't know why he was judging them. He only

knew that, like the picnic, he no longer felt he fit in. And what was worse, he wasn't sure that he *wanted* to fit in anymore…at least, not with these people.

Chad sighed, turning to Lester. "I don't know what happened," he said, feeling completely at a loss.

Lester shook his head. "You had a bad break. You're running low on money, and your family's giving you grief," he said, and for a change, he actually kept his voice respectfully low. "That's enough to rattle anybody. I was there once."

"Really?" To his knowledge, Lester had been rolling in money all his life. His family had invented something crucial, like the fluorescent lightbulb or something, and consequently Lester had never had to work a day in his life.

"Yup. When I graduated from college, and I was bumming around Europe, my parents cut me off. Said that I was just drifting, and that I needed to get some direction. Told me to stop wasting my time and their money."

Chad knew what that felt like. His last family dinner was still burned in his mind. "Then what happened?" he asked with interest.

Lester shrugged. "I sold my cars and a bunch of the stock that was in my name, and just laid low for a while. After six months of being incommunicado, they freaked out and I got in their good graces again," he said, with a touch of pride. "I figured it was just a bluff, and I was right. They might have thought they wanted me to stop drifting, but they don't want you to disappear completely. It worked like a charm."

Chad suddenly had a sour taste in his mouth, and it

had nothing to do with his glass of Syrah. "Really," he said, unsure of what other comment he could make.

"Sure, it gets boring partying sometimes," Lester said shrewdly. "Are all these people my friends? Probably not. But what the hell else are you going to do? I don't give a damn about working."

"But you invested in that movie, just like I did," Chad protested. "And that real estate thing…"

"I already apologized for that," Lester said, rolling his eyes. "But besides, that's not really working. That's like…I don't know. Roulette or poker. That's just something to do."

Chad looked down at the bloodred wine in his glass. His thoughts, again, turned to Honey Ridge. For Leila or Julio or any of them, the vineyard wasn't just something to do.

Which part of this is "no big deal" for you, Chad?

Lester clapped a hand on his shoulder. "You know what? Screw the wine." He took Chad's glass and put it down on the bar. "Your problem is you're thinking too much. Bartender! Get me four rounds of shots. The nastier the better."

The bartender looked at the half-full glass of wine, and Chad could've sworn the man shot him a disappointed look.

"It was very good," Chad said. "Too good to get plastered on."

He nodded but still looked disgusted. "Vodka or whiskey?" he asked in the same monotone he'd used with Lester.

Chad sighed. "Better make it vodka."

CHAPTER FOUR

THE NEXT MORNING, Leila was still roiling with embarrassment over what she was euphemistically calling "The Incident."

So she'd planned on having a little harmless fun, teach a little about wine, and maybe stir her hormones up a bit. Instead, she'd wound up pouncing on the guy, who then saw it as an invitation to go to bed with him and, from a certain standpoint, she wasn't sure she could blame him. Not that she thought she should have slept with him, or regretted not sleeping with him.

At least, I don't entirely *regret not sleeping with him.* She was human enough to admit that, after over a year of celibacy, her body had complained mightily when she'd denied it what was so close at hand. And it was her body's reaction that caused her to slightly regret what she'd done to Chad. She hated the term "tease," but after a kiss like that, and then going cold on him...

Well, she never should've kissed him in the first place, and that was that. Today, she was going to apologize, throw herself on his mercy, and pray that the two of them could just put the whole ugly "Incident" behind them. Especially if it in any way weighted his decision on whether or not to keep Honey Ridge. She'd like to think that he wasn't so petty, that he wasn't here simply because he was attracted to her. That he wouldn't just up and sell the place because she wouldn't give in to temptation.

Of course, that didn't mean he wouldn't decide to sell Honey Ridge for reasons that had nothing to do with her. She winced. At least the painful humiliation of The Incident had taken the edge off her worries, and the dull ache that was the thought of losing Honey Ridge.

She heard the roar of the engine of Chad's sleek silver car as it zoomed toward the parking area, kicking up a dust trail in its wake. She glanced at her watch—nearly noon, she realized. She wasn't about to chastise him for being late, and she hoped that Julio did not give him grief. She wondered if he was as hesitant to come in as she'd been.

This is ridiculous, she chided herself. She hadn't committed murder, after all. So she'd kissed him and wanted him, and then stopped them both. So what? They were not teenagers. They were grown, mature adults, and there was absolutely no reason they couldn't hold a civilized conversation. She'd clear the air, get it out of the way and apologize.

Then, just maybe, ask him point-blank if he's thinking of selling the vineyard.

Her stomach trembled with nerves, but she straightened her shoulders and walked over to where he'd just parked, waiting for him to open the door. He emerged, looking somewhat worse for wear. He had a day's growth of beard, making him look scruffy. It would have made him look rakish, she thought with a private grin, if it weren't accompanied by very bloodshot eyes.

The man was obviously hungover.

"Morning, Chad," Leila murmured. Getting drunk—she hadn't thought of that. Or rather, she'd thought of it but then decided against it, precisely because she hadn't wanted to feel the way Chad was obviously feeling this morning. She still suffered the occasional sore head after friends' wine bashes, and she knew the price of overindulgence. She felt sympathy for him, especially since he still winced at her deliberate whisper.

"Yeah, yeah, I'm here," he said.

"You didn't have to come in, you know," she said, still in the lowest voice possible. "No offense, but you look awful."

"That's funny, I feel awful," he growled sardonically. "But I said I wanted to learn, and I wanted to work. So I'm here, dammit. If you've got a problem, take it up with the *owner*."

She felt her stomach knot. Apparently, the civilized-conversation theory wasn't going to work this morning. He was angry, and he was going to be rude.

"I was going to tell you I was sorry for last night," she said, crossing her arms in front of her and frowning. "But you're not making it easy."

"Didn't I tell you I don't want you to keep apologizing?" Chad slammed his car door shut, then gripped his temples for a moment.

Serves you right, she thought vindictively.

"So what do you want from me?" she asked sharply, and then immediately regretted it when he looked at her with surprise.

"You know exactly what I wanted from you," he said, in a low voice that was both sexy and angry. "But what you don't seem to understand is, what I wanted had nothing to do with business. And if you didn't want to do something, you didn't have to. Period."

Leila swallowed hard against the lump in her throat. "I know you wouldn't force me to do anything," she said, hating that she'd made him feel like such a beast. "But…you've got to admit, Chad, sleeping together would not be the greatest decision on our part. I mean, we've still got the whole vineyard issue to deal with."

"What 'whole vineyard issue' are we talking about?" he snapped irritably. "The fact that I'm the owner? Is that what the problem is? Because you don't want to sleep with your boss?"

Now, her temper leaped to the fore, and all the anxiety that had been churning around since she'd found out Charles had died spilled out of her in a torrent. "The problem is," she shot back, "I have no idea when or if you're going to get rid of the vineyard I've worked so hard for. I don't know if you're going to decide to keep it on a whim, or sell it tomorrow just because you want the cash. *I don't know you.* And I've been walking on eggshells, trying to make sure you're happy and that you enjoy yourself here in the hopes that you're not going to just scrap Honey Ridge like some toy you're bored with!"

The words were loud enough to almost echo, and in the dusty area in front of the house, they were like two gunslingers, staring at each other with narrowed eyes and shallow breaths. He'd started the challenge, she'd answered it. There wasn't any backing down.

"So, what you're telling me," Chad said, his voice lazy even though his eyes were brightly intense, "is that last night was just another example of you trying to keep me happy, so I'd keep Honey Ridge?"

It took her a second to puzzle out his insinuation, but when she did, she gasped with shock. "I did not try to seduce you to keep the vineyard!"

"Well, if you did," he drawled back, "you didn't do a very good job of it."

She felt tears stinging at the corners of her eyes, and stood up even straighter, staring at him with an almost tangible violence. "So, because I didn't seduce you, you're going to sell, is that it?"

"What I feel about you has nothing to do with this damned vineyard," he said, taking a step closer to her. "Can't you understand that?"

"Well, what I feel for you has nothing to do with it, either," Leila countered, not backing down. She looked up into his eyes.

He finally showed a ghost of a smile. "Now we're getting somewhere."

She put a hand on his chest, stopping him from leaning any closer. "But no matter how I feel, or how you feel," she said softly, "the vineyard's *still there*. I can't just pretend it doesn't matter to me. I can't ignore that I might lose it, and that you are the one making that decision."

Chad took a step back, his eyes widening. "You can't possibly ask me just to keep it to make you feel better," he said. "I can't do that."

She felt ice pierce her chest. "No, I couldn't ask you to," she said sorrowfully. "So where does that leave us? Nowhere. We can't get involved as long as Honey Ridge is in limbo, Chad. It wouldn't be right."

He grimaced. "You're making it harder than it needs to be."

"I'm just telling the truth. Everybody knows that the place could shut down any day, on your command. Can you see how stressful that makes everything? If I slept with you, and then you had to shut the place down to-morrow—I don't know. I wouldn't want to blame you," she said honestly, "but some part of me would feel betrayed. That's lousy, I know."

His eyes blazed. "You'd think it was personal."

"No. I wouldn't think it was personal for you." She said, looked down at the ground for a second. "But what I'm saying is I know it would be personal for me."

Chad was silent for a moment, and when she looked up, she could see the muscles in his jaw clenching. He was still angry, although it was a con-tained anger.

"Well, here's one thing that might help you sleep at night, for at least the next month or so. When I inher-ited Honey Ridge, one of the stipulations of the will was that I could not sell the place until you guys bottled one last vintage. No matter what else happens—" and he put particular emphasis on that phrase "—you'll get to finish out the season. I can't make any promises after that, but at least you know you're not out of a job tomorrow, and neither is anybody else."

"So…we have until September?" she asked, feeling bleak. There wasn't much hope, not much at all.

"Yeah," he said, and stalked away, toward the vats. "You've got till September."

"Well, we'll do what we have to do," she said, almost to herself.

"Do that," Chad shot back, even though the statement hadn't been directed at him. "I certainly plan to."

With that, Leila felt her stomach drop. He was going to sell Honey Ridge. Maybe he'd had no intention of even trying to see if it was worth saving. Maybe he was just killing time, and she was one of the diversions. Maybe it was all some big gag.

The tears that had been looming suddenly hit her in a storm, and she disappeared back into the house. At least, she thought, he didn't see her cry.

THAT NIGHT, after cleaning the cellars and helping Julio close the oak barrels that now held the Cabernets, Chad made his way slowly toward the farmhouse. He'd saved cleaning the cellars for last, waiting until everyone else had gone home for the night. He'd had a full day (well, a half day) to think about what had happened the night before and what had happened when he came in that morning. He hadn't meant to be that brutally honest with Leila, nor had he meant to imply that he'd be getting rid of the vineyard, or that he would've sold the place already if it weren't for Great-Uncle Charles's will. It was a stupid, emotional act on his part, pure pettiness. He didn't like the idea of Leila kissing him simply out of fear of reprisal, or because she was so desperate to save her vineyard that she would give herself up for it, physically if need be. He didn't like being accused of being a dumb businessman who thought emotionally more than he thought practically—one who might just toss a money-maker on a whim, simply because he was bored with it.

Or one who might keep it, just because he was un-believably attracted to the head winemaker.

He waited until Julio left, after admonishing him 'not to work too hard,' and then Chad made his way to the farmhouse.

He had to apologize.

He had to make sure Leila was all right.

As he walked toward the farmhouse, he saw that the light in the kitchen was burning. The fireplace was lit, as well. He could smell the rich smoke from the chimney, and the front window glowed with cheery, red-tinged warmth. He knew Leila was home.

Chad hoped she'd let him in, and hear him out.

He knocked on the door. It took a while, and he was starting to lose hope, but eventually she opened it.

She was wearing faded jeans with the right leg torn at the knee—not an artistic, store-bought tear, but one that obviously came from hard work. She also wore a beat-up flannel shirt in a burgundy-and-brown pattern, and her tawny blond hair was up in a ponytail. She didn't look as polished or pulled together as she had last night, when she'd kissed him, he noticed. He could see the smudges beneath her eyes, making her look weary. She was either exhausted, or she'd been crying. Possibly both. Either way, he felt horribly guilty.

"Chad," she said, and her voice was monotone, lacking its usual warmth and openness. "I wasn't expecting to see you here."

"We need to talk," he said. "About this morning. And last night," he added, then sighed. "We need to get things straightened out."

Leila paused, chewing at her full lower lip for a second in a way that would've been sensually distracting if it weren't for the obvious apprehension in her eyes. Finally, after a long pause, she nodded.

"Come in," she said, then walked down the hallway. He closed the door behind him and followed her.

He walked past the living room, noticing that, unlike last night, it was in disarray. Books were piled up on the floor, leaving the built-in bookcases barren. There were a few cardboard boxes leaning against the wall, waiting to be assembled. "What's all this?" he asked, as he followed her toward the kitchen.

"I'm getting ready to move," she said, and the twist of guilt in his guts knotted a degree tighter. "I figured I'd start with stuff I wasn't using—the books, the artwork, stuff like this. Then kitchen items and linens, then clothes. It shouldn't take me that long. I'll probably have to arrange for movers for my furniture, though," she said, and it was as if she were trying to get the whole process straight in her head, explaining it to herself rather than to him.

He felt cornered. "Leila, I didn't say I was going to sell the vineyard. I just said it was an option," he protested. "And nothing's happening till September, and nothing's happening immediately. Besides, I had a headache that could've killed a rhino this morning and I was in a wretched bad mood, and I took it out on you. I had no right to do that."

"You didn't say anything that wasn't true, though," she replied, taking a ceramic mug off the counter. "Did you want some tea?"

He shook his head, then stood closer to her, waiting until she stopped avoiding his eyes, to make sure he got his point across.

"I spent last night at my friend Lester's house—although 'friend' is a loose term for us, I figured out," he said, slowly and gently. "I used to party with his crowd all the time. We did all sorts of things together—crazy trips, big spending. Investments."

She nodded, but she looked puzzled.

Chad sighed. "I haven't had what people would call a 'real job.' I inherited all my money," he explained. "I have a trust fund. My parents funnel money to me from the family accounts."

"Chad, why are you telling me this?" Her voice was soothing.

"Because I want you to understand," he said. "I've made a lot of bad investments over the years. I haven't come up with a single winner, and I'm starting to realize that it was because I played at it. I didn't have any real passion for it. I just went in with other people. I had fun, I dabbled, but they were bound to fail because I didn't care. Not the way you do, about Honey Ridge." He sighed. "Not the way I'm learning to care about this place."

She sighed. "It's only been two weeks."

"I know that," he said, and he gritted his teeth with frustration at himself. "I know. It's too soon to know for sure. And I don't know anything about the winemaking business. So I can't just say I'll keep it, especially when I haven't run all the numbers."

He was quiet for a moment. Then, he was surprised—no, shocked—when Leila placed a gentle hand on his shoulder.

"I didn't know you were beating yourself up so badly about this," she said. "I didn't think past what the place meant to me. I didn't think at all about what this decision meant to you."

It was maybe the kindest thing anybody had ever said to him. Chad couldn't help it. He leaned his head down against her shoulder. After a moment, he felt her fingertips brush against the hair at the nape of his neck, and he enfolded her in a hug that wasn't sexual, but merely comforting—both giving, and receiving, support.

"I didn't want you to think that I was just making this a hobby because I was bored with my life," he said. "I don't know why, or how, but this place matters to me. *You* matter to me, for different reasons. And I feel that one wrong move, and I'm going to ruin everything."

She made a little sympathetic noise, holding him tighter. "You're not going to ruin everything," she said. "It was unfair of me to put that much pressure on you. You're going to do what you feel is right, just like I am. You're not hurtful. I know that and I shouldn't have reacted the way I did."

He inhaled deeply, breathing her in—earthy tones from her work in the vineyard, the subtle aroma of wine and smoke from the fireplace, and her own scent, a woodsy floral combination that was more intoxicating than any wine. They stood like that for a moment, and Chad savored it.

Then, deliberately, he stepped away from her and walked to the far end of the kitchen.

"You weren't wrong, not completely," he said. "It would be complicated if we were to…get involved."

She nodded, but he could've sworn he saw regret on her face, as well.

"It's not final death overtime yet," he said. "I have my financial advisor running numbers. If it's at all viable to keep Honey Ridge going, then that's what I'll do. Not just for you," he added. "For me, because I really do enjoy it. I'm not just saying that."

"I know." Her eyes were luminescent. "You can tell by how you're learning."

He took a deep breath and stuffed his hands in his pockets. "So. Where does that leave us?" he finally asked. "I don't want to make any more mistakes or have any more fights like that one."

Leila nodded vehemently. "Amen to that."

"Hands off, that's a given," he said, almost to himself, and with a real sense of loss. Because if the news was bad, he'd have to sell the vineyard, and he knew what that would mean to her. No way would she want to get together with the man who had destroyed her livelihood and sold her childhood home out from under her. At the same time, if he kept the vineyard, he'd still be her boss. Where would that leave them?

"Maybe we should cancel the private lessons, too," she said tentatively.

His sense of loss doubled. He had enjoyed spending time with her…not just simply from a sensual stand-point, but because she was good company. Granted, he'd only spent the one night purely alone with her…

A flash of what had happened in just that short time hit him. "Good idea," he agreed.

"But we can still hang out when there are other people present," Leila amended, causing him to smile.

"Good," he said. "I'd like that."

"Actually," she said, "toward the end of the season,

there's usually a big winemakers' party at a nearby resort. A lot of the little indies show up there. You might find it fun, if you want to come with me."

Like a date? Chad squashed the question as soon as it leaped to mind. "That sounds great," he said. "I'm glad we talked."

He held out a hand, and she took it…a handshake, to seal their agreement. Her hand was soft and warm in his.

He would've given up half his fortune to be with her the way he wanted to, he thought. But if he screwed this up with her, he got the feeling that he'd be losing a lot more than an inheritance. He wasn't sure what that was, but it was bigger than anything he'd experienced, and it confused the hell out of him.

With that, he said, "Good night, Leila," and let himself out the door.

THREE WEEKS LATER, Leila and her crew had finished bottling most of the vintages. She'd hurried, even though part of her wanted to drag her feet. She didn't want to get caught by an early frost again, which was the whole reason she was finishing early. But she now knew that Charles's will only protected the vineyard until they bottled this final harvest. Soon, Chad would have every right to sell the property and collect his money, if he chose to do so.

She'd spent a good amount of time with Chad in the past three weeks, always observing their agreement. She'd had dinner with Chad, Julio, his wife and Marisol, and they'd had a wonderful long conversation about Honey Ridge's history and legacy, as well as wine in general. There were still picnics every week, and she talked with him then. And they'd worked together. He tried to absorb everything, like the world's most eager student. It was fun to discuss stuff with him, to watch as he grew and learned, and got more and more enthusiastic.

If they happened to go into the wine cellar and walked a little too close to each other, it was her own stupid fault that her heart raced ever so slightly. And if he walked her to her porch, always with other people around…well, it wasn't against the law to daydream.

And if the nights were getting progressively longer, and she was having trouble sleeping…

Leila shook her head. She didn't want to think about it. September was already coming up like a freight train, with the possibility of losing Honey Ridge and everything that entailed.

Including never seeing Chad McFee again.

She needed balance and equilibrium. She needed a reminder of what she was in all this for.

She went to the farmhouse and picked up the phone, gripping the receiver more tightly than she needed to. She heard the phone ring, and heard a familiar voice answer: "Hello?"

"Hi, Mom," Leila said, feeling a wave of relief and comfort just hearing her voice.

"Leila, dear! This is a surprise!" Her mother was bright and cheerful, just the way Leila had always remembered. "We've been so busy, and I've been meaning to call, but I haven't had more than a minute to shoot off an e-mail, you know that. Spring and all, and the time difference…but I'm rambling. How are you?"

"I'm…" Leila thought about how to word it. "Hanging in there."

"Oh, my," her mother said. "What's wrong? I can hear it in your voice."

"You got my e-mail, saying that Charles McFee died, right?"

Her mother clucked sympathetically. "A pity. He was a good man, and he believed in the vineyard. We couldn't have asked for a better patron. Still, I'm sure at his age…well, he wasn't surprised. He was getting tired those last years we knew him. You mentioned that he passed the vineyard on. How's that going?"

Leila sighed. "His great-nephew Chad has taken the place over," she said carefully, "but I'm not sure he'll keep it. He may sell. It hasn't been making money the past few years, after all."

"I know that tone, too," her mother said. "You're blaming yourself, and you should stop it. Force majeure, my dear…acts of God. You didn't cause the drought or the frost."

"Yes, but it was always in the black when you and Dad were running the place," Leila said, feeling childish and whiny but unable to help herself.

"Leila, love," her mother said patiently, "you're a winemaker. You know that a vintage depends on a million different variables. You can plan for some things and you can fix some things, but so much of it is pure, blind, random luck."

"It's frustrating," Leila admitted. "I wanted to do so much with this place. Especially after you and Dad fought to get me the job. I just…I feel like such a failure."

There. She'd said it. Somehow, saying it loosened the lump of lead that had been weighing down her chest, and she wiped at the tears that escaped from her eyes.

"It is frustrating," her mother soothed. "But it's also what makes winemaking so exciting. That's why it's art, instead of just work."

"I know that," Leila snuffled.

"Yes, but you've never really applied it," her mother gently corrected her. "Not at Honey Ridge, and not in your life, from what I've noticed. It's always amazed me how stubbornly focused you can get when you want something." She chuckled. "You get that from your father, you know."

"How is he doing?" Leila said, feeling a little better.

"He's out in the pouring rain, checking on the grapes. You know your dad."

"And how are you doing?"

Her mother gave a sigh of contentment. "Australia was one of the best moves we could've made. It was a huge change, and it took a lot of getting used to, but it's been a blast, as your father would say. I swear, it's like he's twenty years younger," she said. "I guess you're never too old for a new adventure. He thinks that a little risk improves the wine."

Leila thought about the last time she'd used that argument: *I'm just doing this to improve the wine.* Then she'd kissed Chad, and…well, that hadn't turned out so hot.

"A little risk could also turn the wine cheese-worthy," Leila pointed out.

"Glass half-full, sweetie," her mother reminded her. "You'll get through this. Just don't worry about things that are out of your hands. If Honey Ridge's time is up, then it's up. You don't have to sacrifice your whole life. Just learn from it, take the experiences, and move on."

"Yes, Mom."

"When your father gets in, I can have him call you."

"No, I just needed to hear your voice," Leila said. "I'll call again in two weeks. I love you."

"I love you too, sweetie."

Leila hung up the phone, then looked out the window. Chad was working with the other laborers, joking with Ted and Julio about something. He looked like a completely different person lately. He was livelier now, more comfortable in his own skin. When she'd first met him, he'd struck her as a frat boy, a rich guy who was completely clueless. Now, he seemed more mature. Like a wine that had breathed, he'd come into his own, somehow, and was expanding and turning more complicated every second she knew him. He seemed more like *himself*, even if she hadn't known him more than a month and a half.

You need to take more risks, Leila.

Julio had been right, and so had her mother. Leila had been so careful, so rigidly inflexible, that she hadn't made any room in her life for experimentation. She'd been so intent on succeeding, she hadn't wanted to actually *live,* or take the chance of making a fool of herself, of making a mistake. She was so afraid of losing what she had that she was damaging the very thing she had set out to create. She wanted everything perfect.

That was no way to make wine—and it was no way to live.

She was tired of controlling things. She was tired of fighting the attraction. She might never see Chad McFee again after a week from now; she might never work in Napa again, for all she knew.

But one thing she did know was, if she was going to have one regret in life, it wasn't going to be that she had the chance to feel the love of a wonderful man, if only for a night…and that she'd watched that chance pass her by.

CHAPTER FIVE

LEILA SMOOTHED down the skirt on her little black dress. She had her hair up in a chignon, with tendrils escaping to tickle at the back of her neck, and she was wearing makeup. She was also wearing her "CGM's" as Julio's wife Angelina called them…her "come get me" stilettos, with tiny bows at the heels.

She knew what Chad's reaction was when she was just wearing jeans. She couldn't wait to see how he'd feel about her when she was all dressed up and really *trying* to get his attention. She wasn't sure if she was going to seduce him outright, but she knew that the party was just a pretense, a reason for her to be with him alone—and a reason for her to look like this, while she was alone with him.

She got the feeling that they'd make the rounds, say hello, mingle a little…and then she'd gently make sure he took her back to the farmhouse. She'd offer him some wine, and they'd see where it went from there.

Leila glanced in a mirror in the resort lobby, one last check. She watched as her own plum-painted lips curved into a wicked, thoughtful smile. They'd just see how the night shook out.

She walked back to Chad, who had checked their

coats, trying her best to look sexy and not totter in her heels. "So, here we are," she said, taking a deep breath before looping an arm through his. "Your first wine-maker party."

"You look right at home," he said, and he gave her an intense perusal that suggested more than he was saying. His smile was evocative, and she felt warmth hit her right in the pit of her stomach. "You look amazing, actually. The shoes are great, but the dress…"

"Not a lot of call for cocktail dresses at the vineyard," she said, deliberately letting her body brush against his as she dodged another knot of people who were crowding the hallway. She leaned a little closer to him, to be heard. "You clean up pretty well, yourself."

Leila could feel the muscles tense beneath her hand, and for a moment, she felt his breath brush against her neck. She shivered.

"I don't mind dressing up when the occasion calls for it," Chad murmured, stroking her arm. "But I've learned that I prefer a more quiet, private life lately. Like at Honey Ridge."

She smiled. His voice had such an endearing mix of heat and ruefulness. "I would've thought you'd miss the high-society party thing," she said.

"Well, the last party I went to seemed to cure me of that," he said. He hadn't gone into many details about that night, but she got the feeling it had been a turning point for him. She did know that it was the last time she'd seen him hungover. "So no, I don't miss the party life at all."

"I'm glad," she whispered.

"Besides," he said, as he brushed a stray curl away

from her jaw with his fingertips, causing all her nerve endings to jump to attention, "I'd rather spend time with people I genuinely care about…and who genuinely care about me."

For a second, it was as if they were the only two people in the place. Then someone jostled them, and her chest bumped against his. She could feel her cheeks heating with a blush.

Wait till you get home, at least!

Chad cleared his throat. "Want a glass of wine?" he asked. "I mean, I guess that's why we're here, right?"

She nodded, then led him toward the crowded bar. She felt tongue-tied and her heart was still skipping from their contact.

"And maybe," he whispered, and she could feel the heat of his breath against the nape of her neck, "maybe we could duck out early."

The words were music to her ears, but before she could turn and answer, another voice interrupted them.

"Leila Fairmont, where *have* you been hiding yourself?"

Leila sighed, then smiled as a portly, silver-bearded man walked over, clapping her on the shoulder. "Bernard," she greeted him. "How's it going?"

"My dear, I've just bottled a Muscat that would shame any dessert on earth," he enthused, his eyes gleaming. "But don't get me sidetracked. I heard that ancient patron of yours finally got out of the business—in a manner of speaking. What's going on over at Honey Ridge? There's been talk."

She clenched her jaw and stepped back so Chad was included in the conversation. "I should introduce you to the new owner," she said. "Chad McFee, this is Bernard Schwartz, of Nocturne Vineyards."

"Pleased to meet you," Bernard said cordially, his eyes shrewd. "It's a great place, Honey Ridge. They put out one of the best Merlots in the Valley."

"I know," Chad said easily.

"Maniac or tourist?"

Chad blinked. Leila shook her head. "He's asking if you've owned a vineyard before, or if you're new to the business," she said, frowning at Bernard. "This is his first vineyard, Bernard. Be nice."

"No offense intended, honestly," Bernard said. "I'm sorry, I have a chronic case of foot-in-mouth disease. Thankfully, *I* own a vineyard. So I can usually blame it on being plowed."

To Leila's relief, Chad grinned. "That's a perk I hadn't even thought of," he said.

"Trust me, you'll love it. It's hand-to-mouth, especially as an indie, but it's completely addictive. You won't know how you lived any other way after a year or so." Bernard's grin was wide. "Well, this is something we ought to toast. What have you had tonight?"

"We just got here," Chad said. "Should we be trying your Muscat?"

"You can taste some of that later," Bernard said. "Work up to it. It's a dessert wine, after all."

"I didn't know that," Chad admitted.

Bernard's eyes widened. "I see. You really are new to this." He put a heavy hand on Chad's shoulder, his eyes gleaming. "Let's introduce you around."

Leila sighed. So much for the idea of ducking out early. Bernard was practically a social director. Before the night was over, Chad was going to know every single person at the party.

An hour later, as she'd predicted, Chad was ensconced in the "old boys network" of vintners. Leila knew most of the men, after years of being in the business. Bernard pulled her aside.

"Seriously, are you all right?" he asked.

She glanced to make sure Chad wasn't listening. He wasn't—he was learning about the blight that had nearly destroyed all the vineyards in the 1980s, from an old vintner who had started out as a musician in L.A. "I'm hanging in there," she said.

"There's talk that one of the corporate wineries has an eye on your land." Leila's stomach clenched. "You know how much the land is worth, and all. And Chad's new at this. Does he plan on staying with it?"

"I don't know." She felt numb. "I hope so. He seems to really enjoy learning about the wine, the vineyard, the whole nine yards."

"And you two don't exactly look like business associates, if you don't mind me saying," Bernard said.

She wasn't sure if she minded or not, so she just shrugged. "One thing at a time," she said, causing Bernard to laugh.

"He just needs to get bit by the bug," Bernard reassured her. "Do you remember the first time you could tell the difference between a Syrah and a Cab? Or the first time you made a really stellar wine? It's pure adrenaline."

Leila smiled, closing her eyes...remembering. "I could tell the difference when I was thirteen," she admitted. "And I remember the smell of our first really phenomenal Merlot, the taste of it."

"There you go," he said. "Get the guy hooked on that, and he'll never leave."

She gave Bernard a little hug in gratitude, and then walked over to where Chad was sitting. He had a few bulb-shaped glasses in front of them, each with only a little bit of wine. He twirled the ruby liquid in one, then let it slide up the side to watch if the wine clung or not. He put his nose in, inhaling deeply. Then he took a slow sip.

"Wow," he said, after a long moment.

The crowd of men and women around him crowed triumphantly. "You see? Nothing to it," the ancient musician, Simon, said with approval. "You look like an old pro."

"What are you drinking?" Leila asked.

He scooted over on the bench, and she sat next to him as he proffered the glass. She took a sip. It was full-bodied, with hints of raspberry and black cherry and smoke. "Pinot Noir," she said. "Nice. Yours, Simon?"

Simon nodded. "Yup. I was just telling your man here about the clones we've been grafting."

She looked over nervously at Chad, to see how he liked being referred to as "her man."

He didn't even seem to notice, more intent on the conversation. "So, it took you five years to get the balance right?"

"It's a million different elements," another winemaker, a woman named Sylvie, piped in. "There's nature, there's environment, there's the pressing and how you manipulate it once it's off the vine, there's the aging. There's just plain, blind, dumb luck, to boot. It's a lot like gambling."

"It's a work of art," Bernard rumbled, and they toasted each other, smiling broadly. They weren't drunk…not even close, at least not on wine. They were drunk on the process.

Chad was right there with them, looking mesmerized.

"You doing all right?" she whispered, under cover of the raucous laughter. "Still want to leave early?"

"Actually, this is really interesting," he admitted, and he looked at her with a combination of embarrassment and helpless happiness. "Do you mind if we stay a bit?"

Leila thought about why she'd wanted to take him out of here…her plans for him later, at the farmhouse. But when she saw the genuine fascination in his eyes, she realized that as much as she wanted him, she loved this side of him. She loved that he was as interested in what she did as she was. And if he wanted to learn more, why would she take that away?

She sighed softly, just to herself. Besides, the night wasn't over yet.

"I love wine," she said, and it was the simple truth. "And I'm glad you love it, too. Don't worry. We can stay as long as you want."

Later that night, Chad drove Leila back to the farmhouse. He was feeling a warm glow, not so much from the wine he'd imbibed, but from the company. Over the course of three hours, he'd had sips of several different kinds of wine. But he felt he'd learned enough for a college course or two. Of course, he'd never been that interested in any of the college courses he'd taken, way back when, so it probably wasn't a good comparison.

He was riveted by wine.

He looked over to see Leila's face, traced by the bright moonlight, looking like an angel. She didn't catch his glance, but instead watched the landscape, transfixed by the beauty of the vineyards and the softly rolling hills.

He might be riveted by wine, he thought. But he was obsessed with Leila Fairmont.

"You looked like you had a good time tonight," Leila said, not breaking away from the view.

"I did," he said honestly, paying attention to the road. Then he shot another glance her way. "Didn't you?"

"I've been to a million of those parties," she said, causing him a moment's worry—maybe he'd spent way too long there. But her next remark comforted him. "I would have had an okay time, but having you there made it special. You made everything new, and seeing how enthusiastic you've become about wine, in such a short period of time, is just incredible. You probably don't realize just how much you've picked up this month."

This month. Which brought to mind the fact that his self-imposed deadline was fast approaching. His parents and Renaldo were starting to get antsy, too.

He pushed that out of his mind, focused on Leila instead, which wasn't that hard. "I haven't had this much fun in years."

"It shows," she replied.

They were quiet for a moment. "My only regret," he said slowly, "was that I guess I kept you out way too long. But you looked gorgeous. You wouldn't want to waste that outfit just staying at home, right?"

He was trying for a light, teasing tone, and still glancing over occasionally to check on her. So he inadvertently caught the look, shot through with fire and

wicked amusement, that she sent his way at the
question.

"If you had been at the house with me," she said
in a low, husky voice, "believe me, it wouldn't have
been wasted."

His stomach clenched into a ball of desire, causing
the rest of his systems to go haywire.

She wanted him.

Well, he knew that, just as much as she knew he
wanted her. But she wanted him *tonight*. Hell, she
wanted him *now*.

And from the sounds of it, she meant to have him.
Tonight. Now.

Chad swallowed hard.

"You okay?" she asked, still sounding amused. "Or
was I too forward?"

"Well, you might want to save statements like that
for when I'm *not* driving," he said in a choked voice.

Leila chuckled, a sinfully sensual sound. "We're
almost home," she replied. "I figured it was enough time."

He looked—they were on the border of the property.
They'd be at the farmhouse in a matter of minutes.

He wanted her, she wanted him. He shouldn't let it
get more complicated than that.

The only problem was, his conscience muttered with
its implacable logic, they might have one incredible
night, but there would still be all kinds of problems in
the morning. Namely, the fact that he might have to sell
the place, put her friends out of work, put *her* out of a
job and out of her home. She might want him now, but
how could she not look at him like some kind of
monster if he did all that *and* slept with her too?

Of course, maybe you don't have to sell. You don't even want to sell.

He blinked, shocked temporarily out of his lust-soaked recriminations. That wasn't his conscience. That was another inner voice entirely.

You haven't gotten the numbers from Renaldo. You'd love to be with Leila, sure, but you also love the life. You love vineyards. You're enjoying yourself even when you're working. Why screw everything up?

"Chad? Are you okay?"

"Huh?" He noticed that Leila's voice no longer had the sexy, raspy, full-of-longing tone it had. She sounded concerned.

"You've got this faraway look, and we've been parked for a few minutes," she said, her violet eyes dark with worry. "I didn't mean to shock you, or anything. I was just kidding around."

She thought she'd done something wrong. He swallowed, hard. He'd never met someone so fiery, so sweet, so…so *amazing* as Leila, in his whole life. He hated that he had to meet her this way. But maybe, just maybe, everything could work out after all.

He leaned over the stick shift of his now shut-off car, and kissed her, hard, with all the passion and confusion he was feeling. She seemed stunned by it initially, but soon enough she was matching his passion—and then raising him a level. She tasted of wine and heat, her tongue tickling his, causing him to groan. He pressed her into the leather of the passenger seat—and promptly got hit in the hip with the gearstick.

"Ouch, dammit," he said roughly, pulling away and taking a deep, uneven breath. "Okay, not in the car."

She laughed. "Then why don't you come inside?"

The words hung there, heavy with invitation. Chad thought about it...then sighed heavily.

"The thing is—we'll still have some issues hanging between us," he said slowly.

She stared at him. "I was trying not to think about that."

"I know," he said. "And ordinarily, I would ignore absolutely anything to sleep with you. I wouldn't care about tomorrow. I'd just want to make love to you for hours until we were both exhausted, and worry about the consequences later."

Her eyes lit like beacons, and her hand rubbed his thigh gently. "Okay. Okay," she murmured, her breathing going shallow. "I can live with that. That sounds good."

It took every ounce of self-control he had, and some he didn't realize he had, to put his hand on hers, slowing the maddening motion of her fingertips. "But here's the thing," he said, his voice thick with desire. "Ordinarily, tomorrow would suck, and you'd probably be hurt. But I wouldn't care, because I wouldn't be there."

He was ashamed at his own admission, and her hand paused on its own.

"I see," she said, pulling her hand away. He could feel her withdraw, both physically and emotionally.

He leaned over, stroking the petal softness of her cheek. "I'm not proud of who I was, or what I've done. I can say this—I would be there tomorrow, for you," he said. "But that doesn't mean I want to do anything tonight that'll hurt you in the future. I want the way to be perfectly clear before we get together, because when we finally *do* get together, it's not going to be for just one night. Can you understand that?"

He held his breath, waiting for her response.

Leila stared at him, her eyes almost black in the moonlight. Then, he saw her lips curve into a smile, before she pressed a kiss on him, full of tenderness and promise.

"I understand," she said. "But how can we clear the way?"

Chad sighed raggedly. "I need to talk to my family and my accountant tomorrow," he said. "And then I'm going to see what my options are. And I am going to do everything I can to keep the vineyard."

She let out a gasp. Then, slowly, she asked, "It's not…it's not just for me, though, is it?"

"No," he said. "I care about you, more than I could've believed. And I don't want to hurt you. But I care about Honey Ridge, too, now." He sent her a smile, tinged slightly with pain at what he was turning down. "I'll find out definitively tomorrow. Can you wait one night?"

"All right," she said. "I can wait one night."

He kissed her again, and then watched as she got out of the car and went up to the house. He had never wanted anything as badly as to go up to the house with her, and have her. He knew if he so much as opened his car door, all his miraculous self-restraint would evaporate and that's exactly what he would do. But she was too damned important for him to screw this up.

He could wait one night, too, he decided.

Still, it'd be the longest night of his life.

CHAD SAT in his father's study, squirming slightly in the high-backed chair. It was sumptuous leather, but it always felt uncomfortable to him, although he supposed that had more to do with the circumstances than with the seat itself. He never sat in the thing unless he had something really important to discuss or, more to the point, something to justify. He'd sat here after each of his investments had gone down the tubes. Chad had sat here when his father had replenished his trust fund, the first time.

God, I hate this chair.

Today, though, was more important—and more painful—than all of those previous incidents combined.

He'd already spoken to Renaldo this morning, and the verdict was not good.

"Hey, Renaldo," he'd answered his phone, still churning with joy and frustration from the night before. He wanted Leila; he wanted Honey Ridge; he had a definite vision of what he wanted his future to be. He could not remember feeling more impassioned, more happy.

"We need to talk," Renaldo had said. "Chad, you can't keep the vineyard."

Chad had been driving, and he'd gripped his steering wheel. "Why not?"

"It's hemorrhaging money."

Chad had swallowed hard. "I know it's fallen on hard times the past two years, but that's just a fact of the business," he'd said carefully. "This year's bottling went smoothly. And even though last year's crop was small, the wine itself is remarkable."

"This isn't about the wine," Renaldo had countered. "This is about the vineyard itself. It won't survive another year on its own without some serious cash influx. It won't even survive through Christmas at this rate. The collectors are circling, and you haven't given them any money yet. It's overextended. Charles knew that, but Charles had boatloads of money to throw at it. You don't. Your trust fund—even when it was at its peak—isn't enough to bail Honey Ridge out of the hole it's in. And it certainly isn't enough to keep it operational for another year or two, which it would definitely need to help you recoup your losses." Renaldo's voice had been melancholy but firm. "You'd be committing financial suicide, Chad. I can't advise you to do this."

"But…" He'd felt happiness seep from him like blood from a wound.

"At least the sale of the land will more than cover the losses." Renaldo had tried to comfort him. "You'll come out ahead—not a lot, but enough. That land is valuable, more than the vineyard. You'll be all right. It'll replenish what you lost on the movie, probably."

He'd winced. "It's more than the money, Renaldo."

Renaldo had sighed. "Well, unless you can think of a way to suddenly get a few more millions to throw at this, I don't know what to tell you."

After hanging up, Chad had thought about the dilemma, and the only solution he could come up with had led him here…to his father's study, to the dreaded chair.

He imagined police interrogation room furniture was more comfortable.

His father walked in, looking the same as always— vaguely stressed and harried. Even though he'd just come back from a European vacation, even though he was wearing a polo shirt and a pair of khakis, he looked like he had just stepped out of a boardroom, where he'd received bad news. Chad had no idea how his father managed it, since he didn't even work anymore. Hell, he hadn't worked since he was thirty-seven.

"I'm a little surprised that you wanted to meet with me, son." His father sat in the position of authority behind the broad bird's-eye maple desk that dominated the room. "What's going on?"

Chad took a deep breath. This was the painful part.

"I need your help."

His father's eyes widened. "What mess are you in now?"

He gritted his teeth. "It's not a mess. It's a business proposition."

Now his father's eyes shut. "Oh, God," he muttered. "Tell me this isn't another one of your cockamamy investments, Chad. I warned you. I told you before we left that you needed to stop all this nonsense!"

Chad took out his small leather portfolio, containing the numbers he'd pulled together from Leila and Renaldo. "I am asking for you to put money into a business venture," he said. "I'm not asking you to bail me out. I'm asking on behalf of Honey Ridge Vineyards. And I'm not asking you to do it blindly. I've brought research, that shows you why they need the money— why *we* need the money," he corrected, "and how we'll be able to not only pay back your interest, but get you some return on it in the future. This isn't charity. It's business."

His father now stared at him as if he'd never seen him before. "Are you kidding?" he finally asked, bewildered.

"Dad, I know that I've been an idiot and a flake in the past," Chad said, grinding out the admission painfully. "But I also know that I was just playing at business then. You were right about that."

His father looked gratified at Chad's acknowledgment. "So what makes this different? You were only there, what, two months! Tops!"

"I love wine, Dad," Chad said, then grimaced when his father chuckled dismissively. "Not just drinking it. I learned about the whole process. I worked, actually did physical labor. I fell in love."

Now his father scowled at him. "Should've known there was a woman involved in this whole fiasco."

Chad felt his anger bubble at that one, but he shook his head. "I fell in love with *wine*, Dad. And with winemaking."

He'd also fallen in love with Leila, improbably enough. But he was not about to bring her into this— not to face his father's derision. Chad was going to do that on his own.

"Well, I hope you two are very happy together," his father said. "Because I'm not investing a damned dime in your vineyard."

Chad felt his stomach clench. "If you just front us some money, not even the whole investment," Chad said, trying not to plead, "I can reimburse you in the next six months. I just need time to get the vineyard back on its feet. In the next six months, I could get my friends to put the money in, set up my own investment collective. I could pay you back."

"You don't get it, do you?" his father said. "I don't care about your vineyard, and I don't care about the money. *I don't want you to keep throwing yourself into these damned foolish business dreams!"*

Chad stared at his father, aghast.

"Do you know how embarrassing it is, for you, for all of us, when you keep failing?" His father hit the surface of his desk with a balled fist. "I've tried to spare you that, but you keep ignoring me, doing your own thing, falling flat on your face. Well, I've warned and I've talked, and I'm sick of it."

Chad felt his chest burn like acid. "I see." He loaded up his portfolio. His father had been a long shot, anyway, but he'd hoped that, by showing how serious he was, he might relent.

"You're going to try anyway, aren't you?" his father said. "What's your next move? You don't even have one, do you?"

"I'll try my friends," Chad said, wincing at the thought of Lester as one of the vineyard's patrons. "And if that doesn't work, I'll figure out something."

"You don't get it at all," his father said. "You don't know what it's like to be broke, to not have this endless flow of money…to actually *struggle* for something. You think I'm just going to be there to bail you out forever."

"That's not it at all." *You've never struggled for anything, either. You were born into money, same as me!*

"Well, son of mine," his father said, "welcome to the real world."

"I'll make this work," Chad said, stubbornly. "I just wanted to come to you first."

"This isn't about the vineyard," his father snapped. "This is about you. I'm cutting you off. Your trust fund is gone. You're on your own."

Chad sat there a moment, in shock. He had wondered if his father would help, but he hadn't anticipated this.

"So whatever money you've got, you'd better hold on to it, because that's all she wrote," his father said smugly. "You want to know what it's like? You want to ignore your family and go your own way? Well, then, here's your chance."

Chad forced himself to stand up, even though he felt numb. "All right," he said slowly.

"Do you understand? You're cut off!"

"I get it," Chad repeated. And he didn't listen to the rest of his father's tirade as he walked out the door.

He was on his own. His trust fund was gone. He had some possessions, but he had no money, nothing to offer Honey Ridge—or Leila, for that matter, he thought absently. His friends would probably give a little, out of charity, but they would not want to continue to hang out with him. He knew them well enough for that.

He was in a corner.

He thought about Renaldo's assessment. *You'll be able to cover your losses with the sale.*

He was going to have to sell Honey Ridge, he thought, the pain of the realization circling out of him in waves.

And he was going to have to tell Leila. Tonight.

CHAPTER SIX

LEILA SAT IN HER LIVING ROOM, waiting for Chad.

She'd spent the afternoon bottling the last of the year's wines. Each vintage seemed to hold some crucial part of her, some essence of her spirit, if that wasn't too melodramatic a way to put it. After all, there was something of her spirit in every bottle that left the place. But this was different. It would be interesting to see, in a few years, how this year's harvest had fared, whether it would be one of Honey Ridge's best years, or one of its worst.

At the end of the day, though, once it was in the bottle, one couldn't control what happened next. One had to simply hope for the best, and plan for the next vintage.

That was what she was doing, she thought, as she smoothed the skirt of her dusty-rose sundress around her legs. It was all out of her hands now, no point in worrying over something she couldn't control. She could only enjoy what she had, and make the most of it.

She heard the roar of Chad's car and was on her feet before she realized it, heading for the front door and standing on the porch.

She'd always remember the moment afterward... standing on the old porch, her hands on the railing, polished glass-smooth by years of rough hands rubbing over it. Watching Chad step out of his car, his hair tousled by the early autumn breeze. The grape leaves were turning colors, and in the sunset the hills looked aflame. It was one of the most breathtaking things she'd ever seen.

He walked toward her with purpose, almost stern, and then he walked up the steps.

"I missed you," he said simply, and then kissed her, taking her breath away in an entirely different way. She clutched at his shoulders, marveling at their strength, wondering why she'd bothered fighting their attraction for so long.

After a long moment, Leila pulled away, panting slightly, feeling light-headed. Then she looked in his eyes.

They were filled with darkness, and a hint of despair, and while a part of her quavered at the sight of it, the rest of her knew instinctively not to question. He'd get to it, in time. Right now, he needed to sit down. He needed comfort.

"Come in," she said breathlessly. "I've got some wine you might want to try."

He nodded, letting her lead him into the living room and pour him a glass of Syrah. He took a sip, but she knew he wasn't tasting it, wasn't savoring it. He was playing out something in his mind—bracing himself. Just as she was, she realized.

Instead of waiting for him, she sat down next to him, kissing him tenderly, tasting the Syrah on his tongue. Then she stroked the hair on the nape of his neck, tracing her fingers down his neck. "It's all right," she murmured. "It's okay. It's going to be fine."

That seemed to surprise Chad, and he allowed her to take him into her arms, rubbing his shoulders. "How did you know?"

"I just had to look at you," Leila said.

He was silent for a moment, board-stiff, with waves of pain coming off him, and her heart ached for him. "I tried," he said finally. "I wanted to keep Honey Ridge. I had no idea how much money we were losing."

She closed her eyes. She hadn't either—not really. She'd always been more about the grapes and the wine than the ledgers and margins. "So there's no hope?" she said, wanting to be clear.

"I'm selling the vineyard," he said, and he choked on the words. "I am so sorry, Leila. I am so very, very sorry."

"I knew you'd have to," she said, even though she hadn't wanted to believe it. "And it's all right."

"How can you say that?" he said, pulling away from her, studying her face. His looked harsher—older, she realized, in some intangible way. "I know how much this place means to you! I couldn't believe how much this place means to *me*, in just a few months, and you've lived here most of your life! You've always wanted this. So how, exactly, can you look me in the eye and tell me that this is 'all right'?"

He was furious, not at her, but at himself, at the whole situation. Still, his words stabbed, pointing out everything she'd railed against herself. This was what she'd wanted her whole life. This was what she'd dreamed of and planned for, since she was a child. And it was going away.

And yet it really was going to be all right.

"You know," she said, trying to figure out a way to put

it in words, "there's a lot that can go wrong in a season. Frost. Drought. Fire. Bugs. You name it, we've had it."

Chad stared at her, obviously not getting it.

"But you still do it," she said, kissing him on the cheek, "because you love it. And when something happens, you just say 'it'll be better next season.' And you *keep* going."

He leaned into her, and she took comfort in his heat, in his arms around her.

"So you're saying," he said, his voice muffled against her neck, "that it's good that I'm dumping the place, since with the frost, fire, bugs and whatnot, it's a real lemon?"

He surprised a laugh out of her. "You idiot," she said, but realized he wasn't serious—he was just trying to take some of the pain out of the situation by joking. But she wasn't ready to joke, not yet. "I'm saying," she said clearly, framing his face in her hands as he held her hips loosely, "that when you love something, you just find another way."

He smiled. "I can't believe I found you. I can't believe what you mean to me. I think I might be falling in love with you."

Leila couldn't swallow. She could barely breathe. She could only stare at him.

"I know it's sudden," he said, his voice ragged. "And I know I don't have a chance, with all of this. But I thought you should know."

How long had it been since she'd heard those words from a man? And how long had it been since she had felt like this?

She couldn't answer immediately. Instead, she wordlessly took his hand, leading him up to her bedroom.

The covers were turned down. She'd known, no matter what else happened, it would come down to this.

Chad paused in the doorway, staring at her. "It's more than this," he said solemnly. "You know that."

She nodded, still silent. Then she reached to the back of her dress, unzipping it slowly and letting it drop to the floor. She hadn't worn underwear, so nothing was impeding his vision. It had been years since she'd stood, naked and vulnerable, in front of a man in this way.

He looked at her almost reverently. Then he reached for her, with infinite gentleness, stroking her skin, murmuring tender words against the crown of her head as he kissed her.

After some artless fumbling on both their parts, they managed to get his clothes off, too, and slowly made their way to the bed. It was as if they were both nervous, as if it were equally important to both of them, and neither wanted to make a mistake. But soon, his hands smoothing over her bare skin caused her blood to heat and her breathing to go shallow. Her gentle stroking motions turned more ferocious, grasping, wanting. He grew more insistent, kissing her with a furious fire, molding the white-hot planes of his body against hers.

In the moment before he eased into her, she couldn't think of anything about her past, about her future, about what she'd wanted. She didn't care about the vineyard or the wine in the cellar or anything. Her only thoughts were of him, and of how she felt at that instant.

"*Chad*," Leila said, in a rippling murmur, as he moved inside her. She clung to him, clawing her nails down his back. This was perfect, she thought, before all thought fled altogether. This was fiercely, utterly *right*.

They moved against each other with tender passion, and when it was over, she still clutched him to her, as if she couldn't bear to be more than a heartbeat away.

"I might be falling in love with you, too," she murmured, and only by the sudden tightness of his arms around her did she know he'd heard what she said.

That didn't change things. He was selling Honey Ridge. They were both moving, and more than likely moving on.

But she'd had her one night, her last vintage. It was perfect. And if it was all she ever got—so be it.

CHAPTER SEVEN

"HEY, CHAD! Man, did you miss out in Machu Picchu. What a scene!"

Chad sipped at his wine—a little indie out of Oregon, a red blend. It had promise, but it also had some sourness, he noted, and jotted down the observation in a notebook he'd purchased. Then he looked up to address Lester, who was standing beside him in the crowded San Francisco restaurant. "Hey, Les."

"Where the hell have you been hiding yourself?" Lester's eyes gleamed. "We haven't seen you in ages. And I've got a party coming up."

"I can't make it," Chad said quickly, taking another sip, "but thanks anyway."

"What, are you a monk now?"

Actually, Chad thought with a humorless grin, he was. "Just busy."

"Doing what?"

"Selling my vineyard," he said. Even after three months, it still hurt. "Escrow just closed. It's out of my hands now."

"All right! Finally, you'll be back in the black," Lester said, all but rubbing his hands together. "Which is good, because the Christmas party I've got coming up—you won't believe it. You've heard of that ice hotel they set up in Sweden, right?"

"I told you, I'm busy."

"Sounds like you're not busy anymore," Lester said practically. "You sold the place." Then his eyes narrowed perceptively. "Wait, wait, don't tell me. You've got a girl, huh?"

That did cause Chad to wince. "Not at the moment."

And it was true. After their one night, after telling her he was in love with her, Leila had woken him up the next morning, presented him with a cup of the best coffee he'd ever tasted—and then told him that they probably shouldn't see each other again.

"Why not?" he'd asked, stunned to the point of numbness. "I thought you said that you wouldn't hold it against me! I didn't want to sell the vineyard. I just…I *have* to!"

"I know," she'd said, caressing his face, her eyes wet with tears. "But that doesn't stop what has to happen. I have to find a new place to live. I have to get another job. I have to make choices with my life." She'd paused, and she'd gotten that practical tilt to her chin that he loved—or at least, that he'd loved before that moment. "And so do you."

"You can move in with me."

"I'm sure I could, but I need to work with grapes. You live in the city. That's a hell of a commute."

"I could get a place out here," he'd said, with the desperation of a man arguing against a death sentence. "It wouldn't be that hard."

"I care about you. That hasn't changed." She'd sat

next to him. "But I need to get my life sorted out. You can understand that."

"So where does that leave me?"

Leila had stared at him then. "You tell me, Chad. Where does that leave you? What do you want to do now? You can't have the vineyard. And you've got a bunch of financial stuff you're going to need to think of, from what you've just told me. What's your next move?" Her eyes had been expressive. "What do you *want?*"

He'd been pushed off balance. He hadn't thought beyond that. He'd thought the vineyard was the answer to all of his problems, just as he'd thought Leila was a part of that solution. But when one part of the solution failed, it seemed, all of it did.

He still loved Leila, and he hadn't been with anyone since her. But when she'd taken a flight to Australia to visit her parents, he hadn't protested. He still called her but respected her need for space.

True to his word, his father had cut off his trust fund. He'd gone over all the money he had in his personal account, the worth of his condo, and the money he'd make on the sale of the vineyard. He had made some hard decisions.

His days of "playing" were over.

"I'm waiting for someone, Lester," he said, seeing Renaldo entering the restaurant, scanning for him. "But it's been nice catching up."

Lester simply shook his head, walking away. Chad shook Renaldo's hand. "Thanks for making the time to meet."

"Thanks for not calling me at home anymore," Renaldo said. "How are you doing?"

"Hanging in," Chad said. "Listen, I also wanted to thank you for handling the vineyard sale."

"No problem," Renaldo answered. "You got top dollar. Any idea what you want to do with the money? I can put you on to some good investments."

"I've been doing some research, myself," Chad said slowly. "And I've drawn up a plan."

"Really? This *is* news."

Chad didn't laugh, even though he knew Renaldo meant him to. "I'm thinking real estate."

"Okay. Any idea where?"

"California's getting a little too expensive," Chad said. "I was thinking of Oregon."

"Oregon? What's in Oregon that's got you so interested?"

Chad pulled a manila folder out of the briefcase that he hadn't carried for years. He handed it to Renaldo, who opened it, scanning its contents quickly. Then Renaldo looked up at him, surprised.

"Are you sure about this?"

"There are a lot of good wines coming out of Oregon right now," he said. "I know where I can get some quality used equipment cheap. And I've got a guy helping me out as far as scouting the location. He assures me the land's worth it."

"A guy?" Renaldo's voice was skeptical.

"Not one of my old party cronies. Julio Escobar," Chad said. "He was head of the farmlands at Honey Ridge. He's given it the seal of approval. I don't know if I can afford to hire him, but I trust his recommendations."

"Well," Renaldo said, nonplussed. "Well. You know, it wouldn't be a slam dunk."

"I don't expect this to happen overnight," Chad said soberly. "I have the business background, and I've been running some numbers—how long it would take us to be profitable, what it would take to cover payroll, the whole nine yards." He pulled out another manila folder, passing that to Renaldo. "I'd appreciate your help looking it over, though."

"You really have been working," Renaldo said. "Damn, this is comprehensive. You seem to know what you're talking about."

"I know."

Renaldo looked at him for a second, then cleared his throat. "Can I ask you a question for a second? Not as your financial advisor, but as your friend."

Chad nodded. He'd always thought of Renaldo as both, anyway…or else he never would've called him so late at night.

"Is this for you?" Renaldo asked quietly. "Or is this for the girl?"

Chad sighed deeply. "I've asked myself the same question," he said.

"And…?" Renaldo prompted.

"It's for me," he said, and he knew that the truth rang in every word. "I miss her, and I love her, and I won't deny that I'd like to have her with me. But when I worked at the vineyard, for the first time in my life, I loved what I did. I felt like a whole person. I don't think that what you do defines you, or anything like that, but I do know that not doing anything, and wasting my life, was making me miserable. And being miserable and not myself was never going to be good enough for her. She wanted me to get my life together, and she never guaranteed anything. I see now that, the way I was, there was no way I could be with her."

"So you are doing this for her," Renaldo said, and Chad hastily shook his head.

"No. I'm doing this for me. I'm just saying she was right."

Renaldo nodded, then he sighed. "This could take a while to pull together."

"That's okay," Chad said. "My calendar's pretty empty for the foreseeable future."

"I DIDN'T KNOW it got this cold in Oregon in the winter," Julio said to Chad, shivering at the kitchen table, his large hands gripping a large mug of coffee.

"But the vines are going to be okay, right?" Chad said, pouring himself a third cup. It was January. He had been owner of the vineyard for a month. In that time, he'd managed to hire a skeleton staff, and even had a few investors. He spent most of his days planning the next year's vintage and focusing on hiring. He spent most of his nights working himself into oblivion and trying not to focus on the fact that Leila was working in Australia and hadn't returned his calls for a week.

He missed her, with an intensity that he couldn't believe. Still, he had a life, which was more than he could say before he'd met Leila and gone to Honey Ridge, and for that, he thanked her.

"How are we coming on the head winemaker search?" Julio said suddenly.

Chad closed his eyes against the pain of it. "Still looking," he said casually. "I've got a few résumés that look pretty decent."

"It'll get easier, boss." Julio said.

"How's your mom?" Chad asked.

"She's looking forward to trying something new," Julio said, grinning. "Although if she thinks you're not feeding me properly, she may move up here."

"If she'll feed me, too, she has my blessing," Chad said, chuckling. "Go ahead, knock off early. I'm sure your family's waiting for you."

"The kids did want to play in the snow," Julio said. "Thanks, boss." He left.

Chad was alone in the large old house. He'd sold his car, trading it in for a work truck. He'd sold his place in San Francisco. He'd also ditched most of his furnishings—Scandinavian modern looked downright stupid in the relatively rustic wilds of an Oregon vineyard. Still, the place seemed large and empty.

He was in the process of starting a fire when he heard a knock on his front door. Probably a solicitor, he thought, although his heart beat quicker, as always, as he answered it.

Leila stood there on his step, and for a moment he wondered if she were a mirage, something his heartsick imagination had conjured up. Until he realized she was shivering.

"Are you *kidding* me with this cold?" she said, stepping in uninvited.

He closed the door behind her. "It got cold in Napa," he said inanely, still struck with disbelief that the object of his affection was currently dripping the remnants of sleet on his foyer rug.

"Not like this," she said, then stared at him for a moment, as if studying him.

Chad knew he looked nothing like he had the first time she'd seen him. He was wearing a flannel shirt and a pair of jeans, as well as a thick sweat jacket. He wore boots, for God's sake. He hadn't shaved that morning. He probably looked like a mess.

She looked the same as always—her hair tawny and wild, her violet eyes wide. She looked perfect.

"I missed you," he said in a quiet voice.

She threw herself in his arms, and he kissed her with all the passion he'd been shoring up in the months they'd been physically apart. She was tearing at the buttons of his shirt even as he went for her jacket. More by luck and chance than any sort of planning, they wound up in his bedroom, kissing each other fervently, gasping incoherent phrases of longing and love.

"Don't ever, *ever* just vanish on me again," he said, kissing her breast and making her gasp.

"I won't," she promised. "I had to fight to stay away."

"Well, don't do that, either," he warned.

"I had to know that you were doing things for yourself, not just using me as another escape," Leila said breathlessly, as she shucked off her own jeans. Lying there, deliciously naked, her eyes were still serious. "I had to *know*, Chad. I couldn't bear it if you got tired of me because I wasn't the answer to your problems."

He nodded. "I deserve that," he said, lying naked beside her and savoring the warmth of her compact little body. "I didn't know how much I had to learn until I lost Honey Ridge, and you."

"And now?"

He looked around, at his much less luxurious surroundings. "I think I can be happy here," he said.

It was the answer she was looking for, apparently, because she proceeded to make slow, sensual, thorough love to him, as if trying to erase all memories of their being apart.

Afterward, with her lying in his arms, Chad felt just as he had when he'd first come to Honey Ridge. He felt as if he'd come home.

"I hear," she said, pressing a few kisses against his chest, "that you're looking for a head winemaker."

With that, he felt a bubble of happiness. "Yup," he drawled. "Interested?"

"I could be," she said.

"You know, you'll have to turn in a résumé—*ow!*"

He laughed after she punched him in the ribs, then looked at her seriously. "I know, this place is a risk. And it's not Honey Ridge."

"It's got a good feeling to it," she said, smiling. "And I think I could be happy here, too."

He nuzzled her neck. "I'll do everything I can to make sure you are," he said.

"What do you call this place, anyway?"

Chad smiled down at her. "So far...I'm calling it Long Shot Vineyards."

"Sounds like a gamble," Leila said, then pulled him close and kissed him. "Count me in."

ICE CREAM KISSES

Stephanie Doyle

PROLOGUE

Labor Day...present

Gracie McMullen wrapped a hand around her beer and stared at the clock. Ten minutes to go. Her group of friends—minus one—had been counting down with her for the past hour.

"I'm here." Rick, the owner of the establishment where they were all assembled and the last official member of the Labor Day group, joined them at their table. "Finally got everyone out of the bar. I swear, some people just don't know when to leave. Last call was at eleven."

He got a beer for himself and sat down at the round booth in the back of the bar next to his wife, Dottie.

"Ten more minutes," Dottie told him. "Actually, nine."

"Ten more minutes until peace," Elis, the fourth member of the group clarified. Squinting his eyes, he lifted his wineglass half-filled with good chardonnay and studied the rim. "Jeez, Rick there's a lipstick smudge on this glass. I bring my own wine. Is it too much to ask for a clean glass?"

"Sure the lipstick isn't yours?" he drawled.

"Once again a member of the heterosexual community fails to understand his brother on the other side of the sexual spectrum. I'm gay, not a cross-dresser. I don't wear lipstick. And I want a new glass."

Rick grudgingly slid out of the booth and made his way back to the bar.

"Do you think…" Dottie stammered, watching Gracie with a pained expression. She had started and stopped the same sentence five times in the past hour.

"No," Gracie replied curtly. It was a catchall answer. It answered the question Dottie really wanted to ask, and it covered the question she only partially had asked.

Gracie wasn't thinking about anything. She didn't want to think about what had happened this time last year. She didn't want to think about all the winter seasons to come.

She was happy, she told herself. She had friends. She had her own business. Living on Long Beach Island about a mile off the coast of New Jersey provided her with all the income she needed during the crazy summer months between Memorial Day and Labor Day and all the peace and quiet she needed during the off-season. It was a perfect existence.

But the last two off-seasons had been different. They hadn't been peaceful or particularly quiet. They'd been filled with tension and turmoil, as well as fun and love. Not to mention hurt and loss.

Because of him.

She'd sent him away with good reason. There was nothing to make her think he would come back. This was exactly what she didn't want to think about.

"You don't think maybe he might…" Again Dottie let the rest of her question trail off.

"No," Gracie answered. "I don't."

Forgive her? That's what Dottie had been about to say. Gracie supposed that she couldn't very well know what he would or wouldn't do. She supposed there was always a chance that he might understand, but she didn't want to spend her days pining for a chance.

"Leave her alone, Dottie. She's in mourning." Elis reached across the booth and laid his soft manicured hand on top of hers. "I've been there, remember? After Doug, I flew all the way to the opposite end of the country to get away from him. And landed here. In Beach Heaven. Where, I might add, there are no gay bars. But I digress. My point is, I got through it and you were there for me and you'll get through it and we'll be there for you."

"But what if he—" Dottie clamped her mouth shut.

Rick walked up to the table. "Here's your glass. I cleaned it myself. Then of course I spit in it, but you shouldn't let that worry you."

"Oh look, he's cute *and* funny."

"Dottie, Elis is hitting on me again. Make him stop."

But Dottie was still working up the courage to finish at least one sentence. She glanced up at the clock and gasped. "Only one minute to go. And then it will be Tuesday. The first official day of the off-season. We should count down. Ready…twelve, eleven…"

"Ten, nine, eight…" Everyone joined in.

A loud banging on the front door stopped everyone. Gracie turned her head and focused on the door across the other end of the bar. Who would knock on the door of a bar that was obviously closed? A drunk. Or maybe…

"Do you think it's him?"

Gracie stared at the door. Her heart thudded heavily against her ribs. She'd told him to go. He'd said he was happy, but she'd told him to leave. Because she had to know. He had to know, too. Now someone was knocking on the door and she couldn't believe, couldn't hope, that he'd found his answers.

"Go open the door, Gracie," Rick told her. "It's the only way you're going to know."

Gracie slid out of the booth and walked across the bar, winding her way between tables that held upside-down chairs. She reached the door and it rattled from the force of the pounding the person on the other side was giving it.

Maybe she shouldn't open it. Maybe it was better if it stayed closed. When she opened the door the last time it had ended in pain. So much heartache she didn't think she could survive it. What made her think that this time it would be different?

Only a fool would open the door.

Only a coward wouldn't.

Gracie figured she was somewhere in between. Besides that, opening it was the only way to stop all the banging. She turned the lock, took a deep breath and opened the door.

CHAPTER ONE

Labor Day...two years ago

"FOUR, THREE, TWO....one!" The group of four tucked in the back of Rick's Place shouted with joy as the minute hand ticked beyond twelve. It was officially the off-season. And while each of the small business owners gathered around the table loved to see the tourists come, they also loved to see them go.

"Free at last," Gracie sighed.

"I shouldn't be this happy," Elis stated. It was his second off-season since moving to the beach community. The first time September came for him he'd worried and fretted, as most do, wondering if the profits he had made over the summer would last through winter. Elis owned a gift shop stuffed with eclectic pieces that were apparently attractive to tourists. He'd done very well his first year.

Gracie and Dottie, who shared space in the three-storey bungalow-style house next to him, had taken him under their wings and explained how great the off-season could be. At first he hadn't believed them, but when the crowds had deserted the island he discovered a sense of quiet that he'd never known before.

That first year Elis had decided to take up painting as a hobby. But he discovered he couldn't paint.

"You said the same thing last year and it worked out all right, didn't it?" Gracie reminded him.

"I found out that I am not the second coming of van Gogh."

"You found out that you have months of free time to explore your inner self. That is a good thing. And I'm glad you're no van Gogh. I rather like your ears." Gracie winked at him and Elis couldn't help but smile.

"You know if I was straight…"

"We would have already had a passionate affair that ended in tragedy," Gracie finished.

Elis shrugged. "It's true. All my affairs end in tragedy."

"Oh, that's horrible," Dottie sympathized. "You'll see. You'll both find someone you can spend the rest of your life with someday. Just like I found Rick."

Gracie tried to stifle a snort. "Found Rick? Don't you mean flattened Rick?" She referred to the incident where after a night of rather copious drinking, Dottie chased Rick down the beach, tackled him to the sand and flat out demanded that he propose to her.

Since they had been dating for almost a year and Rick really did love her, he said sure. It was one of the more romantic moments Gracie had ever witnessed.

"You're just jealous that I got the last single man under seventy in town."

Gracie smiled because she knew Dottie wasn't serious. Rick, like Gracie, was a native of the island. They were both born here and they both stepped into businesses that their families had owned before them, but never once did their friendship ever take a romantic turn—probably because they had been raised as cousins.

Rick's parents owned the most popular bar in the area and Gracie's father owned the most popular ice cream parlor, the Sea Breeze. Good beer and good ice cream being key to any successful beach vacation spot, both of their businesses had flourished. After Gracie's mom had left her dad, Rick's folks had become a surrogate aunt and uncle to Gracie. Other than one really awkward incident during a spin-the-bottle game when they were twelve, they had never once considered each other anything other than family.

"I'm only teasing," Dottie quickly added because she wanted to make sure she never hurt anyone's feelings by being misunderstood. "I know your time will come, Gracie."

"Ah, Dottie. Our little optimist. Do you think it's all that money that makes her so damn happy?" Elis wondered out loud.

It was a known fact that Dottie was an heiress from the Philadelphia Main Line crowd. She had come to Long Beach Island to escape the suffocating world of the upper class and decided that being a shop owner might be fun. Naturally Gracie, who relied on the Sea Breeze to make a living, instantly hated her downstairs neighbor who had decided to open a coffee shop.

But no one could hate Dottie for long. She was simply too nice. Hating Dottie was like hating candy or…ice cream. It wasn't possible.

"Nope," Rick said. "It's me. Now if you don't mind I'm going to take my wife home, make mad passionate love to her for a few minutes and then sleep until Wednesday."

Elis snickered. "Rick and passionate, two words I would never put together, but I can take a hint. Say good-night, Gracie."

"Good night, Gracie," Gracie parroted.

Dottie giggled. "It gets me every time."

Gracie kissed her friend's cheek and then allowed Elis to walk her home. They stepped out into the street. Already the change was immediately felt. No late-night partygoers. No cars filled with college kids barreling down the road to get to the next bar. No drunken twenty-somethings staggering home in search of the one pizza place that still might be open.

Quiet. So quiet Gracie could hear the roar of the ocean a block away. A mist was descending on them as the seawater mixed with cool air to create a light salty fog. Gracie took a deep breath and smiled. She loved this place.

She loved it when it was filled with people. She loved seeing their overly red faces come into the parlor in search of the perfect beach sundae. She loved the kids who pressed their faces up against her glass cases asking their parents if it was okay to have whatever they wanted. She loved the long days and the long walks along the beach at night.

And then fall came, and then winter, and then spring and she loved them all too.

"It's starting to get chilly," Elis complained. A native of southern California, he hadn't yet grown accustomed to the penetrating cold of a New Jersey winter near the water. Eventually, he would. His bones would thicken. That's what her father would always tell her anytime she complained of the cold.

"It's seventy degrees," Gracie pointed out. Anything over seventy didn't really count as chilly.

"And misty. Don't forget the mist."

"How could I?"

They walked across the street and stopped before they each had to go their separate ways.

"Are you going to keep the Sea Breeze open year-round again?" Elis asked, probably more to make conversation than anything else.

"That's the plan. The folks at the assisted-living home keep me in the black. Plus, I had a good summer. Not to mention there is the added bonus of living above an operating ice cream parlor. It really gets a girl through that time of the month."

"Ew. Women issues. Please stop."

Gracie laughed and gave her friend a playful punch on the shoulder. "You're such a baby. What about Knick&Knacks?"

"It's easy enough for me to keep open, but I'm not planning for much traffic. Since my attempt to paint was such a disaster I thought I would give woodworking a try."

"Woodworking. Good for you."

"The dream obviously is to find some talent for making something that I can sell in the store that will attract so much attention it will became the next nationwide must-have item. Naturally, it will make it all the way across the country to Santa Monica, where Doug will be forced to sell said item in his store for...full price. He'll eventually be so green with envy that he'll seek me out and once he does he'll realize that he is still totally and completely in love with me. He'll fall to his knees in front of me, no sexual innuendo here, but you can imagine where I'm going. He'll beg me to take him back. He'll confess that his profits have gone down since the day I left his shop. And he'll admit that he hasn't had a decent night of sex since. At which point I will laugh in his face and walk away from him, leaving him a wretched mess of a man."

"That's a pretty big dream."

Elis lifted his chin high in haughty pose. "I don't dream small."

Since he sounded seventy-percent serious, she had to bite her lower lip to keep from laughing. "Okay. Well, have a good night. Sleep in."

"Will do."

Elis headed down the block to his new fall rental and Gracie made her way to the top floor of her bungalow.

She turned to wave good-night one last time and saw that Elis was standing on the corner watching her. "What are you doing?"

"Making sure you get inside safely."

His attempt at protection was rather cute since Gracie considered the island just about the safest place on the planet. "I'm fine."

"And I'm a gentleman."

"If you were only straight."

"Remember. Horrible tragedy."

She gave another wave then climbed the outside steps all the way up to the third floor. Dottie's coffee house took up space on the ground level. The Sea Breeze was above it, held up on stilts and her two-room apartment was above the Sea Breeze. The steps led to landings at Dottie's place, then to the Sea Breeze, then followed up to the apartment.

It was a heck of a commute.

Gracie opened the door without using a key and laughed when she thought of Elis waiting to see that she got home safely. No doubt he would be horrified to know that she didn't even lock her door. She didn't see the point. Sure there was crime on Long Beach Island. Here and there a robbery in one of the more affluent communities on the north end of the island. But south of the causeway, the bridge that connected LBI to New Jersey, the police mostly dealt with traffic violations, disturbing-the-peace violations and, of course, the dreaded not-walking-your-dog-on-a-leash violations.

She closed the door behind her and wasn't surprised to see Rufus and Eleanor waiting up for her.

"Miss me?"

"Roof," Rufus replied in half sneeze half snort. He was a mutt she had saved from the pound only last year when she found out that he had been left by a vacationing family. She'd asked him to name names so she could track down the family that deserted him and give them a piece of her mind, but he remained stubbornly quiet on the subject. He got along well with Eleanor, who wasn't the outgoing sort, and he was very good about pretending to walk with a leash anytime he spotted the fuzz.

Eleanor, another rescue from about four summers ago, walked out to greet her mistress with a run up against the legs.

"You know what today is? It's officially the first day of the off-season. It all changes tomorrow. No more traffic lights in town, not that I drive anywhere, but it makes for faster biking. No more surfing only before and after the official beach times. No more 'no dogs on the beach' during beach times."

"Roof!"

Rufus got it. He understood. She moved through the apartment to the brick fireplace that ran the length of the room. For some it might seem odd to have a fireplace in a beach apartment, but when it got cold in the winter sometimes a fire was the only thing to take away the damp chill. She reached for the picture of her father on the mantel and smiled down into his brown and wrinkled face.

Even cancer hadn't diminished his native island tan.

"Another summer over, Dad. Wish you'd been here. We did good. I added two new toppings to the topping menu. Chopped up Peppermint Patties and broken Tasty Cake Peanut Butter Cups. Huge hit on both of them. You would have been proud."

Gracie replaced the picture with a sad smile and used her finger to wipe the dust from the top of it. Fall cleaning, she sighed. Just another part of the post-season ritual. But that could wait for tomorrow.

"Come on, guys. Let's go to bed. Tomorrow we get to sleep in."

Her companions trotted after her and waited patiently while she performed her evening ritual. Gracie considered the cornrows in her hair. She'd had them done at the beginning of the summer as a lark and they were so easy to maintain, she had left them in. Eventually, she needed to return to her normal soft blond locks, but she could do that whenever. Maybe after surfing season was officially over.

Huddled in bed with Eleanor at her head and Rufus at her feet, she took a moment to listen to the faint sound of the ocean as it crashed against the sand. Peaceful. She had a feeling it was going to be one of the most peaceful off-seasons ever.

An odd feeling came over her then. Something akin to…longing. But before Gracie could wonder about it, the purr of her cat and the sound of the ocean lulled her quickly to sleep.

CHAPTER TWO

DEAN ALEXANDER WRIGHT III wanted ice cream. Sitting at his office desk in the house he'd rented for the winter, he literally ran his tongue over his teeth as if he could somehow taste the sweet one.

He checked the time on his computer monitor and saw that it was a little past seven in the evening. He'd eaten leftover pizza just an hour ago and probably shouldn't be this hungry. Then again ice cream cravings rarely had anything to do with hunger. He knew better than to fight it, because the longer he waited out the craving the worse it would get.

The sun had dipped below the ocean's horizon. Dean thought about the places that might be still open on the empty island and frowned. There weren't that many businesses that remained open after the summer, which made sense because there weren't that many people left. Not that he was complaining. It was the very reason he'd chosen this place as his winter retreat. He'd spent his summer in Colorado in a friend's condo near a ski resort that had been blissfully quiet and now he was looking for the same from this island. Peace and quiet were two necessary ingredients for working on a book.

But peace and quiet were really just the result of no

people, which ultimately was what Dean was looking for. If he never saw the inside of a crowded D.C. bar filled with pitying faces, or the crush of cubicles filled with curious little newshounds at the *Washington Post*'s office, or a room filled with the political elite at some house party in Georgetown it would be too soon. That life had betrayed him. Those people had stabbed him in the back.

Dean imagined that eventually he would have to go back if for no other reason than to face all the demons he had left behind, but he didn't have to do that anytime soon. What he needed to do was work on his research, write his book and enjoy the luxuries this beachfront house afforded him.

And he had to track down some ice cream. Now.

Dean decided to leave his Mercedes in the driveway, since the convenience store he had targeted as his best chance for being open was within walking distance. He made his way down the short empty blocks to the main boulevard that ran the length of the island. He stopped when he reached the street, although he wasn't sure why since there weren't any cars traveling in either direction. The traffic light overhead blinked yellow.

He jogged across the main street in the direction of the convenience store that was a block to the right when a sign caught his eye.

Sea Breeze—Ice Cream.

It was neon blue and hung over a door that looked open. Given the option of ice cream out of a carton or a sundae, there really was no choice. A sundae, after all, came with toppings and hot fudge.

Dean turned left and climbed the steps that led to the

second floor of the bungalow. He opened the screen door and stepped into heaven. It was just like an ice cream parlor was supposed to be. White and clean with an ocean fish design painted on the floor and on the walls. There were a few small round tables with wrought-iron chairs around them for those who wanted to linger. But more importantly there was a glass-covered countertop that displayed tub upon tub of ice cream flavors.

A kid walked out from what must have been a back room and nodded. Long and lean and still dark from the summer's tan, he couldn't have been more than sixteen. Dean decided he was a native. That or he'd chosen not to leave his summer job. And why would you if you were surrounded by all this ice cream goodness?

"Hey," the kid said.

"Hey. I'll have a large sundae. Chocolate ice cream, hot fudge and whipped cream." Dean studied the list of toppings that hung on the wall behind the counter. "With peanut butter cups and throw on some Gummy Bears."

"Gummy Bears?"

"Yeah. For color."

The kid shook his head. "Sorry. I can't do that."

"You're out of Gummy Bears?"

"No. I'm just not allowed to mix Gummies and peanut butter cups."

Dean shook his head as he tried to make sense of what he'd just been told.

"What do you mean you're not allowed? I'm a customer. I'm ordering a sundae. You have to give me what I want."

"Yeah. But no." The kid shook his head. "Boss's rules, man."

"The boss made these rules?"

"Yeah. No Gummy Bears and peanut butter cups. For that matter, I'm also supposed to recommend against a chocolate ice cream and Gummy Bear combo."

It was ludicrous. Beyond ludicrous. And maybe if he weren't so completely pissed off at the human race he would have actually found it amusing. In his current mood he did not.

"Is your boss here?"

"Yeah. She's in the back."

"Can you tell her I would like to speak with her?"

"Sure. Gracie! Dude out here wants Gummy Bears and peanut butter cups on chocolate ice cream!"

A second later, a woman came out from the same back room that the kid had emerged from. Dean registered the long blond cornrows first. Then there was her tan, which made her Caribbean-water-blue eyes pop and sparkle. She wore a simple T-Shirt with the Sea Breeze name embroidered over her right breast and cutoff jean-shorts. He followed the length of tan toned legs to her bare feet. He noted a rope anklet and two toe rings.

She reeked of beach bum. And since he pegged her as closer to thirty than away from it, which in his mind was too old to be going around without shoes, he instantly labeled her a flake.

"Gummy Bears and peanut butter cups. Ew. No." She shuddered even as she said it.

"Why do you care?"

"Hey, I don't just sell ice cream, I create sundaes. It's

an art. And I'm telling you the Gummy and cup combo just won't work. You're going for a chocolate flavor with a little bit of salt in the peanut butter. The Bears are too sweet and will throw that off. Here, let me show you."

Dean watched in stunned amazement as she moved behind the counter. She scooped out ice cream then turned around to the toppings counter where he could no longer see what she was doing. He heard the spraying sound of whipped cream, and a second later she turned back to him with a massive sundae in her hands.

For a second he thought about telling her to forget it and leaving on principle. After all, it was unheard-of for a retail business not to cater to what the client wanted. But his craving hadn't gone anywhere and the sundae looked damn good.

"Have a seat and I'll bring you a plastic spoon."

Dean found one of the small round-bottomed iron chairs and sat. It was covered with a cushion but was still uncomfortable. Not that it mattered when a person was eating ice cream. He set the sundae on the table and watched as she brought him a plastic spoon and a paper cup filled with water.

"I'm not sure why it is, but doesn't ice cream always taste better when eaten with a plastic spoon?"

Flake, he thought again silently and took the white spoon with a smirk and a nod. Diving into the sundae, he brought up a large spoonful of chocolate, peanut butter cup and…something else. Something dark and crunchy and chocolaty. He nearly groaned with pleasure, but he didn't want to give her the satisfaction.

"Cookie crumbs," she announced with a satisfied

smile. "Gives the sundae some depth while staying in the chocolate realm. I know what I'm doing. You should learn to trust people who offer good advice."

Since trust was the absolute last thing that Dean had to offer, he said nothing and focused on his sundae. It was good. And the sweet beast within him was soon appeased.

"Let's see. You can't be a tourist. The season is over. You're under sixty-five so you're not a retiree. I know you're not a native. So what brings you to my island?"

She was sitting at the table with him, her legs crossed in a yoga style. He wasn't sure how she maintained her balance on the small chair, but she seemed sturdy. She was smiling at him, waiting for an answer.

Of course it would have been rude not to give her one, but hell, he hadn't come to make small talk with the natives. The last thing he wanted was to have any interaction other than a nod hello and a way to order food. But something inside him said she wasn't going to go away without an answer.

"I'm writing a book. I...wanted the quiet."

"A book. That's interesting. Fiction?"

"Non fiction. A historical biography on the first men who crossed the mountains. You know, the Rockies and Sierra Nevada."

"Wow. Just the men?"

"They were the first," he muttered around the last solid bite of peanut butter cup.

"Yeah, but the women had to follow shortly. Can't imagine men being content on one side of a mountain when all the women are on the other side."

"Really? Sounds like heaven to me," he muttered grimly.

"Ah. I see. Bitter man. Breakup or divorce?"

This time Dean took his attention off the sundae and scowled at his unwelcome guest. "Do you mind?"

Gracie looked around the shop, confused. "Do I mind what?"

"That's personal."

"Oh. Sorry." She shrugged. "We're a tight-knit community around here. I'm sort of used to being in everyone's business. Guess that's a bad habit."

"Guess so," he answered curtly, waiting to see her close down at his blatant rudeness. Instead, she smiled. Smiled as if she had answers about the universe that he would never understand.

"Well, my name is Gracie."

She offered her hand and, for a second, Dean considered ignoring it. Even a simple handshake was a commitment he didn't want to make. Alternatively, he knew that if he avoided the contact it would reveal more than he wanted to give away. He reached out and shook her hand, intending to keep the contact brief.

Her hand was cool and slim and small inside his hand. She wasn't tall, maybe five inches shorter than his own six feet, but her hand gave the impression of delicacy. Instinctively, he looked up to reassess her and locked on her eyes. They truly were a startling blue. So deep.

"You come back again and I'll make you a sundae that really showcases the Gummy Bear's best attributes."

He felt her tug her hand gently and realized he was still holding it. He released it and struggled against the desire to shake his head to clear his thoughts of her.

"What do I owe you for this?" Dean reached for the wallet in his back pocket.

"Nothing. It's on the house."

Worried that she might be flirting with him, he shook his head. "I think I'll pay. Giving away ice cream can't be good for business."

"On the contrary. I'm like a drug pusher in that respect. First taste is free, but next time you're going to have to pay. And there *will* be a next time. You'll wake up tomorrow morning and the first thing you'll remember is how good that sundae was."

He snorted. "It's just ice cream."

"It's shore ice cream. There's a difference. It might have something to do with the salt in the air from the ocean that makes the sweet that much sweeter."

Dean crunched up his brow at the ridiculousness of that statement. Ice cream was ice cream. And her flake status had just been elevated a notch. She might have nice eyes, but she gave the impression of a hippie living in the wrong decade.

"Whatever. Thanks."

Gracie watched him leave and considered the fact that, before he did, he'd picked up his empty container, spoon and cup and had thrown them all away in the wastebasket by the door.

Interesting. It was the sign of a man who knew how to do for himself, but every indication was that he'd recently come out of a relationship. A bad one.

Maybe he thought he was here to write a book, but more likely he was here to escape. It wasn't the first time she'd seen someone do it. Dottie had come to escape from her overwhelming family. Gracie's mother had been an escapee, too. Although Dottie had stayed where her mother had eventually left. Island life wasn't like life anywhere else. It took a certain attitude to survive.

One that her mother hadn't possessed.

"What do you think, Gracie? Are we done for the night?"

Gracie turned at the sound of her employee's voice. Chad worked for practically nothing, since she had very little to pay in the off-season, but he was happy for an excuse to get out of the house during weeknights. His family owned one of the few restaurants that stayed open year-round and it was either dish up ice cream or shuck clams and oysters for the restaurant's raw bar.

"I think so. Doesn't look like anyone else is coming tonight." Gracie didn't like to keep set hours during the week. She closed when she felt it was time to close or stayed open if she thought she might catch a straggler with a craving. Like tonight. She would make a note to stay open a little later tomorrow night. She had no doubt the author who hadn't given his name would be back. Only he would do everything he could to resist the temptation, so she would have to be patient.

Not that she cared if he did come back, she told herself firmly. While attractive men—and he was that— were a rarity on the island, especially in the off-season, Gracie had no time for escapees.

Her father had learned that lesson for the both of them.

"Take forty dollars out of the register, Chad."

"Forty is too much. You only made thirty dollars tonight. I'll take twenty and make it up on the weekend."

Gracie smiled. Pay as you go was a common enough

practice on the island, especially when things slowed to a grinding halt. It took an islander to understand how it worked. Gracie bet it was something Mr. Bitterman would never understand.

A shame.

"Sounds good. You want to lock up?"

"Cool."

As crazy as it was, Chad actually liked the responsibility of locking up. His older brother had yet to be given the task of locking up the restaurant, so it gave Chad a one-up on him.

Gracie gave him a wave and then made her way up the stairs along the side of the bungalow to her apartment. She took a deep breath and nodded her head.

Salt air definitely made ice cream sweeter. She was curious to know how well it would work on Mr. Bitterman.

CHAPTER THREE

"THERE'S A MAN on the island! A man on the island!"

Gracie walked through the door of her friend's coffee shop located on the first floor of the bungalow-style house. The Good Morning offered some of the island's finest coffee, along with homemade muffins, cakes, and pretty much anything a sugar junkie needed to start the day. And for the health conscious, there was always a bagel to be found.

Dottie had redone the place in a mix of birch- and oak-wood tones. There was paneling along the walls and hardwood on the floor. The effect was clean, orderly and square. She had also added some oversize chairs for the late-nighters who preferred a quiet cup of coffee rather than a loud beer. It seemed to be working, as there was always a steady flow during the season.

Then again, Dottie had all the money in the world to spend to make her dream a reality. Gracie had to wonder if Dottie had yet to recover the costs on all the work she'd done to the place. Not that Gracie cared. The place looked great. Plus, sometimes she got spillover upstairs when people were done with their coffee. And Dottie always paid the rent on time.

"Did you hear me?"

Gracie chuckled. "I believe the island heard you."

"But it's true. I got it from Gloria who got it from her sister, Margaret, you know Margaret—real estate Margaret."

"Ah, yes. Real Estate Margaret, the nosiest woman on the island."

"Well, she rented the Barnes house you know, the blue one on the beach with the bird cutouts all along the front, to a single man. Margaret was tight-lipped about his story just to annoy Gloria, I'm sure. But it's true. A *real* man."

"Awesome." Gracie rounded the counter and pulled a mug from the stack of clean ones. She filled it with the coffee of the day. It was part of the rental agreement. Free ice cream anytime Dottie wanted it in exchange for coffee anytime Gracie needed it.

"I can't believe you're not more excited about this," Dottie said accusingly. "This is the first real man-spotting, under the age of sixty-five, on the island during the off-season in…well, since I got here."

Dottie waved her hands excitedly and Gracie had to duck below a flying dish towel. Dottie was a little older than Gracie and had recently married Rick. Gracie figured her friend had yet to shake the single-woman-all-time-is-running-out-for-me flu. Since it no longer applied to her, she was pawning it off on Gracie.

Flinging the towel over her shoulder, Dottie moved into the work area adjacent to the display counter to arrange the blueberry muffins. Gracie leaned her hip on the counter near the register and watched for customers.

"First, we're going to have to get his name," Dottie told her even as she took a pinch out of one of the muffins. "This one is for me."

"I hope so." Gracie smiled. She saw the door open and turned her attention to the customer when suddenly she felt a jolt in her stomach.

Mr. Bitterman. Now why would he make her stomach jolt? Shaking off the sudden weirdness, she plastered a big smile on her face and watched as he stopped two steps before the counter, once he saw who was behind it.

"Good morning. Welcome to the Good Morning."

He sighed. "I'm not going to get what I want, am I?"

"Depends on what you want."

"A vanilla latte."

"Perfectly within reason."

He seemed to relax, which she doubted was the easiest thing in the world for him to do. It was nine o'clock on a Thursday morning and the man was wearing khakis. Probably his idea of casual dress.

"Excellent."

"Except…" Gracie added.

"I knew it."

"While I also love a vanilla latte, from time to time I find that I can get into a rut with it. When that happens I like to mix it up with hazelnut."

"All right. Hazelnut."

"Do you need me?" Dottie called to Gracie from the back room. She was cutting up a cake into even slices and Gracie shook her head as she went about preparing Mr. Bitterman's drink.

"I got it covered."

"Good. We need to talk strategy. How do we go about meeting this new mystery man? Maybe we should just go to his house with a basket of goodies. You know, like a good-neighbor sort of gesture."

Gracie smiled then blushed a little. This could get interesting with the man in question currently at the counter and able to hear every word Dottie was saying. Gracie thought about shushing her friend, but decided there was more fun to be had the other way.

"Ah...maybe."

"I wonder what he looks like. Gloria said nothing about appearances, which means either Margaret didn't tell her or that he's not that much to describe. I'm not saying he's got to be Brad Pitt, but still I have to hope for your sake he isn't a troll."

Gracie turned around with the mug in her hands and slid it across the counter.

"He's not a troll."

"You think?"

"I know." Gracie stared at Mr. Bitterman, who took a cautious sip then nodded satisfactorily.

"How do you know?"

"I met him last night at the Sea Breeze. The man wanted Gummy Bears in his chocolate ice cream of all things."

The man in question instantly lifted his head and stared at Gracie, who shrugged. Then he craned his neck trying to see the person she was talking to.

"You're telling me you've seen him! The first real man to hit the island in the off-season in forever and you've already seen him! And you didn't tell me! Ah, you are so frustrating. Tell me what he looks like right now."

"Well he's about six foot."

"And an inch," Dean added in a low whisper.

"Six foot and an inch. Decent build, but not a gym freak."

Dean raised his right arm and made a bicep curl then squeezed it to validate the "decent" classification.

"He's got dark blond hair. Plenty of it, too. Face is a little scruffy." Gracie leaned over the counter to get a better look. "And he's got coffee-brown eyes. Real dark. No tan at all, though. In fact, he's sort of pasty looking."

Dean scowled, which caused his brow to furrow.

"Plus, he doesn't smile much. I don't think you can trust a man who doesn't smile."

"Well, then you'll just have to make him smile," Dottie declared as she came out from the back with her hands filled with a tray of muffins and a pound cake.

She stopped as she saw the man in front of the counter scowling at Gracie.

"Oh goodness. You're him, aren't you?"

"Dean Wright. Man of mystery."

"Even your name is Mr. Right," Dottie sighed.

"It's spelled with a *W* and trust me I'm nobody's Mr. Anything."

Carefully putting the two dishes on the counter, Dottie proceeded to wring her hands. "I'm very sorry about what I said. I must have sounded like a busybody. It's just that this is sort of a small island. Not that I care, of course. I'm very happy here. I got married six months ago. To Rick. He owns the bar across the way. You should come in for a drink sometime. On the house."

"Thanks, but I'm really not here to be neighborly, if you'll excuse me." Dean Wright, man of mystery, turned and headed back out the door.

It was Gracie's turn to frown as she watched Dottie's face fall.

"That's it. I've ruined it. The first chance you have at finding someone and I've gone and scared him off."

Gracie was about to contradict her friend when she felt a severe pinch on her upper arm which was exposed by the short-sleeve shirt she wore. "Ow! What was that for?"

"It occurs to me that you knew he was there. You could have told me to stop talking."

"Dottie, did you see his scowl? The man's a mess. My guess is mucho emotional baggage due to a breakup. He reeks of bitterness. I wouldn't get anywhere within ten feet of him."

"I suppose. It's just that I want…"

"Me to be as happy as you are with Rick. I know. And someday I will be. I hope."

Dottie nodded, apparently satisfied with Gracie's answer. "Oh look. He forgot his coffee."

Gracie looked out the coffee shop's front door window and saw that Mr. Bitterman, Dean, was standing on the corner, his hands on his hips. It was that horrible moment when you realize you've made the grand exit, but you've left behind the one thing you wanted. No doubt he was contemplating returning for the latte or scrapping it and making a pot of regular coffee at home.

Gracie pulled a to-go cup off the cup holder and poured Dean's coffee into it. She added a spoonful of steam left over from the pitcher of milk and popped a lid on it.

"I'll be back."

She didn't dare turn around to see Dottie's delighted expression. She was performing a service, that's all. There was nothing worse than having a latte on the brain only to be denied.

He was just about to cross the empty street when Gracie called out to him.

"Hey, Dean."

He turned at the sound of his name and instantly zeroed in on the coffee cup in her hand.

"You forgot your coffee."

Cautiously, he reached for it, like a wary animal uncertain whether or not to take an offer of easy food from a human's hand.

When it was safely in his grasp and he saw that he had escaped the encounter without incident, he sighed and a smile tugged at his lips. "Thank you. I really wanted that coffee."

"I know the feeling. So what do you think of the hazelnut?"

He took a sip. "It's good. Different, but still sweet."

"Like I said, nothing against your basic vanilla, but the hazelnut offers a nice change."

"I'll keep that in mind."

"Good. That will be three-fifty."

He seemed shocked. "You mean I don't get this on the house?"

"The Good Morning isn't my house. I own the Sea Breeze. Dottie owns the Good Morning. She doesn't subscribe to my theory of addiction. She likes to get paid instead."

"Hold this." He thrust the coffee back at Gracie and reached for his wallet. He took out four dollars and handed it to her. She returned his coffee.

"Nice doing business with you."

Gracie had turned when he reached out and caught her arm. The hair on the back of her neck stood up, but she dismissed it as having nothing to do with the contact of his hand on her arm.

"What about my change?"

Gracie smiled and waved the four singles like a fan in front of her face. "It's customary to tip in situations like these."

"Like these?"

"I delivered. Have a nice day Mr. Wright with a *W*."

SHE PRACTICALLY SKIPPED her way back to the coffee shop. It was ridiculous. Girls skipped. Grown women shouldn't skip. The very idea of his ex-wife, Elena, skipping…no. He wasn't going to think about her. He wasn't going to spend one damn minute thinking about her. It was going on four months since their split and for the most part he'd been able to dismiss any feelings of loss. It wasn't so much the dissolution of their marriage that hurt.

It was the *incident*. That miserable, awful incident that made his jaw clench and his stomach acid churn until he felt like he was burning up from the inside. All it took was one slip. One flicker of thought about Elena and it all came back.

This was ice cream lady's fault. If she'd walked like a normal person he wouldn't have tried to compare her to his wife. Then he wouldn't be simmering the way he was now. This was exactly why he'd made the conscious decision to avoid people at all costs. The less he had to do with people the more he was able to focus on his work and concentrate on not thinking about his wife. Ex-wife.

But no, the lady with the cornrows and the bare feet

had to skip by him and get him all worked up. And when he'd touched her arm he could have sworn he felt…nothing. He felt nothing. Practically racing back to his house, Dean was comforted by the fact that he was once again alone. He climbed the stairs to his office on the second floor and stared out through the glass wall to the ocean. It truly was a spectacular view.

If he was a less practical person he might have thought that the rolling ocean brought him a measure of peace. But he was sure that was just wishful thinking. A man of facts, he knew that the mountains in Colorado were just big hills and the ocean was simply a large body of water.

He was alone and it was time to get some work done. Another fact. However, when he took a sip of his delicious hazelnut latte all he could think about was that he hadn't given Gracie a big enough tip.

He would have to correct that the next time he saw her.

CHAPTER FOUR

"ELIS! HEY, ELIS!" Gracie popped her head inside the open door of Knick&Knacks but saw no one behind the counter. She was going to have to remind him that if he planned to keep the shop open year-round, it was a good idea to be waiting for customers in case they did come.

Setting her surfboard against a decorative bookshelf, she headed toward the backroom where Elis had set up his art studio. The sound of a lathe carving into wood filled the small space. Elis stood over the machine wearing a pair of goggles for protection and Gracie grabbed earplugs.

Waving her arms in a dramatic fashion over her head, she tried again to get his attention.

"Elis!"

The motion more than the sound attracted his attention and he immediately reached to switch off the lathe. He took his goggles off and Gracie was glad to see had had in one earplug.

"What's up?"

"The surf. Want to come with?"

"You know I only enter the ocean under perfect conditions. No seaweed, no jellyfish, and it must be cool without being cold. It's September so it must be cold."

"Sixty-five degrees according to the weatherman. That's practically balmy."

"Only for a surfing nut like you. I'm fine here with my wood."

Gracie wandered over to the machine and stared at the block of wood that had been rounded into what appeared to be a debarked tree trunk.

"What is it?"

"I'm not telling. It's a surprise. But know that when I'm done with it, it's going to fabulous."

"Make your ex, Doug, cry with envy?"

"Absolutely. I live to make him suffer."

Gracie frowned. "I think this is the point where I'm supposed to tell you that that's not healthy."

Elis sighed. "Maybe not. But for now, without the hope of another man in my life, the need for revenge keeps me warm at night. Speaking of men...word is there's a man on the island and that you've met him."

"Dean Wright. Nonfiction writer."

"Oh, boring. Sex-scandal nonfiction?"

"Historical nonfiction."

Elis practically shuddered. "That's worse. Straight?"

"I don't know," Gracie admitted. "I didn't ask."

"You shouldn't have to ask. If he's straight he'll hit on you and you'll know."

"I don't think he has any intention of hitting on anyone. The man's got baggage. That was clear enough."

"Don't we all."

Gracie reached out and rubbed his arm. "You know you're going to meet someone again. Someone even better than Doug."

Elis tried to smile, but it didn't quite reach his eyes. "I know. You go have a fun time and keep me posted on the nonfiction writer. I want to know the instant his sexuality is confirmed."

Gracie laughed and left the shop, collecting her surfboard on the way out. Unfortunately, she didn't imagine she would be able to provide Elis with any sort of confirmation. Dean had made it very clear that he wanted to be alone and Gracie had no intention of pursuing him.

If he happened to seek her out, then that might be a different story.

HE WAS WATCHING her.

Gracie smiled as she pushed her surfboard into the sand then plopped her bottom down onto the beach for a few minutes to get her wind back. The ocean was perfect today. So perfect she considered seeking out Elis again and forcing him to come with her, but she'd decided that time to herself would be better. It wasn't rough enough that the waves came in too fast to ride or too calm that she got bored. The last one she'd caught had practically ridden her all the way back to the front door of the Sea Breeze.

The air was getting colder, enough that she'd gone with her half wet suit, but the ocean was a massive body of water that took a long time to heat or cool. If she was lucky and the weather held through October, she could potentially surf into November.

Gracie smiled to herself, knowing that each year she made the same prediction and each year it was always too damn cold by November.

But not today. Today was perfect and she planned to enjoy it.

It was about two in the afternoon on a Tuesday. The beach was empty except for a few seniors who were shell collecting. Another older man in sneakers and black socks with his pants rolled up to his ankles dutifully searched for coins with his metal detector. His energetic terrier bounced around beside him when he wasn't chasing the sandpipers that lined up on the wet sand looking for little fish. Maybe tomorrow Gracie would bring Rufus with her. He'd been curled up on her bed around Eleanor when she left and she hadn't the heart to disturb either one of them from their midday nap.

Another surfer caught a wave on the next beach over beyond the jetty. Gracie recognized the red hair and waved as Chad's older brother paddled back into the ocean. He gave a brief wave, but then put his hands in the water, his focus now on the ocean before him. That he'd picked the beach one down from hers meant he wasn't looking for company. For that matter neither was Gracie. Surfing was in many ways like a religion for her. And there were times when a person wanted to pray with a group and there were other times when solitary prayer was needed.

But when she looked back over her shoulder at the glass front on the house that bordered the beach, she saw that Dean was still watching her.

Let him watch, she figured. There was no harm in it. Picking herself up, she pulled her board out of the sand and jogged back to the ocean in search of another ride.

THE NEXT DAY Dean took up his post to watch her on the beach. It was almost October. Two days until

October and she was playing in the water as if it was the middle of July. Maybe by island standards it had been a mild September; he had no way of knowing. Still, September was September and that was pretty darn close to fall. If surfing in the fall wasn't a clear sign that the woman was lacking in mental capabilities he didn't know what was.

She'd done the same the day before and the day before that and each time he thought it was crazy. Even though he'd seen others surfing along with her, for whatever reason, he picked her out as being the most foolish.

Today she had brought her dog, who sat dutifully on the beach while she paddled out into the ocean only to run to her when her board slid onto the sand once the ride was over. Twice, he'd bumped against her so that she had fallen off her surfboard, but each time she'd gotten up laughing and leaned forward to kiss the furry head.

Fun. A flake she may be, but it seemed she knew how to have fun. Dean tried to think about the last time he'd had fun. Instantly, he thought about his old job. Reporting on Capitol Hill for the *Washington Post* had certainly been exciting. It had been challenging and competitive. A job filled with political intrigue where there was always a story beneath the story.

However, he couldn't say that it had been fun. He thought about Elena and wondered when the last time was that they had done something fun together. He could remember parties they'd attended with the political elite. Golf outings they'd participated in with the political elite. Brunches where they ate with the political elite. It was the circle they traveled in together.

Had any of that ever been fun?

A motion caught his attention and pulled him out of his musings. The ice cream lady had caught another wave. She seemed to have a sixth sense for knowing exactly when they would peak and when to make her move. He watched her throw her weight forward onto her arms to push herself up and back until suddenly in a snakelike move she went from belly to feet in one graceful motion. Her arms moved to her side, but not in any kind of exaggerated way like they always showed in the those silly old beach movies. Instead she seemed to move with the wave, crouching low over the board so that she could twist and turn when she needed to, following the wave where it went and letting it take her all the way to the beach.

Move over Gidget. Gracie was good.

Dean realized he was smiling as he watched the dog run down the beach toward his mistress only to collide with her legs and send her sailing off the board onto her butt. Again, she laughed. Again she kissed his furry head.

The cell phone on his desk rang, forcing his attention away from the view. He glanced at the caller ID display on the front of the phone and immediately chose to let it ring. For some time after he stared at the quiet phone.

Then he heard a soft beep. Dean recognized the sound of his laptop going into sleep mode. It was set to do that after an hour of disuse. Since he knew he hadn't been staring at the phone that long, he realized he *had* been staring out the window for quite some time.

"Focus, Wright. You're here to work." Dean took his seat and tapped the computer back to life. He contemplated the blank page on the screen. His goal for the day had been ten pages, but given the distraction, he was lucky to accomplish half that.

Distractions. That was exactly why he had left Washington. Well, that and it seemed everywhere he went he'd become a spectacle. It wasn't an easy thing to make the transition from being the man who wrote the story to being the man who *was* the story. The bottom line, however, was that he was supposed to be working and instead he was distracted by a flake with cornrows in her hair.

This was all her fault. If only she hadn't picked the beach in front of his house to surf he wouldn't be behind. Tomorrow, if she came back to surf, he was going to lower the blind that ran the length of the glass wall and pretend that neither she nor the ocean existed for the day.

It was a good plan.

IT WAS A GOOD PLAN, Gracie decided. She'd had no intention of intruding on Dean's solitude, but after a week of him watching her surf she'd come to the decision that it was time to act. The man was all but daring her to intervene. And she was never one to back down from a dare.

Barefoot, she climbed the steps to the front door, which faced away from the beach. It was sort of backward, but it was how most beachside houses were constructed: with the front entrance facing away from the beach and mostly all glass backs facing toward the ocean to take advantage of the view.

She rang the doorbell and waited. When it seemed forever had passed, she rang the bell again. This time the door opened instantly. The man stood there in loafers, khakis and a white button-down oxford shirt. The very idea of wearing shoes inside unless it was slippers seemed foreign to Gracie.

"What are you doing here?"

"You've been watching me for a week. Either you're stalking me or you're interested in surfing. I'm going with the latter. So I thought you might like to give it a shot."

His jaw dropped for a second before he could recover. "Excuse me? I have not been watching you."

Gracie thought about this and nodded her head. "Yes, you have. From your second-floor window. I recognized you by the long-sleeve shirt. Unless you've got someone else living here."

"Don't be ridiculous. I came here for privacy." He emphasized the word *privacy*.

"Right. So it was you looking out the window."

"Maybe I was staring at the ocean."

"Maybe you were," Gracie conceded, struggling to hold back a smirk. The man was as tightly wound as a yo-yo. "Wouldn't you like to get out in the water? Ride some waves, feel the earth move?"

"I don't surf. Besides, it's freezing. I can't believe that every day you …" He trailed off as he realized that he had officially incriminated himself.

Gracie decided to live up to her name and be gracious in victory and not point that out. "That's what the wet suit is for. You'd be surprised. It keeps you really warm. The ocean itself isn't that cold yet. Maybe sixty-eight degrees. It's the air you have to worry about. But I've got towels and blankets and…"

"I don't have a wet suit. Or a surfboard for that matter."

"I do." Gracie tilted her head toward the bottom of the steps. There was a duffel bag, an extra suit on top of it and two boards leaning up against the wood railing that lined the stairs. "The suit and the board were my dad's."

"He doesn't mind you lending them out to strangers?"

"Oh, he would if he were still alive. In fact, he might come back to haunt me still. His board was sacred to him. But you look like you could use a run on the ocean and I suppose he would be in favor of introducing anyone to the sport he loved."

For a moment he stared at her, then at the paraphernalia at the bottom of the steps. "I'm sorry for your loss. When did he…"

"A year ago," Gracie answered quickly. "Cancer." Because most people wanted to know.

"I'm sorry."

"Thanks. What do you say? Are you game?"

"No. I'm sorry if you mistook my…curiosity for interest," he said flatly.

"I took your curiosity for curiosity, which is why I thought you might be interested in giving it a try. It didn't always kill the cat."

Dean frowned. "Surfing?"

"Curiosity."

He smiled as he followed her train of thought. "No, and it seems it doesn't bother your dog, either."

"Curiosity?"

"Surfing."

"Rufus is a born water dog," Gracie elaborated, having no trouble keeping up.

"Where is he today?"

"He was napping. I don't like to disturb his rest. Besides, Eleanor gets sad when he leaves her to play, but I can't very well take her surfing."

"Eleanor?"

"My cat."

"Right," he groaned. "Because surfing would kill her."

Gracie smiled. "It probably would."

Dean nodded. "You're telling me that your cat gets sad when the dog leaves?"

"And vice versa. Those two are inseparable. Interesting that I found each of them at the pound. Not together. But both had been left by some vacationing family. Can you believe that? I brought Rufus home and introduced him to Eleanor and explained to both of them that they had the pound in common. Next morning, I found them cuddled up on the couch together and they've been inseparable ever since. Except for when Rufus goes for his walks or comes surfing with me. Naturally, Eleanor understands Rufus needs his space, but it still makes her sad."

"Naturally."

Typical, Dean thought silently. Flakes tended to be animal people. They also tended to have soft hearts for strays. That's when it occurred to him why someone like Gracie might encourage him to go surfing when it was clear he didn't want to.

"Look, Ice Cream Lady, I'm not sure what your point to all of this is, but I am not some stray in need of rescuing."

"Really, Mr. Bitterman—"

"Excuse me?"

"I meant Mr. Wright," Gracie quickly corrected. "I only thought you might like to try something new. You're here at the beach for at least the fall it seems. There are only a few weeks left for surfing. You should take advantage of it. Besides, it's fun."

Fun. There was that word again. It resonated in his head and struck a few wrong chords. Almost like his brain couldn't process it. Fun. It actually sounded good.

"I have to work."

"You can work tonight. There's nothing else to do on this island. I promise you."

"I need to work today and tonight. I live in the real world, okay," he snapped in reaction to his weakening resolve. Surfing always had been something he'd wanted to try.

Gracie turned her neck over each shoulder as if checking out the house behind her. "It all looks pretty real to me."

"Ha," Dean barked. "This is an island. A beach resort. This is where people come to play. This place is not reality."

"That's where you are wrong. There's nothing more real than the ocean."

She said it with a soft smile on her face. And there it was again. A knowing that implied she was in on the secret to life that few people would understand even if she told them.

It was a flake's smile. There were no secrets to life. Dean was almost sure of it.

"Well, I'm not going to badger you," Gracie conceded. "I thought you wanted to have a go, but obviously not. I'll leave you to your work."

Maybe it was because she seemed to be giving up on him. Or maybe it was the fact that he really did want to surf. Or maybe it was because he was truly tired of not having any fun. Ever.

"Wait," Dean called to her when she was at the bottom of the steps. "How do I get into that wet suit?"

CHAPTER FIVE

"IT'S FREEZING."

"It's not that cold."

"It's arctic."

Gracie sighed. The man barely had his toe in the water and already he was complaining. "You'll get used to it."

"Before or after I lose my toes to frostbite?"

"Definitely before. But if it's after, you won't feel the cold anymore."

He shot her a look and she smiled back at him innocently. "Come on. Trust me. It will be better once you get in."

Leading by example, Gracie waded into the water with the surfboard under her arm. The board was hooked to a Velcro cuff that wrapped around her ankle, but she had plenty of line to play with. It was low tide so she had to walk pretty far out before the level of the water even hit her knees.

"Okay, once you're waist high you can get on your board, belly down and just paddle."

She twisted around on the board after issuing her directions, only to see that he wasn't nearly as close as she thought. He was still about shin high and looking skeptical, with the board tucked under his arm.

He did, however, fill out that wet suit nicely. He was about the same height as her father, but the suit seemed tight around the shoulders and chest, which led her to conclude the obvious…he had broad shoulders and a nice chest.

Instantly Gracie shut those thoughts down. There was no point in allowing herself to be sexually attracted to someone she had no interest in getting involved with. The point of inviting him surfing was merely to get him to stop watching her from his window, which was mildly creepy if taken at face value.

And of course there was her ingrained instinct to reach out to those who needed help: animal or man. Ironic, too, because she knew without a doubt that if anyone would have asked Dean if he needed help, his answer would have been no.

But he did need it. He'd shut himself up in that house and had become an island hermit. Maybe he said he was here for the quiet so he could work, but Gracie believed he was here to escape.

There was no better escape than the ocean.

"Oh my God, it's cold! Why did I let you talk me into this?"

"I'm very convincing."

"Convincing! More like manipulative." He followed her instructions and laid his belly flat on the board while he paddled to where she was. "The ocean is as real as it gets," he mimicked in a high falsetto voice.

Gracie laughed. "You'll see. Sit up with your legs on either side and your butt just about in the center of the board."

He did as told and they found themselves sitting on

their respective boards, bobbing in the water as small waves formed underneath them. "Now look out there. What do you see?"

"Water."

"Look closer."

Dean squinted his eyes. "I don't know. Maybe there's a motorboat out there."

Gracie shook her head. "You're not looking hard enough."

"Maybe if you gave me a hint."

Gracie turned her head in the direction she had told him to look and watched the ocean move and sway before her eyes. The cloudless blue sky arched over her head like a pretty umbrella until it finally stopped on the horizon. Then the darker more turbulent ocean began and that line—that end-of-the-earth line—was to her the most perfect sight on the planet. She bobbed in the water in a rhythm that was unique to the earth. She could hear the sound of the seagulls diving for fish and calling to one another from the rock jetty. Beneath her feet she imagined scores of tiny fish contemplating whether or not to nibble on her toe while crabs and lobsters shuffled along the sandy bottom ready to pinch any intruders who got in their way.

The ocean. Her ocean. It was magnificent.

Finally, she said, "I can't tell you. If you don't see it and feel it. I can't tell you." A shame, too. She thought it might help him put things in perspective. Make whatever it was he was running from seem not as scary anymore. Anytime she thought her problems were insurmountable or her sorrow was too much to handle, she could always come to the ocean. Once in it, she was reminded that she was a little speck in the big picture of things. Any problems she had seemed to shrink before her eyes.

Dean was carrying a burden. She'd been hoping maybe she could help him shrink it or, at least, give him the opportunity to try.

"Are you kidding me?"

His sharp tone had her turning back to face him but only partially. As a rule, she never completely turned her back on the ocean.

"What?"

"Tell me you didn't bring me out here for some mystical gibberish about the ocean. I'm here to learn how to surf not to find my chi."

"Surfing is mystical. You don't find chi. And I was just trying to show you—"

"Something tangible, right. Something I could actually see?"

"Absolutely," Gracie said, biting her lower lip. She pointed out to nowhere and said, "See that little pointy thing just on the surface, right there at about six o'clock? It's a fin."

Instantly he sat up straighter. "A what?"

Gracie tried not to laugh as he craned his neck forward trying to find an imaginary fin. "You know…Daa dun. Daaa dun. Da dun, da dun."

"Holy shit, stop that."

Ocean newcomers. It got them every time. "Relax. It was probably just a porpoise and besides, it's miles away. Now for your lesson. You're not ready to stand on the board so don't even try. What you want to get used to is the feeling of catching a wave. Basically, you'll use the board as a boogie-board until you get comfortable with that."

She had to give him credit. He was a lousy surfer, but he was a pretty good sport. His first wave he missed. His second wave he didn't even see until it crashed over his head. Ten waves later and he was still staring out to the horizon looking for a shark that wasn't there. But by wave fourteen she had gotten him to paddle for it. Only to miss it.

By wave twenty he had finally caught it but, in his excitement, he paddled so hard he paddled himself right off the surfboard. When she noticed that his lips were turning blue and her own fingertips were shriveled ice prunes, she called an end to their first lesson.

Dragging herself up the beach, Gracie headed toward their mini-camp of blankets on the sand. She turned around, walking backward as she watched him safely reach the soft sand as well. "You're going to want to take a hot shower when you get back to your place. A long one. It will help raise the body temperature."

"No problem. Is three hours too long?"

Tossing him a dry towel, she took another for herself and pulled it along her cornrows.

"Hey, Gracie!"

Gracie turned around at the sound of her name and saw Rick and Dottie walking down the beach hand in hand. She could see Dottie pointing to Dean behind her then turning to Rick to explain who he was. Not the subtlest move in the whole world. Then she broke away from Rick and came jogging up to where they had made camp.

"How was the surfing?" she asked Gracie as she eagerly stared at Dean.

"Okay."

"Cold," Dean answered at the same time.

"Dean," Gracie began, "you remember Dottie. She owns the Good Morning. And this is her husband Rick. He owns Rick's Place."

Rick, who never ran anywhere he could get to by walking, strolled toward them and raised his hand in greeting. "Hey."

"Rick's is one of the few bars on the island that stays open year-round."

"I'll have to check it out," Dean murmured.

"Oh absolutely," Dottie chimed in. "And we also serve food. Like hamburgers and fries and that kind of thing. Bar food. I mean good food. It's just not like cuisine or anything. As a matter of fact, you could come tonight. Gracie usually eats with us on Thursdays and we hang out there and have a few beers after. You could come and the four of us could have dinner and—"

"Sorry." He cut her off quickly. "I really need to work tonight. Thanks for the lesson. I'll see you around sometime."

With that he handed her back the board, slung the towel he'd brought with him over his shoulder and started back up the beach to his glass house. He practically sprinted.

"I don't care if he is the only man on the island. He's rude." Dottie glared at Dean's back and Gracie smiled as her friend stomped her bare foot into the sand on her behalf.

"I think he prefers his privacy," Gracie suggested.

"All I did was invite him for dinner."

"Maybe it was the bar food that did it," Rick said. "He looks like a cuisine guy to me."

"Huh. Well if he's such a snob that he can't enjoy a burger, then Gracie won't want anything to do with him. Right, Gracie?"

Gracie could see that her friend was disappointed for her, but when she looked at Rick his expression matched her thoughts.

"Gracie wouldn't have had anything to do with him anyway. He's a mainlander. Down to his toes. And if he's here for the winter then he's a mainlander escapee."

"He's definitely a mainlander," Gracie repeated without inflection hoping to conceal the disappointment that she felt. "He couldn't even see the ocean."

"When it's right in front of his face," Rick finished. "Fool. Figures you had to try and show it to him."

Dottie glanced at her husband then at her friend. "You know I've been on this island for two years, and there are times I still can't understand what you two are saying."

"Give it a few more years, hon. You'll be talking ocean like a pro." Rick wrapped his arm around his wife and pulled her close until she tumbled into him, smiling.

Dottie too had once been a mainlander looking for escape. Escape from the pressures of her money, her family and all the expectations that went along with it. However, she had managed to adopt island life so quickly that it was clear she was going to be one of the few exceptions. A mainlander convert. They were rare, but they did happen. Two years and she was as happy as the day she arrived. Maybe even happier. So happy she practically glowed.

"Oh my gosh! You're pregnant!" Gracie announced.

Clearly startled, Dottie blinked. Then she blushed. "How did you know? I'm only two months along. We were going to wait another month before we told anyone."

"It was right in front of my face," Gracie said. "I just needed to see it."

"Oh no. Now that you said it…"

"Dottie needs to puke," Rick explained. "You want me to hold your hair?"

"No, I prefer my dignity." She quickly scurried off behind the dunes and a minute later the horrid sounds of retching could be heard.

"You know another reason I didn't want to tell you was because…" Rick shrugged in an attempt to find the right words. "I know your history. I thought it might weird you out a little."

Rick was referring to Gracie's mother, another mainlander escapee who tried to convert, only to have a daughter and then decide she couldn't do it.

"Dottie's not my mother."

"Amen to that. I want you to be happy for us."

"I am. I'm thrilled. Nothing my mother did would ever change that."

He needed to hear that. "Good. Okay, dignity or not, I better go help her."

"Give her a kiss for me," Gracie said as she gathered up her things. "You know, after she brushes her teeth."

"Will do."

Gracie walked along the beach for a while, leaving her boards planted in the sand. She thought about how exciting it would be to have a new baby on the island, and wondered if when Dottie had it, she would be as happy then as she was now.

Her father had convinced her mother to have a baby, thinking that would help her adapt more to the island. He'd told Gracie that, during her mother's first winter, she'd become depressed but after she found out she was expecting it seemed to change everything. She'd been happy.

But only for a while.

The winters continued to come, the isolation continued to wear on her mother, and eventually she couldn't take living on the island anymore.

Or she couldn't take Gracie anymore.

It was a thought that had always dogged Gracie growing up. Maybe she had been just too much to handle. Her mother simply hadn't found a way to love her, so she'd left her.

Shrugging off the old memory, Gracie headed back to where she'd left her boards and tucked each one under her arms as she hiked her way over the dunes back to her place. Instead of thinking about the bad, she tried to remember that it was good news that Dottie was pregnant. And that today had been fun. But if she had to guess, that was likely the last surfing lesson she was going to be giving Dean.

She doubted he would even watch her anymore.

A shame, really. For all his ineptitude, she bet he'd had fun.

CHAPTER SIX

"WHAT IS IT?"

Elis plunked down his wood statue on the counter by the cash register and seemed highly offended.

"You can't tell what this is?"

Gracie studied the squat wood figure with indentations and crazy painting around the top of it and shrugged.

"It's a tiki. Hello, Brady Bunch goes to Hawaii? Cursed tiki?"

Gracie struggled to place the reference. "Were we even born when that show was on?"

"Oh, shut up. That's what reruns are for. Anyway, it's a model of a Hawaiian totem pole."

"Will anyone outside of Hawaii know that?"

"Of course, silly. Again Brady Bunch. Anyway, I plan to make a hundred of them this winter to sell next summer. I've already got my advertising strategy worked out. *Take a tiki*. You know, then I can add ideas like *Take a tiki to work. Take a tiki to school. Take a tiki to college.*"

"Why would anyone want to take a tiki to college?"

Elis huffed. "Because it's cool. I don't ever rain on your new ice cream topping parade, now do I?

Remember when everyone said that pretzel crumbs as a topping would never fly and what did I say?"

"You said it was my business and I should go with my instincts," Gracie quoted.

"Exactly. And how did that work out?"

"Pretzel crumbs have become surprisingly popular with certain flavors, like butter pecan. Okay. I'm on board. Take a tiki. I love it."

"I knew you would love it. Speaking of love, any further update on our mystery nonfiction-writing island man?"

"Nothing new to report. One surfing lesson and that was it."

"Hmm…surfing. Not exactly a gay thing, but I can't confirm straightness. I mean the phrase 'waxing your board' occurs frequently in the sport, which can have all kinds of connotations."

"You've got sex on the brain."

"How could I not? There is a mystery man on the island. Dottie is going to spit out a baby—"

"You know about the baby?"

Elis shrugged. "She figured, since you already knew, there was no point in keeping it a secret. But can I say she didn't plan very well. The baby is due in April, which means she's going to have a newborn on her hip for the summer crush."

"Life shouldn't revolve around tourism."

"Really? Mine does."

There was a moment of silence and Gracie could feel him studying her. "What?"

"I just want to make sure you're okay with all of this. Rick told me about your mother."

"I'm fine. What happened to me isn't going to happen to Rick and Dottie. And I can't wait to get my hands on a baby. So soft and sweet."

"So loud. With diapers filled with you don't want to know what."

"You'll change once he or she is here."

"I'll take your word for it." His attention drifted off and Gracie could see him checking out the case of ice cream tubs under his nose.

"Would you like some?"

"You know I can't. My waist." Elis's waist was probably smaller than Gracie's, but there was no point in arguing.

"I've got a double-churned half-the-fat chocolate that just came in. It's sinful."

"You bitch," he cursed with a smile on his lips. "All right, but half a small cup."

Gracie smiled and had moved to get his order when she heard the bell over the door chime. She glanced up with a ready smile and felt a punch to her gut when she saw Dean.

Acting in accordance with her prediction, he'd never sought her out for another surfing lesson. He had, in fact, shipped her father's wet suit back to her by UPS. Charlie, the island delivery guy, had had a hard time hiding his confusion when he'd dropped off the package. A package he'd just picked up from two blocks away.

The weather turned colder not too soon after that, which ended her surfing days anyway so there was no tempting him even if he still had been watching.

He also hadn't come in for ice cream. Not a good sign. A man with a sweet tooth and he'd managed to avoid her for weeks. Poor guy. He must be making do with Ben & Jerry's. Gracie smiled at the idea—he was so concerned she was out to snare him that he was making do with retail.

Gracie decided to take pity on him. "Well, hello. Welcome back."

Cautiously, he moved into the tiny parlor. His eyes strayed toward Elis, who was clearly giving him the once-over. And the once-over again.

"Please tell me you're gay, Mystery Man," Elis begged.

Dean didn't flinch but shook his head. "Sorry."

"Figures. I'm going home to work wood and make tikis." He leaned over the counter and gave Gracie a loud smooch and turned to leave. "Thanks for the ice cream." He took his half of a small to-go.

"Wait. Your tiki." Gracie held up the wood statue, eager to get the fearsome face out of her store.

"You can keep that one. It's part of my advertising scheme. I want to build suspense for the upcoming line this summer."

He left and Gracie lowered the tiki to the counter with a resounding thunk. The thing was as heavy as it was ugly. "Great."

"What is it?" Dean asked.

"A tiki. You want to take a tiki?"

He studied the sculpture and frowned. "No."

"That's what I thought," Gracie sighed. "So what brings you here? I figured you had conquered your sweet tooth."

Dean shoved his hands into his pockets and lowered his head. "I uh…wanted to try some of the other places on the island."

Other ice cream places on the island. It was almost November. The only place left open along with the Sea Breeze was…"Oh. You went to the Clown-o-rama."

"They sang at me," he stated with disgust. "They brought me what I asked for, but then the clowns sang this song right in front of me and everyone in the place stopped and stared. It was awful. I wanted ice cream and they sang at me. Why did they do that?"

Gracie considered pointing out that singing at someone wasn't quite the torture Dean was making it out to be. The Clown-o-rama was a hot spot for families in the summer and somewhat of a legend on Long Beach Island. Gracie didn't mind the competition because she figured they served two different interests. People went to the Clown for the show. But the day-in and day-out ice cream needs of the island were served by the Sea Breeze.

"I'm sorry you had to experience that," she said solemnly.

"Anyway, I figured I was being an ass for staying away. I left sort of abruptly that day on the beach."

"Yup."

He glanced up at her, a deep frown on his face. "I meant to tell you that I had…fun."

And because he said it as if it was a rarity, her heart ached for him. "I'm glad."

"I don't have fun very often. My work has basically been my life."

"Writing books?"

"Writing. Not books always. I was a reporter for the *Washington Post*."

"Oh."

"You read the *Post*?"

"No," she admitted. "I read *The Beachcomber*. But I've heard of the *Post*. Very prestigious."

He studied her for a minute and Gracie didn't have a clue what he was thinking. Probably, he'd never met anyone who read *The Beachcomber*. It did have a relatively small circulation.

"Anyway, I wanted to apologize for leaving and for not thanking you. Like I said, I felt like an ass. Then I felt like more of an ass when I realized I still had the suit on. I shipped it two blocks and that really made me feel like an ass…"

"Charlie got a kick out of it."

"Charlie?"

"The UPS guy. He recognized the address when he picked it up and just walked it over to me. Excellent service."

"Oh. I think I need to explain. Your friend started talking about dinner and double dating and it freaked me out."

Gracie nodded. She figured it was coming. The reason for the transformation from Dean Wright, reporter, to Mr. Bitterman, recluse. Still behind the counter, she reached for a small foam cup, and then decided this called for a large.

"You have to know Dottie sees two single people walking down the street and starts to imagine them bumping into each other only to fall madly in love. She's a romantic." Gracie found the scooper on the counter behind her and dipped it into a pitcher of hot water for a minute before turning back to the ice cream case.

"Is that how she met her husband? Bumped into him."

"Uh, no. She chased him down like a dog. Rick wanted nothing to do with a mainlander escapee. Chocolate Peanut Butter or Deep Chocolate Explosion?"

"Better give me the Explosion. What's a mainlander escapee?"

With a strength born of habit and hard work, Gracie used the scooper to pull forward two large round balls of ice cream. "A mainlander escapee is someone who decides they're going to leave it all behind and come to the island. It may only be a mile over the causeway that separates us from the mainland, but for whatever reason there is a certain finality to it once you cross it. Most escapees stay for a while, realize they can't handle the quiet and go back. Rick figured Dottie would be one of those people. But she proved him wrong and then she…"

"Chased him down like a dog," Dean finished.

"It was much more romantic to see it than it is to tell it. And now they're going to have a baby. Sprinkles?"

"Please. Tell her I said congratulations." He paused. "Is that what you think I am? An escapee?"

"Partly. You're obviously here to get away, but unlike most M.E.s you're not trying to convince everyone you are here to stay. You plan to leave."

"Right before the summer crush."

"And there you have it." Gracie dripped hot fudge over the concoction she'd assembled and then topped it off with a healthy spray of real whipped cream. Finishing it off with two cherries, she turned back to him and smiled.

"Have what?" he asked, reaching for a spoon in the holder next to the register.

"The reason you don't have to worry about me

chasing you down like a dog. I don't date mainlanders, mainlander escapees or tourists. Not even casually."

"That doesn't give you a lot of choices." Dean looked at her hard and she thought she spotted what might have been disappointment in his expression, but it was quickly gone.

"No, it doesn't. But it's the only choice I have."

"How about you join me?" He nodded his head toward one of the tables and Gracie shrugged with acceptance.

Just because she wasn't going to date him didn't mean they couldn't have a civil conversion over ice cream. After all, she had yet to hear the whole story of his transformation and the small-town meddlesome side to her was convinced he needed to tell it to someone.

Grabbing her own sundae, identical to his, she made her way to the table and sat down across from him.

"This is amazing."

"With the Explosion you don't want to mess with a lot of complicated toppings. Chocolate sprinkles and hot fudge is as far as I go."

Dean smiled around another spoonful. "A sundae maker with integrity. You're a rare breed."

"I aim to satisfy."

"Then we're good? I can start getting my ice cream from now on without the clown entertainment?"

"We were never bad. I hate to be the one to put a pin in your ego, but what makes you think I was ever interested in you in the first place?" She was, but only in a superficial way. The man was hot. Hot enough for Elis to be interested, which made him really very hot.

"You asked me to surf," he reminded her, pointing his plastic spoon at her in an accusatory fashion.

"I asked you to surf because you looked like a man who needed to surf."

Dean shook his head. "More of the woo-woo stuff. One more reason why, if I was ever going to date again, which I'm not, it wouldn't be you."

Gracie smothered the kernel of hurt at his rejection with ice cream and whipped cream. "You said you had fun."

"I did, but I didn't find any answers in the mystical, all-powerful ocean."

"I should have let the shark get you," she muttered under her breath.

"What was that?" he asked suspiciously. "It doesn't matter. As long as you make it clear to your friend Dottie that we're not dating and as long as you don't think you can cure with me sea water, then maybe…"

"Maybe what?"

He paused for a minute as he scraped the remnants of melted Explosion from the bottom of his cup. "I don't know. Maybe we can do it again."

Gracie leaned back in her chair with a casual smile on her face. "It's too cold for surfing now. In fact, winter feels like it might be coming on early. I'm going to need to take the rows out soon so I can keep my head warm." She pointed to the tight braids that ran along her scalp and tumbled about her shoulders.

For a moment he studied her, no doubt wondering what she looked like with real hair. She wondered if the image was a pretty one. "I didn't mean surfing exactly. More like hanging out."

"You want to hang out? With me?"

"After three months in a cabin in the mountains and two months in a house on the beach, I'm getting a little…"

"Stir-crazy?"

"Restless," he modified.

"You seriously don't talk to anyone?"

As if to illustrate the point, Dean's cell phone rang. Gracie watched him pull it out of his pocket to glance at the caller ID display. He didn't answer it and eventually the ringing stopped.

"I guess not," Gracie said, answering her own question.

"It's only ever one of my exes. And I don't want to talk to either of them."

"Multiple exes. No wonder you're so bitter."

"One ex-wife. The other is my ex-editor at the paper. Only one of them wants me back."

Gracie didn't need to guess which one that was. His face said everything. "Obviously you don't want the ex-editor back, but what about her? Do you want her back?"

"No," he answered. Firmly, clearly, with no hesitation or extra speed to indicate he was trying to convince himself.

"Why does she keep calling then?"

"She wants to apologize," he said grimly.

"Oh."

"She cheated on me. With a senator. I was investigating the senator for possible corruption only to discover that my wife, a prominent lobbyist, was sleeping with the senator to gain his vote on a bill she needed to pass. It was ugly. Someone else got the story and I became a character in an old-fashioned Washington, D.C., sex scandal. Instead of reporting the news, I *was* the news. And my editor, my ex-editor, he was just pissed that I hadn't gotten the scoop. It was awful and I can't forgive her."

"You were more upset about the story being written than you were that your wife cheated on you?"

"I guess that sums up the state of my marriage," Dean concluded. "Elena was a social and political climber. Looking back on our relationship, I was nothing more than a step for her. And she was nothing more than an attractive woman on my arm."

"That's sad."

"That's reality for a lot of people. Anyway, I had to get out of that town and more than that, I just wanted to get away from the stink of people."

Gracie lifted her hand to her nose and sniffed. "I think I smell okay."

Dean smiled. "You smell better than okay. You smell like ice cream." He stood up then and pulled a five-dollar bill from his pocket and dropped it on the table. "You got me. I'm addicted."

"Another successful tale of an ice cream pusher and an addict." Gracie beamed.

"Can I stop by sometime? You're easy to talk to."

"Even if you do think I'm a flake."

"Exactly."

Gracie figured she had to give him points for honesty. She wondered if she was really all that interested in being some kind of sounding board for him. But winter was fast approaching, and on a practically empty island it required skill to come up with things to entertain a person.

As stuffy as he was, he still was more exciting than anyone else she knew on the island.

"I'm here every day," Gracie told him. "And now that it's almost November, I can close up at will. I like to think I have a sixth sense for knowing if I'll be getting any business or not."

"You're telling me you can sense when a customer might come?"

She chuckled at the mild level of disgust in his tone. "What? You think that's a little too…woo-woo?"

"I'm leaving."

"But I was just about to get out my tarot cards!" she called after him even as the door closed behind him. Gracie pocketed the five and tossed away the trash. She considered why she had agreed to hang out with a main-lander escapee who thought she was one card shy of a full deck. Possibly two.

She was missing her father. That was it. She was missing her dad. And while she loved her friends, now that Dottie and Rick had a baby on the way, she wanted to make sure they had plenty of time to themselves. It would be their last days as just a couple. Elis would be busy with his tikis all winter. He was a great gal-pal, but sometimes it was nice to mingle with the other side. So Dean would be just another distraction to pass the time. A mainlander escapee that she could hang out with until he left.

The one thing she would not do is fall for him.

CHAPTER SEVEN

Independence Day...one year ago

DEAN LEANED BACK in his leather chair to stretch out the kinks an hour of writing did to his back. He stood and walked around the study of his Aspen condo and stared out at the lush mountain scenery before him. Aspen trees, evergreen firs. Lush and green and mysterious with dark crevices hidden behind bushes and clusters of trees.

It didn't hold a candle to the ocean.

A beep sounded on his computer and the sound triggered an instantly happy reaction. He clicked on the IM button and smiled at Gracie's moniker that she'd chosen just for him.

Mysticaloceangirl—Hey.

"Hey," Dean said aloud to the empty room. WrightIII wrote back the same sentiment.

He checked the time on the computer. It was almost ten at night, which meant it was later back in New Jersey.

WrightIII—Can't sleep?

Mysticaloceangirl—Nope. Too wired. Crazy busy weekend.

That's right. It was the Fourth of July. Dean saw the flyers downtown about a fireworks display, but he hadn't bothered to check it out. He told himself it was because he was too busy, but the truth was he had no interest in going alone.

Now if Gracie had been here…

He tried to squash the thought, but he couldn't deny the veracity of the sentiment. If she'd been here she would have insisted that they go. She would have oohed and aahed with the best of them, and they probably would have had fun.

He missed having fun. No, he missed having fun with Gracie.

They had done so well through the winter just hanging out. They had become friends and the experience was truly unique for him. There was no man-woman game-playing; no point in trying to impress each other. They were simply themselves when they hung out. She dragged him along to the assisted-living home to deliver ice cream and that was fun. He made her go with him to Manhattan when he had to meet up with his editor and that was fun.

He drove her to the hospital the night Dottie had Katie and even that was fun. Rick passed out cigars. Elis passed out when he saw the baby the first time. It was crazy and joyous *and fun*.

Dean stared at the monitor on his screen. It was his turn to reply, but suddenly he wanted more than words on a screen. They had started by exchanging e-mails when he first arrived in Colorado. Then he suggested the instant messaging as a way to talk more freely. Neither of them had considered calling the other, because calling on the phone, talking, implied a certain intimacy that went beyond buddies.

Only now he didn't care. He wanted to hear her voice. He wanted to know how the weekend had gone and how business was doing and how Katie was growing. He wanted to know if Elis was selling his tikis.

Not stopping to think about it, Dean pulled out his cell phone and punched out the number to Gracie's apartment.

It rang a few times before she picked up the phone. "Hello?"

"Hey."

"Hi."

"I've been writing all day and I couldn't get my fingers to move anymore. I figured I would call." It sounded like a logical explanation, he decided. "I didn't mean to disturb you. So it was crazy this weekend."

"Crazier than I ever remember. Of course I say that every year. It's just when you've seen this place in the winter you can't imagine how many people can fit on it in the summer. The weekend was perfect. Not too humid, sun was out, water was great. Everybody and their mother from Pennsylvania, New York and New Jersey were here."

"No one from Delaware?"

"They tend to go south," she chuckled. "But lots of tourists means lots of money. So I can't complain."

"Any sundae-topping rule breakers?"

"Several. But after a quick explanation of my reasons they all readily agreed to my recommendations."

"Of course they did," Dean said smiling. "And Katie?"

"Growing like a weed. Rick stays home with her during the day and then Dottie takes her at night. Rick's mother is enamored. First grandchild and all. So they have a babysitter whenever they need one. And Elis has actually held her. Twice."

"Brave man."

"You've never seen anyone so afraid of holding a baby with a dirty diaper in your life. It's not like we would ask him to change it."

Dean rolled his neck a few times and felt the tension of the day, of the past few months really, drift away. He could almost picture himself back there, in the midst of the normal chaos and the thought of it made him feel lighter.

"I got your gift," he blurted out.

"Good. Do you like it?"

Dean leaned over his desk and picked up the mayonnaise jar filled with the fine white sand. "I do. I'm sending you something in the mail. Charlie should be bringing it by any day. I hope you like it. It's silly but…I saw it and thought of you."

"I'm sure I'll like it."

"I should let you go. It's late. Your days don't get any easier until Labor Day."

"You're right. What about you? Is the book going along well?"

"Very well. I should be done shortly."

"And the exes. Still bothering you?"

They were still phoning him, but Dean had to admit that they weren't bothering him as much. He felt as if he was getting farther and farther away from them with each day and the farther he got the less anger he felt toward either of them for betraying him.

It was good, he decided. He was finally healing. That didn't mean he wanted to go back to Washington, but it could mean that he was ready to come out of seclusion.

"Not so much," he finally said. "No."

There was a pause and then he heard her yawn. "I guess I should go."

"Sleep tight. Sweet dreams." He heard the husky intimacy in his voice and winced. He didn't want to go there. Not with her. He was having too much fun as friends. But the thought of her lying in her bed in probably nothing more than a T-shirt and some panties made his blood heat. He twisted in his chair trying to ease the pressure of his kakis on his erection.

"You too."

He disconnected the phone and thought about how nice it had been to actually talk with her. Their phone rule was stupid, he concluded. Next time if he wanted to talk to her he would just call.

He thought about the gift on its way to her and wondered if she would like it. Then he thought about the fact that the summer was about halfway over and what he was going to do come Labor Day.

Going back could be stupid. Going back could lead to things he wasn't ready for.

But going back was his only option.

Labor Day...

"YOU FELL FOR HIM, didn't you?"

Gracie slowly lowered her mug of beer to the table. "Who are you talking about?"

Elis made a ridiculous face. "Pul-leeze, do not insult my intelligence. You've been checking the door every minute on the minute. Considering that this is a private party and that the sign on the door says Closed, one must conclude that you're waiting for someone in particular."

"You're a regular Sherlock Holmes," Gracie drawled.

"I'm not finished. Rick is behind the bar, Dottie is in the bathroom with the baby—"

"And Colonel Mustard is in the drawing room with a lead pipe."

"My point being that everyone I know who knows about our Labor Day party is here. Which means you must be waiting for someone else who knows about the party. Someone you told during your long and pathetically platonic winter together."

"It completely irks you that I've made a new friend," Gracie said, shaking her finger at him. "You're jealous."

"I'm not jealous, I'm outraged. You spent all winter with him and you didn't have sex. If you weren't going to at least get some action you could have let me attempt to turn him to my side."

Gracie scowled at him. "What is so hard to understand? He didn't want to be involved with me. I didn't want to be involved with him. At least not romantically. So we hung out together as friends."

"Are we talking about Dean?" Dottie asked, as she rejoined the table with a freshly diapered, soundly sleeping baby snuggled against her chest. She placed Katie in her bouncy chair and smiled as the baby quietly cooed then drifted back into a deep sleep.

"Do you think he'll come back this year?"

"Yes, Gracie. Tell us. Do we know if Mr. Wright is coming back?" Elis asked with the tone of someone who already knew the answer.

Gracie shrugged, pushed her beer mug back and forth between her hands in an effort to be as casual as possible. "I think in his last e-mail he might have said something to lead me to believe he was coming back. I'm not exactly sure when or anything, just that he might possibly at some point…"

"Oh, for heaven's sake," Elis snapped. "You've been e-mailing him and talking to him all summer, admit it. You know he's coming back. You told him about our Labor Day party and that is why you've been staring at the door."

Dottie gasped. "Is that true? Is he coming here tonight?"

"Possibly," Gracie muttered.

"I knew it!" Dottie shouted. "You do like him. All that friend stuff was just to throw me off."

"It was not to throw you off. We are friends. That's all it was last winter and if he comes back—which he may or may not do—then that's all it will be again. I'm not falling for a mainlander." To make her point she took a large sip of beer, but she misjudged the distance to her mouth and ended up dumping some down the front of her T-shirt.

"Just friends," Elis repeated suspiciously.

"Just friends," she stated adamantly, even though

her hands shook a little as she cleaned up her shirt with a napkin.

"Hey, will you two leave her alone." Rick joined the group. He turned a chair around and sat on it backward, resting his arm on the back while he casually dangled a beer bottle between his fingers. "She's right about staying away from this guy. Mainlanders are trouble."

Dottie reached out to swat her husband's shoulder. "Do I constantly have to remind you that *I* was a mainlander? If you were as stubborn as Gracie is about not falling for my type then we never would have gotten together. We would never have had Katie."

"I was as stubborn as Gracie. You just happened to be more stubborn. And the bottom line is I got lucky with you. For every ten islanders that fall for mainlanders, at least nine will end up with broken hearts. Gracie should stick to her own."

Elis rolled his eyes. "The only single men left on this island are widowers over seventy and me. Do you want her trapped in a relationship where she is guaranteed never to get laid? Wait a minute, that's what you had all winter, wasn't it?"

Elis smiled at his own joke and Gracie wanted to throttle him. "What I had this winter was a nice platonic friendship."

In response to that, Elis mocked sticking his fingers down his throat.

"I guess that sounds…nice," Dottie said, clearly trying to be supportive.

"Just keep it that way and no one will get hurt," Rick told her.

"But you do think he might be coming tonight?"

Dottie turned and looked at the door. "Because I was going to take Katie home, but I'll wait if there are going to be fireworks."

"There will be no fireworks. However, in my last e-mail, I did mention that I would be here," Gracie said. "But that doesn't mean anything."

"Right. And how often did you e-mail him?" Elis wondered. "Just out of curiosity."

"I don't know. Once a week, maybe. Or maybe a little more than that, but not daily. I don't think." Gracie grimaced. If she were honest with herself it had definitely been daily e-mails. But there was nothing wrong with that. Nothing romantic about an e-mail. The phone calls, the ones late at night that ended with the two of them wishing the other sweet dreams in soft voices. That was something else entirely.

"And Charlie said you were doing an unusual amount of shipping this summer to a place in....Colorado." Elis dropped the bombshell gleefully. He was a man who truly loved his gossip.

"Charlie shouldn't be talking about my packages," Gracie admonished. Then she shrugged. Again, there hadn't been anything romantic about the packages. A how-to DVD on surfing. The mayonnaise jar filled with beach sand. A shipment of frozen Chocolate Explosion. That had been a challenge. Still, nothing that screamed romantic interest. It's not like she had sent him flowers.

His packages to her were equally benign. A few preview chapters of his book for her to read. A winter hat that he picked up for her in Aspen. He'd complained all winter that her cornrows would leave her head exposed to the elements and that she needed a hat. Usually she undid the rows once it got cold, but it got to be such a thing with him that she'd left them in for fun.

A snow globe. That was the present he'd sent her the Fourth of July. The one he'd bought thinking about her.

She had once told him that as an islander she rarely saw snow. Most of it turned to wet rain by the time it hit the sand. She said it was the only thing she missed from the mainland.

So he had sent her a snow globe.

Gracie looked around at her friends and took their teasing in stride. But as she defended the packages she had sent to him, and kept quiet on everything he had sent to her, and told herself that none of it meant anything…she still turned and looked at the door every other second.

Maybe it would be better if he didn't come back. Maybe she had gone a little further than she intended to go. Having a pleasant evening out with an intelligent and attractive man her own age had been a novelty. She knew he'd needed the distraction and she believed, because of the situation, she would be able to keep her distance.

And she had to an extent. The weekend before Memorial Day he'd come to say goodbye. She'd smiled easily and told him to have a nice trip back into the woods. Then the summer crush came, and for days she didn't think about how he was doing. Okay, sure she thought about him when she sent the gifts. And of course she thought about him when she read his e-mails, but for the most part he'd lifted out of her life as easily as he'd dropped in to it and that was a sure sign that she hadn't lost her heart to him.

She turned to check the door again.

"It's too late now," Rick told her. "It's almost one in the morning. And a good thing too. I might have had to run him off."

"Stop," Dottie warned. "You sound like her father. Just because her mother left doesn't mean that everyone…oh I'm sorry, Gracie. I didn't mean that."

"It's okay."

"It's not okay. Especially now. When I think about how I feel about Katie…oh darn. I did it again."

Gracie hadn't been able to hide her wince. It had been harder lately to think about her mother. Seeing how well Dottie was thriving in her new home, with her new daughter, it seemed to make less and less sense to Gracie how her mother could have left.

Her father had given her all sorts of reasons. The island was too isolated, too quiet; the winters were too cold and damp. There was a disconnection that happened to the people who lived here year-round that some embraced while others grew steadily nervous about it. As if they feared they might be lost to the rest of humanity.

Her mother had started out wanting that separation from the rest of the world as a mainlander escapee, but at some point it had changed. She had grown sad and lonely and not even a happy toddler had been able to make her happy.

Maybe that was what hurt most of all. Gracie hadn't been able to make her happy enough to stay, and her mother hadn't loved her enough to want to take her with her when she left.

Over the years there had been a few letters from her

mother that tried to offer an explanation. She spoke of depression and how it could control a person and how much better she was doing back in Chicago, where her family was from. There were a few birthday cards that were signed "Love Mom." But there hadn't been anything serious enough to bring her mother back to the island she'd grown to hate so much.

Not even when she lost her dad. Her mom had sent a condolence card, but she hadn't come. Gracie tried to understand why that made sense, too. Being on the island again might trigger another bout of depression. Seeing the daughter she abandoned would be too painful for her.

Eventually, Gracie decided she didn't care. Her father had been her family and he'd died. From that moment forward, the moment that she had tossed her mother's card into the trash, Gracie had known that she was alone.

"You can't fall for this guy." Without her realizing it, Rick had sat down, and placed another beer in front of her. "I don't care what he looks like."

Dottie sighed. "Really? Not that he's as handsome as you, but he definitely has something. A little ruggedness. A lot of smarts. Some stiffness and a dash of..."

"Dottie, he's a man not a recipe," Elis chimed in. "And you forgot his really tight buns."

"Well, either way it doesn't matter," Gracie announced. "He's obviously not coming. Not that I thought he would. If I see him again this winter, I see him. If I don't, I don't. Because as Rick so elegantly warned me, I cannot fall for this guy. Because as Dottie so succinctly reminded me, my mother was a runner and I don't want to have to suffer what my father did. There. Is everyone happy?"

Knock. Knock. Knock.

The pounding on the door got everyone's attention. All heads turned toward it, but no one actually got up to answer it.

Knock. Knock. Knock.

"You don't think…" Dottie's voice trailed off.

"I do indeed," Elis stated. "Go open that door."

"Do not open the door," Rick countered. "If we pretend we're not here, he'll eventually go away."

Knock. Knock. Knock.

Gracie frowned at Rick. "You don't even know who it is."

"You're right. We might be really lucky and it might be just a robber with a gun. I still vote not to let him in."

But Gracie stood up from the table and pushed her chair back. Almost as if pulled by some unseen force from beyond the other side of the door, she walked to it. Standing before it, she waited while her head and her desires warred with one another.

Then the knocking stopped.

In a rush of speed she twisted the dead bolt and pulled open the door. She thought he might have left, but there he was, Dean Wright III standing there with his hand in midair ready for his next knock.

She couldn't remember when she'd seen anything that made her so happy.

"Hey," Dean muttered.

"Hi," Gracie responded.

"I didn't know if you would still be here. You mentioned you guys hang out until late every Labor Day."

"I did. We do. We're still here."

"I can see that."

"Right," she laughed awkwardly. "Otherwise I wouldn't have opened the door."

"Yeah. This is weird," he said, stating the obvious.

"I know."

"I didn't want to come here. I knew this would be a mistake."

"I didn't want to open the door," Gracie admitted.

"But it was like I didn't have a choice."

Gracie sighed. "I didn't either."

Dean crossed his arms over his chest and frowned. "I can't offer you anything but short-term."

"I wouldn't believe any offer of anything else."

He nodded as he accepted her words. "So what happens now?"

Gracie turned and waved to her friends. "We're going to head out and catch up. I'll see you tomorrow."

Her friends stared back at her. Rick looked resigned. Dottie looked hopeful and Elis looked... well, frankly he looked jealous, probably because he knew what would soon be transpiring between them.

Katie remained fast asleep.

Gracie stepped outside and allowed the door to swing behind her. She was pretty sure she heard Elis curse, "Lucky bitch" before the door closed, but she wasn't entirely certain.

Dean waited for her at the end of the sidewalk and reached out to touch the hair, which flowed loosely around her shoulders. "I like it."

"Thanks."

"You never answered my question. What happens now?"

"Well, I've never been a fan of clichés but this one seems apropos. Your place or mine?"

He smiled. "Yours."

"Yes," she said. "I think so, too."

He reached for her hand and clasped it in his as they walked the short distance across the main street to her apartment above the Sea Breeze.

Dean stopped at the bottom of the stairs that would take them to her place. "I should tell you up front this probably isn't going to end well."

Gracie didn't have to be warned. "No, it probably isn't."

"If we were smart we would stop this now before either of us got hurt."

"That would be the sensible decision." But her heart was pounding in her chest and her arm was heating up just from the feel of his hand in hers.

"You know what my problem is with that?" Dean asked as he lowered his head, his lips coming perilously close to hers.

"What's that?" she whispered back, feeling his breath touch hers.

"I've always been a real dumb-ass."

CHAPTER EIGHT

ONCE THEY REACHED the conclusion that neither of them was smart enough to avoid the inevitable train wreck that would be their relationship, it made things much easier.

Dean kissed her. As soon as his lips met hers with serious intent, as soon as her tongue felt the push of his and the heat of his mouth, it was like a wave had suddenly overtaken her. Gracie felt it shake her body. And like any other wave, there was that sudden moment of fear when she wondered if the power of it would be too much and she would drown.

However, alongside the fear was exhilaration. She knew that the only way to get her head above the water would be to give it everything she had. Just like a wave, she embraced the power of Dean's kiss, knowing that the best way to survive it was simply to hang on.

She couldn't say how long it took them to get to the top of the stairs. They climbed a stair and then kissed again. Another stair another kiss, this time with her hand in his hair and his hand on her bottom cupping her and squeezing her through the cutoff jean shorts she'd worn that night.

Finally, either frustrated with their slow pace or eager

to get on with what was to come, Dean hauled her up into his arms. Instinctively, she wrapped her legs around his waist. In response to her tight hold, he groaned.

"Too tight?" she wondered as she leaned in to nibble on his ear.

"No such thing," he grunted in return.

He carried her with ease up the stairs to her apartment, despite every attempt she made to distract him. When they reached the landing outside her apartment door, the moon gave off enough light to see by. She pulled away from him and turned the knob.

"It's not locked."

"I'm not really a door locker," she confessed.

"Remind me to give you a very stern lecture after."

"After what?" she asked innocently, smiling as she watched his face drop.

He seemed to catch on to her teasing, because once again the grip on her bottom tightened and she found herself snuggling deeper into his hold. "She's funny, ladies and gentlemen. Very funny. Because you are joking, right? I mean, I would need to know now if we're not going to do what I so desperately want to do."

"Oh, we're going to do it. When I said 'after' I just meant after which part?"

"After all of the parts. And there will be many."

"Okay, but if that's the case I think you're going to be way too tired to give me a lecture."

"Honey, you have no idea how much stamina I have. It comes from a long summer of waiting." He moved them through the door and Gracie leaned over his body to shut the door behind her, but their progress was stopped by a large hairy mutt who wasn't exactly sure what he was supposed to do to the man holding his mistress.

He barked.

"It's okay Rufus, he's a friend. You remember him."

"See, nice man," Dean added. "From last winter."

That seemed enough to satisfy the animal. He turned around, hopped onto the couch, spun twice and crumpled into a ball after a long doggy sigh.

"Bedroom?"

"To your right."

Dean followed the short hallway to the open bedroom door. Through the haze of his desire he could make out the color pink on the walls, mixed with a lavender bedspread. He spotted a surfboard in the corner and framed pictures over a lot of the walls but couldn't say what was in them. He dropped Gracie on the bed, then jerked when something bounced off one of her pillows and went streaking from the room.

"What the hell was that?"

"My cat Eleanor, remember. You startled her, but Rufus will take care of her."

"Good to know. Rufus is a pal. Is there anybody else besides Rufus or Eleanor I need to worry about? Any birds that might come flying about."

"Nope."

"Good." Now that he had her where he wanted her— he hoped, without further distractions—it suddenly occurred to him what they were about to do.

Sex.

He told himself he hadn't missed it in the months since his divorce. Not that he didn't miss sex—no man in his right mind could go a day without missing sex—

but he hadn't missed the involvement with another person. He certainly hadn't missed Elena. Sex with her had always been physically hot but emotionally cold. She never backed away from a new position, but as soon as it was over she was in the shower or a bath. Alone. Not with him.

That really should have been a tip-off.

Now he was here with Gracie, about to get involved, and it was a little unnerving. Gracie, who he had tried to convince himself that he hadn't been attracted to the first time he saw her. Gracie, who had become his friend over what had seemed to him a very short winter.

Maybe they'd both understood that there was an attraction there, but together they seemed committed to not acting on it. Just friends. Platonic friends. It had been their motto. And they'd both done that for a reason. They'd both known that sex between them wouldn't just be sex. Gracie simply wasn't the type a man could have for a night then walk away from and Dean still didn't trust anyone enough to commit himself to more than a night.

So what had changed in three months?

Nothing. That was the worst of it. He still had no idea if he was anywhere near ready for this, which meant that the only thing that had changed was the willpower to deny himself. Here he was staring down at Gracie, who was stretched out on the bed, her blond hair floating around her, her tan deeper than he remembered when he left her in May. Her legs bare and smooth with her arms reaching out to hold him.

Gracie who had sent him the sand. Gracie whose e-mails had made him feel good each time he read them.

And reread them. Hurting her wasn't an option. But walking away from her when he'd done nothing but think about her like this for three months wasn't an option, either.

"I don't want to hurt you," he said gruffly, the words being forced out of his throat.

Gracie sat up a bit, leaning on her elbows. "You won't. It's been a while, a real long while, but I think I'll still be able to get the hang of it once we get started."

That wasn't what he meant, but her eyes were dancing with mischief and promise and he found himself smiling as he reached for the buttons on his shirt. He undid them and tossed the shirt aside watching as her eyes roamed over his chest and body. She sat up and touched him, placing her hands gently on his chest as if to not startle him.

The contact was electric and a surge of power went straight below the belt. Immediately his jeans became too tight. He closed his eyes as he felt her hands slide down his body to his belt. She tugged and pulled and he let her, despite the extra time it took because of her fumbling hands. He loved the sensation of having her undress him. Then she was sliding her hands over his hips, dragging down his pants and briefs. He felt his sex spring free from the material and hoped she wasn't startled by how aroused he already was.

But Gracie didn't comment. Instead she moved off the bed and followed the trail of his jeans down his legs. He managed to kick off his sneakers and let her pull the bunched material from one leg and then the other. Then just as slowly, she moved her hands back up his legs, gliding her fingers around the back of his knees to his thighs. She brushed over his buttocks then moved her hands forward until they caressed the spot where his stomach met his groin, all the while staying away from where he most needed her touch.

It drove him crazy, but he loved it. He hadn't felt as cherished since…never.

He watched her raise her baggy sweatshirt over her body, and marveled at the sleek figure in the tank top underneath. She wore no bra and his hand instantly sought out the small but perfect mounds on her chest even before the sweatshirt was completely over her head.

Her nipples puckered through the thin cotton and he teased her for a bit with his thumbs as he rubbed them both relentlessly over her tight buds. Soon the cotton became more of a barrier than a tease, and this time it was his turn to undress her. First the white tank over her head, then a simple tug of a few buttons and the oversize shorts dropped to the floor.

His gaze roamed her body, along with his hands. She wore a lavender thong that drove him absolutely wild. By the time he stripped her completely of the flimsy silk material, she was blushing furiously. That blush went straight to his heart.

Reverently, he scooped her up in his arms and placed her in the center of the bed. For a brief second he thought back to all the tricks that he had learned and had taught his ex-wife in an effort to make the sex more pleasurable than their actual relationship. Quickly, he disregarded all of them. He didn't want to perform tricks. He didn't want them performed on him.

All Gracie was doing was touching him. Her hands were stroking his back. Her head was coming off the pillow to kiss where she could reach. His neck. His jaw. His mouth. For a minute or maybe for an hour they did nothing but let their bodies touch at every juncture while they kissed. Hot, openmouthed, endless kisses as her hands rested on the small of his back. While his hands cradled her face and his chest rubbed from side to side over her sensitive breasts. While the insides of her smooth thighs glided against his hips.

It was unlike anything he had ever known. His body was tight with urgency as his erection continually brushed against her soft center. He could feel the puff of damp wispy curls tantalizing him, giving him a sense of what was to come, but he wasn't ready to give up the sheer un-diluted pleasure of what they were currently doing.

Then her hips started tilting up toward him, tempting him beyond reason. Without leaving the taste of her mouth, he allowed one hand to drift over her body to find her center. He felt the heat before his fingers dis-covered how wet she was, how ready after nothing more than a gentle rubbing of two bodies together.

With another minor shift, he angled his hips so that he was at the entrance to her body. He moved his hand away and waited. Again her hips tilted up and this time he slid inside her just a little. She arched her back and he slid deeper. She groaned and twisted her head on the bed in a parody of agony that he knew instinctively was pleasure and waited until she thrust herself up into him again. This time he slid all the way home.

Once inside her he couldn't remain still. His hips began to match her movements, his down, hers up. Not a furious thrusting motion, but more a steady rocking that had both of them gasping with every tug and pull. Dean reached for her hands and linked his fingers between hers, stretching their arms high over her head letting her feel completely the contact of his oversized body on top of hers. Her legs circled his calves, then slid lower until their ankles locked together. Her whole body tightened and seemed to hold him in a way that felt like, even though he was holding her hands, even though he was pushing inside her, that she was somehow possessing him.

It was like sinking into quicksand. Deeper and deeper he drove himself into her and deeper and deeper he fell into the endless well of comfort and acceptance that she seemed to be offering. If his whole body meshed into hers, he wouldn't have been surprised.

He might have even welcomed it.

"Dean," she called softly as she rolled her body in a fluid movement that had him sliding even closer to her core.

His eyes were pinned on her closed ones and he was grateful that she couldn't see him. He had a sudden fear that if let himself keep falling into her, if he didn't pull back now, he might never be able to, and he was certain that if she opened her eyes that's what would happen. Her mouth fell open on a sigh. Her face was flushed and, when he glanced down, he could see a red blush creeping up her breasts and over her neck.

He snapped his hips and drove into her with more purpose. He felt the tension inside her body as her walls locked around him, squeezing him while his body finally gave him the release he sought with her.

As soon as the storm was over, he carefully unlocked his fingers from hers, then pulled his body away from hers, rolling onto his back with an arm draped over his eyes. The sense of separation, even though they continued to touch at points along their bodies, was crushing. But he forced himself to remain still.

In the next second Gracie turned to him and eased her body over his. Dean wasn't sure what he was expecting. Confrontation over having pulled away so quickly. Soft, sexy words about how amazing it had been. Or worse. Words of love.

Instead, she nestled her head into the crook between his neck and shoulder and let her legs fall to either side of his. Behind her, she reached for the bedspread and pulled it over their sweat-damp bodies.

"Rufus and Eleanor will want to sleep with us. If they crowd you, you can push them off the bed. Just say you're sorry when you do it or Rufus will be upset all day tomorrow."

And with that she fell asleep.

Okay, he thought. No reason to worry. They'd had good sex, great sex, really amazing sex, and now they could crash for a while. Maybe they could do this a few more times over the winter, he thought. Not every night or anything. Maybe just an occasional date that ended in a pleasant romp. Nothing that would get either one of them in too deep so that when he left next summer it would be as easy as it had been last summer.

Dean could feel himself quickly following her into sleep, but he promised himself that it would only be for a minute or two and then he would leave to go back to his house.

Sleeping together would absolutely send the wrong message.

CHAPTER NINE

"ARE YOU GOING to do this every morning?" Gracie was sitting in the bed, the covers pulled up over her body although she wasn't sure why she was bothering with modesty at this point. Over the past week, he'd seen, touched and worshipped every inch of her body. It had been, in a word, delicious. Like an ice cream kiss.

They'd practically been cocooned in her apartment, relying on takeout and ice cream for sustenance. Chad had taken care of the shop and Dean had forgotten about any work that he'd brought with him. They made love, ate, slept and talked. But just when she thought everything was about as perfect as it could be, he would get weird. It reminded her that they were only temporary.

"What? I need clothes."

Dean was stepping into the jeans he'd worn the day before. As soon as they were over his hips, he looked around for the shirt he'd worn.

"I understand that. But you know you could just bring your suitcase up from the trunk of your car and leave it here so that every morning you wouldn't have to go down to your car to get your clothes only to come back up here to shower and change."

Dean pulled the polo shirt over his head but said

nothing. His face, however, was serious. "Gracie, we discussed this. We both agreed that neither one of us wants to do serious."

Gracie nodded, but she already knew that for her it was too late. Like running full speed into a brick wall, she knew the crash was going to be particularly painful, but she couldn't slow herself down. She was serious about him. "And moving your suitcase a total of thirty-two steps and five feet makes a difference…how?"

"It would be like I'm staying here. Living here."

"You've been here every night since you got back. You haven't even seen the inside of the house you rented. Rufus and Eleanor have found a way to sleep around you on the bed. How much more living here would it be like if you moved your suitcase upstairs?"

He said nothing, but she knew he could see the ridiculousness of what he was doing. Of course, she did run the risk that he might decide the best course of action was to retreat and go back to the house he had rented. Since she didn't want that, she opened her mouth to give him the out he wanted, but his cell phone rang interrupting her.

Dean picked up the phone to check the incoming call, then immediately turned it off. Gracie frowned. Mainlander escapees. They all had that in common. It was easy to run, but it was hard to leave behind whatever was chasing them.

"You know you're going to have to deal with them eventually."

"Who?" Dean grumbled, shoving the phone into his back pocket as he checked the floor for his sneakers.

"Both of them. Ex Number One and Ex Number Two."

"There's nothing to deal with. Ex Number One is officially behind me and Ex Number Two will get over losing his top writer. Seriously, that's the first time he's called in a while. I think they're as ready to move on as I am."

"Really?"

Dean put his hands on hips. "Really," he repeated. "You think I'm not moving on with my life?"

"If you were really moving on like you say, it wouldn't bother you to speak with either of them. You might even consider going back to Washington to—"

"I'm not going back to that world."

Gracie closed her eyes then opened them. "You may think you don't want to go back now and that's understandable. You were humiliated by the person you were supposed to trust…"

"This isn't about what Elena did. It was the way it all went down. The lies, the corruption. Reporters, friends I knew who suddenly didn't give a damn about me, just the story that unfolded. That included my ex-editor."

"Maybe he's calling to apologize, too."

"Maybe he is, but I simply don't care anymore. The life was getting to me. It was my job to uncover the dirt, but every time I caught a politician in a lie or a lobbyist making a slimy deal it got harder to take. Elena was simply the last straw. I'm a writer now and happy with it." He walked over and placed a kiss on her forehead. "I'll be back in a minute and if I happen to find you in the shower waiting for me…"

"Yes?"

"Well, let's just say I won't kick you out."

She smiled as she watched him leave and wondered how much she could trust what he said. Her heart beat heavy in her chest. The way he sounded when he said he wasn't going back seemed sincere. For the first time, she began to wonder if it was possible for another mainlander escapee to become an islander.

But her mind knew better. He'd only been away from his life for a little more than a year. This winter it would start to change. He would start to miss the action, his old friends and the people. By Memorial Day, if he even lasted that long, he would be ready to go back and then, like most mainlander escapees who returned to the mainland, she doubted she would ever see him again.

Gracie could only hope that she would survive having another person in her life leave her behind.

AFTER A LONG HOT SHOWER that had nothing to do with the water temperature, Dean and Gracie headed downstairs for some coffee. Elis was at the counter waiting for his decaf nonfat sugar-free vanilla latte.

"Hey Elis, I never had a chance to find out. How did those tikis go over this summer?"

Elis scowled and looked to Gracie. "He's mocking me, isn't he? Are you mocking me?"

"Not well, I take it."

"It's a sore subject," Gracie whispered.

"That's a shame. I thought that last one you did, the purple one, was pretty nice."

"Woodworking is out. Glass cutting is in. I'm thinking butterflies. What do you think about butterflies?"

Dean winced, but quickly hid his expression when

Gracie elbowed him in the ribs. "I think butterflies are…" He had no idea what he thought about butterflies. "Cool?"

"Excellent. Glass butterflies. They're going to be all the rage. You'll see." With his coffee in hand, he practically sprinted out of the coffee house, no doubt in a hurry to get to his glass.

"Do you think we should tell him that he doesn't seem to have any creative talent?" Dottie bit her lower lip. "I mean, maybe then he wouldn't get so upset when his work doesn't sell."

"Tell Elis he's not artistic? Not me," Gracie concluded. "Besides, maybe glass will be his thing."

"I suppose you're right. We find talents in the strangest places. For example, I'm an amazing mother and I never thought I would be. My mother was so distant and proper that part of me was afraid I wouldn't know how to be any different. And yet, I'm perfect. See, you don't have a thing to worry about in that regard, Gracie."

Dean was about to ask what that meant, but he could tell by Gracie's expression it was best to drop the topic.

"I take it that means Katie is doing well?"

"Thriving." Dottie beamed. "Have you seen a picture? She was there the night you came to collect Gracie at Rick's. Not that I'm going to do that again. I wanted her to be part of the group, but next year I think I'll leave her with Rick's mom. That way if there are any fireworks I won't have to worry about missing them."

"Fireworks?" Dean repeated.

"You know! How you came barging in to whisk Gracie off to bed, where you've kept her for practically a week. Why can't I find her picture?"

Dottie dug into the purse under the counter for the picture while Dean smiled over Gracie's blush.

"Here it is," she declared. Dean did the obligatory smile and nod as Dottie held up the small picture with the small face smack in the middle of it.

"She's beautiful."

"I know." Dottie said with a sigh.

A ripple of a strange emotion lanced through his body. Dean wasn't sure, but it might have been parental longing. Which was crazy since he'd never considered himself parental material. Instantly he looked away from the picture and gave Gracie a single-man-save-me-from-baby-picture look.

"Two vanilla lattes to-go," Gracie told Dottie.

Relieved, but slightly disappointed as he'd planned on lingering over his morning coffee, Dean asked, "Why to go?"

"We're in a hurry."

A hurry didn't sit well with him. He had finished his book on the mountain men and was waiting for revisions from his editor. He'd already picked his next project, a retrospective of life in the city of Philadelphia in the year of 1776. But he had decided a break wouldn't be a bad thing. He planned on more surfing, more love-making, and lots of peace and quiet. Hurrying anywhere didn't fit into that picture.

"We've got the Sunset Village run to make," Gracie told him. "I promised Joe I would have the ice cream delivered before noon this time."

Dean nodded. He'd helped Gracie with the ice cream deliveries to the assisted-living home last winter and knew that it wasn't wise to get between seniors and their ice cream. The look in those people's eyes the one time Gracie was late was enough to make a strong man fear for his life.

"Then I guess it will have to be to-go."

Dottie put the first cup then the second coffee on the counter in front of them. "So I guess this means you're here for another winter, Dean?"

"Yep." Dean heard the subtle fishing in Dottie's question, but for whatever reason it didn't seem to bother him this time. He was with Gracie and he planned to be, for the next several months. There was no point in hiding it. He'd come to grips with the fear of his involvement with her the night they first made love. Once he'd woken up the next morning still in her bed, warm and sated, and the world hadn't crashed around his head he'd figured he would go with it, wherever that took him.

He thought about the suitcase in the trunk of his car and realized it was stupid not to move it upstairs. Just like it was stupid not to admit he planned on living with Gracie for the winter.

"Wait for me, I'll be right back."

Gracie picked up the coffees. "Where are you going?"

"I need to move my suitcase upstairs. It's stupid to leave it in the car when I'm basically living with you, isn't it?"

Her expression was inscrutable and it suddenly made him nervous. She'd been the one to suggest he move in, but now that he was putting it out there, it was possible she was getting cold feet.

"You should. And you should call—"

"The rental people. Right. No point in paying for a house I'm not going to use."

This was good, Dean decided as he left the coffee house and made his way to his car. This was a positive step forward. No, he wasn't ready for any serious commitments and he wasn't sure that he ever would be, but what he told Gracie this morning was true. He didn't want to go back to his old life. He was happy here. Happier than he could ever remember being. There was no point in not embracing that happiness for as long as it lasted.

THE TWO OF THEM were in Rick's borrowed pickup truck heading back to the house after the ice cream drop-off. They had barely made it in time for lunch, and Dean and Gracie were forced to pitch in and do some of the scooping in order to get everyone their two scoops.

Gracie had laughed and smiled. She'd flirted with the older men and confided with the older women that she'd been lucky enough to snag herself a man for the winter. She'd assured Joe, the administrator, that he could take an extra few weeks to make payment on the ice cream and promised him a steady supply at the same rate they had agreed upon last year.

A generous woman.

But something was missing. There was a tightness around her mouth that wasn't part of her usual expression and in her eyes he was sure he sensed sadness.

"Something bother you at the home today?" he asked, while she kept the wheel steady down the main boulevard that separated oceanside from bayside homes.

"No, why do you ask?"

"It just seems...call me crazy but you look a little

sad. You're not worried someday you're going to end up in Sunset Village, are you?"

"I should be so lucky. Joe takes great care of them. No, not at all. I'm fine."

But she wasn't fine. The more he pressed, the more he realized that was true. Then he remembered something from earlier this morning. "This is about what Dottie said. That crack about you not having to worry when you're a mom. It didn't make sense to me."

"You didn't know my mother," Gracie mumbled.

"Was she cruel to you?" The thought made him instantly irate. The idea of anyone hurting Gracie was abhorrent to him.

"No, she wasn't around."

"I see."

Gracie sighed. "She was a mainlander escapee, okay? She came to run away, fell in love with my father, had me, then decided she couldn't take it anymore and left."

Wow. Didn't that just about explain everything, Dean thought. Why she didn't date mainlanders, or mainlander escapees. Why she seemed to be pushing him to go back to a world he truly didn't belong to anymore.

"I'm sorry."

"Thanks. I'm really over it. I had my dad and he was everything and that's all I needed."

"Right," he said. Then he had to add. "Dottie's not your mother."

"I know that," Gracie snapped. "She's wonderful with Katie. She would never leave her."

"I'm not your mother either."

To that she said nothing. Dean decided to let it drop. For now.

THE LABOR DAY GANG plus Dean celebrated Thanksgiving at Rick and Dottie's home. Rick cooked the turkey, Dottie did the trimmings, Gracie and Dean brought desserts, and Katie sat around looking cute as she showed off her new tooth.

Elis arrived with homemade appetizers that were inedible. It appeared that he had as little talent for cooking as he did for woodworking, but everyone was still holding out hope that his glass butterflies would be a hit.

When they each received one for a Christmas gift at the party he hosted on Christmas Eve, they all learned otherwise.

"He really doesn't think it looks like a butterfly, does he?" Dean was in bed while Gracie was in the bathroom trying on one of her Christmas gifts.

"Like he said, it's a work in progress," she called to him.

"But it's all crooked and cracked. It looks more like a butterfly that ran into a glass window and shattered to pieces. Maybe that's how he should market them."

"Sure, because lots of people want to buy a dead glass butterfly. Now, are you ready?"

"I am ready," Dean said, eagerly rubbing his hands together.

"Ta-da!" Gracie jumped out in a pink piece of silk froth that clung to every delicious curve of her body.

"Oh yeah. Merry Christmas," Dean groaned.

She did a pirouette first so he could get the full effect and, when she turned back his gaze had shifted from fun and sexy to lustful and needy just the way she liked it. She was about to skip toward the bed when a phone ringing stopped her progress. She knew the sound of that ring all too well. Turning, she saw Dean's cell phone on top of her dresser vibrating with each ring. She walked over to it and picked it up. She knew the number well enough, too.

"Ex Number One. Guess she wants to say Merry Christmas."

"Put the phone down and come over here."

"Maybe if you just talked to her," Gracie suggested. She wasn't sure what would happen, but the idea of Elena still being there. One phone call away. It was driving her a little crazy.

"About what? We have nothing to talk about. The woman's got a guilt complex the size of a crater. That's not my problem."

"So let her say she's sorry."

"What's the point? It won't change what happened. It won't change anything. Now put the phone down and forget about her. She's the last person I want to be thinking about tonight."

She was the last person Gracie wanted to be thinking of as well, but it seemed no matter how many steps they had taken together, sleeping together, moving in together, sharing holidays together, there was still this past life calling out to him at the most inconvenient times.

Eventually, he was going to have to answer the call.

"HEY, ELIS! You here?"

"In back!"

Gracie let herself into Knick&Knacks and headed for his studio.

"What's up?" he asked, lifting his goggles over his eyes.

"My butterfly broke," Gracie told him. The glass

figure he'd given her had snapped in half where the wings met. "Rufus started chasing Eleanor and then Dean started chasing Rufus and then someone, they won't tell me who, banged into where it was hanging on the wall. It fell and broke."

Elis looked at the two pieces of glass in her hand. "And you want a new one?"

"Of course. It was my Christmas gift. I know it's only January and already it's broken. But I promise to be more careful with the next one."

"No, I mean it's ugly. Why do you want another one?"

"It's not ugly," Gracie countered. "It's unique."

Elis glanced at the glass. "You really think so?"

"I do. I wouldn't be here for another one if I didn't."

"I've got a bunch of them over on that counter. Take any one you want."

Gracie wandered over to the counter and studied the pieces as if she were choosing which Degas she wanted to take home.

"You're too sweet for your own good." Elis smiled. "I know they're horrible. Frankly, I'm ready to give up the whole idea of creating some incredible must-have item just to get even with my ex. If I were over him, really over him, it wouldn't matter. I think I need to move on."

"Exactly!" Gracie shouted. "That's what I keep telling Dean."

"Dean?"

"An ex-wife and an ex-editor. He says different, but I think they both want him back. The only way he's really going to know that he doesn't want them back is to confront them. On their own turf. He needs to go back to his old life and—"

"Hold on a second," Elis interrupted. "You want him to go back to his old life?"

"It's the only way to prove he's over them. To move on, like you said."

"No, I said *I* need to move on. That doesn't mean going back to Doug and working with him again. My life with him is over. It's here now. Moving on means not letting my past dictate what I do. Which, by the way my dear, sounds suspiciously like what you're doing."

"Me?" Gracie put a hand to her chest, offended that he would even suggest such a thing.

"Yes, you. You're letting what happened in your past dictate your relationship with Dean. You think he's going to leave like your mother did, so you're trying to push him away first. It's a classic defense mechanism. You really can't blame yourself."

"You're wrong. This isn't about my mother. This is about his ex-life."

"If you say so," Elis said, then put the goggles back on over his eyes

Gracie snatched a piece from his counter and left without a word. It was only when she hung the damn thing up that she realized she'd grabbed a yellow butterfly.

She hated yellow.

FEBRUARY CAME with its typical dreary and cold weather. Dean had finished the bulk of his research on Philadelphia and was now working on putting the book together. March started to bring warmer temperatures.

Gracie usually took that time to contemplate the upcoming summer season, but this March all she could think about was when Dean was leaving.

He hadn't given her any time frame. He didn't seem to be in any hurry to leave. It wasn't what she'd predicted. She'd planned that by February he would finally begin to feel the effects of the isolation. Instead, he seemed more than content to spend his days writing, or helping out with chores, or spending time with her on her errands.

He'd talked her into joining him on a few day trips to Philadelphia for research. He'd talked her into a weekend in New York for a Broadway show and a fine dinner. While they were in those cities, she always made sure to pay close attention to his reactions, waiting to see if these trips were somehow a precursor to him getting ready to return to his old life, but he always appeared happy to arrive and just as happy to return to the island.

Gracie didn't know what to think, which only made things worse. If he was leaving, then she could start to push him away, start to build the walls that would help protect her when he finally said goodbye. The fact that he wasn't saying anything made her feel vulnerable and it wasn't a feeling she was comfortable with.

But it wasn't until April that she began to get really nervous. It was a warm day and they had decided to take a walk on the beach with Rufus. Dean reached for her hand and she thought about how wonderful that moment was, but in the next instant it all changed.

"I've decided I'm not going back to Colorado for the summer."

Gracie stopped in her tracks.

"I'm going to stay here," Dean told her.

She pulled her hand away from his and folded both over her chest.

"If that's okay with you."

Glancing up at him, she could see he was confused by her withdrawal. No doubt he thought she would be thrilled to death that he was staying. She wasn't the best at hiding her feelings; he had to know she was in love with him.

"I thought we agreed at the beginning that this—" she waved her hand in the space between them "—was only going to be temporary. You didn't want a commitment."

"That was then. I'm not saying I'm ready for marriage, but we're doing great. We've got a great life here and I don't want to leave."

"*I* have a great life here. You're just visiting."

She watched his expression fall, and she knew she'd hurt him, but she couldn't seem to help it. "Your life is back in Washington," she insisted, and heard the shrill quality in her voice as she said it. "Just because you pretend it isn't there doesn't mean it's gone away."

"It *is* gone. I'm not going back to that life."

"Your wife still calls. Your editor still calls. If all that were truly behind you, you would pick up the phone and tell them. You would let her say she's sorry and move on and you would tell your editor to stop calling because you're never going back to the paper, but you don't."

"You think just because I don't want to listen to whatever pitch they have to sell, it means I'm still clinging to that life? You're wrong."

Gracie could feel the tears burning her eyes and she struggled to hold them back. "Yes. That's what I think. And I think you might like it here now, but in another year or two you'll realize what you left behind and you'll want it back and then you'll leave."

"For the last time, I'm not your damn mother, Gracie."

She gasped and physically stumbled back a few steps on the sand. He reached for her, but she moved beyond his grasp. "That's not fair!"

"It is fair. Because it's what you're doing. You're pushing me away because you're afraid I'll hurt you like she did. But I won't, Gracie. I'm happy here."

Gracie snorted indelicately. "She was happy, too, in the beginning. Everyone is happy in the beginning. Because it's easy then. But it quickly gets hard. Much harder if you have a life that's waiting for you back in D.C. You need to leave. Now. It's better that we do this sooner rather than later. Any later and you leaving me will…it will hurt."

Dean moved forward and reached for her, shaking her with his sudden fury. "And you're not going to hurt now? You can't be serious, Gracie. You love me. I know it. I know it every time I come inside you and you hold me like you're never going to let me go. Don't do this. Don't let me go now."

"Let go of me," she ordered. Instantly his hands came off her arms and again she moved out of his reach. "I'm going to Dottie's. You need to get your things from the apartment and leave. You need to go back to D.C. and see if you mean it. See if you can live without all of that. Without the exes."

"What if I can't live without you?" he asked gruffly.

"Then you'll come back. You know where I'll be on Labor Day."

"You're making a mistake. We don't have to do this. We're happy, for crying out loud!"

"You'll never be happy until you've let the past go, and I'll definitely never be happy until I know for certain that you have. That you're not just another mainlander escapee who thinks running away will fix everything. You say you're not my mother. Prove it."

His arms dropped to his sides and his shoulders slumped slightly in defeat. The wind blew his hair about his face and she thought that he should probably get it cut when he got back to D.C. Long hair was an island thing.

"Come on, Rufus, we need to go." The dog came running up to his mistress and followed her as she walked away from Dean. He stopped a few times, turning back to the man who had become his master. He whimpered, but Gracie kept walking so he followed.

She continued to walk. She walked the beach until she could turn around and not see him. She walked even farther so she wouldn't be tempted to run back to him, pleading with him to stay and never leave. She walked until her legs trembled underneath her and finally she dropped to the soft sand. Rufus rested his face on her legs while she stared out at her beautiful ocean and wondered if she'd done the right thing.

Only today it had no answers for her.

CHAPTER TEN

Labor Day...present

GRACIE STARED at the door. Her heart thudded heavily against her ribs. She'd told him to go. He'd said he was happy, but she'd told him to leave. Because she had to know he wasn't like her mother. For that matter, he had to know, too. Now someone was knocking on the door and she couldn't believe, couldn't hope, that he'd found his answers.

"Go open the door, Gracie," Rick told her. "It's the only way you're going to know."

Gracie slid out of the booth and walked across the bar, winding her way between tables that held upside-down chairs. She reached the door and it rattled from the force of the pounding the person on the other side of door was giving it.

Maybe she shouldn't open it. Maybe it was better if it stayed closed. When she opened the door the last time it had ended in pain. So much heartache she didn't think she could survive it. What made her think that this time it would be different?

Only a fool would open the door.

Only a coward wouldn't.

Gracie figured she was somewhere in between and after all opening it was the only way to stop all the banging. She turned the lock, took a deep breath and opened the door.

Dean stood on the other side of it. The first thing she noticed was his angry expression. That and his hair hadn't been cut.

"Are you happy now? Four months. Four months I've been away and it's been four months of hell. I couldn't eat. I couldn't sleep. Forget any real work on the book." He stormed through the door and stopped when he saw the crowd assembled around a familiar table.

"Hi Dean." Dottie waved shyly.

"Dottie, Rick. How's Katie?"

"Good. She's with Rick's folks tonight. You know, in case of fireworks."

"I appreciated the pictures," he said, then turned to Gracie. "At least someone was nice enough to keep me in the loop around here."

"Hey," Elis stopped him. "Don't forget, I sent you some extra butterflies."

"Right. They were…you know. Anyway Gracie, there are a couple of people who want to talk to you."

Dean reached into his back pocket and popped open his cell phone. He hit a button and waited for it to ring. Then he thrust the phone at her. "Say hello, Gracie."

"Hello, Gracie," she murmured instinctively. She waited then listened to a woman's voice on the other end saying how grateful she was that she'd finally forced Dean to confront what had happened. That apologies were given, the matter was settled and that everyone was free to go on and live their lives.

Gracie barely got out a goodbye before Dean was pulling the phone back and hitting another button. He thrust the phone back at Gracie. "I should warn you Steve is not at all as happy with you as Elena is."

"Hello?" Gracie answered, then listened to a gruff smoke-filled voice rail at her for several minutes at how she'd ruined one of the best political reporters the *Post* had by turning him into a nonfiction-writing island-living idiot. And that he hoped she was happy!

Dean took the phone back and closed it. "There? Satisfied?"

Her head was in a whirl. "It's really true? You really went back there, saw everything you had, and decided you didn't want it anymore?"

"I knew it the first day I was back, but I also knew you wouldn't believe me unless I served my time. I hated not being able to walk on the beach anytime I wanted. I hated that I couldn't hear the ocean. I hated sleeping in my bed without you, Rufus and Eleanor. I hated the crush of people and, most of all, I missed the ice cream. You know it's the salt air that makes the ice cream taste so good."

Gracie looked up at him, smiling through watery eyes. "Is that all you missed?"

"No. I hated not being with you. I missed you, Gracie. I missed your wacko woo-woo ways. I missed your face. I missed your smile and your warmth. I thought I was done with people forever and for the most part I still am. Except for you. Only you. I love you."

"I wasn't sure," she whispered. "I had to be sure. My own mother left me."

"Because she was mentally sick, Gracie. She had to

be. Only someone hurting really bad on the inside could not love you. I know. Because I thought I was hurting on the inside and I still managed to fall in love with you."

"You're sure?"

He leaned down to kiss her softly on the lips. "Absolutely. Now you are sure, too. I'm not going anywhere. I'm officially an island convert. I'm even thinking of buying my own surfboard and wearing cutoff jean shorts."

"Let's take it one day at a time, shall we." Gracie smiled.

He kissed that smile then picked his head up to wave to the rest of the group. "We're going to take off now. Say good-night, Gracie."

"Good night, Gracie."

She heard Dottie giggle behind her as Dean took her hand and led her home.

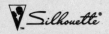

Silhouette® Desire®

**Introducing an exciting appearance
by legendary
New York Times bestselling author**

DIANA PALMER
HEARTBREAKER

He's the ultimate bachelor…
but he may have just met
the one woman to change his ways!

Join the drama in the story of a confirmed
bachelor, an amnesiac beauty and their
unexpected passionate romance.

"Diana Palmer is a mesmerizing storyteller
who captures the essence of what
a romance should be."—*Affaire de Coeur*

---

*Heartbreaker is available from Silhouette Desire
in September 2006.*

Silhouette® BOMBSHELL™

On their twenty-first birthday,
the Crosse triplets discover
that each of them is destined
to carry their family's legacy
with the dark side.

DARKHEART & CROSSE

A new miniseries
from author

Harper ALLEN

Follow each triplet's story:

Dressed to Slay—October 2006
Unveiled family secrets lead sophisticated
Megan Crosse into the world of
shape-shifters and slayers.

Vampaholic—November 2006
Sexy Kat Crosse fears her dark future as a vampire
until a special encounter reveals her true fate.

Dead Is the New Black—January 2007
Tash Crosse will need to become the strongest
of them all to face a deadly enemy.

Available at your favorite retail outlet.

SAVE UP TO $30! SIGN UP TODAY!

 INSIDE *Romance*

The complete guide to your favorite
Harlequin®, Silhouette® and Love Inspired® books.

✓ Newsletter ABSOLUTELY FREE! No purchase necessary.

✓ Valuable coupons for future purchases of Harlequin, Silhouette and Love Inspired books in every issue!

✓ Special excerpts & previews in each issue. Learn about all the hottest titles before they arrive in stores.

✓ No hassle—mailed directly to your door!

✓ Comes complete with a handy shopping checklist so you won't miss out on any titles.

- -

SIGN ME UP TO RECEIVE INSIDE ROMANCE
ABSOLUTELY FREE
(Please print clearly)

_____

Name

_____

Address

_____

City/Town   State/Province   Zip/Postal Code

(098 KKM EJL9)

Please mail this form to:
In the U.S.A.: Inside Romance, P.O. Box 9057, Buffalo, NY 14269-9057
In Canada: Inside Romance, P.O. Box 622, Fort Erie, ON L2A 5X3
OR visit http://www.eHarlequin.com/insideromance

IRNBPA06R   ® and ™ are trademarks owned and used by the trademark owner and/or its licensee.

THE PART-TIME WIFE

by *USA TODAY* bestselling author

Maureen Child

Abby Talbot was the belle of Eastwick society; the perfect hostess and wife. If only her husband were more attentiive. But when she sets out to teach him a lesson and files for divorce, Abby quickly learns her husband's true identity...and exposes them to scandals and drama galore!

On sale October 2006 from Silhouette Desire!

Available wherever books are sold, including most bookstores, supermarkets, discount stores and drug stores.